**She stood on her toes and kissed him lightly on the lips.**

Oric groaned and pushed her away, holding her at arm's length. "I should not allow this. If I had not been distracted today, I would have discovered the assassin earlier."

"I was distracting you?"

"You do distract me."

She dropped her gaze. "I wasn't in any real danger just now, Oric." Uncertainty crept into her voice despite her best efforts.

"Arlana." His voice dropped to a harsh whisper. He closed the space he'd placed between them in a single step and wrapped her in his arms. "I should never have allowed this," he said roughly, "but I'm afraid I cannot stop it now."

He claimed her mouth again, liquefying her body once more.

*This is but the beginning, Arlana.*

# Titles By Author


**Fate's Hand Series**
Thief's Desire
Destiny's Seduction

Bonfire Night

**Fire and Tears Series**
Brightarrow Burning
Darkness Singed
Dawn Ignited

Kellyn's Sacrifice
The Last Guardian

# DESTINY'S SEDUCTION

## FATE'S HAND SERIES

## ISABO KELLY

T&D PUBLISHING

# DESTINY'S SEDUCTION

## FATE'S HAND SERIES

## ISABO KELLY

# PROLOGUE

Morning sun sneaked in past the curtains, collecting in a thin line across the wooden floor of the bedroom. Catarin watched the line slowly form, watched the new day being born and was overwhelmed by a sense of impending disaster. Her eyes felt heavy and swollen from lack of sleep, and the beginnings of a headache pricked at her temples.

Today of all days she should have been well rested, but knowing she needed to sleep hadn't helped shut her eyes during the long night.

She felt Owen's movements just before his arm fell across her waist.

"Morning, sweetheart," he murmured in her ear, pulling her back against his chest.

She squeezed the arm around her waist in wordless greeting. But her silence must have given her away.

"You didn't sleep, did you?"

With a sigh, Catarin rolled over to face him. He was propped up on one elbow, his other hand still resting warmly on her waist. She looked for a long time into his brilliantly blue eyes and studied the sweep of his white-blond hair against the long, handsome lines of his face. Her sense of foreboding clutched tightly around her throat, making it hard to swallow.

Owen leaned over and touched her forehead with a gentle kiss. "Everything will be all right, love. We've spent long months preparing this spell. The others are fully committed. And they're the most powerful magicians in the empire. What could go wrong?"

"Oh, Owen, all kinds of things could go wrong. You're expecting all one hundred and ninety-nine of them will follow through with the spell. And you…you'll be most vulnerable."

"Being chosen to take up the task of Guardian is a great honor. You've been my apprentice and my heart's treasure for long enough to know that I couldn't shun this."

"I know." She sighed, feeling the first sting of tears behind her tired eyes. "I'm so very proud of you. But I can't let go of this feeling that something isn't right."

"You're worried about him, aren't you?"

Catarin's lip curled in an involuntary snarl. "Yes. Gavin is selfish and power-hungry. He's the only blood mage among the one ninety-nine—"

"We have taken that into consideration, love."

"Owen, he's a blood mage because he craves power. More than any other, he covets the power and influence of being a strong sorcerer. Yet now we must believe he'll sacrifice his physical existence to the completion of the spell?"

"That's precisely the reason he'll go through with it," he said, squeezing her waist. "Because he craves power. And the power he'll have will be beyond even his wildest dreams."

"But he won't be able to control that power." Catarin threw the silk sheet from her body and rolled away from Owen, out of bed. She stood, naked, hands on hips with the early morning light warm against her back. "*You* will control the power. *You* will be the one focusing and using the strength of this thing you'll create. What good will that power be to Gavin if he can't use it?"

Owen slowly rose from the bed and approached, but when he would have folded her into his arms, she spun away. Her knee-length hair whipped around in an angry cloud. "Don't try to console or patronize me, Owen. I may not be as powerful as you and the others, but I understand the seductive nature of magic, the temptations of wielding unimaginable power. It's why the emperor agreed to this… this experiment. For the power he'll bring to the wars, for the power he thinks he'll hold over the conquered countries."

She paced to the wardrobe, stiff with helplessness and frustration. "I know. I know what the emperor doesn't realize. That the Guardian— you—will be the real power." With her back still to him, she murmured, "I trust you and your ethics implicitly with this power, my love. I know you won't abuse it. But I do not trust the others."

The feel of his large, warm hands on her shoulders made her shudder. Her irritation fled and she leaned back against his chest. He wrapped his arms around her, hugging her tightly and rubbing his cheek against the top of her head.

"I'm sorry," she whispered after a quiet moment. "I didn't mean to trouble you with my fears today. I love you so much, Owen."

"And I love you, Catarin. More than my life. I would that I could quiet your fears."

She turned in his embrace and wrapped her arms around his waist. She took a determined breath, then looked up into his blue eyes and said with a conviction she didn't feel, "All will go well. And I'll be standing there in the shrine to watch as you cast the most incredible spell ever attempted."

His soft, full mouth curved upward. He tightened his arms at her back and lowered his head to hers, kissing her long and deeply.

Catarin knew in that moment that it would be the last kiss they ever shared.

# Chapter One

Arlana stared at the white marble wall shot through with golden patterns. Watched the gold shift and meld, blend into almost-shapes then dissolve into nothing. Here an arm, there a smile, just there a dragon, next to it a wing, beyond that two bodies intertwined, above that an eye. So familiar. So alien. She closed her eyes and breathed in slowly. Sandalwood. It always smelled like sandalwood. Her heart skipped once, then started to beat fast.

He was near.

She opened her eyes. The white marble was the same, never changed. But the air now surged with white fog. Her breathing sped and her stomach clenched.

And she could feel him. Across her skin, in her pulse, along her spine, she could feel him.

She turned slowly, unbalanced and wavering, the ground beneath her invisible in the fog. She knew what she would see—had seen it before—but her heart still jumped.

"I've been waiting for you."

The sound of his voice reverberating through the heavy air made her shiver. Low, deep, husky. Enticing. Terrifying. She watched, unable to move as he emerged from the fog.

White. His snug trousers, fluttering silk shirt, knee-high suede boots. Everything was white. Except his hair. Except his eyes.

Those were black.

And those black eyes caught and held her, as they always did. He circled her slowly, never taking his gaze from hers, never stepping close enough to touch. But she felt his touch. Felt the breath of a caress on her neck, her cheek, her shoulder, her breast. Felt his velvety lips brush hers.

Her heart slammed into her ribs.

She couldn't blink. Couldn't breathe. Couldn't look away. She stood in place, turning as he stalked around her, pulled by the power of his black eyes.

When he stopped, she stopped. Only a foot of white marble remained between them.

He stepped forward. "Arlana."

Arlana bolted upright in bed, choking on the cry that came with her out of the dream. Her name, murmured by that voice, followed her into consciousness, lingering like the afterimage left in front of the eyes when all light is suddenly snuffed out. Sweat clung to her skin and soaked through her thin nightshift. Her heartbeat raced as if she'd run the length of the barony. She could smell her fear mixed with the faint scent of sandalwood.

Squeezing her eyes closed, she drew her thoughts down to her heartbeat, gently urging it to slow. With the return of her heart's regular cadence, her breathing also returned to normal. An extra breath, deep and cleansing, wiped away the last of her panic, and she opened her eyes.

Her bedroom always looked so mundane after the dream. Stone walls lined with pale cream silk to insulate the room. Sunlight just beginning to slide through the crack in the heavy, lavender velvet curtains. The oak posts of her bed, the lavender bed curtains that had been pulled apart by her maid just before sunrise. The low fire in the gray stone fireplace to the right of her bed just beginning to warm the room. Everything was the same as it had been when she'd gone to sleep the night before.

But everything always felt disjointed when she awoke from the dream.

Before she could blink away the last of the fog and white marble dancing in her mind, her maid, Jill, entered, moving silently to avoid waking her mistress.

"Oh," Jill exclaimed, "my lady, you're up early this morning. You'll be wanting your bath now, then?"

"Thank you, Jill. Yes." Arlana smiled, trying to disguise the unease still creeping through her veins.

"Would you like coffee or juice with your breakfast, my lady? Mistress Leshar has had a fresh batch of apple juice mixed up for this morning."

"Some of Aunt Becky's apple juice? How could I refuse?"

Jill grinned and bobbed her head once before disappearing through the side door that led to Arlana's washroom.

Her mother's love of hot baths had prompted her father to expand on the castle plumbing, which already ran to a few communal bath areas. Now several rooms, including her own, had the convenience of hot and cold water pumped directly to their bathtubs. Jill had been so excited by the prospect of never having to haul another bucket of heated water that she'd prepared Arlana three baths the day the final pipe connections had been made.

Arlana had never had the heart to tell Jill she could heat the water magically. By the time she'd learned that trick, just after her sixth birthday, the piping was nearly in place. She preferred the maid didn't know anyway. Jill was one of the few people who didn't tremble, bow and scrape the instant Arlana stepped into a room, so Arlana went out of her way to keep from using her magic while Jill was around.

"The bath's ready, my lady."

Arlana climbed out from under her thick blankets, shivering as she shuffled past the cheery fire to the washroom. The smell of wood smoke followed her into the jasmine-scented steam. Arlana loved that combination of smells. But the steam reminded her of the dream, and when Jill stepped out of that swirling wall of white, Arlana jumped and let loose a strangled yelp.

"My lady?"

She shook her head and tried to laugh away her reaction. "Sorry, Jill. I'm fine. Just a little tired this morning."

Jill's answering smile was hesitant but accepting. The maid left Arlana to her bath and went down to the kitchens to get her breakfast.

Alone again, Arlana stripped and climbed into water that was almost hot enough to scald her skin. She welcomed the heat. Slowly, the cold in her veins warmed. She hadn't even realized how cold she was until the bathwater stung her skin.

"Let's see," she mused, "what color today?" She fingered a wet lock of hair falling across her breast. "Maybe red. Red seems a good color. Bright. Lively." Without meaning to, she added silently, *Not white or black.* "Yes. Today will be red."

***

Oric stood before the Fordin court, his face a perfect mask of neutrality, betraying nothing of the chaos in his mind. At least he'd

8

been able to master that outward calm before this journey had become necessary. Only another Browan would know he was anything but calm and in control.

The audience hall buzzed with conversations all centering on the Browan soldiers and diplomats, the first Browans besides the ambassador and his household to enter Karasnia in more than two hundred years. Oric, in turn, surreptitiously studied the hall and the Karasnians filling it as his translator exchanged the proper greetings with Baron Fordin.

The castle itself had impressed Oric from the beginning. He'd heard of the castle designs of Karasnia from Ambassador Rowkan. Fordin Castle hadn't disappointed. It had been designed, built and rebuilt over the centuries, but always with an obvious concern for defense. Even after two centuries of peace, Fordin Castle was still capable of withstanding a long siege.

The audience hall where he stood waiting for the end of the formal greetings was simple, functional and adequate, if not overly majestic. Oak panels lined the long walls, four candle-filled brass chandeliers ran the length of the hall and the galleries contained simple cushion-covered wooden benches. Atop the dais at the end of the hall sat a large, carved oak chair padded in velvet of Fordin blue.

The Karasnian nobility were, for the most part, as Oric had expected. Ambassador Rowkan had instructed him on the proper mode of dress for Karasnia. The men wore hose, woolen or leather breeches and tunics of wool or heavy silk. Women's dresses were tight-bodiced, low-waisted and brushed the ground. The range of color was brilliant, if not overly ornamented, and the styles were less extravagant, perhaps, than his country's fashions, but they were attractive in a foreign way.

Then there was the variety of eye color in Karasnians. That was intriguingly exotic. Fascinating.

Oric pulled his attention away from his study of the Karasnians to focus once more on the dais. The people there were people he'd been studying for many years now—people whose cooperation was essential to his mission.

In the single chair sat a young man a little less than four years Oric's junior, with long dark brown hair, green eyes and the build of a warrior. From the reports, Baron Aaron Fordin was an agile and cunning man with a sword, but was still uneasy in his new role as baron. That might cause problems if the man decided to make things difficult for Oric.

Lord Kevin Fordin, former guardian of the barony and now Baron Fordin's chancellor, stood to the right of the younger man. Lord Fordin was quite probably the largest man Oric had ever seen, standing head and shoulders over Oric's own six-foot-one. The resemblance to his nephew was obvious in the green eyes and strong, sharp features. Not for the first time, Oric wondered why the powerful lord had never made a play for the Karasnian throne. He certainly had the bearing of a king. Though he wasn't related to the current king by blood, he was the son of the king's second wife and second cousin to the king's first wife. For the last twenty years he'd commanded the second largest barony in the kingdom. Yet he'd sworn allegiance to the regent and peacefully handed the barony over to his nephew when Aaron Fordin reached his majority. That spoke of Lord Fordin's character. But how would a man of that character react to Oric's mission? And did his political honor reflect his attributes as a father?

To the left of the dais stood Baron Fordin's aunt, one of the strongest sorceresses in all of Karasnia. Lady Tiya Von Fordin—the daughter of a bookbinder, heroine of the realm and wife to Lord Fordin—was quite simply stunning. White-blonde hair cascaded down to the small of her back. Blue eyes like those of his own countrymen looked out of angular features. She wore a simple black robe cinched at the waist by a gold rope belt—the uniform of a Karasnian magician.

He couldn't help but wonder if the daughter would look like her mother.

He murmured a few words to his translator. The man beside him, Ferdinand of Claousin, was young for a diplomatic translator, but he'd mastered the nuances of Karasnian far faster than Oric. And for the moment, Oric didn't want any of these people to know he spoke their language.

"My lord, Baron Fordin," Ferdinand intoned, his voice commanding attention and conveying courtesy at the same time. "Lord Commander Oric of Czanri of Myseen of Browan thanks you for your kind greeting."

Oric kept his gaze focused on Baron Fordin, who in turn watched Oric intently, as if they were talking directly with one another, two fighters sizing up their opponent.

"I wish to request a private meeting with his lordship, Baron Fordin, Lord Kevin Fordin, Lady Sorceress Tiya Von Fordin and the sorcerer Merig," Oric said.

"Might I ask," Baron Fordin said, "what topic you wish to discuss, Lord Commander Oric?"

Ferdinand made a show of translating. Oric murmured a single word. Ferdinand in turn said, "The sorceress, Lady Arlana Von Fordin."

Baron Fordin's eyes flashed with what Oric suspected was a defensiveness honed by instinct. To the young baron's credit, he suppressed the urge to challenge Oric to single combat then and there. Instead, he nodded for a moment to confer with his chancellor.

The room's already irritating hum grew stronger. Oric controlled his intense desire to wince and doubled his efforts to block out the thoughts of so many uncontrolled minds. *I don't know how the blasted ambassador manages it.*

*His ability to hear the thoughts of others isn't as strong as yours, Lord Commander*, Ferdinand replied in Browan, then switched languages. *I also find the crowd less difficult than you do. And don't forget to use Karasnian. You need the practice.*

Oric managed not to scowl at the edge of amusement in the translator's mental voice. But it took an effort. Then, more resigned, he thought, in Karasnian, *At least none of these people can overhear us.* He couldn't seem to prevent the smug confidence that filtered into his mind voice.

Ferdinand lifted his lips in a smile only Oric was close enough to see.

The conversation on the dais ended and Baron Fordin turned back to the Browans. "Lord Commander Oric, my steward will show your guard to the guest quarters. If you and your translator will follow me, we shall adjourn to my private audience chamber."

The murmuring among the gathered nobility resonated with unease, conjecture, suspicion and blatant curiosity. Oric strengthened his defenses and blocked out most of the mental muttering, but he couldn't wait to get away from the crowd.

He was one of the strongest, if not *the* strongest, telepaths in his country—a country where every person had telepathic abilities of some strength. He'd been learning how to block out the mental noise of uncontrolled minds since the age of fifteen. But he'd never had to use the skill under real circumstances. Blocking out the thoughts of others was much more difficult than keeping one's own thoughts shielded. In Browan, children learned to shield their thoughts before they learned to eat solid food. It was necessary to protect the privacy of the individual, as well as the sanity of the populous. One unrestrained telepathic mind in Browan could cause a great deal of mental turmoil. Millions of such minds could…

Oric preferred not to think about what had happened before Browans had learned to shield their thoughts.

If he chose, he was strong enough to penetrate most of the shields of his countrymen. But from a very young age, he'd been inundated with the unwritten rules of social protocol. He would no more think of penetrating those shields under normal circumstances than he'd think to strip an unwilling stranger of their clothing.

If the circumstances weren't normal, Oric wasn't so sure. But only the most dire of situations would force him to break with social customs and taboos to read the thoughts of the unwilling. Or the unknowing.

As he and Ferdinand were led through a short hall to Baron Fordin's private chamber, Oric briefly entertained the idea of reading the thoughts of his hosts. It would serve them right for all the mental noise they made. But no. It wouldn't be honorable.

And if nothing else, Oric still had his honor.

The room they were shown was another functional, moderately attractive room of oak paneling and Fordin blue. The Fordin banner—a blue flag sporting a wild boar embroidered in silver—hung behind a large desk. Before the desk, two velvet-lined chairs had been placed for Oric and Ferdinand. Baron Fordin sat behind the desk. At the right edge of the desk, Lady Tiya sat in a high-backed chair, her husband standing just behind her, his large hands resting on the chair. Another high-backed chair remained empty at the opposite side of the desk.

And to the left and just behind Baron Fordin stood the ancient, ageless sorcerer, Merig. His white hair and beard could as easily have come from age as from the immense amount of magical power he possessed. His eyes, the brilliant crystal blue of powerful magic, were surprisingly kind even in the face of the potential threat Oric represented. A neutral expression occupied features that should have been far more wrinkled.

Oric bowed briefly to the small group, and at Baron Fordin's gesture, took a seat before the desk. He leaned close to Ferdinand and murmured in his native language, "We'll tell them only what we must for now."

"Lord Commander," Baron Fordin began when Oric straightened in his seat. "You've approached us on a very delicate subject. What is it about my cousin that you wish to discuss?"

After Ferdinand's translation, Oric answered, "There is a prophecy." A collective gasp and one colorful curse issued by the baron preceded a pregnant silence. Oric let the silence draw out a moment before continuing. "A thousand-year-old prophecy of a child born of power so great she will control all magic and hold the fate of the world in the palm of her hand. She will control that which cannot be controlled and command what will not be commanded." Oric paused, giving the Karasnians time to absorb the words Ferdinand translated into their language.

Then very quietly, he said, "The time has come to bring Lady Arlana Von Fordin to her destiny."

The baron shot out of his seat, his hand reaching instinctively to his hip for a sword that wasn't there. "You dare come into my barony—?"

"Aaron." Lady Tiya's voice was quiet, just above a whisper.

Oric could almost feel her power flowing out on that single word.

The young baron looked at his aunt, then glared at Oric, but he returned to his seat.

"Explain, please, Lord Commander," Lady Tiya said.

Oric took a minute to compose what he would allow them to know. To gain their assistance, he'd have to tell them something of the secret his country had kept for two hundred years. But not everything. He didn't dare tell them everything.

"My lady," Oric started as Ferdinand unobtrusively translated, "this prophecy has been known in my country for centuries, but the meaning behind the words was a mystery. Until two hundred years ago. At that time, there was an accident—an accident that killed the most powerful of our magicians. Only one survived, though he survived for just a few days. This one spent much of his remaining days muttering nonsense. But on the last day of his life, he grew more lucid. He had the high counselors brought to him and bade them memorize his final words. He reminded them of this prophecy, whose source had been lost to time, and he said, 'Look to her. This is why she will be born. Only she can fix what we have started. Only she can succeed where we have failed.' With these words, he died."

Lady Tiya and Lord Kevin exchanged a long look, then turned to Merig. His expression remained neutral and unreadable.

Lady Tiya met Oric's gaze once again and said, "What has this to do with my daughter?"

"We know that your daughter is the prophesied one, my lady. It is time for her to take up that which she was born to take up. She must be brought to the Browan Shrine in Czanri."

"To do what?" Baron Fordin growled. "To fix the mistake made by your magicians two hundred years ago? Based on the mutterings of a dying man!" Lord Aaron half rose from his seat again. "Fix your own mistakes, Lord Commander. I will not allow my cousin to be carried off to Browan by—" The baron stopped abruptly when Merig placed a hand on his shoulder. He settled back in his chair, but his gaze burned into Oric.

"Perhaps," Merig said in a quiet, melodious voice, "you'd better explain further, Lord Commander."

"Yes." Lady Tiya leaned forward. "How do you know my daughter is the child of this prophecy? How can you be sure?"

"Her birth was felt by our strongest sorceress. She was able to pinpoint the location."

"Location maybe," Lord Aaron snarled, "but not a specific person."

Oric met the man's gaze. "Baron Fordin, if we had any doubts—which we do not, but if we had—you would have waylaid any fears by reacting as you have. You know of the prophecy, you treat the topic of Lady Arlana delicately and you prove by your hesitance that you know she is the prophesied one."

"We haven't made this public, Lord Commander," Merig said, his hand visibly tightening on Baron Fordin's shoulder, "but the degree of her power has been impossible to hide. You wouldn't be the first to approach us with a request that Lady Arlana carry out some 'magical miracle' to solve someone else's problem. You can understand why we would be hesitant."

"Of course," Oric acknowledged with a nod, "but have any previous applicants mentioned the prophecy?"

Merig pursed his lips and answered with the barest shake of his head.

"That doesn't prove anything," Lord Aaron snapped.

"I'd like to know," Lord Kevin Fordin said, "more about this 'accident', Lord Commander."

Oric turned to meet Lord Fordin's sharp green gaze. "I can tell you that it was an act of magic gone wrong. The effects are still present in our country. If the…damage is not repaired, it may have repercussions for the rest of the world. There is no one besides the prophesied one strong enough for this task."

Lady Tiya sucked in a sharp breath, turning to Merig. "What do you think? Does this sound right to you? Does it feel right?"

Oric turned slowly to meet the sorcerer's gaze. He sat unflinching as Merig studied him for a long, quiet moment.

"Perhaps," Merig murmured finally, "we should send for Lady Arlana. This does concern her, after all."

Baron Fordin tensed visibly, and a muscle in his jaw jumped. Lady Tiya's eyes widened and her mouth tightened, but after a moment she schooled her expression and nodded her assent. Lord Kevin leaned down to murmur something in his wife's ear, taking her hand in his and squeezing it.

The baron pulled a small cord that hung beside the banner behind his desk, and a moment later a young girl poked her head into the room. "Please ask my cousin to join us," Lord Aaron commanded. The girl scurried out of the room, closing the door without making a sound.

As they waited, Oric met Merig's gaze. He was surprised by what he saw in the depths of those blue eyes. Of all the people in the room, Oric had hoped for this man's support, knowing his counsel would be heeded by Lady Arlana's family. He'd been sure the mage's support would be the hardest to obtain. Now, he wasn't so sure. So far, he hadn't been forced to reveal too much, though it was more than most Browans would wish outsiders to know. But he wasn't at all confident that either the young baron, Lady Tiya or Lord Kevin would allow Lady Arlana to leave the barony without more of an explanation. With Merig's support, however, he might not have to reveal too much more.

They sat silently staring at one another for long minutes, the tension in the room mounting with each breath. Oric studied each of the faces before him, looking for clues to their thoughts, their feelings. He heard the door open behind him, watched the four before him look toward the door, but he didn't turn. After a long pause, he realized the newcomer hadn't moved from the door.

Baron Fordin noticed the hesitancy at the same instant. "Arlana?"

Seeing the concern in the baron's eyes made Oric frown. His movements controlled, his facial expression schooled, Oric rose and turned to face Lady Arlana Von Fordin.

Only years of military and diplomatic training kept the shock from reaching his face.

For the last twenty years, Oric had imagined what Arlana Von Fordin would look like. He'd pictured her fat, skinny, short, tall, plain, beautiful, and in his more bitter moments, hideously ugly or deformed. He'd pictured short hair and long, round features and angled, big boned and a delicate frame. He had known when she turned thirteen and wondered if she was gangly as a colt or pudgy as a gopher. When she turned sixteen, he'd wondered if she still looked like a child or if the woman she would be had begun to show.

More often than he cared to admit over the past five years, Oric had lain awake at night, staring at his bedroom ceiling trying to picture the sorceress who would dominate his future, the woman responsible for the direction his life was forced to take. He knew almost everything about her from his spies, but he'd always been afraid to ask specifically what she looked like—afraid he would give away his inner obsession and torment.

But in all the years, through all the various images he'd concocted, two things had remained unaltered. Two things had passed consistently from one image to the next. White-blonde hair and blue crystal eyes— the coloring of strong magic.

The red-haired, green-eyed beauty blinking in the doorway was absolutely the last thing he'd expected to face.

Their gazes locked. Oric saw the panic that quickly passed through relief and into confusion. For a very long moment, he held her gaze, incapable of looking away. Fleetingly, he thought she might not be Lady Arlana—just a servant or perhaps Lady Arlana's maid. The brief hope that the breathtaking woman wasn't Arlana Von Fordin died quietly when Baron Fordin said, "Please, Arlana, come in and meet our guests. Lady Arlana Von Fordin, Lord Commander Oric of Czanri of Myseen of Browan. Lord Commander Oric, my cousin, Lady Arlana."

Ferdinand translated the introductions as Arlana dropped into a graceful curtsey. Oric, in turn, bowed low from the waist, as was the Karasnian custom. He studied the young sorceress as she moved into the room and took the seat to the left of Aaron's desk. He could see now the strong resemblance to her mother in the fairylike, angular facial features. Her body was thin, almost too thin, but still surprisingly voluptuous wrapped in the emerald silk of her tightly bodiced gown. Her pale skin, brushed with faint freckles, pinkened under his scrutiny.

Her blush pulled a reluctant smile through his controlled expression. So she was human after all. And capable of embarrassment. Quite the most charming embarrassment he'd ever seen, if he wanted to be honest with himself.

Which he didn't.

Her gaze dropped to her lap and Oric noticed the small mole on her right jawline. He had an almost uncontrollable urge to run his fingertip over that small dot.

Exerting a considerable effort, Oric pulled his attention back to the matter at hand, irritated by his response. When he faced Baron Fordin, the young man regarded him with storm clouds racing in his eyes. Oric hazarded a quick glance at Lady Tiya and Lord Kevin, who both looked suspicious and scared. Then he met the thunderclap of Baron Fordin's gaze again.

"Arlana," Lord Aaron began without taking his gaze from Oric, "the Lord Commander is here to request your presence in Browan's capital city, Czanri." The baron's eyes flicked to his cousin's face when her head snapped up. His voice gentled as he said, "He claims it's the prophecy, cousin. Your fate might finally have found you."

Oric watched Arlana's face closely as Ferdinand quietly translated the baron's words.

She sat perfectly still, gaze locked with her cousin's, no expression touching her features. Then her gaze slid to her mother and father. Lord Kevin, still holding his wife's hand, nodded once. Lady Tiya echoed his affirmation with a reluctant nod.

Oric hid his astonishment. They seemed to accept, however reluctantly, that this was part of Arlana's future. That she'd been born for this. Or at the very least, they were willing to listen to more. His relief was like a blow to the stomach.

Jaw set, Arlana looked up at Merig. "It's time, little magic," the ageless sorcerer said in a voice like soft music.

Her mouth quivered for a second before she controlled her reaction. She turned a steady gaze to her cousin. "Tell me."

# CHAPTER TWO

Aaron stopped walking and faced Arlana, taking her hands in his. Around them, the air was filled with the scent of spring flowers and the music of birdsong. In the distance, Arlana could just hear the waters of the fountain at the center of the family gardens.

"Arlana, are you sure?"

She looked down to where Aaron's large hands engulfed her own and nodded.

"You don't have to do this. We can't be certain this was what the prophecy intended for you."

The urgency and protectiveness in his tone made her smile. "I do have to do this, Aaron. Merig feels fairly certain this is what the prophecy intended, at least in part, and I trust his judgment. In the past, his feelings have rarely been wrong. We've wondered for years now why I was given so much power, what purpose was served by my birth. This trip into Browan may finally answer those questions."

"What if this is a ruse, concocted by the same person who arranged your kidnapping? Have you considered that? What if you're walking into the very hands of the person or people we've been trying to protect you from for all these years? The people who took you knew you were the prophesied one too."

"I was carried into Bthak, not Browan, and we both know there's no love lost between those two countries."

"But if you hadn't stopped it, you would have been gated from the place in Bthak where you were rescued. Who's to say you wouldn't have been gated to Browan?"

"I suppose it's possible. But then how would you explain the assistance of the GeMorin if the people responsible for my kidnapping were from Browan? A treaty between anyone in Browan and the GeMorin—a treaty that would force the Browans to cross into Bthak or the GeMorin to cross into Browan—would have been discovered some time in the last twenty years, don't you think? Especially with Merig looking for that sort of movement."

Arlana took a deep breath. "The Lord Commander has come with letters of introduction and commendation from the Browan senate as well as Ambassador Rowkan. The seals on both letters are authentic. And the ambassador has the king and queen's recommendation. We both know how good the queen is at judging character." Arlana smiled, forcing a reluctant nod from Aaron. It was well-known throughout the kingdom that their grandmother instinctively knew things about people.

"I still don't trust this Lord Commander Oric." Aaron's handsome face crinkled into a scowl.

"You don't trust anyone but family around me. I am perfectly capable of taking care of myself." She chuckled and squeezed his hands. "Ever since you were old enough to use a real sword, you've treated me like delicate porcelain. When we were kids, you were never this concerned about my wellbeing. You were more concerned with teasing me mercilessly."

Aaron grinned. "You were too easy to goad into fights."

"That was very dangerous, you know," she said, frowning in the same way her mother did when she scolded them. "I could have turned you into a snake."

"You did turn my practice sword into a snake once!"

"Well, you kept poking me. What'd you expect me to do?"

Aaron chuckled and kissed her cheek. "I thought it was fun the way you could do things like that. And I always knew you'd never hurt me. That's why I teased so much."

"You're just lucky I love you."

"I know. I love you too, Arlana. And I can't help worrying about you." His grin dissolved once more into a worried frown. "I don't like the idea of you going beyond the Karasnian borders without an escort."

"You heard the Lord Commander. No Karasnian but myself will be allowed to accompany the group."

"And that's the part I don't like. That man trying to get you alone in a foreign country where you don't even speak the language."

Arlana raised an eyebrow. "Are you more worried about my life or my virtue?"

Looking directly into her eyes, he said, "Both."

"Aaron, I'm twenty years old. And I have a destiny to face." She shook her head, a crooked smile turning up her mouth. "I've supposedly got more magical power than any other human on the planet, and my cousin is worried about—" A hesitant cough cut off the rest of her sentence.

She glanced up to see one of the castle's servants standing nearby. He shifted from foot to foot, looking distinctly uncomfortable. Behind him stood Lord Commander Oric and his translator.

Aaron scowled at the two Browans before addressing the servant. "Yes?"

"My lord, the Lord Commander wishes a word with her ladyship." The servant's dark eyes darted from Arlana to Aaron, then dropped to the ground.

"Thank you, Gretch. You can return to the castle now."

The man hurried away at Aaron's quiet order, looking almost painfully relieved.

"What did you wish to discuss with the lady?" Aaron asked Oric directly.

The translator murmured his translation and the Lord Commander answered without taking his gaze from Aaron's. "I wish to speak to Lady Arlana alone, Baron Fordin."

Both Aaron and the Lord Commander stood with legs braced, hands ready at their sides, their mouths hard lines of distrust and barely contained animosity.

At the Lord Commander's declaration, Arlana watched Aaron's eyes darken. His hands fisted into tight balls and his jaw clenched. She'd seen that look before. Aaron was spoiling for a fight. She placed a calming hand on his biceps, felt the muscles flexing, and forced him to look down. "I'll speak with him, Aaron."

His eyes narrowed. "Arlana…"

"I'll be fine, cousin." She held his gaze for a full minute before he nodded. She let out a relieved sigh. The last thing she wanted to do was break up a fight between the two men. The necessary spell would reveal too much of her powers to strangers.

With one last dark glare at Oric, Aaron walked stiffly from the gardens. She shook her head and faced the two strangers. The translator was a handsome man around Aaron's age. His black skin and straight black hair were a stunning contrast to the vibrant blue of his eyes. But she noted him only in passing. Her gaze was drawn almost unconsciously to Lord Commander Oric—to the black hair that dusted the top of his high-collared white tunic. She had to suppress a shudder. When she'd walked into Aaron's private audience chambers earlier, the sight of that black hair against the white tunic had stopped her breath and started her heart hammering. Flashes of her dreams had crashed down as panic closed her throat.

And then he'd stood and looked at her with those wonderful blue eyes.

Blue eyes that were studying her even now. Arlana felt her cheeks warming again under the Lord Commander's brazen stare. No man in Fordin dared look at her in that particular way.

Forcing back her natural shyness and ignoring the funny dance of her stomach, she took a moment to return his scrutiny. He was a few years older than Aaron and handsome in a hard way. The strong lines of his face looked incapable of softening even when he smiled, unlike Aaron who could still look like a boy when he grinned. Though the same height as her cousin, Lord Commander Oric was broader, his muscles denser, but his size belied the negligently graceful way he moved. *A lot like Father and Jacob*, she thought absently.

*You don't look like a powerful sorceress, Lady Arlana.*

Arlana froze. She'd been looking directly at his lips and knew he hadn't spoken aloud. But it'd been years since she'd overheard another person's thoughts, years since she'd allowed other thoughts into her mind. And he'd spoken Karasnian! That final realization quelled her shock and fanned her anger.

"Why do you use a translator if you can speak our language?" she demanded without thinking.

Oric's assessing gaze flicked to wary surprise. He looked at his translator, who shrugged, looking equally confused. *Perhaps she can hear us.*

Arlana gasped. This voice was different—Ferdinand's mental voice. He'd also spoken in Karasnian, but his comment had been directed to Oric.

Oric faced her again, his brow furrowed deeply. *You can hear this, can you not, my lady?*

"How do you do that?" she demanded. "You can speak to each other?"

*Please, do not speak of this aloud.*

The brush of Oric's mental voice was rich and warm in her mind, sparking tiny shivers down her spine. "Stop that."

*If you would please speak this way, it would—*

"I can't speak in someone else's mind."

Oric's blue eyes narrowed to slits. *You can hear, but you cannot speak? How do you know?*

"First, tell me why you've been using a translator when you can speak my language." Arlana had never admitted to anyone, not even Merig or her mother, that she could hear the thoughts of other people. She'd learned at a very young age how to shield against those thoughts—it hurt too much to hear what went on in other people's minds. Now here stood two people who talked freely to each other with their minds and spoke to her in the same way. The shock of discovery was quickly followed by curiosity and instantly after that a wariness that counseled caution.

"I do not speak your language as well as Ferdinand," Oric answered aloud with only a faint accent. "And this was a delicate diplomatic mission."

His accent made her language sound exotic and sensual. "Your Karasnian sounds perfect." His smile brought another wash of heat to her cheeks.

"My lady is kind. But I have not mastered the nuances of your language as well as my translator." Oric glanced at Ferdinand and the man walked away without another word, leaving Arlana and Oric alone in the gardens.

She watched the translator's back with a sudden sense of panic. She didn't want to be left alone with a man who might be able to read her thoughts. As if he'd done just that, Oric's sultry smile deepened and he sauntered closer. Arlana took an involuntary step backward. Then, annoyed by her retreat, she lifted her chin and refused to move another inch, even when he stopped entirely too close.

*Now, my lady*, Oric's mental voice whispered into her mind, *perhaps you will explain why you believe you cannot speak this way.*

There was something much too intimate about this form of speech—something that made Arlana's nerves tingle. "Stop that," she said with as much command as she could muster. "Speak aloud."

*Why should I when this works just as well?*

"Stay out of my head!"

His smile was smugly gracious. "As my lady wishes."

The look in his eyes made Arlana nervous. He might be speaking aloud, but that didn't mean he would stay out of her thoughts. She closed her eyes briefly and added an extra layer to the shield that protected her mind from outside thoughts. When she opened her eyes, Oric was staring, surprise clear in the set of his mouth and jaw.

His surprise made her smile. "Now," she said congenially, "perhaps you'll explain how you're able to speak with your mind."

He studied her for a long moment, his face schooled into a neutral mask. Finally, he said, "I will explain, my lady, but not now. Not here."

She was about to protest, when he stepped closer and took her arm. The contact froze her voice in her throat.

"Will you walk with me a moment, my lady?" Without waiting

for her answer, he guided her farther into the gardens, in the general direction of the fountain.

This close, his scent wafted around her. A heady mix of musk and pine smoke and something exotic she couldn't quite place. "Why did you wish to speak with me, Lord Commander?" She could only manage to get her voice just above a whisper. The feel of his large, warm hand on her elbow was almost as disconcerting as her first view of his black hair against his white tunic.

"I wish to discuss my reason for being here, my lady."

She frowned. "You've already made it quite clear why you're here. To take me back to Czanri."

"Of course. Perhaps I should have said that I wished to discuss your reaction to my presence."

Arlana looked away as her cheeks heated again and her heartbeat jumped. Her reaction to his presence was nothing short of disturbing. "Are you asking me if I'll agree to accompany you to Czanri, Lord Commander?"

He chuckled softly, and Arlana had the distinct impression he knew exactly what she'd really been thinking. She stopped and turned to face him, forcing him to drop his hold on her arm.

"Yes, my lady," he murmured. "That is what I am asking."

"Why do you think I don't look like a sorceress?" she asked abruptly.

He reached out and brushed a lock of her hair. "Red hair, green eyes. I had expected…I had expected you to have coloring more like Lady Tiya."

"My father has green eyes. Why shouldn't I?"

"True. But this," he ran a finger over the hair near her shoulder, "is not the coloring of great magical power."

"And how much do you know about magic, Lord Commander?"

"Enough."

"In that case, you'd know that it's a simple thing for a magician to alter the color of their hair and eyes. The spell is basic and takes a negligible amount of energy."

He acquiesced with a slight dip of his head. "As you say, my lady. But I cannot help wondering why. Why would a sorceress of your power cover the physical signs of that power?"

"Why not?"

For a silent moment, Oric studied her. Then his expression returned to the neutral mask of diplomacy. "Have you made your decision? Will you travel with my party to Czanri?"

She didn't even pause before answering, "Yes."

***

"Arlana, I don't want you traveling into Browan without at least a small Fordin guard." Kevin Fordin paced his sitting room.

On the couch set into the bay window—the only bay window built into Fordin castle's defensive façade—Arlana sat with her mother, watching her father pace restlessly through the room.

"The Lord Commander can't expect me to send my only daughter into a foreign land without so much as a maid."

"Da, I can protect myself. And although having a familiar face with me would be nice, it's far from necessary."

Tiya squeezed her daughter's hands. "It's just that we've spent so much time trying to keep you safe. You can't expect us to stop being concerned after twenty years of making your safety a priority in our lives."

Arlana chuckled. "I know you'll worry. But I'm not a six-month-old baby now. I've had twenty years to train my power."

"I'd still feel better if you had a few Fordin soldiers with you,"

Kevin muttered, still pacing.

"So would Aaron. But there's nothing a few soldiers can do to protect me that I can't do for myself."

"Sweetheart," Tiya said, "you've never been outside of our protection before. Don't underestimate the dangers posed by physical attacks."

Arlana sighed and looked down at her hands. "You've both spent the last twenty years trying to protect me, to keep me safe from…from everything. And in that time you've raised me to be a good person, and you've seen my power well trained." She looked up, meeting both of their gazes in turn. "But it's time to face my fate. I wasn't given this power to spend the rest of my life hiding behind these castle walls. This is something I have to do."

Tiya reached up and caressed her daughter's cheek. Tears welled in her eyes without spilling over. "I was younger than you when I faced the first big challenge of my life," she murmured. "But knowing that doesn't make this any easier. I'll miss you."

Arlana let herself be folded into her mother's arms. "I'll miss you too, Mom."

***

Oric stared into his jug and ignored the stares, mumbled questions and comments of the other pub customers. The Blue Dragon was full at this time of the evening with merchants, traders and farmers alike. And Oric was the main topic of discussion.

He was too deep in his own thoughts to care much about the people surrounding him. He gulped down the rest of his ale and signaled to the barmaid. This Karasnian ale had turned out to be better than Ambassador Rowkan said it would be. Less bitter than the equivalent drink in his country.

"Bright ale," he told the barmaid when she reached his table.

She raised an eyebrow at his empty cup. "You sure you wouldn't like the gold, m'lord? Better flavor to that one."

"Bright ale," he repeated evenly.

The woman bobbed her head and hurried back to the bar.

Oric returned to his thoughts. All of which centered on Arlana Von Fordin. Though, he admitted with an inward grimace, that wasn't anything new. He'd spent his life shadowed by her specter, anticipating this moment with a combination of dread and intrigue. He should hate her for the life she took from him, the life she'd forced on him.

There'd been times when he had hated her.

The corners of his mouth lifted with the barest of smiles as he remembered the blush that had crept over her cheeks when he'd looked at her, when he'd touched her arm. Hate her or not, he was drawn to her. Powerfully. Now more than ever. Seeing and talking to her finally, after twenty years, hadn't lessened his obsession. If anything, his obsession was taking on new dimensions, turning in a direction he'd have only admitted to in his most secret of fantasies.

And for that he wanted to hate her even more.

The barmaid returned with his ale, his fourth for the evening, and scurried away, eyes averted. He could imagine what he must look like to the woman—a dark, brooding stranger taking up an entire table, drinking ale as if it were little more than water. He glanced up, taking in the rest of the pub's common room for the first time since entering. The multiple pairs of eyes that had been covertly watching him quickly turned away, focused on the tables before them or the person across from them. Their mental noise hummed just at the edge of his mind. With a snarl, he reinforced his blocks and cut the irritating noise down to almost nothing.

He gulped his ale in three large swallows and thunked the jug onto the table, then pulled out a handful of gold coins—Karasnian kern. The coins were as strange as everything else in this country. He fingered them a moment, then dropped three on the table—probably much more than was required—and left the dark tavern.

Outside, the spring air was cool, funneling through the quiet cobblestone streets in gentle waves. Beneath the lingering smell of smoke and ale from the pub, Oric could just detect the scent of the spring flowers that decorated the windows of nearby homes. Only a few people moved along the dim street. Every one of them crossed the road to avoid him.

He stood just outside the circle of light from a streetlamp, debating whether to go back to the castle or walk through the city. They were leaving first thing in the morning, a departure he both looked forward to and vaguely regretted. He'd have liked a few more days to explore this strange new place, but the relief of getting away from so many untrained minds was almost tangible.

He looked down the hill at the buildings bracketing the street, tempted not to waste this last opportunity to see the city. He focused inward, judging the hour. Late—nearing middle night. His innate sense of time forced him to admit that he should return to the castle for a full night's rest.

With an exhalation that was almost a sigh, he pushed away from the shadowed wall of The Blue Dragon and turned back toward the castle. Only to bump hard into a townswoman. He caught her upper arms when she stumbled back from the impact, supporting her while she regained her balance. She wore a simple brown dress, the snug bodice showing a small waist and voluptuous curves. Her face was turned toward the ground as she worked to right herself.

"Pardon me," he said in Karasnian, dropping his hands when she straightened.

The woman looked up, eyes wide, then glanced away quickly and started to walk around him.

Oric frowned. Taking hold of her arm, he turned her toward him again and lifted her chin. "Lady Arlana?"

Her hair was now a deep brown, pulled back in a loose braid that hung down her back. Her eyes were a brown so dark that in the faint light they looked almost black. But there was no mistaking her fairylike features—the pretty, full mouth, the dusting of freckles across her nose, the small mole on her right jaw.

Without conscious thought, Oric gently took hold of a strand of her silky hair where it had escaped the braid and brushed against her cheek. Arlana took a step back, pulling herself up to her full height, which was still half a foot shorter than his, and gave him an offended look that he found quite delicious.

"What are you doing here?" she demanded, her voice pitched low.

"Having a drink." *And if you wish for this conversation to remain private, this way of talking is much easier than whispering.*

She glared, which only made him smile. He couldn't seem to help it. No matter the color, her eyes caught fire when she was irritated. And he liked that fire a lot.

"I told you already," she hissed, "I can't do that."

"Very well. Aloud then." He stepped close again and recaptured the loose lock of her hair. "Is there a reason for this change?"

"In the dark, it's harder to recognize me this way."

"I recognized you."

"You wouldn't have if you hadn't nearly knocked me off my feet."

"Perhaps." But he doubted it. She was far too beautiful to go unnoticed, no matter what color her hair and eyes.

"If you'll excuse me." She tried to step around him again.

He blocked her with his body. "Where do you go so late at night, my lady? Is it safe for you to walk the streets unescorted?"

"Perfectly safe so long as you stop saying my name aloud and referring to me as 'my lady.'"

"What shall I call you then?" His smile turned wicked and that charming pink blush colored her cheeks.

"There's no need to call me anything. If you'll step aside, I'll be on my way."

"You never told me why you are walking so late at night." He didn't bother stepping out of her way.

Hands on her hips, she threw her chin higher. "If you must know, I wanted to see the city one last time before leaving." A slight quivering of her bottom lip belied her haughty pose.

He cupped her cheek in one hand, running his thumb gently over her soft skin.

Her hands fell back to her sides and her gaze dropped to the street.

"I will walk with you," he murmured. "Perhaps you will show me the city as you see it?"

She looked up again, her eyes wet and luminous in the faint light of the streetlamp. A small smile curved her mouth and she nodded.

They turned down the street, walking away from the castle. Fordin was built atop a large hill. It covered the hillside and was just starting to spill out past the city walls. The roads curved and circled around between stone and wooden buildings. The roofs were tiled or wooden beamed, mainly peaked. Most of the windows were shuttered against the night, but flower boxes hung from houses and merchant buildings alike. In the day, the streets would be filled with people, animals, merchant traffic and the noise of daily life. Now the only sounds were those spilling out of the occasional pub or the shuffle of Oric and Arlana's passage.

They walked in silence while Arlana took in the familiar sights of her home. She stopped in front of a two-story shop, the wooden sign above the door showing an open book embossed in red with the name Debber. She smiled at the dark window front. "This is my grandfather's store."

"Your mother's father. The bookbinder."

"Yes," she said, a touch of surprise in her quiet voice. "He doesn't really work much anymore. Mostly he supervises. But he's still here every day."

Oric glanced down. She was looking at the storefront, but her gaze was turned to some inner thought.

"When I was a child, I thought I'd make a very good bookbinder. I wanted to be…"

She sucked in her lower lip, but not before Oric noticed the slight quiver. The urge to comfort that sadness with his arms and his lips was overpowering. And damned annoying.

She took in a deep breath and started back down the street. "I came here a lot as a child. When I could get out of the castle. I used to follow Aaron when he came to watch Grandpa work."

"You are very close with your cousin?"

"Most of the time." She smiled. "He's as much a brother to me as my own brother."

"Nickolas is in the city now?"

Arlana's head jerked up. "You know my brother's name?"

Oric's brow arched. "It is not a secret, my lady."

"He's at the university in Meth," she said after a pause.

"Ah, yes. I remember now. He's been gone for a year. Studying diplomacy, if I remember correctly."

"How do you know so much about my family?" She stopped to face him, hands on hips.

Oric's amusement vanished. "It has been my duty for many years to learn everything I could about you and your family. You might be surprised at how much I know."

"Why?"

"Because, Lady Arlana, it was my position. My duty."

They glared at each other for a heartbeat before Arlana turned and began walking again, faster this time.

Oric kept up without effort. He was so busy thinking of all the reasons he had to despise the woman next to him that her sudden laughter took him completely by surprise.

She'd stopped at the foot of an alley that dead-ended into a wooden fence. She clapped her hands together and trotted into the alley.

Oric was so nonplussed by the change he simply stood and stared after her for several minutes. He finally followed when she bent down at the wooden fence and picked something up.

"What is that?" he demanded, his tone harsher than necessary.

She grinned, all of her previous hostility vanished. She held up a piece of weather-worn wood that had been carved into the shape of a throwing knife the size of his palm. "I didn't think any of these would still be here," she said. She flipped the wooden dagger in her fingers from tip to handle and back to tip. "Vic taught me how to throw knives using these. We had to sneak off to practice because my mom would never understand. But Vic thought I should learn how to use a physical weapon, even if I was the most powerful sorceress in the world. Those were her words. She said you never could tell when you might need a good throwing dart."

Oric had to remind himself to breathe. Her face was glowing with memories and laughter. When he could find his voice again, he asked, "Vic?"

"Victoria Flash. Well, that was her street name. She's Victoria Von Marin now."

"General Marin's wife."

"You've heard of Jacob, too?"

"Of course. But I've heard more about his wife. She's gambled Ambassador Rowkan out of quite a bit of gold. He swears she cheats."

Arlana laughed. "She does. When she feels like it. She used to be a thief and a street con and a spy, and she started a gang war once and… And she helped save my life when I was a baby." She looked back down at the wooden knife, stroking the warped wood fondly.

Oric stared at her fingers as they brushed along the wood. When he realized what he was doing, and the direction his thoughts had turned, he pulled away his gaze. What the hell was he doing here? He was fanning the flames of an obsession that already endangered his mission.

"Why are you scowling?"

Her voice startled him. "I am not scowling," he shot back. In truth, he hadn't even realized he'd been looking at her.

"Yes, you are. You're frowning, and you've got these wrinkles right here." She tapped his forehead just above the bridge of his nose. "That's called a scowl."

Oric stared, incredulous. And then, slowly, his mouth turned up into a smile, relaxing the creases on his brow. Hate her or not, she was quite probably the most charming woman he'd ever met. With a sigh, he murmured, "Good night, my lady," and walked back up the alley, leaving Arlana to gawk at his retreating back. He had a sinking feeling her charm would be his doom.

# CHAPTER THREE

Her mother was crying. Arlana couldn't remember the last time she'd seen her mother let tears escape her perfect blue eyes. Around them, the Browan entourage waited for her to say her final goodbyes. Half the town gathered outside the castle gates. The rest lined the streets she would follow as she left the city.

But all she could see was the sadness in her giant father's eyes and the tears on her mother's cheeks.

Tears that reflected the bright spring sunlight like tiny prisms, breaking the light into a thousand colored rainbows. With a kind of helpless fascination, she watched the colors dance and grow and twist out toward her. In the small stretch of air that separated her from her parents, the rainbow colors began to coalesce into a square. The square grew, elongated, and the colors condensed until the space before her was black—a blackness that swallowed light.

Around her, silence filled the courtyard. She barely noticed. She could no longer see her parents. That didn't seem to matter either. All of her attention was focused on the center of that black rectangle from which she was powerless to step away. For one heart-stopping instant, she knew it would grow until it swallowed her, her city, her world.

Then something moved within.

And he stepped out of the blackness.

He was no longer wearing white. His black tunic and hose matched his hair and eyes. Matched the darkness at his back. His face seemed a thing without a body against the black. But his jet eyes were luminous, filled with a light that couldn't come through the hole. A terrifying and captivating light.

He stood only inches away. The scent of sandalwood filled the air. She stared up into those black eyes and felt herself begin to fall.

"It is time at last, my love."

His voice brushed over her, a caress. A threat.

He reached forward, looked into her very soul, touched her hand and whispered, "Come to me, Arlana."

Arlana lurched upward, flinging her fur blankets across the tent. The sound of a scream—her scream—hung in the air, but she wasn't sure whether she'd cried out in her dream or aloud. The scent of sandalwood permeated the narrow space, choking her, forcing her to gasp in quick, deep breaths. She blinked into the darkness, spots of color dancing before her eyes, and hugged her arms to her chest.

"My lady? Are you well?"

She stifled a startled yelp at the sound of the quiet voice. She looked around, her heart thumping, and verified her surroundings, assuring herself she was awake. After a moment, she remembered the guard placed outside her tent—a Fordin guard. "I'm fine," she whispered back through the canvas wall. "I was dreaming."

They were still in Fordin Forest. Only a day since leaving her home and already it felt like she'd been away forever. Her father and Aaron had insisted that a regiment of Fordin soldiers accompany the group to the Karasnian-Browan border. From there, they'd have to leave her. Oric had made it abundantly clear that no Karasnian but herself would be allowed into Browan.

But for the night, she was still in her own country, with loyal soldiers surrounding her tent. If she chose, she could return home. That thought was her only comfort in the face of her dream.

Her hand trembled. The skin where he'd touched her felt icy and feverishly hot all at once. She rubbed her palms together, calming her heartbeat with an effort. He'd never touched her in the dreams before. Not physically.

As her body relaxed, weariness overwhelmed her. Dawn felt far away. Afraid to close her eyes but craving more sleep, Arlana pulled her furs around her, tucking them tightly under her chin. She stared at the wall of her tent, fighting a losing battle. Her eyes finally closed, and she slept too deeply to dream.

The sounds of rustling footsteps pulled Arlana back out of sleep. Light filtered dully through the tent, and the scent of cooking fires mingled with the pines. Her eyes were gritty and swollen, as if she hadn't slept at all. Groaning, she rolled out of her furs and shuffled through her trunk for something to wear. On her departure from Fordin, ceremony had demanded she wear the black robes of a magician. Today, she decided tunic and hose would be infinitely more comfortable.

Sunlight dappled the forest floor and lit the green boughs when she finally stepped out of her tent. She took in a deep breath, clearing away the last of the sandalwood scent from her nostrils. Around her, the camp was busy making ready for the day. Small cooking fires dotted the area, and the welcome smell of coffee carried on a cool morning breeze.

Arlana stretched until her spine popped, then began breaking down her tent. Two Fordin soldiers hurried over and carried her trunk back to one of the wagons. She'd just collapsed her tent and was thinking about how good a cup of coffee would taste when a hand dropped onto her shoulder.

She jumped and had to bite back a yelp.

"We have people to do that for you, my lady," Oric said.

She took a deep breath, making sure she was under control before she turned. "I don't mind doing it myself. I… What?"

His brow furrowed with his frown. "You did not sleep well, my lady?"

Arlana chuckled. "Does it show?" She rubbed her eyes and shrugged.

He cupped her chin and lifted her face. "Perhaps it would be best if you journeyed in the carriage today."

"No. I'll ride." The one point that Oric and Aaron had agreed on was that she should travel by carriage. Oric had brought a well-appointed coach from Browan for that very reason. Unfortunately for both her cousin and the Lord Commander, Arlana flatly refused to travel tucked away from the sun and insisted on riding her mare, Esmerelda.

"My lady, if the journey is too hard—"

"It's not the travel, Lord Commander," she said, pulling her chin away from his hand. "I just didn't sleep well last night."

For a moment, he looked as if he'd say more, then he nodded sharply. "Come and eat then. I did not bring servants all the way from Czanri for you to let them sit idle."

He took her arm and led her toward a fire before she could protest.

"Lord Commander—"

"Oric."

"What?"

"It is too early for titles."

"Very well. Oric, then. I don't require servants to take care of my every need. I am capable of taking down my own tent."

He looked at her sideways, the faintest of smiles on his hard mouth. For some reason, that look made her stomach dance.

"Would you like some coffee, my lady?"

Arlana frowned. "Well, you might as well call me Arlana. As you said, it's too early for titles. And yes, I'd love a cup of coffee."

She sat on a dew and moss-covered rock, the thick material of her long tunic keeping out the damp, and accepted the steaming cup he handed her. She let her gaze wander around the rest of the camp. Her first sip of the coffee brought a contented sigh. She turned back to Oric. He was still dressed in Karasnian-style clothing, but subtle differences marked his apparel as foreign. His black leather riding trousers were laced with purple and his violet high-collared tunic was embroidered with yellow, green and black designs the likes of which she'd never seen before.

He looked entirely too good for Arlana's comfort.

Because he was still standing, looking down with a curious expression on his face, she asked, "What?"

"Is this closer to your natural coloring?" He gestured at her hair.

She glanced at the bright golden strand falling across her shoulder. "No. I borrowed this color from Baroness Georna. The eye color too. She has beautiful eyes."

"They are naturally violet?"

"Um hmm."

He tilted his head to one side, examining her but keeping his thoughts hidden. Then quietly he asked, "Do you ever simply wear your natural colors, Arlana?"

"Not if I can help it." She looked into her mug and gulped down more coffee. "Are you going to sit or are you just going to stand over me?" She took a deep breath and met his brilliant blue-eyed gaze again.

"I must see to my company. We will leave within the hour." He stared into her eyes for a heartbeat longer, then walked away.

Arlana finished her coffee and ate the biscuits offered to her while watching the camp activity. Between the Browan entourage and the Fordin garrison, there were over a hundred people moving about. A lot of people to escort one woman to the Browan border and beyond. Oric's company—a full seventy people—was made up of soldiers, a handful of servants and his translator. There were four supply wagons, not including the wagon for the Fordin soldiers, the carriage meant to carry her and enough horses to carry every soldier.

Arlana couldn't help but wonder why she merited such a large group. Just to supply them all for the six-week trip seemed more costly than could possibly be worthwhile for escorting a single person. Unless, of course, they were afraid of her. She sighed. That was all too likely. And all too familiar.

As Oric promised, the camp was packed and ready to depart before a full hour passed. Arlana climbed onto Esmerelda's back and led the company at Oric's side. He scowled but didn't comment.

They traveled along a wide, rough road through Fordin Forest. Only a very few ever journeyed between Browan and Karasnia, so the road had fallen into disrepair. Arlana had never been through this part of the forest before. She spent the morning watching the trees, trying to catch sight of the forest's inhabitants.

At midmorning, they passed through a small village, or what was left of it. At one time, the village had housed a garrison of soldiers to patrol the borders and hold the inner forest against Browan invaders. It had been one of several villages strung through the length of the forest for that purpose. After two hundred years of peace, the villages had ceased to have a purpose and all but the hardiest of forest dwellers moved to less isolated villages or to Fordin city.

As they passed the few remaining stone and thatch houses, a handful of Karasnians came outside to watch the procession. Most gawked at the strange foreigners that made up the majority of the group, but one person—an old woman, bent and withered—waved enthusiastically as they approached.

"My lady!" The woman's voice crackled above the sound of their passage. "Gonna go stir up some trouble for the Browans are ye?" She screeched out a loud laugh and raised a crooked brown hand.

Caught between embarrassment and amusement, Arlana smiled weakly and waved back. She paused mid-wave and looked closer at the woman. She looked familiar. Well, sort of familiar. But it couldn't be the same woman she'd met when she ran away six years ago. This was the wrong part of the forest. There was no reason to think the old woman she'd met would move from one isolated part of Fordin Forest to another. Besides, this woman wasn't greeting her like she knew her personally. Arlana looked again, and the old woman winked. Taken aback, Arlana turned in her saddle to watch the woman as she continued waving at the passing line of soldiers. When the woman made no further effort to talk directly to her, Arlana settled back into her saddle and shrugged. That couldn't possibly have been the same woman.

She glanced at Oric. He was watching both the road and the few villagers as if expecting an attack. "They won't hurt anyone," she told him.

He spared her an unreadable glance before turning back to his vigilant scan of the area. Arlana sighed.

They stopped briefly at midday to eat and water the horses at a narrow stream. Arlana squatted down near Esmerelda's head while the mare drank and watched the trees on the opposite bank. "They're out there today, Esmerelda," she whispered. "Can you feel them? I think they might just be following us." The mare answered with a quiet snuffle and dipped her nose back into the cold water.

Arlana chuckled and returned her attention to the trees. She stretched out her senses, touching the layers of magic that surrounded her, breathing it in as other people breathed in air. They were out there. She couldn't see them. Couldn't even hear them above the sounds of humans and horses. But she could feel them. She smiled and giggled.

For the rest of the afternoon, she tried to catch sight of them. She could tell when they got closer to the group, but they were too elusive for even a watchful eye.

Oric stopped the group for the night well before the sun touched the horizon. She suspected he ordered the early halt out of deference to her. She'd have told him the consideration wasn't necessary, but he didn't give her the chance. By the time she'd taken care of Esmerelda and seen her settled for the evening, all of the tents, including hers, had been raised and a series of cooking fires speckled the area. Torn between hunger and curiosity, Arlana's growling stomach won out, and she sauntered over to a fire. She could go fairy hunting later.

She sat on a log beside a fire with several Fordin soldiers and chatted while a dinner of beans and fresh rabbit cooked. The smell of the sizzling meat had her mouth watering long before the rabbit was finished. One of the soldiers—a woman only a few years older than Arlana—handed her a wineskin then launched into a story about one of the farmers who lived outside the city, a man known to wander into town on rare occasions mumbling about chickens, bees and poison.

Arlana grinned as she listened to the story and didn't realize quite how much wine she'd drained from the wineskin until she tried to stand. A wash of dizziness sat her back on the log, hard. The woman telling the story smiled and handed her a plate of food.

"Too much on an empty stomach does the same thing to me," she told Arlana in a conspiratorial whisper.

Arlana smiled, then ducked her head and dug into her dinner. Under normal circumstances, the people of Fordin were kind to her— friendly, but in a deferential way. An undercurrent of fear usually accompanied their conversations with her. For reasons she could only guess at, though, this group treated her not like a powerful sorceress and the cousin of their baron, but simply like another countryman. She suspected their reasons had to do with being surrounded and outnumbered by a group of mysterious foreigners.

Despite the camaraderie, the soldiers were still extremely protective of her, glaring off any Browan that ventured too close. She thought the effort a bit pointless since after tomorrow night she'd be alone with those same Browans, but since they were probably acting on orders handed down directly from Aaron, she couldn't blame them.

By the time she finished eating, the effects of the wine had dimmed and she could stand without stumbling. The sun had set, filling the forest with a darkness broken only by the campfires. With her belly full and a good amount of wine running through her veins, sleepiness suddenly swamped her. She wished the soldiers at her fire a pleasant night and wandered toward her tent, hiding a yawn behind her hand.

Oric stopped her as she was pulling back the flap.

"My lady, may we speak a moment?"

Her mouth quirked. "Back to titles, are we? Very well. What did you wish to speak about, Lord Commander?"

His eyes narrowed. Even in the limited light, his eyes shone brilliantly blue beneath the heavy weight of his lowered brows.

"You're scowling at me again, Lord Commander. Why?"

"I am not— Lady Arlana, I must ask you to order your soldiers to refrain from provoking my guard."

"What? What are you talking about?"

"I just separated a potential fight between several Fordin soldiers and a few members of my guard."

"And why do you assume the Fordin soldiers began the argument?"

"They did not realize that several of my people speak your language—"

"I didn't know that either."

"And made comments not intended to flatter," he finished delicately, ignoring her interruption.

"And they did this on purpose? Perhaps the Browan soldiers misunderstood."

"They did not."

Arlana stared up into his hard face, into eyes that were almost too blue to be real, and saw he wasn't going to listen to anything she had to say in her soldiers' defense. His obstinacy annoyed her. She pursed her lips. "I'll speak to the lieutenant of the Fordin garrison, Lord Commander, but I suggest you speak with your guard as well. A fight is generally made up of more than one side." When she turned back toward her tent, he took hold of her arm and spun her around.

She glared, her hands fisted and her jaw clenched. She was so prepared to argue for the honor of her soldiers, Oric's next words caught her completely off guard.

"Why did you not tell me you were having nightmares?"

Her mouth dropped open. With an effort, she snapped it shut. His voice had lost its hard edge, softening into a deep, warming baritone. Where his hand still clasped her upper arm, heat spread through her tunic and raced across her body. The sensation mingled pleasantly with the wine already coursing through her.

"I…I didn't see any need to tell you," she murmured. "It isn't really important."

"It is important."

His hand squeezed just a bit tighter—not enough to hurt, but enough to emphasize his point.

"Why?" she asked.

*Because everything concerning you is important.*

His mental voice caressed her mind even as his hand reached up to touch her cheek. "Don't do that."

*As my lady wishes.* His hand fell away.

"Not that. Speak aloud."

The corners of his mouth tilted upward. His hand returned to gently caress her cheek.

And for several heartbeats, Arlana was too flustered to speak. Finally, panic and embarrassment had her demand, "How did you know I had a nightmare last night?" She sucked in a sharp breath. "You didn't…You weren't inside my head?"

His seductive half-smile disappeared and his hand pulled away. "Your soldiers are not the only ones guarding your tent, my lady. The Browan soldier on watch last night spoke enough Karasnian to understand why you woke up with a scream." He turned abruptly and stalked across camp.

Arlana stood for a long minute staring at the darkness. Then, with a curse colorful enough to have surprised her mother, she ducked into her tent. She was too tired and had too much wine in her system to worry about Oric. Or why he'd changed moods so suddenly. Was it her fault the man sent to escort her turned grumpy at the blink of an eye? She closed her thoughts to the look of insult on his face just before he'd stalked away. Or she tried to.

She was tired, she assured herself as she undressed for bed. And she really had had too much wine. She'd think about their conversation in the morning with a clear head. Yes. She would deal with the Lord Commander tomorrow. But as she cuddled beneath her furs, her errant mind insisted on taking her into sleep with thoughts of Lord Commander Oric of Czanri of Myseen of Browan.

The next morning Arlana woke feeling no more rested than she had when she'd gone to sleep. Between her sporadic dreams of Oric and Browan, and another haunting dream of *him*, she felt more like she'd spent the night in heavy activity. She forced herself to get up and get dressed. She had two very important things to do before they got moving. First, she had to ask Lieutenant Freemon to talk to the Fordin soldiers and urge them to avoid fights with the Browans.

Second, she had to apologize to Oric.

After a great deal of reluctant thought during the night, she realized she'd insulted his honor by accusing him of eavesdropping on her thoughts and dreams. She was quickly coming to realize that Oric ranked duty and honor very high in his life. Too high to resort to spying on other people's thoughts. He was a lot like Aaron in that way. Her cousin took great pride in his honor and would have been offended to have someone question it.

So she owed the Lord Commander an apology.

The instant she emerged from her tent, servants surrounded it, taking care of her belongings and packing up the tent in a matter of minutes. She sighed and went to find Lieutenant Freemon. The older guard stood near the Fordin supply wagon, supervising the reloading of their equipment.

The lieutenant's first reaction to Arlana's retelling of Oric's story was outrage that her soldiers would be accused of starting a fight with the bloody foreigners. But hard-earned discipline reasserted itself.

After a few deep breaths, with her jaw clenched tight, she agreed to talk to the soldiers. They only had one more day of travel and a night to spend with the Browans. She assured Arlana her garrison could avoid a fight for that long.

Satisfied, Arlana went to find Oric, but her stomach danced uncomfortably as she wandered the camp. She was hungry and needed coffee. She couldn't talk to him while she was still so groggy. As she ate, she tried to convince herself she wasn't really delaying. No matter that she kept her face turned to the ground in hopes that he wouldn't notice her and approach her first.

When she'd finished two mugs of coffee and was too full to eat any more, she went back to her search. She found him in less than a minute. He stood near the center of activity around the wagons. One of his soldiers passed as Arlana watched, and Oric suddenly started laughing, a sound that made Arlana's stomach flutter for reasons other than nervousness. The soldier looked back, grinning, then kept walking. Oric continued to chuckle, shaking his head as if he'd just heard a very amusing joke.

Arlana stood very still for a moment as her mind absorbed what she'd just witnessed. Then, for the first time in years, she lowered the shield that protected her from overhearing other people's thoughts. Listening passively, she could hear the Browans holding entire conversations with their minds. They could all do it, she realized with a start.

Even more startling, she couldn't hear them when they weren't "talking" to one another, unlike the Karasnians who were a constant noise in her head while her shield was lowered. The Browans kept their own thoughts shielded, protected from others listening in, instead of shielding against other thoughts the way she did.

Amazing. Gaping at the passing Browans, she very nearly forgot why she'd been looking for Oric. When she turned back in his direction, she found him staring at her, no trace of humor left in his hard face. She swallowed, trying to calm her suddenly jumping pulse, and forced herself the last few yards.

"Good morning, Lord Commander," she greeted, trying to smile and not succeeding very well.

"My lady." His expression never changed.

Well, damn it, you're not going to make this easy, are you? She took a deep breath. "I wanted to apologize for last night. I didn't mean to insult you by implying that you would listen in on my dreams. That was very rude of me, and I do hope you'll forgive me."

His expression remained the same—unreadable. But something changed in his eyes. Something crossed over the blue depths.

When he didn't comment, Arlana said, "You see, I have dreams, nightmares sometimes, and I don't like to discuss them. They really aren't that big a deal. I'm actually embarrassed to admit I still have nightmares, which is why I was so rude to you."

He raised one eyebrow, a slightly amused look wiping away his previous implacable expression. She stopped talking and heat flooded her face when she realized she'd been rambling. But he held her gaze so she couldn't turn away and hide her embarrassment.

"I accept your apology, my lady," he said. "I did not expect it, but I thank you for it."

He looked her over slowly, which only made her cheeks flame hotter.

"You have decided to stay with Baroness Georna's coloring?"

A heartbeat passed before she could answer. "Yes. This is one of my favorite hair and eye colors. It's different, but not too different." She bit her lip before the urge to ramble took hold again.

Oric ran the fingers of one hand through the loose locks of her hair, brushing the skin of her neck gently. Arlana hoped he didn't notice the shiver that raced up her spine at that brief contact. From the slight smile curving his lips, she was pretty sure he did notice her cheeks reddening and her breath hitching.

"One day," he said, "I would like very much to see your natural coloring."

Too flustered to speak now, she stared helplessly, wondering how other women would handle this situation. His hand fell back to his side and Arlana felt bereft.

"We leave soon, my lady. Your mare has been readied."

His voice returned to the neutral, hard strength of command.

Arlana nodded and walked toward Esmerelda in a daze. Lord Commander Oric was having a very peculiar effect on her. And she wasn't sure if that was a good thing or a bad thing. She did know that outside of her nightmare, she'd never in her life felt so insecure and so excited at the same time. The difference, however, between Oric and the man in the dreams was that she wasn't afraid of Oric.

She was terrified of the man in her dreams even as she was helpless to resist him.

The day was again warm and sunny with enough of a breeze to keep the forest from getting uncomfortably humid. They passed the last of the sparse population just before midday—a small shack that housed a hunter and his family. Arlana watched the building and realized it would be the last Karasnian home she'd see for a long time. The next group of people they'd encounter would be Browans.

She felt an instant twinge of sadness, but the feeling was quickly overshadowed by a thrumming excitement. The adventure ahead held an irresistible appeal after a lifetime of relative isolation. With her excitement came a renewed desire to watch for fairies. She stretched out her magical senses. And there they were again. Near this time.

Following close to the train of travelers.

She felt them close all the rest of the day, felt them watching. When the train was forced to a stop so a fallen tree could be removed from the center of the road, Arlana moved away from the milling people and horses and closer to the densely packed trees. Just above the sounds of her group she heard it—a faint echoing laughter like the sound of a thousand tiny bells.

"My lady?"

She spun in her saddle to see Oric riding up beside her. "Listen," she whispered, grinning. "Can you hear them?"

For several minutes they sat, listening. Oric's brow furrowed deeply with his concentration. The last of the echoing laughter died off just after they fell silent and didn't start again. At Oric's questioning glance, Arlana shrugged.

"What was that?" he whispered, still staring into the trees.

"Fairies. They're almost impossible to see. But sometimes you can hear them laughing. And I usually know when they're around."

"Have you seen them before?"

"I caught sight of one once, when I was very young. It was a fleeting glance, barely enough to be able to tell that what I'd seen was a fairy."

He tilted his head to one side, a slight smile lifting his mouth. "You and your mother both have the features of the fairy folk. At least the way fairies are described in stories and drawn in books."

"That's what my father always says. He used to call us his two forest fairies."

Oric smiled fully and started to say more, but a shout from behind them brought their attention to the train. The tree had been cleared from the road. They rode together in silence back to the head of the group. Although Oric remained relatively quiet for the rest of the day, Arlana noticed him looking into the woods, his ear tilted toward the trees.

# Chapter Four

Oric called an early halt again that evening, only an hour's ride from the border. Camp went up with the same speedy efficiency of the days before, leaving Arlana nothing to do but tend to Esmerelda.

Despite the fact that she should have been exhausted, the fairy laughter left her energized. And curious. She scanned the camp from where the horses were picketed. Everyone was busy with some occupation or other and meat was already roasting on spits over cooking fires. Dinner wouldn't be ready for awhile. She didn't want to make the same mistake as yesterday by drinking most of a wineskin on an empty stomach.

Giving Esmerelda a parting pat on the shoulder, she walked further into the forest, away from the noise of the camp.

She continued until she couldn't hear the camp anymore. Stretching out her senses, she felt the fairies again, all around now that she was deep into the trees. Then she felt them move, streaming past to converge at some point ahead. She followed at a trot, laughing as she ran, heedless of the direction.

She popped out into a clearing. And froze. The bonfire blazed high in the center of the dirt and twig-strewn space. The circling trees seemed to stretch out and upward in the dancing shadows from the flames. Here, this deep into the woods, much of the evening light was cut off so that the bonfire was dazzling against the growing dark.

Around the fire, they danced. Circling, twirling, leaping and running. They skipped and pirouetted at a dizzying speed to music Arlana could only hear when she reached out to the surrounding magics. The music colored the magics in bright, living rainbows that she saw as clearly as felt. The sound, the feel, the sight of the fairy dance made her heart thrum faster. Giddiness and energy flowed through her, around her, so she could think of nothing but the dance. And every muscle, every fiber of her body pulsed with the need to join.

The change came so suddenly she only had an instant to notice, to feel the coalescing power before the rectangle of impenetrable black opened at the opposite end of the clearing. Arlana blinked. He stepped from the blackness and stood for a moment simply looking into her eyes.

She couldn't turn away. The living light of black that was his eyes moved into her, over her, held her in place. He walked toward her then with the grace of a mountain cat, slowly circling the fire until he stood only a few feet away. Then he stopped. Annoyance and something that could have been anger waved through his black eyes.

The shift in his gaze freed her, allowed her to look away, and she noticed for the first time that the fairies no longer danced around the fire. They danced and circled her, making her their fire. She looked back at the man from her dreams. He tried to take a step closer and snarled viciously when he couldn't get near.

The anger was replaced by a beseeching look that shot into her soul, pulling her toward him.

*Come to me, my love.*

In that instant, Arlana felt helpless to prevent her body from moving forward. And she didn't care. She wanted, needed to go to him.

The fairy dance whirled wildly around her as she took her first step toward him. The music in the magic surrounding her pulsed and clashed and screamed. But nothing stopped her forward movement, until she stood an arm's length from him. And went no further. The fairies now spun in a tight circle, preventing her from moving any closer to him. When he reached out, his hand couldn't move beyond the ring of whirling dancers.

*Arlana? Please.*

She stared into the black depths of his eyes and trembled.

Just beyond the throbbing of her own pulse and the now frantic fairy music, Arlana heard her name again. Spoken aloud by a familiar voice. He flicked a glance past her shoulder toward the forest. His upper lip drew back.

Arlana turned her head. She heard her name being shouted again, this time closer. When she looked back at the man from her nightmares, he was backing away, retreating to the black door through which he'd first appeared. Just before stepping into that light-devouring darkness, he met her gaze. *Next time, my love.*

Her knees weakened and her pulse raced at his promise. She stared numbly as he disappeared inside the door and it collapsed in on itself. A deafening silence filled the clearing. She stood with her mind a blank and her ears ringing in the oppressive quiet.

When hands clasped her shoulders from behind, she screamed.

"Arlana!"

Oric's voice broke through her numb panic. She looked around wildly as if she'd just come out of a dream. The clearing was empty. No fairies. No fairy music. No sign of the bonfire. And no black-eyed man. She started to shake so hard her teeth chattered together.

"Arlana?"

She looked up. Oric's brow creased and his brilliant blue eyes narrowed as he studied her. She took a long, shaky breath and straightened, gaining control by an act of pure will. After several moments, her body stopped trembling and her heartbeat slowed. She glanced around one last time. Nothing to indicate that anything but Arlana had been in the clearing only moments before. She gave Oric a weak smile and said, "You startled me, Lord Commander."

"What's wrong? What happened?"

"Nothing. Nothing. I was just…just thinking. Not paying attention to my surroundings."

"I do not think you are telling me everything, my lady," he said quietly and evenly. His entire body quivered with tension, as if the slightest movement would snap his control.

"Nothing happened," she insisted.

"What are you doing here alone?"

His voice was so gruff, it was almost unintelligible. She swallowed. "Walking."

He grabbed hold of her shoulders and pulled her roughly against him, the move so fast she couldn't react.

"Never, ever leave the camp without an escort, Arlana. Do you understand? Never."

"I'm not a child." An edge of resentment crept in under her shock. "I'm perfectly able to take care of myself on a short walk in my home forest."

His jaw muscles jumped and his teeth ground together. Bringing his face very close to hers, he hissed, "I am responsible for your safety. And while your safety is my responsibility, you will do as I say. Never again leave the camp without an escort."

His breath was hot against her face. His eyes and the set of his hard mouth left no room for argument. Instinctively, she wanted to argue with his high-handed command. She wasn't a child, damn it. But the breeze shifted and the scent of sandalwood washed over her. She swallowed hard against a renewed rush of panic. "Very well, my lord," she mumbled, forcing words through a throat closing with fear.

Her sudden acquiescence deepened his frown. "You are not well, my lady. What happened? Are you injured?"

"I'm not injured. But I'd like to return to the camp now, if we could."

The hands clamped on her shoulders relaxed. "As my lady wishes." He took a single step away from her, took her arm in his and led her wordlessly back to camp.

***

Oric sat outside the entrance to Arlana's tent and watched the night. The darkness in the forest was almost complete. Through the tree boughs, he could just make out the star-speckled midnight sky. Nearby, two Fordin soldiers stood, hands on the hilts of their swords, eyes trained on him. Behind the tent, two Browan guards stood in similar poses, watching the Fordin soldiers. Oric ignored all of them.

He was worried. Something had happened in the woods today. Something had scared her. The memory of her panic-stricken eyes brought back a surge of protectiveness. Not so much the urge to protect her physically, though that was a part of it. But that was his duty. This was more a deep need to protect her emotionally. He wanted to erase the fear he'd seen in her eyes. Though why he should feel this overwhelming need to protect the emotions of the most powerful sorceress in the world, he didn't know.

And that worried him too.

He sat outside her tent because of this need, personally guarding her while she slept, despite the objections of the Fordin guard and the confusion of his own. His duty didn't necessarily translate into all-night vigils after a full day's travel. But he didn't trust anyone else to keep her safe tonight. Though just what it was he kept her safe from, he couldn't have said.

Oric turned that part over and over in his mind. He could feel the threat in the air. But threat from what? He hadn't seen signs of an attack when he'd found her in the forest. He hadn't seen signs of anything. What threat could make the hair on his forearms rise and bring out this violent protectiveness for the woman who'd stolen his life simply by existing? A woman he had, only days before, wanted desperately to hate.

He couldn't hate her anymore. It was hard to admit that to himself. But he couldn't see her face, remember the terror in her falsely violet eyes, and hate her. Knowing her, spending time with her, listening to Karasnian fairy laughter with her, had robbed him of his preconceived prejudices. Arlana Von Fordin was no longer some vague image to be scorned, but a real woman who laughed and smiled and feared.

He'd spent the better part of a lifetime resenting her existence, resenting her for being who and what she was. And he still resented, only now he had no outlet for that resentment. All he had was regret for the life that might have been, and an anger directed at everything and nothing.

A rustling inside the tent brought Oric out of his brooding thoughts. He focused inward long enough to use his innate sense of time to judge the hour. A little more than an hour past middle night. He frowned and listened expectantly until the movements inside the tent settled again. When she fell quiet, he looked around, marking the Fordin soldiers. Their vigilance and protectiveness for their mistress earned Oric's respect. He nodded, a quick acknowledgement that was returned in kind.

He turned his mind back to his own soldiers. *All is well?*

*Yes, Lord Commander.*

Oric gave a mental grunt of approval and closed off his thoughts again. Out in the forest, away from the thickly inhabited city, it was easier to block out the mental hum of the Karasnians. He could talk with his fellow Browans without getting a headache from the background noise.

He'd have to teach Arlana how to shield her thoughts after they entered Browan. She controlled her mind instinctively, and the blocks she'd put up to keep from overhearing all the thoughts around her helped prevent her own mental voice from intruding on the telepathic Browans most of the time. But every once in awhile, that instinctive control slipped and he'd inadvertently catch clipped phrases or images. Oric suspected he was the only one in the group powerful enough to overhear these lapses, but for her own privacy, and his sanity, he'd have to teach her a better control.

He was secretly anticipating these mental lessons and the intimate contact it required when a scream pierced the night. Oric was on his feet and inside the tent before any of the other soldiers moved. He found Arlana sitting on her fur bed, her thin shift wet with sweat, her face deathly pale. Wide violet eyes looked wildly around the tent. When she glanced at him, she gasped and her hands clenched into the furs tangled in her lap.

Oric knelt beside her, noting an odd scent in the air—sandalwood?—but her trembling shock kept him from thinking much about the smell. "Arlana?"

She stared for a heartbeat, and then recognition flooded her gaze.

"Oh," she squeaked and fell against him, clutching at his tunic and dragging in long, shaky breaths.

He wrapped her in his arms and rocked her gently, murmuring soothing nonsense in his own language.

"Lord Commander?" From the entrance to the tent, a Browan soldier and a Fordin soldier looked in, both with similar expressions of bewilderment and concern.

"She is all right." He spoke in Karasnian for the benefit of the Fordin soldier. "I will stay until she sleeps again. Back to the watch."

The Browan guard nodded and retreated immediately. The Fordin soldier hesitated, a lingering suspicion in his dark eyes. He glanced back at Arlana. She was quiet but still clutching at Oric's tunic. The guard finally nodded and returned to his station.

When they were alone, Oric squeezed her tighter, wanting to still her quaking body.

"They didn't stop him this time," she mumbled against his chest. "Why didn't they stop him this time?"

"Shhh, fayria. You're safe now. Everything will be all right." He slipped back into Browan then, mumbling reassurances until he felt her body relax.

She lifted her head from his chest and met his gaze. "I'm sorry," she whispered. "I didn't mean to—"

"Shhh. You have no reason to apologize." He rubbed one thumb over her cheek, caressing the soft skin, circling the small mole on her jaw. "Lie down now, fayria. I will stay until you sleep."

He pulled the furs up under her chin, letting one hand linger on her cheek. Then he sat back against the canvas wall across from her and she closed her eyes.

***

When Arlana awoke that morning, Oric's scent still lingered in the air. And just beneath, less oppressive than the night before but still present, was the scent of sandalwood. *I wonder when he left*, she thought as she climbed out from beneath the furs.

She emerged from her tent, groggy and uneasy, to see a change in camp. All of the Browans had returned to their native fashions. Brightly embroidered patterns and bits of metal and colored stones decorated vests, shirts and loose-fitting trousers of every color. Many of the soldiers donned headwraps or embroidered caps. Though the style and cut of clothing was similar for all of the soldiers, the outfits were a chaotic blend of patterns, colors and textures, more brilliant and exotic than her native fashions.

Unable to suppress the urge, she looked through the camp for Oric. She stared in helpless wonder at his change. The clothing should have looked odd, but on him it seemed perfect. And very sexy. His loose-legged trousers of deep purple, embroidered with mahogany thread, were tucked into the tops of tan suede knee-high boots. His shirt was a simple white full-sleeved garment with a high collar. But the vest… the vest was a collage of colors, patters and materials on a tan base. Above the armholes of the vest, a stiff vee of material stuck out over his shoulders, and from the edges hung a series of copper chains decorated with colored stones. A wide sash of decorative copper chain mail circled his waist, accenting his lean hips and broad chest. His black hair curved around the high white collar, but the mix of colors and different materials made confusing him for the man in her dreams impossible.

And the most amazing part was that he was dressed somberly compared to most of his guard. The Fordin soldiers looked drab in comparison in their uniforms of Fordin blue tunics and black leather pants.

While they prepared to leave, Arlana couldn't help studying the variations in the Browan clothing. Each new outfit was a feast for the eyes. *Maybe I can arrange for some new clothes*, she thought, overly conscious of her simple teal tunic and thick gray hose.

They rode the final hour to the border in a quiet, dew-wet morning. The sky was again brilliantly blue, the air heavy with moisture and the promise of a warm day. At the border, Arlana wished the Fordin guard a fair journey home and sent messages to her family. The guard stayed at the border, watching as she crossed into a country where no foreigner had entered in more than two hundred years.

Just as they crossed the border, Arlana felt a change. A subtle change, but a change nonetheless. She stretched out her physical and magical senses and saw the reason for the shift immediately. The magical energy surrounding her was… *Tainted* was the only way she could think to describe it. It flowed just a bit differently, felt just a little off, looked a touch wrong. It wasn't a good change or a bad change from the forces she was used to working with, as far as she could tell. It was merely different.

She glanced at Oric, wondering if he could tell. He wasn't a magician, so he probably didn't notice. There was a strained look to his expression, a crinkling around the eyes, like he was listening to something. Or like he had a headache. She chided herself for letting her imagination run. He'd probably been up most of the night, so of course he'd look strained. This was his homeland, the country he'd been born in and grown up in. The very air wouldn't trouble him.

It did bother her, though. Not a lot. But enough to notice. It was like a thought at the back of her mind, one she knew was there but couldn't quite remember. A little annoying, but not painful. The difference in the magical energy would make using that energy more difficult, however. Until she could trace the differences and understand the new flow, she'd have to rely on her internal power to do anything requiring magic.

She cast another sideways glance at Oric. Should she tell him? It left her temporarily vulnerable. Her internal power was greater than most, probably the greatest ever found in a human being, but it wasn't endless. Without being able to draw energy from her surroundings, casting any large spells, doing any great magics could drain her internal power, which would in turn leave her physically exhausted. If drained enough, she might even pass out for an extended period of time. That had happened to her mother before. It wasn't something Arlana wanted to experience for herself.

Oric's expression was serious but detached, his mind turned toward some inner thoughts. After a long, hesitant moment, she decided against telling him. He already thought she required a constant guard, and after last night… Well, he no doubt thought her too skittish to handle any real danger.

Thoughts of the previous night brought a renewed wash of embarrassment. And the panic she'd felt in the dream. The nightmare was almost an exact replay of the incident in the woods—so exact that she was no longer sure the earlier encounter had been real. A waking dream, perhaps. But in her nighttime encounter, the fairies hadn't surrounded her. They hadn't prevented him from coming near her. And she'd stood helpless, watching him approach, falling into the black depths of his eyes even as he reached out and circled his hand around her upper arm. That contact had brought her awake screaming.

Oric would never understand, so she'd never explain, but even now the thought of that touch chilled her and excited her in a way that was more terrifying than anything she'd ever experienced.

With an effort, she pushed away images of the nightmares and the man that haunted her, and turned her attention to her surroundings.

They were still traveling through a pine, oak and beech forest. The road they followed was as wide and as rough as it had been on the Karasnian side of the border. The forest was quiet but for the occasional chatter of birds. Except for the odd magic, she could have been in Fordin.

There was one other difference she was only just beginning to notice. But the sensation was so faint, she wasn't sure if she was imagining things again. Just at the edge of her senses, she felt a pulling, an almost physical line drawing her forward, toward…something.

They stopped at midday to water the horses and eat. The place Oric chose was marked by a tall wooden platform. "What's that?" she asked him as they dismounted.

"A border guard tower. When there was movement between our countries, it served alternately as a tax collection point and a primary warning system against invaders."

"Tax collection point? You taxed for passage into your country?"

"Many of our roads are taxed, my lady. It is a source of funding for the senate."

"The senate is your governing body?"

He nodded. "They took control of the country a little over a century and a half ago. After the overthrow of the emperor."

Arlana stared at the tower. "We know so little about your country," she sighed. Abruptly, she turned and asked, "Will you teach me Browan?"

"Why?"

His harsh, suspicious question took her by surprise. "If I'm to spend time here, don't you think it'd be helpful if I spoke the language?"

"There will always be a Browan with you. There is no need for you to learn the language."

"But what if I find myself with a Browan who doesn't speak Karasnian?"

"It will never be an issue, my lady."

"Why won't you teach me?" Anger and frustration boiled up at his offhanded refusal. "Why don't you want me to know your language? I may have to be here for a while, and—"

"My lady, you will probably be here for the rest of your life. And I will not teach you the language because it is not necessary that you know it."

"What do you mean the rest of my life?" Her voice rose.

"You will understand in time. It is your destiny."

"And if I refuse?"

"I do not think you can, my lady. You cannot escape your fate any more than I could escape mine."

"I am not talking about your fate." At the flexing of his jaw muscles, Arlana changed back to the original topic. She'd deal with how long she stayed in this country when it became necessary. "And whether I stay here for a year or a lifetime, I'll need to know Browan."

Oric cursed hotly under his breath—something in his own language, she noted irritably.

"Enough! I will not teach you Browan because you do not need to know it. I am not a teacher, Lady Arlana. I am a diplomat and a soldier. And we will not discuss this further."

Arlana gaped for a heartbeat, then hissed, "If you won't teach me, Lord Commander, then I'll learn on my own. I'm a sorceress, remember? There's a spell. All I have to do is listen to your language long enough, and I'll know it as well as you do."

"Then why bother asking me to teach you?" His voice was low, ground out through his teeth.

She hesitated a minute, looking away from the intensity in his blue eyes. There were a lot of reasons. None of which she wanted to admit to.

"Well?"

"I asked you to teach me, because…because I thought it'd make you more comfortable. I thought…you'd be less suspicious of me, my…power. The extent of my power makes people nervous."

She couldn't look at him. Admitting this insecurity wasn't easy. Her mother and Merig both knew she tried not to use magic much, especially in front of others. Her mother even understood. It wasn't easy to face the fear in other people's eyes when what they feared was you. But she'd never mentioned it to anyone else. Even Aaron and Nickolas didn't realize how infrequently she really used magic.

"Excuse me," she mumbled when he didn't respond to her admission. "I have to see to Esmerelda." Keeping her gaze down, she turned away before he could say anything.

Oric cursed again, low and colorfully, when he saw her lip begin to quiver. "Sergeant!" he bellowed in Browan. "Take care of our horses. The lady and I have a few things to discuss." He grabbed her arm, ignoring her protests, and pulled her deep into the forest, out of hearing range of the soldiers.

He spun her to face him, but she kept her gaze downcast, refusing to look up even at the rough treatment. Gray eyes today, he thought, surrounded by a mass of soft brown waves. He cupped her face in both hands and lifted until she was forced to meet his gaze. The slight tremor of her bottom lip almost undid him.

"Arlana," he said, harsh and quiet, "I will not teach you my language because I may not. It is not a matter of choice. It is against our customs and our laws to allow outsiders to know our language." His gaze darted briefly away from hers. "It is one of many secrets we guard."

When he looked back, her gray eyes were narrowed, but the hurt had faded from her expression. He took a deep breath and the tension in his muscles eased. "Even if you were to learn our language, it would be considered a grievous insult to the people of Browan for you to use it. And the person to teach you would, at the least, be ostracized by society."

"At the least?" she asked.

She spoke so quietly it was difficult to hear her.

"The teacher would risk much more than merely being outcast," he said. "Uprisings and lynchings have started over less."

Her eyes widened. "Oh, Oric, I'm sorry. I didn't know. I'd never have asked…"

"You could not have known. It is not something we discuss with outsiders. Even the reason behind our refusal to teach others our language is not discussed." Still cradling her face in his hands, he began caressing her cheeks with his thumbs. Her skin felt like rose petals, cool and soft. "I could not tell you in front of my soldiers because this admission is also not done."

She nodded and a small smile replaced the trembling frown. "I understand. I won't use the language spell. It takes too much energy anyway."

He frowned, but she didn't explain. And the longer he stood close to her, the more his thinking fractured. He couldn't focus enough to care about an explanation. "Thank you for not using your magic in this," he murmured as his gaze dropped to her mouth. Her scent overwhelmed him. Jasmine and something else—a scent both basic and wholly female. "Was that the only reason you asked me to teach you my language? Because you were afraid to use your power in my presence?" He moved one thumb to trace the edge of her lower lip, feeling a predatory delight when her breathing hitched.

"It…it wasn't the only reason, but…"

"You need not worry. I do not fear your power, Arlana. I respect it, but I am not afraid of it." He lowered his mouth to hers, replacing his thumb with his lips.

There was an instant of hesitation—a brief moment of unease. Then she relaxed. And her tentative kiss was sweeter and more intoxicating than Myseen ice wine.

Only the knowledge that his soldiers were so near, that they could be interrupted at any moment, kept Oric from losing himself in the taste and touch of her mouth. But he couldn't stop from wrapping his arms around her and pulling her close. And when her kiss grew more confident, he couldn't keep from deepening the contact or squeezing her tighter against his body.

The curious but uncertain play of her tongue against his threatened to tumble years of hard-won discipline beneath an earthquake of desire. He pulled his mouth away from hers, gently but with a great deal of effort. His hands flexed on her waist, a testament to the amount of control he was exerting.

To his relief, Arlana seemed to understand his retreat. Her hands, where they clenched his vest, relaxed, and she splayed her fingers over his chest.

"May I ask the meaning of one Browan word?" she murmured.

He nodded.

"Fayria."

"You remembered that?"

"What does it mean?"

"It is the Browan word for a fairy's laughter."

He felt her slow, knowing smile in every inch of his body. "I should not have kissed you," he told her as his hands ran up the length of her spine.

"Why?"

"It is difficult enough to do my job in your presence. Now that I have tasted you, I will not be satisfied with only this one kiss." He brushed her lips with his, then pulled back before the temptation to linger grew too strong to resist. "It would be best if we returned now."

She nodded. He held her for a few moments longer, loath to let her go, then he dropped his arms. She took a single step back. Their gazes locked together for another breathless moment. She dropped hers first. Wordlessly, they returned to their horses.

# CHAPTER FIVE

W e've been followed." Oric spoke quietly with Ferdinand, his telepathic hearing turned toward the errant sound.

"I can just hear him." Ferdinand's brow creased.

The translator was the strongest telepath among Oric's group, but he was like a pebble to the boulder of Oric's strength.

"You didn't notice him until now?"

Oric snarled. Ferdinand's diplomatically trained voice was neutral, but the rebuke underlying it well understood. "I was distracted," he hissed.

"Yes."

"Don't think that smirk will go unanswered, Ferdinand. But I'll deal with this intruder first."

"Yes, Lord Commander. Suggestions?"

*Captain Voquz,* Oric called telepathically to his second-in-command.

*My lord?*

*We've an intruder. A foreigner. Probably one of those damned Fordin soldiers, but I can't be sure. Deploy half the men, quietly, to the west half a mile then turn north and come back down toward the camp. He's not far away now, but he's moving, so I can't pinpoint his location. Can you hear him yet?*

*Not yet, sir.*

*You'll hear him when you get closer. His mental noise is giving me a headache.*

*Yes, sir. When we catch him?*

*Bring him back to camp. Unharmed. If he is an overzealous Fordin guard, we'll escort him back to the border.*

*Yes, sir.*

"Ferdinand," Oric returned his attention to his translator. "Stay with Lady Arlana. This intruder probably isn't a threat, but just in case, I want someone other than the servants here to protect her while we track him."

"Of course." Ferdinand started to move away, then hesitated. "Oric? She wasn't the only reason you were distracted earlier today, was she?"

"No. But I'll deal with that later too."

Ferdinand nodded and walked back to the campfire where Arlana sat turning a spit holding a large wild turkey—one of the many they'd brought with them from Fordin.

Oric pushed his unease aside and telepathically deployed the remaining guard into the woods. The intruder didn't know his mental noise made him easy to track, but a clever person could still elude capture if Oric's soldiers weren't careful.

Arlana watched the movement of the soldiers. When Ferdinand sat beside her, she asked, "What's happening?"

"It is nothing, my lady. A scouting excursion."

"You're lying to me, translator. But I suspect I know why, so I won't press. I do expect a truthful answer later."

Ferdinand's reed-thin body shook with laughter. "Very well, my lady. Later, when I have the Lord Commander's permission, I will give you a truthful answer. Your perception is very acute. You would have made a good diplomat."

"My brother will be the diplomat." She looked back at the fire and forced her smile to stay in place. "I really didn't have a choice of professions. My profession chose me."

Ferdinand was silent a moment. "You and the Lord Commander have a lot in common then, my lady."

"What do you mean?"

"It is, perhaps, better that he tell you himself."

"Very diplomatic of you, Ferdinand."

He bowed his head. "My lady is too kind."

Arlana chuckled. "May I ask a question, Ferdinand?"

"Or course, my lady. I can't guarantee the answer of course, but you may ask."

"This one won't interfere with your duty. Oric mentioned something in passing about staying at an inn, but he didn't say when."

"We will camp for two more nights. After that, there is a series of inns that will house us for most of the rest of our journey. We'll be forced to camp I think a few more nights, but we will have the comfort of real beds during the remaining nights."

"You don't like camping?"

"Not particularly. I find that travel bedding doesn't provide nearly enough padding against the hard ground."

"Then for your sake, I'm glad we'll—" Ferdinand's frown stopped Arlana in mid-sentence. "What?"

*I'm afraid there may be a problem, my lady,* he told her telepathically.

Arlana winced, but for some reason, Ferdinand's mental voice didn't disturb her as much as Oric's.

*If you would, please remain here. I will return in a few moments.*
Aloud, he said, "It's nothing, my lady. But I am feeling quite thirsty. If you'll excuse me for a moment, I'll go fetch us some wine."

Arlana nodded and pretended to smile, but her heart hammered. When Ferdinand left, she called up a small amount of her internal power to scan the area. Unfortunately, with all of the soldiers moving through the woods and the servants shuffling around the camp, she couldn't pinpoint any one person or even several people that might have caused the general disturbance.

She was debating her options, trying to decide whether to lower her mental blocks to listen to the Browans or to put up a protective shield, when the sound of running feet spun her around. In her mind, she heard someone shout her name, but it was peripheral to the image she faced.

A Browan soldier charged her, a dagger poised to leave his fingers. She threw up a shield against physical attack. But before she could do more, the soldier's eyes bulged and he staggered to a halt. He stared at her while his eyes clouded over, then he dropped face forward onto the packed earth, a small dart protruding from the base of his neck.

She looked into the eyes of the man who had killed her attacker, and an instant later, soldiers surrounded her. Her savior was also encircled, but the Browans had drawn swords trained on him. Arlana stood as Oric stalked into the group. He knelt at the side of the dead man, pulled the dart from his neck, looked for a long moment at the dagger still clenched in the man's fingers then looked up at the stranger.

Arlana pushed past her guard to Oric's side.

"Are you injured?" he asked without taking his gaze off the stranger.

"No. This man saved me." She studied the stranger. He was maybe an inch or two shorter than her five foot seven and covered in sinewy muscle. His brown hair was long and pulled back in a low tail. Brown eyes looked out of a pleasant brown face that was marred by a single white scar across his left cheekbone. He wasn't unhandsome, but he wasn't what she would call obvious, either. He was, however, familiar. "I know you, don't I?"

The man smiled widely and bowed low from the waist. "My lady Arlana, I believe you know me as a member of Becky Leshar's kitchen staff."

"Yes! Now I remember. Whypp, isn't it? But…what are you doing here?"

"Ah, well that is something of a story. Perhaps if you could ask these gentle soldiers to lower their weapons, we could talk over a bit of wine?"

Arlana looked up at Oric. His expression was hard and unflinching, but he nodded. After a moment, the soldiers lowered their weapons and moved aside. He must have given a mental order. How convenient.

Oric escorted the man to a log near Arlana's fire while a servant ran to fetch wine. Whypp studied the Lord Commander with an amused detachment. "He speaks Karasnian, then?" Whypp asked Arlana.

"Yes," Oric answered in his nearly perfect Karasnian, "I speak your language."

Whypp grinned and shrugged. "Well, that makes it easier, doesn't it?"

Arlana sat across from him, but Oric remained standing, his hands relaxed and ready at his sides. Whypp continued to grin but didn't say anything else until he was handed a wineskin. He took a long swallow, sighed and looked back at her.

"I'm Silver Silence, my lady," he said simply.

She gasped. "Silence…" She swallowed. "Silence the assassin group, Silence?"

Whypp nodded.

"But…I don't understand. Why would—"

"What is this Silence?" Oric demanded.

"They're an assassin group that works out of Dareelia," Arlana told him, still stunned by the news. The members of Silence remained anonymous until they chose to reveal themselves. When they did, that usually meant you were about to die. "Vic's told me a little about them, but even she didn't know much. She said it was better that way."

"And she was right," Whypp added. "But then Flash has always been pretty smart. Actually, I think she's more cunning and quick than smart, but that's a personal observation, and no reflection on her personally. She's one hell of a gambler, that lady. I understand she used to be a hell of a thief too. Before she married that King's Own."

Arlana almost smiled.

"Why are you here?" Oric's voice was very quiet.

Whypp spared him a negligent glance, then looked back at Arlana. "Funny you should mention Flash, my lady, 'cause it's her doing that I'm here."

"What?"

"She's been worrying about you for the last couple of years. Vic's got an instinct, you know, when it comes to danger. She's pretty good at knowing when something's wrong or when something's gonna happen. Gets these twitches. So she arranged to have me take up a new profession, so to speak."

"New profession?"

"Bodyguard." Whypp beamed with amusement.

"I still don't understand. How could Vic hire you—"

"Oh, she didn't hire me," the assassin interrupted. "If she'd hired me, I'd be looking to quietly kill someone right now. Nope. She's just got a special…professional association with someone high in our order. I was sent to bodyguard at his instruction, out of professional courtesy to Flash."

"Then you've been watching over me for two years?"

"About that."

Arlana shook her head, stunned. She glanced at Oric. His thoughts were carefully hidden. "Oric?" she murmured, trying to pull his gaze to her. He hesitated a moment. Whypp grinned and took another long drink from his wineskin. Oric frowned, but finally looked away from the man.

"He cannot stay."

Arlana raised a brow at the order. "But, if Vic sent him…"

"He is an assassin. He is Karasnian—"

"Actually, I'm originally from Depnie," Whypp provided.

Oric ignored him. "No other foreigner but you was to be allowed past our borders. He cannot stay."

"Well now, big fella, I'm afraid you don't have any say in the matter. I've been ordered by my organization to watch the lady's back. And I intend to carry out those orders until such time as either my organization calls me back to Dareelia or her ladyship dies. And since it's my duty to see she doesn't die anytime soon, I suspect I'll be watching her back for awhile yet."

"And if I simply have you killed?"

Whypp's ever-present grin vanished. "I'm not so easy to kill, Lord Commander Oric. And I make a very dangerous enemy."

Arlana didn't like the direction the conversation was going. She stood and placed a hand on Oric's arm. "Oric, if he was sent by Vic, then he isn't a threat to me. And he did kill the man that was attempting to kill me just now. I think he's proven himself an ally. It'd be easier to allow him to accompany us, don't you think?"

"No."

Arlana sucked in her bottom lip, then tried again. "It would please me if you'd allow him to stay."

Oric looked sharply at her. The muscle under her hand flexed.

"If he's sworn to guard me then he will, despite your customs and laws. I'd rather no more blood was spilled today." Very quietly, so that only Oric could hear, she murmured, "Especially not yours. He's a professional killer, Oric. He's very dangerous."

*That is why I do not want him around you, Arlana.*

"He's not a danger to me," she breathed. "But that doesn't mean he wouldn't kill you." She cast a sideways glance at the assassin. He'd relaxed again and was steadily draining the wineskin, but his gaze was trained on their faces.

She looked back into Oric's eyes, pleading silently with her gaze.

*I do not like this, Arlana. And my people will not like it. But I will allow him to stay until he does something that forces me to kill him. I do not do this for my safety, fayria.*

Arlana's heart fluttered to hear him call her by the Browan endearment again. She smiled and her shoulders relaxed.

"Perhaps," Whypp said, "you should be concentrating more on the fact that one of your soldiers just tried to stick a dagger in the lady?"

Oric turned back to the assassin, his brow creased. "Captain Voquz. Search him." He nodded toward the dead Browan.

Oric's second motioned two other soldiers to strip the body. When the man's tunic was removed, a collective gasp filtered through the surrounding Browans, and Oric's frown turned murderous.

"What is it?" Arlana asked.

"Do you see the tattoos on his shoulders?"

She looked closer. On one shoulder, a single line of black spiraled into an irregularly shaped sphere. A series of black and red dashes and dots decorated the other shoulder. "What do they mean?"

Oric looked at Whypp. "This is not knowledge that may leave this land."

Whypp raised an eyebrow and his mouth quirked at one corner.

"Lord Commander, I'm not a spy. I don't deal in information for any reason except to help me do my job. I couldn't care less about the reasons behind that man's tattoos. Unless it applies to her ladyship's life. Then we've encountered a bit of information I need to know."

Oric's eyes narrowed. "Those tattoos represent a small faction of…political radicals. They have very specific reasons to wish Lady Arlana dead."

"And those reasons?" Whypp asked.

"Are not important to you, assassin. The only information that is necessary for you to know is that any Browan with those tattoos will try to kill Lady Arlana."

Arlana gaped at Oric and the matter-of-fact way he talked of this threat to her life. "Why would a political faction want to kill me?"

*I will explain at a later time, fayria.* Aloud, he said, "It is enough for you to know that those tattoos represent a threat, my lady. I did not think they would strike this quickly." He mumbled this last more to himself. He addressed his second in his own language. A few moments later, the shoulders of all the people in the camp were being exposed.

Arlana watched in fearful silence, but no one refused the order to display their shoulders. And no one else wore the distinctive tattoos.

When every person in the camp had been inspected, Whypp nodded at Oric. "And now, Lord Commander, I believe it's your turn."

Arlana felt Oric tensing beside her and for an instant thought he'd refuse. Instead, he stripped off his vest, then pulled his shirt over his head. His broad, muscled shoulders were free of design, but tattooed in blue ink just above his left breast was the outline of a dome, across which grapevines climbed. In the center of the dome, a solid, irregularly shaped sphere was drawn in red. Arlana found herself staring at the strange symbol, watching in fascination as it jumped with each flex of his chest muscles.

*I will explain that later also, fayria.*

She looked up, saw his slight, knowing smile and felt her cheeks heat.

"Are you satisfied now, assassin?"

Whypp nodded and went back to his wineskin. Oric issued a series of orders in Browan to Captain Voquz, then said in Karasnian for Whypp's benefit, "The captain will escort you to retrieve your gear. We will arrange for accommodations within the camp."

"Accommodations aren't necessary, Lord Commander. But I'll be happy to share your wine. Come on, Captain." Whypp lunged up from the log. "Let's go see about collecting my stuff."

The camp flowed back into the normal evening patterns with one exception. A small detachment of soldiers carried the body of the dead man into the woods. "What will they do with him?" Arlana stepped closer to Oric to ask. The heat from his skin pulsed through her, making her shiver.

"It is our custom to place the dead in family crypts, but for his crime, he will be left deep in the forest for the animals."

"I see."

Oric scanned the camp, then turned his attention fully on her. "I believe it is time for us to speak, my lady."

# CHAPTER SIX

Taking her arm, Oric led Arlana away from camp. To her relief, they walked in the opposite direction from the soldiers carrying the dead man.

Once alone, she opened her mouth to ask one of the many questions running through her mind, but Oric didn't give her a chance to speak. Taking hold of her shoulders, he pulled her against his still bare chest and kissed her, hard. Arlana's entire body turned to liquid heat the instant their lips touched. Every question she'd had disappeared behind a single thought—getting as close as she could to Oric. She relaxed, letting him ravish her mouth as she teased and encouraged him with her tongue and lips. The thrill of his heat, his scent, his taste was like an explosion of brilliant colors behind her closed eyes. Too intense to look at, too beautiful to turn away.

He pulled back from her as quickly as he'd pulled her close and met her gaze. "You were not hurt?"

"No." She blinked, trying to think past her rapid heart rate and ragged breath. "No. I wasn't really in any danger."

"What?"

"He made too much noise, the Browan. I heard him coming, saw him coming in time to put up a shield. It would have stopped the dagger."

He ran one hand over her hair and buried his fingers in the masses at the base of her neck. "It is good to know you think fast, fayria, but next time, you may not hear the attack coming. Why wasn't Ferdinand with you?"

"He must have heard or seen something. He got very serious suddenly and told me there was a problem. He went to investigate."

"He should not have left you alone."

Arlana reached up and touched his cheek. "He thought he was doing the right thing for my safety. Don't be mad."

His hand clenched in her hair. "I am mad at myself. I did not expect this."

"And you think you should have?"

"Yes."

Arlana nestled closer, running her palms across his pectoral muscles, feeling them flex beneath her touch. She took a very feminine satisfaction in hearing his sharp intake of air. "So you won't make that mistake again."

"Can you be so sure?"

"Yes." She stood on her toes and kissed him lightly on the lips.

Oric groaned and pushed her away, holding her at arm's length. "I should not allow this. If I had not been distracted today, I would have discovered that Karasnian assassin earlier."

"I was distracting you?"

"You do distract me."

She dropped her gaze. "I wasn't in any real danger just now, Oric. And if you'd found Whypp sooner, he might not have been there to kill the Browan traitor." Uncertainty crept into her voice despite her best efforts. All of the feelings Oric stirred in her, all of the desires and needs, were so new. She didn't have any idea how to deal with them or with him. She only knew that she never wanted him to stop kissing her.

"Arlana." His voice dropped to a harsh whisper. He closed the space he'd placed between them in a single step and wrapped her in his arms. "I should never have allowed this," he said roughly, "but I'm afraid I cannot stop it now."

He claimed her mouth again, liquefying her body once more.

*This is but the beginning, Arlana.*

"Don't," she gasped into his mouth.

He stopped her protest by deepening his kiss. *But this is one of the pleasures of this form of communication, fayria. I can tell you how beautiful you are, how delicious you taste, how soft you feel in my arms without ever having to take my mouth away from your skin.*

Arlana quivered at the erotic, sumptuous experience of kissing him and hearing him speak in her mind at the same time. She was grateful for the strength of the arms holding her because her knees weakened with each simultaneous caress of his tongue and his mind.

He lifted his head. *You have never told me why you believe you cannot speak this way.*

"I…" She swallowed, working hard to think beyond kissing him again. "I tried. When I was younger. With both Merig and my mother. They couldn't hear me."

*If they could not hear, it was not because you could not speak. It was because they did not have the ability to hear. Hearing requires a sort of internal ear. You have this. And only those with this internal ear can speak. You are capable of this too.*

"But—"

*Try, fayria. Try to speak to me this way.*

She frowned and bunched her brow. *Can you hear this?*

Oric winced. *Quieter. You have a strong talent. It does not take so much…exertion on your part for me to hear you.*

*You mean you can actually hear this?* She'd mentally lowered her voice to a whisper.

*Yes, I can hear that. Now you are whispering. And it is a very erotic sound, fayria, one I hope you will use with me often in the future, but I would not approve of you speaking with Ferdinand this way. Try just a little louder.*

She laughed and tried again. *How's this?*

*Perfect.* He punctuated his point by kissing her. *Say something else, Arlana.*

*I…I can't think of…*

*Whisper. Anything.*

*You've got my thinking too muddled.* She felt his mental chuckle like a bolt of heat through her core.

*Even your muddled thoughts feel delicious. Unfortunately,* he lifted his head, *this is not the only lesson you must learn tonight.*

She raised an eyebrow and cocked her head to one side. *What else is there to learn?*

He took a deep breath, his gaze moving past her shoulder as he thought. *There is a very specific reason why we do not allow outsiders into our country, Arlana.*

"Wait, does this—" *Does this have anything to do with the fact that all Browans have the ability to speak this way?*

*You already know?*

*I sort of overheard. Yesterday morning.*

*Overheard?*

*I lowered my blocks, the ones that keep me from hearing other thoughts, and I heard the different conversations as if they were being spoken aloud. Also, I couldn't hear anything from the Browans when they weren't talking to one another. Why is that?*

Oric's brow furrowed. *You could not hear them when they were not talking because they were blocking their own thoughts, keeping their own thoughts behind a shield.*

*Why do you look disturbed? I put my blocks back up right away. I didn't listen to the conversations for very long.*

*It is not that, fayria. It is that you should only have heard those who were speaking generally to a group of people. You should not have been able to hear individual conversations. There is a way to speak so that only the two speaking can hear. Browan children learn this, as well as how to shield their thoughts, before they can eat solid food. Only a very strong talent can overhear private conversations. I can do it. Though I do not. But even Ferdinand cannot, and he is a very strong talent.*

*What does that mean, Oric?* Arlana could feel her throat tightening, afraid she already knew what he would say.

*It means, fayria, that you are a very, very strong talent. Stronger than I suspected. Perhaps as strong as I am. Until now, I had never met a talent as strong as myself.*

*Oh.* Arlana dropped her gaze to his shoulder.

*What's wrong, Arlana?*

"I just…" She didn't know how to explain. She knew the full extent of her powers was still untapped. To keep from scaring people, she'd spent too much time suppressing her abilities. She'd never really stretched to discover her limits. If she had any. To learn that she had yet another powerful talent to deal with was…upsetting.

Oric lifted her chin with his fingers. *I will teach you to use your talent so that you need never reveal your strength. Will that make you feel better?*

She smiled weakly and nodded. *It would help.*

*Then to the first lesson.* He stepped over to a fallen tree trunk and sat, pulling her onto his lap. *This is something that Browan children learn almost from birth and it is the reason foreigners may not enter Browan. You have noticed that we all have this ability. To protect our individual privacy and our collective sanity, it is necessary for individuals to shield their own thoughts. It is easier than trying to block out the thoughts of everyone else around you. When I entered your country, it was difficult for me to be around so many untrained minds. Because of the strength of my particular talent, I had to work hard to block out mental noise. You have been practicing this skill since you were a child. Now you must learn to block your own thoughts so that they do not slip out for anyone to hear.*

"Oh, have you—" *Have you been hearing my thoughts?* Her heart thumped in panic.

*Only occasionally and very briefly. The shields you have constructed to keep mental noise out do help in keeping your thoughts in, but not always.*

Arlana's cheeks flamed. He chuckled both aloud and mentally, which only made her face flush hotter.

*I did not hear anything too incriminating, fayria. But for my own sanity and self-control, it would be best if you learned to keep your thoughts private.*

*You know,* she shot out to cover her embarrassment, *if anyone were to come across us like this, they'd think it very suspicious.*

*I believe we were in a more…compromising pose earlier.*

*Not that.* Her cheeks had to be glowing they felt so warm now. *I mean that we haven't been speaking aloud. I assume you don't want Whypp to know about this. What if he were to see us?*

*He will not. Captain Voquz has orders to keep your pet assassin occupied for the evening so that I could teach you to shield your thoughts.*

*Is that what you told the captain we'd be doing?*

His smile was wickedly dangerous. *But that is what we're doing, Arlana. Or would you prefer to postpone the lesson until the morning?*

His innuendo sent a rush of giddy tingles coursing directly to the area between her thighs. Arlana squirmed on his lap with a mixture of embarrassment and something else she couldn't quite put a name to.

Oric closed his eyes and groaned aloud. He stilled her with a firm hold on her hips. *It would be better if you did not do that, fayria, or we really will have to delay the lesson.*

She nodded, a flare of panic and excitement making her pulse race. She made every effort to sit perfectly still with her hands in her lap while Oric took several long, deep breaths. When he opened his eyes again, she could still see the effort he was exerting to remain in control by the clenching of his jaw and the flexing of his chest muscles.

*I think it best if we make this a quick lesson, fayria. Watch carefully and I will show you how to alter the shield you now have in place so that it keeps your thoughts protected.*

Used to working with mental images and shields of different functions, Arlana mastered the new block quickly. It was simply a variation on the one she'd already constructed, and it took no more energy to maintain than the previous block.

*Very good, my lady.*

Their gazes locked in the deepening darkness. Arlana felt another surge of those giddy tingles and had to force herself not to squirm. For a long, quiet moment, they said nothing. Promise and desire were thick in the air, blanketing them against the growing chill of evening.

*It is perhaps best if we returned to camp now, Arlana.*

She nodded, dropping her gaze to his chest. *First, what does this mean?* She ran a finger over the tattoo, tracing the arc of the dome.

His muscles tensed, but he didn't stop her. *It is a symbol of my position as First Protector to the Guardian.*

*You protect the…Guardian?*

*No. As First Protector, I am sent by her to protect.*

*And who is she, this Guardian?*

He fell silent. Arlana pulled her gaze up from his chest and the tattooed symbol she'd been tracing to look into his blazingly blue eyes.

*Among other things,* his mind's voice was just above a whisper, *she is my mother.*

***

Oric lay awake in his tent that night, long after the rest of the camp had fallen asleep. Arlana's innocent questions about his tattoo and the Guardian had brought the imperatives of his duty surging back. A duty he was endangering by allowing his relationship with Arlana to become physical.

His duty wasn't the only thing endangered by this change in his relationship with her.

Arlana was destined for something not even the Guardian could name. He was destined to be her protector, to die in her defense if necessary. He'd grown up knowing he had to give his life and his death to this woman. He no longer resented that requirement.

But his need to be with her, to hold her, did interfere with his ability to guard her. He'd been distracted for the better part of the day. True, she hadn't been the only distraction. The reoccurrence of the strange mental song he'd been hearing all his life had occupied his mind for much of the morning after crossing the border. It had also followed his predicted calculations exactly and ended just before they stopped at midday.

Leaving his entire afternoon free for the contemplation of Lady Arlana Von Fordin. Kissing her had only turned his vague distraction into more specific fantasies. He'd indulged his imagination until it'd made riding too uncomfortable. Even then he'd had trouble thinking of anything beyond Arlana's sweet kiss. Just before he'd called a halt for the night, when his body was too tense and hard, he'd managed to distract himself by turning his thoughts outward. Only then did he hear the foreign intruder.

His distraction very nearly caused Arlana injury if not endangered her very life. She claimed she hadn't been in any real danger, but what if she hadn't heard the traitor's approach? What if that blasted assassin hadn't been near?

Sorceress or no, she was still vulnerable to physical attacks. It was his honor-bound responsibility to prevent those attacks. At least her magical powers gave her some defense. It was comforting to know that had the Karasnian assassin not been there, the traitor's dagger still wouldn't have harmed her.

But that wasn't enough.

She wouldn't always hear the killer's approach. And if he had anything to say about it, that assassin wouldn't always be at her back. Despite Whypp's actions, Oric didn't trust the man enough to allow him to stay near Arlana for any longer than was necessary. Whypp could have been sent for some other, more sinister reason than to protect her. Saving her this time might even have been a way to gain acceptance into the group.

He couldn't guess Whypp's motives or loyalties. He couldn't trust a hired killer to protect Arlana when the time came. He couldn't trust anyone with that job but himself.

And he questioned even his own competence now.

Oric ran a hand down his face and blew out a frustrated breath. Until Arlana faced the destiny waiting for her, he must be First Protector. It was his duty, his position. For both their sakes, he had to prevent his relationship with Arlana from going any further.

He just wasn't sure he could.

# CHAPTER SEVEN

ady Arlana." The innkeeper greeted her in heavily accented
Karasnian, then dropped to her knees and bowed her head to
the ground.

A quiet mental warning from Ferdinand was the only thing that kept
Arlana from protesting the servile gesture and lifting the innkeeper
back to her feet. For the last two days, the translator had been schooling
her on Browan protocol. He'd forgotten to mention the difference in
bowing techniques.

The squat woman rose easily to her feet and began speaking
rapidly in Browan. Ferdinand, as Arlana's official translator, related
the woman's list of compliments and honors—a traditional greeting
for someone of Arlana's position.

Though Arlana still wasn't sure what her position in Browan
society was, exactly. Ferdinand had never seen fit to elaborate, only
telling her that she was ranked very high among the people. Despite
being a foreigner.

They stood just outside the inn, waiting patiently for the litany of
compliments to end. Arlana's first view of Browan architecture was

enough to keep her mind occupied during the innkeeper's speech. Still located in the woods, though just at the edge of them, this particular inn marked the beginning of civilization in this part of the country. It was a three-story stone building, topped with a collection of domes and spires for which Arlana could see no practical use. Each dome was a different color, from sky blue to sunflower yellow. The spires were covered in patterns created by different colored rocks. The walls of the inn were a plain gray, but each window sported a different style of balcony—some of wrought iron, others of colored stone.

It was an amazing and gaudy sight. Arlana found it absolutely delightful.

When the dark-haired, pale-skinned innkeeper completed her speech and Ferdinand obediently translated it, the group was escorted into the inn's commons. The entire first story was made up of a series of areas divided by low wooden walls. In some of these rooms sat tables for food and drink. In others, low divans of brightly colored silk surrounded large stone fireplaces. The commons was empty, despite the late evening hour. Arlana suspected they had the entire inn to themselves.

The innkeeper, whose name was Wyzima, personally showed Arlana to her room and, through Ferdinand, told her that dinner would be served within the hour.

"Ah, no more travel rations," Ferdinand sighed.

Arlana chuckled. "Over dinner, I think you'll have to tell me where you're from, Ferdinand, and why you dislike travel so much."

"It's not the travel, my lady. It is the camping." He waved a friendly goodbye before disappearing into his own room opposite hers.

Arlana glanced at Oric. He'd been standing silently at her back since they'd arrived. He nodded and walked past her to his own room without saying a word. Arlana felt her bottom lip begin to quiver. She hurried into her room and locked the door.

Ever since the night of the attack, since the night he'd taught her to shield her own thoughts and learned the extent of her talent, Oric had pulled away. He was never in her presence for longer than necessary, and they were never, ever alone. Oh, he was still polite and cordial, but in a distant, formal way.

And it hurt.

For two days, she'd wondered why. Why pull away now? The only answer she could find was the answer that brought back old pains she'd thought in remission. Oric found the extent of her power intimidating and frightening.

At a very young age, she'd learned to push aside the pain of knowing that other people feared her, feared what she might do with her magic. She hadn't felt the pain quite this acutely in years. Pride dictated she fall back on bravado, pretending his distance didn't bother her. Another technique she'd learned at a young age. But the minute she was alone, her throat closed and her lips trembled with her effort to hold back hurt tears.

Ferdinand had noticed the difference. He never said anything. But Arlana knew he noticed. She suspected he'd gone out of his way to keep her distracted for the last two days to keep her away from Oric. With a sigh, she stripped off her tunic and hose, removed the knife scabbard buckled to her left forearm and walked to the washbasin at the far corner of the small room. Pouring fresh water into the porcelain pan, she stepped into the small wooden tub designed to catch dirty water and sponged the travel dust from her body while she examined the rest of the room.

Against one wall, a low wooden dais supported a thick mattress covered by an embroidered lavender silk blanket. A pile of pastel-colored pillows took up one side of the bed and were the only evidence that that was the head of the bed. Against the wall opposite was what looked like a tall pale green tiled box. Heat radiated out of the tiles. On one side of the rectangular heater was a small metal door through which Arlana assumed the heater's fire was fed.

When she was relatively free of dirt and grime, she crossed to the foot of the low bed where her trunk had been placed. She pulled out a floor-length evening dress of gray-blue velvet and silver detailing. The sleeves of the dress were loose enough to allow her to put her knife scabbard back in place.

She pulled on a light shift and retrieved her scabbard. The knife had been a gift from Vic and Jacob Marin on her eighteenth birthday. Arlana ran her hands over the black leather hilt, fingering the thin wires of gold that circled it. Jacob had it specially designed to suit Arlana's grip and throwing style. She smiled at the memory. He'd had it made by the same smith who made all the knives he bought for Vic. The scabbard, Vic's contribution to the gift, was a soft black leather with straps that circled Arlana's forearm and fastened with small, unobtrusive buckles.

She'd never worn the knife out of any real need. Three nights ago, she pulled it from the bottom of her trunk and strapped it on. Just in case. As Vic had warned her time and again, even a sorceress could use a little extra help. The attack on her life had scared her more than even she'd realized at first. No one had ever tried to kill her before. Kidnap her, yes. But not kill.

She fastened the scabbard and returned to the bed to slip into her dress. She was pretty sure her insecurity stemmed from the fact that she still hadn't figured out this country's magical forces. She was close. Within the next couple of days, she should be able to understand them, to use them. Until then, she focused on conserving her internal power.

The few small spells she maintained—her altered hair and eye color, the shield that surrounded her center of power, the shield that contained her thoughts—all took only a little energy. And that energy was replaced naturally without tapping into external forces. But the process of natural replacement of internal power was slow. Without access to external magical energies, Arlana was at the mercy of her body's natural recovery rate. So far, that hadn't been a problem. But she wasn't taking chances.

She tightened the laces running down the sides of her gown until the bodice fit snugly, then brushed out her hair, deciding against pulling it up. The innkeeper had left her hair loose and Ferdinand had never mention any customs associated with female hairstyle, so she went with comfort.

Clean and in fresh clothes, she felt infinitely better. She wandered down to the commons, hunger just starting to make itself known. Whypp was sitting in one of the conversation rooms before the stone fire pit, drinking from an ever-present wineskin. He grinned when she took a seat across from him. She'd barely relaxed into the low divan when a small boy appeared with a glass and silver goblet of deep burgundy wine.

Arlana's first sip was sheer ecstasy. Her deep, satisfied sigh brought a chuckle from Whypp.

"Good, isn't it? These Browans know how to ferment fruit, that's for damned sure."

Arlana nodded and greedily gulped down half the glass before she decided it would be best if she didn't drink so fast on an empty stomach. "How do you like your first view of Browan civilization, Whypp?"

"Lovely and gaudy, my lady. Reminds me a bit of Upper Market, but with less coordination."

"Do you miss Dareelia?"

"I miss my card games some. But my line of work takes me to all areas of the country and beyond, so I don't much get what you'd call homesick."

"May I ask you a question?"

"Well now, you just asked me several, didn't you, my lady?"

"You know you can call me Arlana, Whypp."

"I know."

"What level is Silver in Silence? Vic told me once that there were different…grades of assassins, but she didn't know which order the levels ranked. She didn't even know all the names for all the levels. She said it was better not to know."

"That Flash is a mighty bright woman when it comes to self-preservation. There are things about Silence it's best not to know. That's one of 'em."

She shrugged. "I thought I'd ask." She took another huge swallow of the deliciously tangy wine and felt her eyelids begin to droop.

"You might want to go easy on that stuff, my lady. Tastes damned good, but packs a solid jolt."

"You drink a lot. And all the time."

"This is my only source of nutrition, you might say." Whypp grinned. "I have to keep drinking just to stay alive."

"I don't believe that for a minute." She tried to send him a reproachful glare, but it dissolved into a giggle.

As the commons filled with Browan soldiers, Arlana surreptitiously watched for Oric, though she tried to convince herself she was just waiting for everyone to come down so they could eat. The innkeeper called everyone to the dining tables before Arlana caught sight of the one Browan she wanted to see. Pushing away her disappointment, she lunged upward from the low divan, wobbled a moment and almost found herself sitting again but for a pair of quick arms.

"Careful, my lady." Ferdinand smiled. *Browan wine is stronger than your Karasnian wine.*

"Thank you." She felt her already warm cheeks growing hotter and knew from his mischievous grin she'd turned a brilliant shade of red.

"Food should help."

He took her arm, more to keep her steady than anything else, and they walked to the dining area of the commons.

Standing on the threshold, Arlana took a blurry look around, hoping for a seat near the door, only to find Wyzima the innkeeper waving her to a seat at the head of a long table. A very long table. A seat of honor that would force her to walk the entire length of the room.

Arlana took a deep, resigned breath, and Ferdinand chuckled quietly.

*Perhaps my lady should not indulge in so much wine in the future. Especially considering the current circumstances.*

Oric's mental voice made her jump.

When she'd recovered her balance, she glanced over her shoulder. Oric loomed less than a foot away, looking big and serious and much too handsome, and it irritated her to no end. *Well, Lord Commander, I don't see that it's any of your business.* She firmed her grip on Ferdinand's arm and began the arduous walk to the head of the table.

To her credit, she made it to her seat without tripping once.

Ferdinand had been right. Food helped. Dinner was a mixture of meat dishes and vegetables with names she couldn't pronounce even after Ferdinand told them to her, and a large selection of cheeses and breads. She sipped at the wine she'd been given with dinner, and by the time most of her meal was done, she felt far less dizzy.

"Where're you from, Ferdinand?" She took a bite from a large fruit that would have looked like an apple but for its purple color.

"I am of Claousin, my lady. It is a coastal city in the south."

"Is it beautiful?"

"So many say. I, myself, am not that fond of sea air."

"What do you like, Ferdinand?"

*I like Czanri, my lady. It's a large, diverse, active city. Full of life and culture, politics and intrigue. A most exciting place to live.*

*Why did you just switch to communicating like this?*

"Did I? I'm sorry. Sometimes I switch unconsciously. It happens often in conversations between two Browans."

"This is all so different from anything I'm used to. I hope you don't mind me asking so many questions."

*Never, Lady Arlana. I am happy to answer any question you have.*

Arlana grinned. *Thank you.* She sat back in her chair, full and warm. Without meaning to, she looked across the table to where Oric sat at the opposite end facing her. She couldn't read his carefully neutral expression, but his eyes blazed with what looked like anger.

*And what have you to look so angry about*, she thought, careful to keep her sentiments to herself. *You're the one who hasn't spoken more than a few words to me in the last two days, Lord Commander Oric.*

She was tempted to tell him to stop looking at her, but the last thing she wanted was to cause a scene her first night in a civilized part of Browan.

She had no idea why he was glaring, and she didn't want to know. If he was mad she'd had too much to drink, well, that was his problem, wasn't it? She was old enough to get drunk if she damned well felt like it. And since he'd decided she wasn't fit for his company, she didn't give a damn if he disapproved of her behavior. To prove her point, she gulped down the rest of her goblet of wine in a single swallow.

Ferdinand raised an eyebrow but remained quiet. Oric's expression never changed. Whypp, who sat along the center of the table, his back to the wall, grinned and raised his cup to her in a silent salute.

She frowned. The wine was making her feel petulant and more volatile than usual. But who was he to glare? She was the one with the hurt feelings. Suddenly the room felt hot and stuffy. She needed air. And she needed to be alone.

*Would it be a breach of protocol if I stepped out to the garden for a bit, Ferdinand? I need some fresh air after all the food and wine.*

*I will make your excuses, my lady.*

He stood when she labored to her feet and smiled in understanding. He turned to the table and their hostess, who came charging out of the kitchens when Arlana stood, and began speaking in Browan. Arlana ignored the scene.

She walked on unsteady but determined feet to the rear door and out into a laboriously groomed garden. Patterned areas filled with multicolored flowers and decorative foliage were interwoven with gravel paths. Everything in the garden was low to the ground, making the designs created by the flowers and paths easily visible. It was beautiful, even in the half moonlight of a cloudy night. She imagined it would be breathtaking by the light of day.

Wandering along the paths, not paying attention to where her feet took her, she let her mind drift away from thoughts of any kind. She didn't want to think anymore. She took in deep lungfuls of humid air and opened herself to the magic around her. She still couldn't use it, of course, but feeling it, flowing down the waves and through the layers was comforting.

A touch on her shoulder made her yelp and spin around. She threw up a partial shield on instinct, dropping it an instant later. "What do you want?" she demanded. Without noticing, she'd come to a stop in the middle of the garden. She'd been so focused on wandering through the levels of magic she hadn't even heard him come outside.

Oric's mouth stretched into a hard, solid line. "You should not be out here alone, my lady. Especially in your state. You did not even hear me approach, did you?"

"It wasn't because of the wine, Lord Commander. I was…I was doing sorceress things."

The amused quirk of his mouth and brow were as irritating as his earlier anger.

"Sorceress things?" he said. "I hope that at the least these 'things' would have protected your tender skin if an assassin had tried to damage it."

"Of course," she lied with a perfectly straight face—the shield she'd thrown up was too late to stop a determined assassin. She'd seen Vic lie convincingly. If Vic could do it, so could she.

Oric's mildly amused expression softened into a warm smile. Arlana's heart lurched. The realization that they were alone for the first time in two days was slow in coming, but when it did, it set off an explosive series of emotions—dominated by anticipation and unease.

"Why're you here?" she asked to fill a growing silence.

"I am making sure you are well. I thought the wine might have made you ill."

"I'm not ill, Lord Commander. As you can see, I'm perfectly fine."

"Perfect," he agreed in a low voice.

His gaze slipped down across her dress and the curves of her body, then back again, taking in each detail. Arlana's mind told her she should be offended. Her body thought something else entirely.

When his gaze settled on her face again, he tilted his head to the side and reached out to touch a lock of her hair. "You like this light brown color, my lady? And the gray eyes?"

"Why do you ask?"

"You have not changed it for several days."

"Yes. I like it very much. I love it, in fact." She wasn't about to tell him it took less energy to maintain this coloring than to change to new shades. "Why, don't you like it, Lord Commander?"

He was quiet for a long moment. Then, "It's lovely, my lady. But then, you are always lovely, no matter the color of your hair."

Arlana stopped breathing for just a second, but her heart slammed into her ribs. In an instant, all of her hurt feelings were forgotten. She wanted him to kiss her, and it didn't matter that he'd been distant for days now. She leaned closer, just enough to feel the warmth pulsing from his body, to smell that combination of musk, wood smoke and something else that was so uniquely Oric.

"Excuse me, my lady. I will leave you alone now."

He spun around and stalked back to the inn so fast that Arlana hardly had a chance to absorb his words.

Her lower lip began to quiver and tears stung her eyes. She squeezed her lids shut and bit down hard on her lip, forcing back the hurt and rejection. She wouldn't cry. She would not cry. Her throat felt raw under the pressure of trying to maintain her control. Pain knifed through her heart, constricting her chest. *Damn it, I will not cry!* She stood in the garden for another quarter hour, until she felt in control of her emotions. When she returned to the inn, she went straight to her room, repeating to herself, "I will not cry. I will not cry."

***

"He's kissed you."

Arlana spun around. He was sitting in a large black stone throne on a high dais. She blinked at the white marble room, the golden lines etched in the stone. "Why do you say that?"

He stood, resplendent in a black velvet tunic and hose, holding her gaze with his black, black eyes.

"He has, hasn't he? This Protector." He took long, graceful strides toward her.

In his expression she saw something she never expected to see. Hurt.

"Yes. He has."

"And now he has retreated."

"You know that too?"

He paced slowly around her. She turned with him, unable to look anywhere but into his eyes.

"I know everything about you, Arlana."

"Who are you?"

"Your future. As you are mine. My destiny. I have waited a very long time for you to come to me, my love."

"You've waited for me?"

"Of course." He stopped.

"Why?"

"Because you're mine. You belong to me. And I belong to you."

"You don't like that he's kissed me, do you?"

"It is…painful, my love. To know that another man has touched your lips."

Arlana felt a gentle caress over her lips, though he didn't touch her physically. She began to tremble.

"For love of you, I would deny you nothing. If he pleases you, then I would not forbid him to you."

Another soft, invisible touch on her lips, over her cheek.

"But he's retreated. Because he fears you. Because he's threatened by your strength, your power."

"Yes." Her voice came out as a choked whisper and a single tear slipped over her cheek.

"He's unworthy of your tears. He's unworthy of your notice. For the pain he's caused you, I would kill him."

"No. No, please." She felt invisible fingers wipe away her tear and touch her lips, lingering this time.

"Even as you wish it. I'm yours to command. He won't be harmed because you've seen fit to show benevolence."

Fingers of warmth caressed her neck, moved across her shoulders, tingled down her spine to the small of her back. All around her, the scent of sandalwood drifted in the air. He stood only a breath away.

"My beloved. My destiny." He leaned forward, lowered his mouth to hers while keeping her gaze locked to his. She fell into the deep black abyss of his gaze, felt her world overturn and spin. Out of control. Her mind screamed. His lips touched hers. And the world shattered into a million shards of marble.

Arlana bolted upright, struggling to breathe, fire burning her lungs. Everything was dark, too dark, closing in around her. Blindly, she reached out until she felt the wall next to her bed.

The feel of cool stone and the brush of embroidered silk brought her memory back. The inn. Browan. She blinked into the darkness and realized it wasn't as complete as she'd thought. A thin edge of gray worked its way past the window shutters.

Arlana began to shiver uncontrollably. Dropping back onto the low, soft mattress, she pulled the silk blankets under her chin. Her body was wet with perspiration, but she felt as cold as if she'd just come in from the snow. Her lips felt swollen, tingling and hot despite her chill.

Her heart slowed, her breathing eased. And then her tears began to fall. She curled her knees up to her chest and cried very softly from the depths of her soul until she was drained and hollow. She fell into an exhausted sleep with the taste of salt on her tongue and the scent of sandalwood heavy in the air.

# CHAPTER EIGHT

*Ferdinand, are you sure she's all right? She looks so drained.*

*I am sure that, physically, she is tired,* Ferdinand said, *but other than that she's fine.*

*What do you mean, physically?* Oric glanced over at Arlana. She rode comfortably enough, relaxed in the saddle, her hands loose on the reins. But her face was drawn and dark smudges curved beneath her eyes. She barely glanced at the countryside that had fascinated her days earlier. She'd been withdrawing into her thoughts for days, but she seemed to have gone even deeper into herself since the night at the first inn two days ago. Oric was worried.

*You know what I mean by physically. But since you've told me repeatedly over the past four days to keep my nose out of it, I won't bring the subject up again.*

Ferdinand sounded as irritated as he ever allowed himself to get. His tone softened when he asked, *How are you doing, Oric? You're looking a little tired yourself.*

*Me? I'm fine. Worried that we haven't seen any sign of the Mokrez yet. I know they must have planned more than that single attack. They might be radical, but they aren't short-sighted.*

*True. The scouts haven't spotted any signs of ambush?*

*Nothing.*

Ferdinand fell silent for several minutes. Oric was about to ask what was bothering the translator when Ferdinand spoke.

*Have you...have you heard it again?*

Now Oric understood his pause. *Twice now.*

*It's following the pattern?*

*Exactly as I predicted. I expect it to occur again tomorrow.*

*It's increasing.*

*It's been increasing in frequency for a long time now, Ferdinand. I suspect if I'd figured out the mathematics of it earlier, I'd have seen the increasing patterns from the beginning.*

*And what happens when it hits the peak, Oric? That point, the... what did you call it, the collapse? That's coming soon. What happens then?*

*I don't know. I don't know what the sound is, so I can't begin to understand what it portends.*

*What does your mother say? Now that the time is so near?*

*The same as she's always said. She doesn't know either. She only knows it has to do with the orb.*

Ferdinand sighed long and low in Oric's mind. *As if we didn't have enough to worry about.*

Oric chuckled. *Don't worry so much my friend. I'll take care of it.*

*Ha! You can't even take care of yourself.*

*And what's that supposed to mean?*

*You told me not to talk about it.*

*Ferdinand...* Oric warned.

*I know, I know. I said I wouldn't bring it up again, and I won't.*

*You just did.* Oric scowled over his shoulder at his friend. Ferdinand met the glare with a "you'll see" lifting of his brow. Oric rolled his eyes and turned back to study the countryside.

They'd passed out of the forest two days earlier, entering the soft, rolling hills of farm and sheep country. Shades of green, yellow and purple quilted the hills where crops were planted. Low stone walls fenced in the flocks of sheep.

As they neared the inn that would house them for the night, they rode through a large fruit and nut orchard. Around them the trees were covered in fragrant white and pink flowers. The scent of green grass, fresh rain and flowers hung thick in the air. Blue sky was scattered with gray and white clouds behind which the sun occasionally hid.

Arlana looked up for the first time in several hours and took a deep breath. The change, any change, drew his attention.

"Mmm. This is beautiful," she said to no one in particular.

Oric watched the contented glow filling her expression as she studied the trees, then had to look away. He focused on the orchard, keeping his mouth shut for fear the strain would show in his voice. Gods, but she was beautiful.

"How much longer until we reach the inn?"

He glanced over again. Her gray eyes were focused on him. He couldn't ignore her direct question. Under the pretense of studying the angle of the sun—something he didn't need to do thanks to his innate sense of time—he swallowed hard, took a deep breath and said, "We should reach the Black Swan very soon, my lady. It is just past the next rise." His voice came out steady, much to his relief.

Her lips parted as if she intended to say something more. He suppressed his groan with a great deal of effort and pulled his gaze from the temptation of her mouth. After a moment, she smiled and turned back to the scenery. He wasn't sure if he was relieved or disappointed by her silence.

The Black Swan was another typical western Browan inn. Stone walls, multicolored domes and spires covering the roof and myriad balconies decorating the façade. Dressed in their finest garb, the innkeeper and his family waited in the front courtyard. Though not quite as varied in textures as Oric's guards' clothing, the innkeeper and his family made up for it with a flamboyant array of colors and patterns.

Oric glanced at Arlana. Her cream silk robe was split down the front and back of the skirt for riding. The hem, long sleeves and neckline were embroidered in a subtly patterned gold and the waist was cinched with a thick gold and cream sash. Brief glimpses of the burgundy hose and calf-high boots beneath her robe revealed the only other color in her Karasnian attire. Her hair was pulled away from her face with a gold and ruby comb, but the rest of the sandy brown waves hung down past her waist.

She should have looked bland compared to the Browans she was being introduced to. She should have looked dull and lifeless next to Oric's soldiers. She didn't. She looked luminous.

Oric paid only enough attention to the official greeting to notice when it ended. He was grateful that, in this one thing at least, he played no part. He stood in his place as First Protector just behind and to the right of Arlana, but he didn't have to make any elaborate formal greeting. That was Ferdinand's job.

Instead, Oric was left free to contemplate the curve of Arlana's shoulders and hips, the way her hair shifted in the gentle evening breeze, the glimpses of her suede-clad calf when her robe drifted in the air currents and the faint sent of jasmine that followed her. He even indulged in a single moment of unshielded listening just to see if he could catch a stray thought. He couldn't, of course. He'd taught her well.

The fact that she was just as much of a distraction now as she'd ever been wasn't something he failed to realize. He should never have kissed her. It added too many dimensions to his fantasies, and he couldn't afford those fantasies now. Not while they were traveling and vulnerable to Mokrez attack.

In an effort to focus on something other than Arlana, he turned his attention to their surroundings. Orchards filled the hills around the Black Swan just beyond its low stone fence. Plenty of tree cover for an assassin. His scouts had only just returned with a negative report of any potential threat. But suddenly, looking out at all of those trees, with their thick flower and leaf-covered branches, Oric's instincts jumped to full attention.

That sudden awareness gave him the seconds he needed to pull Arlana to the ground as the first arrow whizzed over their heads and struck the inn wall just at heart level.

The soldiers scrambled for cover behind the low fence surrounding the courtyard and the innkeeper's family dove back inside the front door. Shouts and the zing of arrows split the quiet spring evening. Oric bodily hauled Arlana through the inn door, staying as low to the ground as he could. They ducked past the doorframe, taking cover behind the thick stone walls in time to see an arrow fly past into the inn's commons.

Arlana's eyes were huge as she stared at the black and red feathers of the arrow sticking in a wooden pillar. He opened his mouth to demand she move farther into cover, but stopped when she closed her eyes and began to quietly mouth words he couldn't understand. Another scream of pain from outside and then...

The dull thunk of arrows bouncing off a barrier.

Oric hazarded a glance around the doorframe. His soldiers were all staring in wide-eyed confusion as arrows continued to fly toward their lines only to stop several feet from the fence and fall harmlessly to the ground. Two volleys of arrows were wasted against the barrier. Then the attack stopped. An instant later, black-garbed silhouettes dropped from the distant trees.

"Half of you pursue!" Oric ordered, stepping out of the inn. "The rest of you, split into groups to sweep the orchards and patrol the inn walls. I want prisoners!"

The soldiers hesitated for a heartbeat before charging off to their tasks. The pursuing guards passed easily through the place that had just moments before been a solid shield between the soldiers and the assassins' arrows.

Oric stepped back into the inn, intent on demanding an answer from the sorceress. She was nowhere to be seen. Fury and fear crashed over him. *Arlana!* His mental bellow made the closest soldiers cringe.

*In the back. Don't shout! The innkeeper's son's been wounded. I need your help.*

Despite the calm, controlled tenor of her mental voice, Oric sprinted to the rear of the commons, into a small room with a single bed and a small tile heater. At the head of the bed, the innkeeper's wife was wailing, wringing her hands together and crying out a string of hopeless doom. Her husband stood beside her, motionless, his face blank. In the bed lay a young boy, maybe twelve years old. The side of his face, neck and shoulder was covered with blood.

Arlana knelt beside the bed with her hands covering a still gushing wound at the boy's throat. The front of her cream robe was spattered with thick spots of blood. *Get rid of the parents.* She spoke privately to him, but her attention was on the boy.

*What are you going to do?*

*Heal him. Get the parents out of here. I've sent Ferdinand for boiled water and washcloths. Bring them in when he returns, then allow no one else in.* She was quiet for a moment, then added almost as an afterthought, *You may stay. I'll need someone to explain what's happened to his parents later.*

He wanted to ask what was happening. Instead, he led the parents from the room. He had to physically force the mother, but the father walked out placidly, his eyes glassy and unfocused. Ferdinand appeared just when Oric passed the mother off to one of her older daughters. Oric took the pitcher of hot water and the cloths and went back into the room, closing the door. Mentally, he told Ferdinand to make sure no one entered until Oric himself said it was all right.

He crossed to the bedside, set the pitcher on the floor next to Arlana and kept hold of the cloths to make sure they stayed clean. Then he took one step away and watched. Her head was bowed, her eyes closed, and her hands still covered the boy's torn neck. The boy was as pale as death and unconscious now. But the blood that had been gushing between Arlana's fingers had stilled.

A long time passed as Oric watched in silence. Arlana never moved, but the strain of her concentration showed around her eyes and the line of her mouth. He couldn't tell if she was breathing. He wanted to touch her, to make sure she was still warm and her pulse still beat, but he didn't dare. Tension vibrated around him in a silence so complete it was deafening. The minutes flowed by. As he watched, Arlana grew pale and her head dipped lower. When he realized nearly an hour had passed, his worry edged toward panic.

And then her hands fell away from the boy's wound. She slouched with her forehead against the mattress, her arms heavy at her sides.

Oric stared in disbelief. The boy's neck was still wet with blood, but where the wound should have been, he saw only a jagged purple scar.

"Wash away the blood," Arlana whispered. She didn't lift her head from the mattress.

He knelt beside her and did as she asked. "Arlana?"

"Tell his parents the boy will be fine." She still didn't raise her head. "That the all-powerful sorceress cast a healing spell."

This last carried a note of biting irony. And hurt. She took a deep breath and lifted her head just as Oric finished washing away most of the blood from the boy. She nodded her approval and started to rise.

He jumped up, giving her his hand. She pushed against the mattress and with his help made it to her feet. Only to collapse into his arms. "Arlana?" He ran a hand over her forehead, pushing back hair that had escaped her comb. When she didn't answer, he shook her gently. Arlana? He tilted her face up. She'd passed out.

*Ferdinand!* Oric called as he lifted Arlana into his arms. *Send in the parents. Their son will recover.*

*Oric, the boy had a mortal wound.*

Ferdinand actually sounded scared. Oric awkwardly eased the door open while still cradling Arlana close to his chest. "Where is her ladyship's room?" he asked the older daughter who was still comforting her mother.

The commons was filled with the soldiers not on guard around the inn. All turned to stare at the unconscious woman. Ferdinand recovered more quickly than the rest. Using a skill born of years of training, he ushered the boy's parents into the room while gently explaining that their son would live. The daughter watched her parents a moment, then led Oric to the rear stairs. Oric felt the gazes of the soldiers following him.

*Captain Voquz, give me a quarter hour. Then I want a full report. I'll be in Lady Arlana's room.* With this final order, he turned up the stairs and away from his guard's blatant curiosity and fear.

***

"Oric, the boy should have died." Ferdinand paced the room, glancing occasionally at the unconscious form on the low divan.

"She healed him." Oric sat on the dais next to her head, watching Ferdinand pace.

"I've never seen anything like it. That was a mortal wound. Your mother couldn't have done that."

"My mother isn't a magic healer. That particular skill is rare. You know that as well as I do, Ferdinand. Why are you so upset?"

"Because she should not have been able to heal that wound." The translator kept his voice low, but his movements were stiff and jerky. "No magic healer I've ever even heard of could have healed that wound. Not so completely. And not before the boy died."

Oric stared into his friend's eyes for a quiet moment. Then in a low, even tone, he quoted the prophecy. "'She will control all magics. She will hold the fate of the world in the palm of her hand. She will control that which cannot be controlled and command what will not be commanded.' She's the prophesied one, Ferdinand."

Ferdinand ran a hand over his black hair and rested it against the back of his neck. "I know. I just never thought… I didn't realize." He looked back at Arlana. "Will she be all right?"

"I'm not sure." Oric turned his attention to her. Her color was returning. He'd had the innkeeper's daughter remove Arlana's blood-soaked robe and replace it with a clean linen nightgown from the trunk at the edge of her bed. He'd personally washed the blood from her hands and face. Now, clean and tucked beneath the blue silk blankets, she looked asleep. "I think she's in what the Guardian calls a recovering sleep."

"How long will it last?"

"It depends on her. I can't say for certain. She may wake in an hour. She may sleep for several days."

"Days! Oric, the Mokrez are still out there somewhere."

Oric growled low in his throat. All but one of the attackers had escaped. And that one had been killed by Whypp's dagger. He forced down his anger and said, "Captain Grunveld has been sent for?"

"Yes. Runners went out to the garrison just before I came up. Captain Voquz says we should have reinforcements by morning."

*Then in the morning, we'll continue on.*

*What? Oric, they'll be watching. They'll ambush us again. And with her like this, she's as vulnerable as a normal woman.*

"If we stay here, they can lay siege to the inn. Attack again and again until they get through."

"From here we can defend. We have walls, supplies. With the addition of Captain Grunveld's garrison, we can probably even hunt them down."

"If we stay here, they'll know something is wrong."

"If we ride out of here and she's not at the head of the train as she always is, they'll know something is wrong. They must be watching us. They've probably been watching us since we entered Browan."

"We can't delay until she recovers. We don't have time." Oric whispered the last sentence. He ran a hand over her cheek, pushing away a stray lock of hair. It took him a moment of staring before he realized her hair was lighter now. A dusty blonde instead of brown. He twisted the strand in his fingers, frowning.

"Oric?"

He glanced up at the translator.

"They'll be expecting us to continue on as we have. And when they see she's not at the front of the train, they'll know she's vulnerable. If we stay here, she has time to recover and we have a solid place to defend from."

"We don't have the time." Oric's eyes narrowed. "Is Brigit still with Grunveld's garrison?"

"Yes. Why?"

Oric's mouth curved upward. It wasn't a smile. "As soon as Grunveld gets here have him send Brigit up."

"What are you planning?"

"A diversion."

Ferdinand folded his hands together and took a deep breath. "Grunveld's garrison disguised as ours, with Brigit pretending to be Arlana."

*Precisely.*

*You're endangering Brigit.*

"Brigit is too good a warrior to be easily killed. Besides, it's my duty as First Protector to guarantee Arlana's safety, and to that end, I can use whatever means I deem necessary. Brigit will do her duty as a soldier."

Ferdinand pursed his lips but nodded. "And what will we do?"

"We turn up the northern road."

"The northern road goes through the Pillars."

"Yes."

"Oric, that's insane. Even if we can get through the Pillars alive, the Timeless Forest is just on the other side and there's no way to get back down to the bypass road."

"I don't plan on bypassing the forest. We won't have time anyway. Going straight through this direction will even get us to Czanri a week early."

Ferdinand's black skin actually paled. "You plan on going through the Timeless Forest as well! We'd stand a better chance against the Mokrez."

"Not so long as she's like this we won't. You admitted it earlier, Ferdinand. Like this, she's as vulnerable as any woman without magic and without military training." Oric purposefully left out the fact that the innkeeper's daughter had found a knife strapped to Arlana's left forearm. "And until she wakes up, she can't even run and hide if we're attacked. By the time we reach the Pillars, she should be recovered. We'll deal with the difficulties then."

"And if she's not recovered?"

"She will be." Oric turned to stare into her peacefully sleeping face. "She'll be fine."

# Chapter Nine

The first thing she noticed was the crick in her neck. The next, the sound of carriage wheels on hard-packed earth and the clomp of horse hooves. Arlana blinked her eyes open only to squeeze them shut again with a grimace. She put a hand up to shade against the bright glare.

The light sneaking in past her lids dimmed and a deep voice murmured, "Better?"

Tentatively, she opened her eyes again, still shading them with one hand. The curtains on the carriage windows had been pulled closed. "Much better. Thank you." She moved her hand away, still squinting. She was lying on her side, knees bent, on one carriage seat. Oric sat across from her. She blinked and slowly rose.

"How long have I been asleep?"

"Two days."

Groaning, she dropped her head into her hands.

"Are you ill?" he asked, leaning forward.

"No. Well, I have a crick in my neck, but I knew what I was doing so no headaches, thank the Goddess. I am starving. And I could drink a lake." She looked up hopefully. "I don't suppose…"

Oric handed her a neatly wrapped bundle and a wineskin. "Just in case you woke up before we reached the inn."

"Thanks." She pulled the cap off the skin and took a long swallow. "The wine is watered."

"Didn't want me getting drunk again?"

"I was afraid unwatered wine might make you sick."

"Very thoughtful of you. This is perfect." She untied the bundle and dug into the cheese round and loaf of bread like she'd been without food for a year.

"Your hair has lightened."

She glanced down at the strands falling over her shoulders. They were a very light blonde now. "The spell degraded. I'll bet my eyes are more blue than gray now."

"They are."

"I'll fix it as soon as I finish eating." She noticed then that she was wearing her nightgown. "Who changed my clothes for me?" She met his gaze without accusation. She knew Oric wouldn't have taken the liberty himself.

"The innkeeper's daughter."

"Next time you see her, tell her I said thank you."

"I think saving her brother's life was more than enough."

"No, it wasn't. Give her my thanks, please." She dropped her gaze, making a show of examining her food and stuffing a few bites into her mouth. "How's the boy?"

"Despite his mother's protests, he helped us reload the wagons and carriages the morning we left."

"I'm glad he's okay. Was anyone else injured?"

"One guard was killed."

"Damn," she breathed, dropping the chunk of bread she held back to her lap. "I didn't react quickly enough."

"He died in the first volley, Arlana. You could not have helped him."

She snorted and shook her head. She should have been quicker.

"The boy's parents want to send you a herd of sheep and the next several harvests of fruit from their orchards in repayment. The innkeeper's wife already restocked our supplies from her own stores."

"She shouldn't have done that. And tell them not to send me anything."

"They owe you their son's life."

"No," she ground out, "they don't."

"Arlana, you healed him when he was mortally wounded. And you saved the rest of my garrison with that shield you erected. No one else was even injured thanks to you."

"One man died and a boy almost died thanks to me."

"Arlana…"

"Oric, do not let them send me anything. I didn't heal the boy because I wanted their offerings or even their gratitude. I healed him because it was my fault he was injured in the first place. It's my fault the other man died. I don't deserve any gratitude."

"You can hardly be blamed for the delusional actions of a small group of fanatics."

Oric's voice was hard enough to make her flinch. "If I hadn't been there," she murmured, "the boy would never have been injured. He wouldn't have a scar for the rest of his life to show how he had almost died because he was too near me. And the soldier would still be alive."

"The soldier accepted that he might die during this mission from the first. It was his duty. One he accepted proudly. And the boy will brag about that scar in years to come. He'll not regret receiving it."

Arlana fell silent. She stared down at her food without seeing it.

"Finish eating," he ordered.

"I'm not hungry anymore."

"You need your strength. You haven't eaten in two days."

She knew he was right. It didn't matter. She didn't want the food anymore. "You said, 'reload' the wagons and carriages. Why? When did we leave?"

"We left the morning after the attack. A nearby garrison was called in for support. And as a diversion."

"A diversion?"

"A decoy. They are set up to look like our party, to give us time to get away from the inn without alerting the Mokrez to our presence."

"So more people are in danger because of me."

"That is what soldiers do, Arlana."

"What about the person pretending to be me?"

"Brigit is a highly skilled warrior."

"Oric, this faction, the Mokrez, will think they're attacking a powerful sorceress. What good will warrior skills do against that?"

Oric stared, not answering, his expression unrelenting and confident.

Finally, Arlana dropped her gaze. She picked at the food in her lap, forcing bits into her mouth, down her throat. The wine was easier to swallow than the food. She drained the wineskin long before she finished the bread and cheese.

As the silence in the small carriage stretched, her still weary body became acutely aware of Oric's closeness. She shifted on her seat and pushed aside the curtain. The countryside was still rolling hills, but these were home to small herds of cattle and dotted with copses of bushy trees. "How long 'til we reach the inn?"

"We should be arriving soon. Are you still tired?"

"A little."

"Perhaps you should sleep more."

"No. I'd rather not." A slight hint of wry humor worked its way into her voice when she said, "I have enough of a crick in my neck as it is." She looked along the line of the train toward the direction of the inn. She could just make out the shape of the building from here.

"Earlier, you said the spell for your hair and eye color had degraded. What did you mean by that?"

She eased back against her seat. "Once that spell is in place, it remains in place until I change it or release it. But it does require a small amount of power to continue working. I drained too much power working those two spells. There wasn't enough to maintain the illusion, so it degraded."

"I like these colors."

His comment took her completely by surprise, as did his intent stare. Her heart galloped a few beats. Memory made her look away and say more harshly than she meant to, "Don't get used to them. They'll be different again by tomorrow."

They both fell silent again, riding the rest of the way to the inn without another word. As they passed through the low fence into the inn's colorfully decorated courtyard, Oric handed her a long red cloak. "I did not think you would care to meet the innkeeper in your nightgown."

"Thank you," she mumbled, working the thick folds around her shoulders. "Will I have to stand through a formal greeting?"

"No. We've sent runners ahead announcing that you are not well and will be taken directly to your room."

"'Will be taken'?"

One side of his mouth edged up. "My lady, you have been unconscious for two days. You have been in no condition to walk to your room."

"You've had to carry me." She grimaced. "Sorry."

"There is no need to be. You are very slight of frame. Perhaps you should eat more."

The humor in his deep rich voice made her chuckle. It felt good to laugh. She smiled gratefully and prepared to face the others. Self-consciously, she brushed her hair with her fingers, pushing it away from her face. Oric's hand stilled hers and sent a line of heat down her arm.

"There is no need for that, my lady. You look lovely."

The carriage lurched to a stop and the door opened, giving her an excuse to look away and hide her flushed cheeks. She was still too tired, too drained to deal with the tumbling mix of emotions and reactions Oric stirred.

The soldier who opened the door looked in and visibly flinched when he saw her awake. He took a step back, dropped to his knees and lowered his forehead to the gravel-strewn ground. She turned to Oric as panic made her pulse race. He ignored the question she asked with her gaze, took her arm and helped her step from the carriage.

Outside, the sky had turned a brilliant shade of red. The air was cool, almost cold when the breeze caressed her face. On the eastern horizon, where the sky was purple, a thin line of fog hugged the tops of the low grassy hills.

Arlana hugged the red cloak around her body and started toward the inn's front door with Oric at her back. Around her, the gathered soldiers began dropping to their knees, bowing their foreheads to the ground. The innkeeper and her two sons were already bent in the Browan bow of respect and reverence.

The first sting of tears prickled Arlana's eyes. Ferdinand stepped up as she neared the door, careful not to block her path. He stared for a long moment with that combination of fear and awe that made her stomach roll.

Then he said, "My lady, I know that our gesture of respect makes you uncomfortable." He motioned to the prostrate soldiers. "So I will humbly adopt your custom in this." He dropped to one knee, resting one arm on his bent knee, and bowed his head, keeping his gaze to the ground.

She looked on in horrified amazement. Her bottom lip began to quiver as her gaze darted to the bent forms around her. She made a strangled sound in the back of her throat and rushed into the inn, desperate to escape their fear and their awe. She ran to the stairs, up to the first floor, and ducked into the first unlocked room she encountered. Slamming the door behind her, she collapsed on the low bed set against one wall of the room.

Tears flowed over her cheeks and anguish burned her throat. She couldn't stop the sobs that shuddered through her. Even at the sound of someone knocking on the door. She ignored the intruder and buried her face in an orange silk pillow.

The knock grew more insistent. "Go away," she sputtered.

*Arlana, let me come in.*

Oric's mental voice felt like an invasion in her raw state. "No! Leave me alone."

The door opened and slammed shut before she could finish.

"What the hell do you think you're doing?" she demanded, sitting up on the low bed and rubbing her wet eyes.

"I should ask you the same question." He locked the door.

"And I should think that what I'm doing is obvious. I'm crying. And I would prefer to do it alone. Get out."

"No."

That one simple word, said with such a quiet intensity, stopped her flowing tears. "What do you mean, 'no'?"

"I mean I am not leaving until we have talked."

"Aren't you afraid I'll zap you for not doing as I wish?"

A mildly amused smirk shifted across his mouth. "No one who saves the life of a dying boy would 'zap' a man simply for refusing to accommodate her wishes."

"Can you be so sure?" she retorted.

"Yes."

"Well, no one else can." She turned away, hiding the new tears leaking from her eyes. "They're all afraid of me now. And worse, they're in awe of me."

"You did something they have never seen before."

"Oh yes," she grated out, "the all-powerful sorceress. Foils the plot of assassins with a flick of her hand. Defies death with impudence."

"And paid the price for it."

Her head whipped around. He hadn't moved away from the door. "What do you mean?"

"The 'all-powerful sorceress' fell unconscious after healing that boy and stayed unconscious for two days. You are not unlimited in power."

She spit out a harsh laugh. "The only reason that happened, Oric, was because I can't draw on external magics yet. I had to use my internal power. And even then, no other mage I've heard of could have healed that boy after constructing a shield around an entire inn using only their internal power."

She stood from the bed and prowled toward him. "Is that why you don't show the same fear and reverence, Lord Commander? Because you believed my healing sleep showed how vulnerable I really am, how human I really am? That I couldn't possibly be too dangerous if my power could actually be drained?" She stopped an arm's length away and her voice dropped low. "You'd be wrong to assume so, Oric. When I can use the magic energy around me, I have never found my limits. I may very well not have any."

She spun away, intent on returning to the consoling comfort of the bed, but strong hands on her shoulders forced her to face him again. His blue eyes were hard as marble, his jaw set.

"What do you mean 'when I can use the magic energy around me'?" he asked, his voice low and dangerous.

"Exactly what I said. I can't use the Browan magics yet. They're different. Something about them—"

"Are you telling me you've been vulnerable since entering Browan?"

His hands clenched on her shoulders, digging in painfully. "You could say that," she sneered. "If a person who can heal an impossible wound and shield an entire building can be called vulnerable."

"Is that why you were wearing the knife?"

"You found it?"

"Answer me, Arlana."

"Yes. All right. I was wearing the knife as a precaution. I'd hoped to avoid the sort of power drain I just exerted until I figured out the differences in Browan magic."

"Why did you not tell me?" He grated out each word as if they raked over broken glass.

"It wasn't important."

He cursed violently in Browan and released her so suddenly she stumbled.

"'It wasn't important', she says. Except that it placed you in a potentially dangerous position. How can I protect you if I do not know your weaknesses?"

"You didn't have any trouble protecting me at the inn, did you?" She paced toward the bed, keeping her back to him. "You kept that first arrow from me without knowing my weaknesses."

"I was almost too slow," he whispered.

"But you weren't. You were too aware of your surroundings to be taken by surprise. No distractions to bother you." Her hurt feelings at his retreat crept out into her words, lacing them with sarcasm. "You were the perfect First Protector."

He whipped her around so fast it made her dizzy. "I was not! Do you know why I was almost too slow?"

"Why?"

"Because of you."

"Me? How?"

"I was too busy thinking of you in ways that I should not have been. I endangered your life because I was not doing my job properly."

"'Thinking of you in ways I should not'," she mimicked. "Should not because you don't want anything to do with the accident of fate. Isn't that right, Oric? I'm not human, am I?" Her voice rose with each hurt-filled question. "Why should you want anything to do with me? You even admit you regret kissing me."

"Oh, I regret kissing you all right, Arlana. But it has nothing to do with you being an 'accident of fate'. It was a distraction I could not afford if I am to bring you safely to Czanri. But you are still a distraction."

"Obviously. I've been distracting you so much you've barely spoken to me since then."

He snaked his arms around her waist and jerked her against his chest. "That is precisely it, my lady," he ground out through a tight jaw.

And then his mouth closed over hers in brutal, bruising possession.

# Chapter Ten

Arlana moaned and gave in to Oric's possessive kiss, his fiery demand. She wanted to pull away. She never wanted him to stop. When he forced his tongue past her lips, she whimpered her surrender. Her fingers splayed across his chest and clenched when he dropped one hand to her buttocks to force her hips closer.

*Never again doubt how much I want you, Arlana.*

His mental voice sounded strained even as it rubbed deliciously through her mind. Her knees weakened under the heat pulsing through her blood, across her skin. But fear and hurt wouldn't let her go so easily. *Will you regret this later, Oric?* She pulled her mouth free of his with an effort. "Will you retreat again? I've spent my life refusing to feel hurt every time someone retreated from me because of what I am. It happened too often. But with you, I felt that pain again. For the first time in years. I don't like it, Oric. And I don't want to feel it again."

"I cannot make you any promises, Arlana. I cannot predict what my duty will require of me. I don't want to hurt you. And I will not willingly retreat again. I don't think I could even if I did want to, fayria. But I cannot promise anything."

She stared up into the depths of his brilliant blue eyes, fear and desire raging equally in her blood. "You're going to hurt me again, Oric. And I can't prevent it from happening." She buried her fingers in his thick black hair and pulled his face back to hers. As his lips sealed over hers, Arlana abandoned herself to her desire. And her fear.

Oric's hunger scorched her, seared through her until her body felt too hot. Anger and uncertainty, hurt and desperation mingled in their hard kisses and demanding hands. He clutched her so tightly it should have hurt, but she softened under his strength, molding along the contours of his tense, firm muscles.

Her cloak thumped onto the floor before she realized his hand had moved to her neck. He walked her backward toward the bed, kissing a hot, wet line down her jaw to the curve of her neck. Arlana's head dropped back with a moan as he sucked and nibbled the skin of her throat.

*Open to me, fayria.*

The caress of his thoughts was decadent. Arlana began to tremble.

*Open your thoughts to me. I want to feel everything you feel. I want you to know all that I feel, all that I need.*

*Oric,* she whispered and opened. The rush of sensations, the heat of his passions and desires collided with her own, mingled—and erupted. A cry ripped from her throat and her body arched against his. She clung to his shoulders to keep from collapsing beneath the torrent of sensations storming through her.

She felt his every kiss, his every caress of her skin, and in her mind she felt his reaction, knew the taste of her own skin in his mouth, the feel of her flesh beneath his hands, the aching hunger he only barely kept under control.

And he knew. He knew, even without the desperate sounds rising from deep in her throat, how the nip of his teeth on her erect nipples through the barrier of her nightgown laced heat through her blood, how each touch of his knowing fingers made her desperate for more. How much she hungered…and how much she feared.

He pulled away long enough to strip her nightgown over her head, then he collected her close again. The press of his copper sash against her bare stomach was an odd sensation that should have been uncomfortable and was instead deliciously sensual. The smooth, cool links were a heady contrast to the heat of her skin. She thrust her body closer, rubbing herself against the thick hardness that pressed against her belly.

And it wasn't enough. She wanted to feel his skin, to know how he tasted. Mentally, she curled around him, demanding to be closer. Savagely he tore off his vest and shirt, a part of his mind resenting the obstacle of his clothing before his hands once more sought out the pliant softness of her flesh.

*More*, she whispered in his mind as he ravaged her mouth. She slid her hands down the straining muscles of his back, pushing at the copper sash and the top of his trousers. *I want to see all of you.* The vibrating tension in his body echoed the low growl that rumbled from his throat and the sizzling heat that engulfed her mind.

He removed the remainder of his clothes with a frightening speed. Arlana gasped at the sight of his naked body—the magnificent bulging muscles, the coarse hair covering his legs, the line of dark hair running down the washboard rungs of his stomach and the thick length of his erection.

Oric felt her reaction to his body even as she felt his reaction to her curious stare. She reeled beneath the mingling of physical and mental sensations, impossible to tell which were hers and which were his. He caught her as her knees weakened and lowered them both to the mattress, covering her with hungry kisses.

She struggled with the need to close her mind and escape the intensity of feelings crashing through her, to hide the fear that still lurked beneath her violent need. But she couldn't pull away. She needed to know how much he loved the taste of her, the scent of her skin, the caress of her hair as it tangled between his fingers. She needed to know that he wanted her as a man wants a woman. That he thought of her only as a woman and not as an abomination to be shunned and despised.

*Believe how much I want you, fayria,* he growled into her tumbling thoughts. *From the moment I saw you. I knew even then who and what you were and none of that mattered. All I wanted was to possess you, to make you as desperate for me as I am for you. To do this.* He licked a circle around the mole on her jaw, traced a line over her chin to the hollow of her throat. *And this.* His hand slipped over her belly to the pale triangle of hair at the apex of her thighs as his mouth closed over one straining nipple.

*Oric, oh yes. Please.* Hungry sounds of desperation gasped from her throat.

*Do you doubt me, fayria? Do you doubt that I want you as a man wants a woman?*

*No.* The single, whispered word was thick with pleading.

*Tell me you want this, Arlana. I want to hear the words. In your mind, from your throat. Tell me you want me.*

*Yes.* "Oh Goddess, Oric, yes." Her voice was raw and breathless. *I want you.*

Coherent thought splintered beneath the surge of primitive hunger that pulsed from him, through her. Images blended with sensations, desires and longings until Arlana was overwhelmed. She no longer tried to sort through the different levels, the different senses. She was swallowed up by the delicious flows of heat and passion and went a willing victim to her doom.

The invasion of her flesh, the violent ripping of her virgin skin was just one more sensation in the sensual flood. Only vaguely aware of the scream that escaped her clenched teeth, she didn't think to separate the feeling, to isolate it as something separate from the myriad physical and mental sensations swamping her. Until Oric went still.

*Arlana?*

Tentative, apprehensive, his thoughts were a contradiction of desperately needing to move and an almost equally desperate desire to keep from hurting her. She allowed her body a moment to adjust to the feel of him inside her, the way he filled her so completely. Then she rocked her hips once and whispered in his mind, *Don't stop, Oric. I need to feel you moving inside me. Please.*

He buried his face in the curve of her neck, groaned into the tangle of her hair and plunged into her again. She made no effort to control the sounds tumbling from her throat or the primitive hunger pulsing through her thoughts, raging through her blood. Knowing he felt it all only made her want to give more. Knowing how tight she felt around his erection made her want to squeeze him tighter. Feeling the loosening grip he had on his control made her want to tear that grip free.

With each thrust she urged him to take more, to let go of everything, to fulfill her longing and his. She willed him to know her as a woman and only a woman. And when she could no longer contain the violence that had built with each thrust, she willed him to come with her, to fall into that shattering abyss that spun with brilliant colors.

***

Arlana didn't remember falling asleep. She only realized she had when she woke up. Blinking, she opened her eyes and looked into the amazing blue of Oric's eyes. He was beside her, holding her securely and running one hand through her tangled hair. They remained locked in each other's gaze for a quiet moment. Then he brushed her swollen lips with a gentle kiss.

"Did I sleep long?"

"Not long." *You make me forget myself, fayria. You have only just recovered from a draining experience, and I give you no time to regain your strength before taking you like a barbarian.*

*Actually, I rather liked the way you took me, my barbarian. And I recover a lot faster than you might think.* She snuggled closer into his heat.

He lifted her chin with the side of his hand. "I hurt you, fayria."

It took Arlana a moment to realize what he was talking about. "Oric, that was inevitable. Besides, I can't really remember the pain right now."

*I can.*

She reached up to gently squeeze his arm. "I'm fine, Oric. I wouldn't have changed anything." She lifted the hand that still held her chin and moved it to her waist while she kissed him firmly on the mouth. He gave over to her persistent lips and tightened his hold.

*Something else is bothering you.* She refused to release his mouth, but she could feel his conflict. *What is it?* He pulled back despite her whimper of protest.

"What if I have made you pregnant, Arlana?"

"Oh, that. That isn't something we have to worry about. Since my first bleeding, my mother has taken pains to make sure I don't get pregnant before I'm fully prepared. I regularly take a drink that prevents pregnancy."

"What do you mean before you are 'fully prepared'?"

"A sorceress, particularly one of my power, has to take certain...

precautions and take into account special considerations to ensure a safe pregnancy for both mother and child."

The tension in his frame relaxed, but the furrows in his brow deepened. "I did not realize that. My mother never… But you can have children?"

"As far as I know. But only when I'm prepared for them."

He rubbed his forehead against hers and kissed her again. *I am relieved to hear this, fayria.*

She wanted to ask what he was relieved about—the fact that he couldn't have gotten her pregnant or that she could have children one day? But she was afraid of the answer. Instead, she concentrated on his kiss, pushing doubts aside.

She snuggled under his chin again, feeling warm and protected. But reality intruded once more. Her stomach rumbled.

"Guess I need more food," she said, chuckling.

"Of course."

He was out of bed and getting dressed in the next instant. She grinned at his enthusiasm. He'd just pulled his trousers on when a knock on the door startled them both.

She watched as Oric's gaze turned inward, a sure sign he was talking telepathically with the person on the other side of the door. His body relaxed. He mouthed Ferdinand's name. After a moment, he came back to the bed and sat. "What did he want?" she asked.

"The same thing I did when I followed you earlier."

She raised an eyebrow and glanced at her body, naked beneath the silk blanket.

Oric scowled. "He wanted to make sure you were all right. Your hasty departure from the courtyard confused the others."

"It was either run or break down crying in front of everyone. I opted for running."

He cupped her cheek in his hand, his thumb drawing small circles on her skin. "I understand now, fayria. Ferdinand is having food sent up."

"What did you tell him?"

"That you were resting."

"And…"

"And I would be staying in here tonight to watch over you."

"Convenient answer."

"Honest answer."

"First Protector." She closed her eyes and nestled her cheek against his palm. "Oric?"

*Yes, fayria?*

"You said you'd explain, but we've never had a chance to discuss it. Why does this faction want me dead?"

He took a long, deep breath. *That is something of a story, Arlana. In Karasnia, I told you and your family that two centuries ago we had an…accident.*

*An accident that killed most of your powerful magicians.*

*This was true, to a point. The accident was a spell gone wrong. It is best if the Guardian explains the entire story to you, fayria. I can say that in that spell, an object was created. The orb. A thing of such lethal and unpredictable power it has been feared and worshiped by Browans since its creation. The Guardian is the only thing standing between the orb and the total destruction of everything we know. And her ability to contain the orb is waning.*

A second knock interrupted his story. He slipped into his vest and boots and answered the door. Arlana curled farther beneath the silk blankets and closed her eyes, pretending to sleep so she didn't have to see the mixture of fear and awe that had sent her running in the first place. She kept her eyes closed until she heard the door close and lock.

Oric set the tray of food on the dais next to the bed. Fruits and cut vegetables, two bowls of stew and a basket of bread filled the platter. A crystal and brass decanter held ruby-colored wine. She sat, wrapping the blankets around her, and took a bowl of stew gratefully.

*What does this creation, this orb, have to do with me?*

*That is also something the Guardian can better explain, fayria. If she knows. We are not sure except that the magician who was last to die prophesied you would be the one to fix what they began. I have always assumed you would be the one to take over the role of Guardian, that your power would replace the current Guardian's waning strength.* He poured a small amount of wine into a crystal and brass goblet and handed it to her.

*Then why would this political group want me dead? What do they have to do with all of this?*

Oric's brow furrowed. He took a long drink from his own goblet before answering. *When you were born, Arlana, the orb...reacted. Violently. We knew then that you were tied to it. We still did not understand why or how—only that the connection was there. The Mokrez believe your death will lead to the destruction of the orb.*

*But why destroy it?*

*As I said, it is a thing much feared by my people. We have been its captives for two hundred years. Keeping its secret, concealing its existence for fear of what could happen if the wrong person gained control of it. The Guardian has assured the people more than once that the orb cannot be used, cannot be controlled by any but the most powerful of magicians. But this only increases their fear. The orb, a thing of such destructive power, in the hands of a powerful magician? Until your birth, all believed that the orb could not be destroyed.*

*And after?* She sipped her wine and watched his face closely as he studied the bottom of his own goblet.

*After, this group arose. Believing that your tie to the orb was the orb's weakness. That to kill you would be to kill the orb once and for all. To free our people from a two-hundred-year-old despot.*

*They're wrong.*

He looked up sharply. *That is what the Guardian has said. But…*

*Oric, my death wouldn't destroy the orb. I'm tied to it, that's true. I can feel it. But my death would only cause a cataclysmic reaction. A reaction that might well do the very thing they most fear.*

*You are sure, fayria? You have only just learned of the orb's existence.*

*I've felt it since entering Browan. A pull toward… Well, now I know toward the orb. I've been able to feel the tie between me and something since entering your country. Now I know what that something is. And I know that my death wouldn't destroy it. I can't explain how. I just know.*

He sat silently for a long moment, the goblet held loose in his grip. Then he said, "They would not believe you, Arlana. Even if you explained that your death could cause a cataclysm. They would not believe. This makes my duty as First Protector even more imperative, fayria."

Arlana blinked and looked away. "Yes. I…I don't like the idea of placing people in danger because of me, but knowing my death could cause unimaginable destruction, I suppose I have to stay alive. I hadn't thought of it like that until this moment," she whispered.

Oric set his stew and wine aside and crawled up next to her on the bed. He set her goblet and empty bowl back on the tray then pulled her into his arms, kissing her swollen lips with a tenderness that closed her throat. He eased her back, kissing his way to her breasts as he once again removed the confines of his own clothing.

*I will keep you safe, fayria. Now and always. I'll protect you.*

# CHAPTER ELEVEN

Arlana woke up feeling completely refreshed for the first time in weeks. No dreams had haunted her sleep. No scent of sandalwood followed her into her waking life. Only the scent of Oric and sex and fresh coffee mingled in the air. A much better way to wake up in the morning.

With a yawn, she rolled over. Oric wasn't in the room. She felt a momentary twinge of anxiety, then pushed it aside. He'd made her no promises. She'd take what he gave and expect no more.

A tray of coffee and sweetbread sat on the floor next to the bed. And against the opposite wall a washbasin and a fresh jug of water sat on a small table next to a bright purple towel. She climbed out of bed to wash for the day and noticed her trunk had been brought up.

Atop the trunk lay her knife and wrist scabbard.

She dressed in a long-sleeved rose-colored robe, edged in lavender, the skirt slit for riding. Beneath, she wore tan hose and calf-high suede boots. She cinched the waist of the robe with a thick gold belt. Inspecting her outfit, Arlana couldn't help but feel another wash of self-consciousness. Her clothing was so bland next to the Browans'.

As she fitted the wrist scabbard to her forearm, she promised herself she'd buy some Browan clothes as soon as time permitted. The promise was becoming a morning ritual. She liked the mixtures of color and texture in Browan fashions. And she loved that no one wore only white or black.

She combed her hair and pulled the top back with a golden clip, leaving the rest to hang down her back. She ate a quick breakfast and left the room, telling herself she was rushing to see Esmerelda. She wasn't really in a hurry to see Oric.

When she stepped out into the inn courtyard, a hush fell over the milling soldiers. Her lip quivered for just a moment before she steeled herself and walked toward Esmerelda with her head high. She'd faced this reaction before. She could face it again.

She was standing at the mare's nose, trying hard to ignore the stares and whispers, when a hand landed gently on her shoulder.

"My lady."

Oric's voice brought an instant flush to her cheeks and a rush of excitement. She turned around, smiling. But the softness of his voice wasn't anywhere in his face. Instead, she looked into hard lines and unreadable eyes. Her smile dropped away.

"You will travel in the carriage again today, my lady. And perhaps tomorrow."

"That's not necessary—"

"It is necessary." He took her arm and ushered her toward the carriage.

"Oric, I'll ride Esmerelda today. I'm—"

"You will continue on in the carriage until I can be sure of your health, my lady."

She stopped in her tracks and glared. *What the hell do you think you're doing? I am perfectly capable of riding today.*

"My lady, you will do as I say. And you will get into the carriage now."

*Oric, if you think you can issue ridiculous commands and expect me to follow without argument just because of last night—*

*That is not why I do this, fayria.* "My lady." He gestured to the open door of the carriage, his expression resolute.

Arlana stared in outrage. How dare he order her about like some, some… The utter silence around them edged into her anger. She covertly glanced around the courtyard. All of the soldiers looked on, eyes wide, gazes focused on the scene between her and Oric. She could see their shock. And the fear. Their commander dared to order the sorceress? What if she called down something horrible in her wrath?

Her lips twitched up at one corner.

She hardened her mouth, glared at Oric for another heartbeat, then turned around and stomped into the carriage, giving in very visibly to his command. She couldn't hold back her chuckle once the carriage doors closed, but she laughed silently.

*Keep that mental chuckle quiet too, fayria,* Oric's voice brushed through her mind, *or our show will have been for naught.*

Arlana reinforced the shields on her thoughts, but not before she sent Oric a mental kiss of gratitude. The mental image he sent back made her blush.

She waited patiently for the train to get underway. To her surprise and pleasure, Oric stepped into the carriage and closed the door just as they began to move forward. "You're riding in here today?"

"Of course. I am First Protector. My duty is to you, not the garrison."

*Thank you for the performance, Oric. Did it help?*

He shifted from the seat opposite to sit next to her. He picked up one of her hands and brought it to his lips. *Yes. They are amazed that I survived that confrontation.* His thoughts vibrated with amusement.

*But more relieved now to know that you will not…zap them the instant you are angered. It has not helped the awe I am afraid, fayria. But the fear is no longer so pronounced.*

*That's something at least. We'll just have to work on the awe. Maybe I should suddenly become clumsy. It's hard to be in awe of someone who's constantly tripping over their own feet.*

*I do not think that would work.* He chuckled and pulled her into the circle of his arms, kissing the top of her head. *You've proven far too agile and graceful so far. But perhaps something along those lines.*

She nestled her head beneath his chin and breathed in the fresh scent of soap mixing with his natural scent. *Mmm. You smell good.* His groan made her smile.

*Careful, fayria. I will not be able to protect you properly if I am busy seducing you.*

*What if I seduce you?* She lifted her head to kiss him, but when his lips dropped to hers she pulled back, instead placing little kisses along his jawline. She stretched up and nibbled at his ear while her hand inched up his thigh.

Oric sucked in a sharp breath and cursed in Browan. He grasped the wrist of her wandering hand and gently pulled his head away from her teasing mouth. "My lady." His voice was low and rough as gravel. "I must be ready to defend and protect at any moment while we are traveling." He squeezed her shoulders. *But I will repay this torment tonight.*

The erotic promise in his thoughts sent white-hot anticipation shooting through her. She didn't want to wait. But she knew he was right. While they traveled, they were vulnerable and had to be ready for anything. And when Oric did fulfill his promise to repay her for tormenting him, the last thing she wanted to worry about was interruptions.

She tried turning her mind to other things—tried without much success to ignore the hard feel of his arm across her shoulders and the soft, unconscious caress of his fingers on her wrist. Then suddenly she remembered something. She straightened a little so she could face him.

"Where's Whypp? I haven't seen him since the attack."

"Whypp has decided not to travel with us for a while."

There was just a hint of superiority in his voice. She frowned. "Why?"

"After the attack, when we were planning our departure and the decoy, I told Whypp of the mental noise he created. I explained how easy it was for a Browan to track him and until he learned to control his thoughts, he would lead the Mokrez right to us."

"I…I didn't think you wanted him to know."

"It became necessary. And as he said, he is not a spy. So far as we know."

"But if he doesn't have any telepathic abilities, how can he control his thoughts?"

"Anyone can control their thoughts with practice, fayria. It takes a talent to hear and speak mentally, but not to keep your thoughts from intruding on others. If there is no inherent telepathic ability, however, it is not an easy lesson to learn. We taught Whypp the basics, Ferdinand and I, but he will need time to practice before he can conceal his thoughts sufficiently."

"Where is he now?"

Oric was silent for a moment, his eyes narrowed. *He is a league south and west of here, traveling through unpopulated areas until he has perfected his blocks. I think he was displeased with the fact that he could be so easily distinguished. It would make the job of an assassin difficult.*

"He's that easy to find now?"

"No. Most would have to be closer to hear him. But I am stronger than most. You could probably hear him as well."

Arlana opened up her shields and listened. She couldn't hear anything but the few Browan conversations going on around her. "I can't."

Oric's brow arched. "I am surprised."

"Well, I'm not unhappy about it. To tell you the truth, I'm rather pleased to know you have a stronger talent than I do." She nestled her head beneath his chin again so she could ignore the question in his eyes. "Will Whypp rejoin us? He's obviously not leaving the country."

"He will begin traveling with us again when I can no longer hear him so easily."

"Would you be able to hear him even with his thoughts protected?"

"Yes. With only a little effort. But I would rather not make the effort. Whypp's thoughts can be unsavory."

"Really? In what way?"

"In the way that any professional killer's thoughts might be unsavory."

She waited for him to elaborate. When he didn't, she let the subject drop. She didn't really want to know the types of things a professional killer might think about anyway.

She let her mind wander through the Browan magic energies, a practice she'd fallen into to occupy her thoughts as they traveled. After a few moments, she noticed Oric playing with a strand of her hair, twirling it between his fingers. He examined the strand with intense interest, as if he'd discovered something new and fascinating. She watched for a few minutes, smiling at his frown of concentration.

"I didn't realize my hair was that interesting," she teased, nodding to the lock he held.

He glanced up and blinked. "Hmm?"

"You're studying my hair." She pointed out the obvious. "Any special reason?"

"It is still light blonde. You did not fix the spell?"

"No. I fixed it this morning."

"You are leaving your hair and eyes these colors?"

"Yes."

"Because I like this look?"

Arlana shifted her gaze to the opposite wall of the carriage and shrugged. "I thought…" She sucked in her bottom lip and fell silent.

Oric gently pulled her chin around so she was forced to meet his gaze. *You are always beautiful to me, fayria.* He kissed her softly.

Arlana sighed and leaned into the kiss, opening her mouth to tease his lips apart with her tongue.

*Arlana…*

*Hmm?* she murmured in his mind as she tempted him to deepen the kiss. He pushed her back roughly, startling her.

"It is not wise for you to tease me like this, Arlana. I am not unlimited in self-control."

She nodded and murmured, "I'm sorry." She was amazed by her own lack of self-control.

He cursed, soft and colorfully, jerked her close and kissed her hard, overwhelming her senses with the demands of his mouth and tongue. Just as suddenly, he pushed away and shifted to the opposite side of the carriage.

When she started to move close again, he held up a hand. "No. You will stay on that side."

Arlana wasn't sure whether to be hurt or amused. She ended up feeling a mixture of both as she turned her attention to the countryside flowing past the carriage window. But amusement was the stronger of the two emotions.

She glanced at him once. He was staring with his jaw clenched, his blue eyes hungry, his mouth a determined line. When she raised an inquiring brow, he glared in answer. Amusement toppled any hurt she felt. She grinned and turned to look out the window.

This was his idea, after all. If he was having trouble with the decision, that wasn't her fault. Just as it wasn't her fault the split in the center of her robe fell apart when she shifted in her seat, giving him an excellent view of her legs. Or that the carriage was too small and their knees kept brushing.

None of it was her fault. But that didn't mean she couldn't enjoy it.

The heat in the carriage climbed despite both their efforts to ignore one another. Arlana's mind kept shifting from her study of the surrounding magical energies to the way Oric's hands would feel on her body. The things he might say. The places he might touch. The tension went unrelieved until they stopped at midday.

Once outside the confines of the carriage, Arlana found it easier to ignore the physical lure of him. He put distance between them the minute he stepped from the carriage, on the pretense of having to confer with Captain Voquz. She couldn't help but grin at the slight stiffness of his stride.

She walked a short distance from the group, stepping out onto the grassy foot of a hill covered with white wildflowers. Breathing in deeply, she did her best to ignore the stares.

A servant hesitantly approached and gestured back to the train. The girl was young, maybe thirteen years old, and dressed as lavishly as any of the soldiers to Arlana's foreign eye. Her bright blue eyes darted from Arlana's chin back to the train, and she rushed out a questioning sentence in Browan.

Arlana shook her head and shrugged to show she didn't understand. The girl's eyes widened in pure animal panic. She gestured with a trembling hand back to the train again and repeated her Browan question. The girl's fear and panic were like salt in a wound. She was a heartbeat from turning her back on the girl to hide her own trembling when a quiet voice translated.

"She wants to know if you're ready to eat, my lady," Ferdinand said from just behind her.

Arlana turned, almost afraid to face him. Until he'd discovered the extent of her power, he'd treated her as a friend. She didn't want to see the awe that had filled his expression the night before.

"Please tell her I'll be ready to eat in a few minutes." Arlana watched his face as he talked to the servant girl, knew the girl had gone when his gaze shifted back to hers. In the depths of his blue, blue eyes, Arlana saw a mixture of confusion and hesitancy that surprised her. Surprised her because there was no awe.

"My lady," he began quietly, "I…I offended you last evening. It was not my intent—"

"Ferdinand, no," she interrupted, "it wasn't—"

He held up a hand to quiet her. "You must understand, Lady Arlana, that in my position as diplomat and translator I am trained to respond correctly in all situations, to read individuals and to be able to predict their reactions to a word or gesture. I failed to do this in your case and it resulted in a grievous insult to you."

"Not an insult, Ferdinand. You couldn't have known how I'd react. You tried not to offend me by adopting my own country's custom."

"I should have known, my lady." His brow creased. "And I'm afraid I still do not understand. This is a hard thing for me to ask because I fear I'll offend you again. That is truly the last thing I want. But why did our gestures of respect cause you to run from the courtyard?"

Arlana sucked in her bottom lip, trying to find the right words. She owed Ferdinand an honest answer. But in answering his question, she opened up her own fears and insecurities, revealing a weakness she kept hidden from most.

"I ran," she started slowly, "because I didn't want to cry in front of the entire group. It may be difficult to understand, Ferdinand, but the combination of fear and awe shown by what you considered gestures of respect hurt me. All my life, people have been afraid of my power, despite the fact that I rarely use it and I've never harmed anyone. In fact, when I've been forced into using my power, it was always to help or heal. It's…difficult to be placed separate, to be isolated because of something you were born with, when all you ever really wanted was to be…normal."

With a great deal of effort, she kept her gaze on his, unflinching during the quiet moments of his appraising stare. She barely resisted the urge to shift her feet and clench her hands as the silent minutes stretched.

Finally, he said, "It's true at first, I was afraid of your power. And then I was in awe. But neither of those reactions prompted me to bow to you last evening. That was a show of respect not for the amount of power you wield, but the way in which you wield it. You protected a garrison of soldiers and saved a young boy's life." He raised a hand again when she opened her mouth.

"I don't know your reasons for those acts," he continued, "nor do I wish to know. You saved lives. You did not have to. But you did, despite knowing, I'm sure, that it would drain you, leave you vulnerable. Many other kinds of people would not have done what you did, even if they could. I pay respect to your humanity, Lady Arlana, and your kind spirit, not your power."

Tears welled in her eyes but not, this time, because of hurt. "Thank you, Ferdinand," she murmured. "I don't think you realize how much your words mean to me. To know that you see me as human, despite my power." She took a stuttering breath and said, "I'd like to call you friend, if I may."

"Of course, Lady Arlana. It would be my honor to have a friend such as you."

She smiled. "At least now I know one person in the camp isn't afraid of me."

"If you're referring to Szeali, remember she is still young and quite naïve for her age. She frightens easily, but she would be reacting the same way to any great person, magician or no."

She nodded and didn't bother pointing out that the servant girl wasn't the only one in the group treating her that way. Simply knowing Ferdinand was no longer afraid made her feel better. She even made it through lunch without feeling too hurt by Szeali's wary, fearful glances.

***

The afternoon enclosed in the carriage with Oric proved to be as fraught with tension as the morning. They both remained staunchly silent, gazes focused on anything and everything but each other.

Arlana once again sent her mind out into the magical forces, tracing the flows, the ebbs and eddies. She was beginning to see a pattern she hadn't expected. At first, it seemed a striped effect, the changes occurring in alternating lines that affected the whole. But the more she studied, the more she realized the lines actually radiated out from a single point like the spokes on a wheel.

All at once, she realized what she was sensing and she sighed in amazement. "I've got it," she said aloud, keeping her eyes closed. "I've figured it out." She popped her eyes open and grinned.

"The differences in the magics," she explained when Oric frowned. "The reason why, until now, I didn't dare use external forces. It's the orb!" She laughed. "It should have been obvious. In hindsight, it is. That must have been what killed the powerful magicians," she mumbled this last more to herself. Then to Oric again, "The creation of the orb, the mistake in the spell, caused a reaction throughout the magic forces here. Not like a stone in a pond, not growing ripples. This is like millions of rays shot out from a central point—shot with such force that they literally ripped apart the cohesive magic forces. What I'm feeling is something like…like scars. The damage didn't heal without leaving evidence of the injury."

She leaned forward in her excitement, dropping her hands onto Oric's knees. When she stopped for a breath, she realized what she was doing and hastily sat back, folding her hands harmlessly into her lap. Despite a sudden rush of heat to her cheeks, she continued to grin.

Her enthusiasm was catching, but Oric's slow smile showed a very different kind of excitement, an excitement that made her stomach dance.

"So," his tone was easy and conversational, belying the heat in his eyes, "this means that you will be able to use Browan magics now? That you will no longer suffer from that vulnerability?"

"Exactly! Well, it'll take me another day to work everything out before I'll feel safe tapping the energy flows, but by tomorrow I won't have to worry about draining away my internal power." Her brow crinkled with a sudden thought. "You know, I still don't know why the change stops at the border. Magic doesn't follow the lines and boundaries set up by humans. At the very least, some damage should have extended past the borders into Karasnia and Bthak."

"Perhaps the Guardian will have an explanation. I'm afraid my knowledge in this area is very basic."

"May I ask a question?"

"Certainly."

"Why do you refer to her as the Guardian more often than as your mother? I think I've only heard you use the word 'mother' twice."

Oric's expression turned thoughtful. After a quiet moment, he said, "She was the Guardian long before she was my mother. And, of necessity, that post must be her first priority. I grew up thinking of her as the Guardian first also. It is only rarely that I think of her as my mother."

"But didn't she raise you?"

"She was always there. But I was raised by my older sister."

His jaw clenched and he turned his gaze to the window. Hundreds of questions begged to be asked, but Arlana kept quiet. There was pain in the creases around his eyes and mouth. She didn't want to poke at the injury. She'd wait until he was ready to talk about his sister, if ever. Perhaps she'd even meet the woman who'd raised Oric once they reached Czanri.

Though she didn't want to pry, her need to comfort was overwhelming. Before he could object, she shifted across the carriage and cuddled against his side. His body tensed, but his arm encircled her shoulders.

"You should not be this near, fayria," he whispered into her hair. *I have been anticipating the night to come all day. I am in no condition to exercise much restraint.*

*I could shield the carriage.* She laced her thoughts with tempting currents of desire and hope. *We'd be safe from an attack. Otherwise, we have to wait at least three hours until we reach the inn and can be alone.*

He groaned and his hand clenched her shoulder. *You could do that? Shield the carriage from attack?*

*Mmm hmm,* she purred into his mind.

*But you said it would be tomorrow before you could use Browan magic.*

He kissed his way from her brow down to her lips, despite the hesitancy in his mind voice. When she parted her lips, he plundered her mouth and closed both arms around her, pulling her tight against his chest.

*That's true.* Her mind voice was a passion-glazed murmur. Oric slowly lowered her back onto the seat, one hand firmly around her waist, the other pressed against the seat's edge. Arlana clung to his neck and answered his intense kisses. *I'll have to use internal power.* Even as she thought it, she pulled a part of her mind away from Oric to tap into her center of power.

Abruptly, he pulled away, bracing his body above hers with the hand still pressed into the seat edge. She lay on the seat looking up, her brows raised in question.

"Then," he cleared his throat, "then to create this shield, you would be draining yourself again. As you did during the last attack."

Where her hands slid to his chest, she could feel the rapid thump of his heart along her arms. "It wouldn't be as much of a drain."

"Would you risk unconsciousness?"

"No." She worked at the strings crisscrossing the front of his shirt, intent on pulling the material apart to get at the warm skin beneath.

"I cannot allow you to do that." His voice was raw and gruff. He sat and gently disentangled her fingers from his shirt.

"But, I just told you—"

"No, Arlana." He squeezed his eyes shut and hauled her into a sitting position. "Ah, fayria," he breathed, opening his eyes again. "You are making my duty as First Protector both more difficult and far easier than it once was." He hugged her close. "For your safety, I cannot allow you to weaken yourself again. Especially not for the selfish reason of satisfying my desire."

"What about my desire?" She could actually feel the petulance in her voice and it made her wince. "I'm sorry. You're right. But at this minute, I can't help wishing you were less honorable." His chuckle was a warm breath across the top of her head.

"I must admit to being glad you desire me as much as I you. There was a moment last night when I feared you would wake to regret your choice."

"There was? When?"

"After the second time we made love, just after you fell asleep. I remembered your words, that I would hurt you again." *I thought then that you might view the night as a mistake. That perhaps it had been a mistake.*

"You think it was a mistake?" She couldn't seem to control the catch in her voice.

*It likely was, Arlana. But even so, it is not a mistake I would change. In fact, it is one I will continue to make for as long as I can.*

*I can't consider it a mistake.* The warm rush of pleasure she felt from him at her defiant words made her entire body tingle. She squeezed close and wished she could hurry them to the inn.

# Chapter Twelve

❦

Oric set about his duties after dinner with brisk efficiency, barking out orders and checking security as if preparing for imminent battle. Every word, every movement was calculated to move him through his required tasks in the quickest possible time. The entire evening—hell, the entire day—had been excruciatingly long. He couldn't tolerate any further delays.

"Four shifts of twelve, Captain." He rushed out his final order for the evening. "Remind them to sound the general alarm if anything suspicious happens."

"Aye, sir." Captain Voquz gave a sharp salute and strode off to deploy the guards.

If Oric weren't positive the man's years of training would prevent it, he'd have sworn he saw a hint of amusement in the captain's eyes.

That was something he'd deal with later.

Oric was almost to the inn's rear stairs, his stride so swift and determined it should have discouraged interference, when the innkeeper stepped into his path. Oric nearly snarled. The man was small, brown, wrinkled and could try the patience of the gods.

"Lord Commander," the little man greeted, "I may be assured that everything was to your pleasure this evening?"

The man's creaky, nasal voice set Oric's teeth on edge. "Yes." He tried to move around him, but the innkeeper wasn't easily deterred.

"Because," he hastily continued, "with the warning of only a day to prepare my humble establishment for your coming, I fear I have not been able to provide the appropriate—"

"Everything was perfect, sir," Oric interrupted. "Now, if you'll excuse me."

"Lord Commander, Lord Commander." The little innkeeper shot around to block Oric's path once again and threw up his hands, both to placate and to forestall. "Lord Commander, it was understood that you would be following the more southerly route to the bypass road."

Oric's suspicions jumped to full alert, but he continued to glower impatiently. "There was a change," he stated flatly, letting the man see his gaze dart to the rear stairs.

"A change. A change, yes…well, those do happen, I am told. And will this change keep you along the northern road, do you think? If that's the case," he added in a rush, "then perhaps I could send one of my men ahead, to announce your approach?"

"That won't be necessary." Oric watched the barely contained eagerness in the man's eyes and for the first time in many years was tempted to ignore the mental blocks of one of his own countrymen and listen to his private thoughts. "However," he added in a distracted, annoyed tone, "you may send someone to fetch Captain Voquz." He once again let his gaze dart to the rear stairs, making it obvious he would rather be up those stairs than talking to the innkeeper. While making a show of not looking at the innkeeper, Oric studied the little man's reactions. The hunch of his shoulders—a contrived humble stance—was belied by the gleam in his blue eyes.

"Right away, Lord Commander." He bowed away, his gaze focused on the floor.

*Ferdinand?* Oric sent the questioning thought toward the translator's room. It was a controlled, quiet inquiry that only Ferdinand—and perhaps Arlana—would be able to hear.

*Oric?* The translator also used a quiet and highly confidential tone.

*We may have a problem with the innkeeper. He questioned me about our future route. At this point there's only one direction we could be going, so his questions were redundant.*

*A member of the Mokrez?*

*Perhaps. Or possibly just an eager spy. In either case, I need him watched, but I can't risk giving the orders myself or he might grow suspicious. I'm getting ready to send Captain Voquz up to you on the pretext of finalizing supplies requested by Lady Arlana. Give him a list aloud. Very quietly pass the word that the innkeeper is to be watched closely. I don't want the little man out of sight. Understood?*

*Perfectly. Where will you be?*

*Arlana's room.* Oric's tone dared Ferdinand to comment.

*I'll send word immediately if we uncover anything.*

There was neither a hint of surprise nor amusement in Ferdinand's tone—only brisk efficiency and an undercurrent of concern.

During the time it took to give Captain Voquz the new order, under the careful scrutiny of the innkeeper, and to get to Arlana's room, Oric's thoughts were focused on the new and disturbing threat the innkeeper posed. He knocked at her door absently while he called to Ferdinand again. *All is arranged?*

*We're organizing the watch even now. Any further orders?*

As Ferdinand answered, Arlana's door opened.

Oric stepped into the room, quickly trying to decide if there was anything he might be missing. Then he looked up. Arlana stood beside the door. Her long, wavy hair brushed to smooth, pale silk cascaded to the small of her back. She wore a thin white linen nightgown. The light of a single lantern shone through the thin material, silhouetting her figure, creating an image both innocent and electrifyingly erotic.

His entire body tensed and heated. As he watched her close the door, a low, predatory growl rose up in his throat.

*Oric?* Ferdinand mentally prodded.

*No further orders,* Oric growled before closing his mind off from the translator.

Arlana had barely closed the door before he yanked her into his arms and covered her lips with his, the near violence of his desire barely held in check. The day's tension and anticipation exploded in his blood.

*What took you so long?*

Her mental murmur only fed the heat consuming him. *We'll discuss it later.* His hands worked roughly over her back and buttocks, trying to force her closer, needing to feel all of her at once. *Open to me.*

Her mind opened wide instantly, and he clutched with proprietary greed at her helpless, eager hunger even as he clutched at her body. To know and feel all that she experienced was a potent, intoxicating elixir. And despite his desperation to bury himself in her, he couldn't resist the challenge of making her feel more, of driving her into a state of such mindless passion that she'd be his completely.

The potential threat of the innkeeper was pushed into a small spot in the back of his mind. He lifted Arlana into his arms and carried her to the bed, kneeling on the mattress and setting her gently onto the satin cover. Her impatient fingers worked at the laces of his shirt and pushed restlessly at his vest. He allowed her this much, removing his vest, shirt and copper sash before catching her hands and pinning them above her head against the pillows. Her slight whimper of protest made him smile.

*Oric, I want to touch you.*

She twisted beneath him, a delicious sensation, and tried without success to pull her hands free.

*Not yet, fayria,* he murmured into her restless, needy thoughts as he kissed his way down her throat. He stopped at the curve between her shoulder and neck to nibble her jasmine-scented skin before working back to her ear. He sucked teasingly at the tender lobe, then grazed it with his teeth. He reveled in the feel of her body trembling beneath his, in the almost painful delight coloring her mind.

He trailed his lips to the hollow of her throat, traced circles with the tip of his tongue, licked down to the embroidered neckline of her nightgown. *I still owe you for the torment you caused me in the carriage today, my lady.* Through the cloth of her gown, he captured one straining nipple in his teeth and bit. She arched upward and moaned.

He sucked roughly at the hard peak of her breast, but the barrier of the gown was a frustration he couldn't tolerate long. With one hand still securing her wrists over her head, he unlaced the ribbon holding the top of her gown together and jerked the material aside, capturing her exposed breast once again with his lips while his free hand kneaded the other. Each helpless whimper she made, each twist of her body, each pleading caress of her thoughts enflamed his hunger, urging him to take more. With the help of her lifted hips, he worked her gown up around her waist. Pulling her up into a sitting position, he stripped the garment over her head and tossed it aside. Her long hair tangled around her face and tumbled across one shoulder and over one full breast.

The minute her hands were released, her fingers sought out the tensed muscles of his chest and shoulders, massaging the lines of his stomach to the top of his pants. Her lips followed the path of her fingers, sucking and kissing. He stayed on his knees, burying his hands in the disheveled mass of her hair, and let her explore his body while he rode the sensations in her mind.

He felt her intent in the currents of her thoughts the instant before her teeth closed on his nipple, returning the bite he'd given her earlier. He hissed out a curse and recaptured her hands. Her blue eyes sparkled with mischievous mirth and triumph.

*You think you have paid me back, fayria?* he asked as he slid off the bed to remove his boots and trousers. She smiled wickedly, reaching for him once more when he returned to the bed. He grabbed hold of her hands and answered her smile with a slow, dangerous lifting of his lips. The touch of apprehension in her eyes brought a low, warm chuckle rumbling up from the back of his throat.

He leaned forward and kissed her, deep and probing, feeling her apprehension mingling with an even stronger anticipation as he settled her back onto the mattress. He pinioned her hands above her head again and resumed his torturous exploration of her body with his mouth. She writhed and squirmed, her every thought, her every moan a pleading she wouldn't put into words. The challenge had been issued silently and answered in kind.

When his hands joined his mouth in the delicious journey down her body, her freed hands moved immediately to him. *No,* he commanded without ceasing his deliberate movement of lips and hands over the quivering length of her stomach.

*Oric, I have to touch you.*

*No.* He nipped the skin of her inner thigh. She threw her head back and clenched her teeth against another whimper. He chuckled before moving to the apex of her legs. *I have not done with repaying you, fayria.* His lips brushed ever so gently against her slick heat.

Arlana's hips bucked off the mattress, her surprised gasp followed quickly by a groan of pleasure as his lips closed over her again. With tongue, lips and fingers, he brought her to a point of such mindless, basic, desperate need it was very close to being painful for both of them.

*Oric!* Her mental voice resounded with pleading.

*Shall I stop?* he taunted.

*Goddess, no.* Her breath came in ragged gasps. *Don't ever stop, Oric. Please.*

Her mentally whispered plea was more than his straining body could take. As he felt her nearing her peak, felt the first contractions of her inner muscles, he replaced his mouth with his erection in one swift, hard thrust. Her body and mind splintered instantly with the force of her orgasm. He remained still inside her, riding the delicious feel of her muscles clenching around him and her mind tumbling through the spasms of release. Feeling her both mentally and physically almost snapped his control.

Just as he felt her start to descend from her orgasm, he moved, stroking her once, then again, driving her back up. Surprise and disbelief widened her eyes and tangled with her passions. He felt her try to pull away from the sensation, to deny what was happening to her body again so soon. Cupping her face in his hands, he kissed her swollen lips, desperate to keep her with him. *Don't pull back, fayria. Let go. I'll be here when you come back down.*

She tangled her fingers in his hair, pulling his face close as the last of her control slipped away. She gave herself over to him in every way, and in doing so, captured him completely, breaking apart what was left of his own restraint. And when they reached that knife-edged peak, they tumbled over into the brilliant, devastating colors of release together.

For a long time after, Oric lay tangled in her arms, too tired to move, the sweat cooling on his skin. When she shivered and tried to snuggle deeper into the heat of his body, he shifted to the side and covered them both with the satin coverlet, then pulled her into his arms again. His eyes were dropping shut when she spoke.

"Oric, what did keep you? Earlier."

The reminder brought him sharply awake. He remained silent, trying to decide how much to tell her. Finally, he said, *I have reason to be suspicious of the innkeeper.*

She levered up beside him, supporting herself on her elbow. *What kind of suspicions?*

*I am not sure. He questioned our future route. He could simply be overeager to please me, but he could also be an informer or even a member of the Mokrez. He is being watched.*

*Are we in danger right now? Should I—*

*No.* He shook his head and pulled her face close for a gentle kiss. *The matter is being seen to. You should rest now.* The uncertainty in her eyes made him regret telling her. He collected her close, keeping her securely pressed against his chest, and kissed the top of her head. *Sleep, Arlana,* he coaxed. *We are safe.*

She kissed his chest and snuggled under his chin with a tired but contented sigh. He ran a soothing hand up and down her back, listening as her breathing evened into sleep. The sleep that had nearly claimed him earlier had fled, leaving him tensely alert. He debated checking with Ferdinand again, then decided against it. All that could be done was being done. He'd be the first alerted to any trouble.

He turned his attention to the woman in his arms. He was getting used to the feeling of protectiveness that filled him whenever he looked at her. But his need to have her continued to cloud his thinking. If he were a wise man, he'd be out on guard himself tonight, following the innkeeper's movements. He squeezed Arlana tighter reflexively and she murmured something vague in her sleep. He smiled. As sleep once again willed him to join her, Oric accepted with a sigh that he wasn't a very wise man.

# Chapter Thirteen



Arlana stared wonderingly at the fog churning around her ankles, clutching at her with icy hands only to waft away the next instant. In a detached part of her mind, she marveled at how closely her long white hair blended with her white nightgown and the white fog. Raising her head, she looked on the familiar white marble walls. But they were no longer lined with gold. They were laced through with a deep blood red.

The scent of sandalwood blew around her. She felt the burning touch of his gaze on her shoulders. Trembling, she turned to face him. He sat slouched in the high-backed ebony stone throne. The black velvet of his hose and long-sleeved, high-collared tunic blended seamlessly with the throne so that only the pale skin of his face and his hands where they rested on the throne's armrests could be seen distinctly. His head was bowed, dropping the silk of his hair forward to frame frighteningly handsome features. But though his face was angled toward his lap, his black, luminous eyes looked up from under dark brows, latching onto her gaze like a sprung trap.

Anger whirled through the room in gusts, churning the fog and billowing through her hair, wrapping around her trembling limbs. Challenging. Threatening. They stayed an eternity locked in the other's gaze—his unrelenting, hers unprotected—as his anger pelted her like hail.

An age and a moment passed before he rose, fluid and graceful, and stalked toward her, holding her gaze mercilessly. He stopped several paces away, glowering, his anger rolling out like the dry, cold air of a frigid winter day.

Beneath the press of that cold, she whimpered, "Why?" and wasn't sure which of her many questions she hoped he'd answer.

Though he didn't move closer, she suddenly felt the grip of a hand on the back of her neck.

Very quietly and evenly he said, "You are mine. I have been waiting for you for centuries."

She took an involuntary step forward, pulled by the unseen hand on her neck.

"And he has touched you."

Something dangerous and wholly alien to Arlana's experience glittered in the fathomless depths of his eyes. She shuddered and that invisible touch pulled her another step closer.

"He will die for his insolence."

"No!" Her voice broke over the single word. She stretched out her hands, beseeching, almost touching him. "Please, you can't."

"Believe me, my love, I could."

"But you said you'd deny me nothing," she whispered.

The grip on her neck dropped abruptly, rocking her back on her heels. He began circling her.

"You wish me to sit by idly, knowing that man is touching you, caressing you, making love to you when you are mine!"

"But you said…" Her voice grew weaker with each attempt at protest.

He stopped, staring hard into her eyes. "You care for this pet of yours. For this simple thing alone, I should destroy him."

Two steps and he stood an arm's length away. The fog at their ankles shifted and billowed with ever-increasing speed and violence.

A part of her mind screamed to defend herself, to protect Oric from the terrifying man before her. Another part wanted to beg his forgiveness and throw herself at his mercy. That part made her shiver with horror…and dread.

"After he has hurt you once, this pet, this Protector, you still go into his bed willingly."

All at once his hands were gripping her arms, bruising the tender flesh above her elbows as he dragged her against his body.

"Why? What does he promise you? Does he claim to care for you? Does he say he loves you? He can never give you what I can, be to you as I am. He will lie to you as I would not. And you want me to watch this without answering his challenge!"

He lowered his face very close to hers, and she fell into the black pools of his eyes.

"I will not allow this, Arlana. You and I are destined for each other. I will not allow him to interfere."

He let his hurt and his pain wash over her with his anger. She felt her knees weaken under the onslaught of emotion, felt an odd, unfounded sense of guilt for causing him sorrow even as her stomach clenched with unnamable fear.

His mouth closed over hers, searing her lips with his passion and his pain. She sobbed against his mouth, helpless to stop him, not sure she wanted to try. In her mind, his voice caressed her like the velvet beneath her fingertips.

*I will have you, Arlana. You are mine and no other's.*

If there was any space left between them, he closed it, pulling her so tightly against him it felt as if their bodies would melt together. And she wondered, absently, if this time it wasn't a dream. If this time, she would never wake up.

*I will give you what he never can. I will give you everything. I love you, Arlana...*

"No!" Arlana lurched up and stumbled out of bed, getting no more than a few steps before she fell to her knees on the hard, wooden floor. She hugged her arms to her shivering body, the cascade of her hair covering her bare shoulders and curtaining her face. She rocked back and forth and sobbed.

*Arlana?*

The feel of Oric's thoughts touching hers made her gasp in pain. "Stay out," she hissed and built up the barriers and shields around her mind.

"What is wrong?"

The concern in his voice was hardened by wary suspicion.

What's wrong? She choked on another sob. Confusion tangled her mind and made it impossible to think. All she could see was the dark anger in his eyes, feel the press of his lips, hear the sound of his voice. "Oh Goddess."

The sudden touch of hands on her shoulders made her jump. She jerked away.

He will die for his insolence.

"Damn it, Arlana," Oric ground out. "What's wrong?"

He pulled her around to face him despite her protesting grunt. "Stay away, Oric. Don't touch me."

"Like hell I won't."

He lifted her to her feet by her shoulders. She tried jerking away, but he grabbed her wrists.

"Tell me what's happened. Another nightmare?"

He will die for his insolence.

"Leave me," she choked. "Go."

"No. Explain."

Using one hand to hold both her wrists, he pushed her hair back over her shoulders with the other. His hand stopped in mid-motion and he stared at her arm. Grabbing hold of her forearms, he pulled her to the still glowing light of the single lantern.

She looked down to see what he examined. Dark bruises in the distinct shape of fingers circled her arms just above her elbows. She stared at the bruises as if they belonged to someone else. Then she began to shake.

"Arlana? Arlana, how was this done? Fayria?"

The hard edge of Oric's voice was now coated by apprehension and what could almost have been fear. Dazed and aching, she glanced up into his eyes. The bright blue depths were wide, searching her face for an explanation. His grip relaxed, and she stumbled away, putting the room's length between them.

"I…I can't…" Her voice caught. She sucked in a deep breath, tried to swallow against the closing of her throat and knew she could never explain. He would think her mad. Or worse.

I will give you what he never can…

"No." She bit hard on her trembling bottom lip, tasting blood. She turned her back to Oric.

He will die for his insolence.

"Go, Oric," she whispered. "Please."

She stood hugging herself, her back to him, her head bowed so her hair hid her face. She listened as he wordlessly collected his clothes and dressed while tears leaked over her cheeks, their salty tang catching on her lips and mingling with the taste of blood in her mouth. Once he was dressed, he remained staring at her back for a silent moment. Then he left the room.

Arlana remained motionless for a long time after the door closed, shrouded by the smell of sandalwood in her hair and the faint echo of a haunting voice.

I love you, Arlana…

***

Arlana's first view of the Pillars stole her breath. For three days, they'd traveled through a low, rocky range of mountains. The tension in the group had been thick with the fear of ambush. But nothing had happened. No sign of the Mokrez, no indication that the innkeeper of three nights ago had betrayed their party.

That morning, they rode down through a narrow canyon out of the low range. When they emerged from the walls of rock, a mile of grassland spread out before them. And at the edge of the grassy plain stood the Pillars.

Giant columns of rugged rock scattered across the horizon. From their place a mile away, Arlana could just see a hint of more of these mammoth stone cylinders behind the first irregular line. The Pillars were like nothing she'd seen before—a disorganized army of stone towers preparing to march across the grasslands.

"They're beautiful," she murmured.

Beside her, Oric remained chillingly silent as he had since the night she'd begged him to leave her room. She glanced at him then quickly looked away, unable to face the hard, emotionless mask his face had become. He hadn't so much as muttered a word to her for the last three days. All of his requests and orders came through Ferdinand.

She couldn't blame him for his reaction. But that didn't help lessen the ache in her chest. She clenched her jaw, holding in her turbulent emotions, and urged Esmerelda forward as they started across the grasslands.

Three days had done little to right her confused mix of feelings. Terror, longing, guilt, pain, need, desire and helplessness all mingled together. She couldn't assign any one emotion to any specific cause, yet they all seemed in equal parts due to Oric and the man who invaded her dreams. She couldn't even give name to the exact reason she'd forced Oric away. Fear for his life had certainly been part of it. The bruises on her arms, now faded to an angry yellow, proved that whatever the man in her dreams was, he was capable of affecting her physical world. And he'd all but promised to kill Oric.

But that wasn't the only reason. And it was this other reason that kept her confused, kept her from explaining everything to Oric. This reason closed her throat when she would have apologized. She didn't want to admit to this other explanation. She refused to put words to it, even to herself. But it haunted her even as the sound of the black-eyed man's voice echoed in her ears.

I love you, Arlana…

After three days of emotional storms and sleepless nights, she was exhausted. The ache in her chest had become so much a part of her, she'd stopped noticing it most of the time. Her eyes were sore and tender, but her tears were all used up. She had no answers, no way to resolve her emotions and still the ache. Even her dreams had ceased. She floated through the days and nights in a daze. And with each passing minute, she became hollow. Numb.

The sky dazzled a blinding blue as they crossed the open tracks. Hot waves of sun and a dry wind batted at them through the knee-high grass. The road they followed was all rough dirt and rain-washed holes. The closer they rode to the Pillars, the larger the rock columns seemed and the stronger the hot wind blew.

Arlana forced her attention to the looming rocks. Ferdinand had told her the Pillars was a place to fear, but he'd never told her why. Only that it was a place of mysteries where many who entered never left. She'd wanted to ask Oric about the dangers they'd face, but…

At the foot of the first two Pillars, Oric stopped the company. The road moved through these two roughly cylindrical columns as if passing a gate, then turned and twisted out of sight into the forest of stone. Arlana craned her head back to try to see the tops of the columns, but they were lost in the unrelenting blue above.

She looked back to the road before them. Despite the bright day, the ground between the towers was filled with gloomy shadows. She wondered if the sun ever reached that soil. From the sparse weeds and scattered patches of small purple flowers, she was certain that whether the sun hit the ground or not, only the most determined vegetation grew beneath the shadows of the Pillars.

She stared for a long moment into that gloom. From the edge of her vision, she thought she saw movement, shadowy shapes looming close, but when she turned to look directly at the movement, the shapes vanished. She glanced at Oric, but his face betrayed no hint that he saw those shadows too. He looked forward into the stone forest, motionless in the saddle.

He turned his head suddenly and caught her gaze, holding it. Nothing in his face changed, no emotion showed on his features, but in his eyes something shifted. He blinked and the change was gone, his thoughts carefully concealed again.

"You are back to your full strength, my lady? Able to use Browan magic?" Those were the first words he'd spoken directly to her in days.

"Yes."

He looked back to the stone sentries beside the road. "There will be many dangers here. Some will be illusions—most will not. But nothing is as it seems. Even time itself shifts and changes within the Pillars." He raised his voice to address the entire company, speaking now in Browan as Ferdinand quietly translated for Arlana. "Once we enter, we can't turn back. To leave the trail for any reason is to be lost to the Pillars. Stay close together and alert. And no matter the oddity, stick to the path."

He switched to Karasnian and said, "My lady, it will take us four days to travel through to the other side. We will need your skills to successfully negotiate this trail. Is there anything you require before we proceed?"

Arlana stared into the gloom for a long moment, then closed her eyes. She carefully touched the flows of magic surrounding her and followed them out into the Pillars. Those energies weren't any more different than the rest of Browan's magic, but one of the largest scars she had yet to encounter ran directly through the area. She traced the scar, pulled its energy toward her and knew she could use it. But the damage it had caused inside the Pillars was obvious and beyond her ability to predict. When she opened her eyes, she was no closer to knowing what they might face. She only knew it would be dangerous.

"I won't need anything special," she murmured.

Oric gave a curt nod and the group moved forward, taking their first steps along a one-way path.

# CHAPTER FOURTEEN

Oric cast surreptitious glances at Arlana when he wasn't
scanning the path ahead. She was silent, alert, her face
furrowed in concentration. And something inside him twisted. Again.
He could barely look at her, barely speak to her without that gut-
wrenching pain spearing him.

Part of that pain was fear. Fear for her life, fear of the dream that
bruised her flesh. Fear that she'd be inaccessible forever. He wanted to
demand answers but was terrified of what she might say.

And, may the gods help him, he still wanted her with a passion that
stole his sleep and robbed his appetite. Even the danger all around
them couldn't distract his mind and body enough. His life, her life,
the lives of everyone in his command were in danger because of his
preoccupation. And there was nothing he could do about it.

He tried again to hate her.

He still couldn't.

Looking around the cool, silent shadows of the Pillars, he became
acutely aware that what he felt for Arlana went beyond physical,
beyond even his obsession before their first meeting. What he felt

went soul-deep, too deep for mere words. And he knew it would kill him one day.

He forced himself to take in the spaces between the Pillars, to pay heed to the danger surrounding them. Stories of the Pillars were told late at night around campfires in hushed voices. Time itself was twisted and distorted inside the stone towers. He'd said it would take four days for the crossing—that was an estimate based on reports from the few who'd made it to the other side. The distance straight through wasn't that far, a couple of leagues, but the only safe path twisted and curved. By the time a traveler emerged at the far end, four days had passed. For the traveler, however, it could have felt like hours or weeks. One small group of travelers came out the other side after spending what they thought was several months inside the Pillars. They were half starved, having run out of food three weeks earlier, and verging on insanity when they finally broke free. They never discussed what they'd eaten to survive those three weeks.

Oric's internal clock, which had a mathematical precision more accurate than most mechanically made forms of marking time, told him that they'd been inside the Pillars for half a day. The sun should have been nearing the horizon. It hung just past midday. He'd never doubted his uncanny ability to know precisely what time of the day or night it was. He doubted it now.

Though, if he heard the song when his calculations and internal timing system told him he should, he'd stop doubting. He expected the song some time near midnight. Until then, he could only wait and hope.

Distraction and doubts kept his body humming and tense. His mind shifted restlessly between the sorceress at his side, the future he faced and the paradoxes of time within the Pillars. He even gave a few minutes to contemplating the sound that had followed him his entire life, arriving at predictable and ever increasing frequencies. But mainly, he thought about Arlana.

They turned a blind corner between two thick columns of stone, and Oric blamed the tension of the day and his distracted thoughts for being taken by surprised when they came face-to-face with a dragon blocking their path.

Shouts and screams erupted from the group. Oric snatched automatically for his sword as the huge orange head swung around to face them. Arlana stilled him with a hand gesture and a harshly whispered warning. He spared her a glance, saw her mouth moving soundlessly, her gaze locked on the dragon. He returned his focus to the beast without taking his hand from his sword. He sent a telepathic order to his people to stand ready but to await his command. The ripple of terror that came back left a sour tang in the back of his throat.

The dragon was a glittering metallic orange, not quite the color of copper. Its head was the size of a small house, the wings folded along its back would probably stretch the length of a medium-sized village. Its purple and gold multifaceted eyes stared unblinkingly at their group as a sharp mane of scaly armor rose just behind its skull and under its jaw. Oric had never seen anything like it before in his life.

He hazarded another glance at the sorceress, wondering why she hadn't struck the beast down yet. Her mouth wasn't moving anymore, but her gaze was still fixed unflinchingly on the creature. "Arlana," he breathed out, his fist flexing on his sword grip.

She raised a silencing hand again, keeping her focus on the dragon.

Long minutes ticked by as Arlana and the dragon stared at each other, both unmoving. Sweat trickled across Oric's neck and back and his palm hurt from clenching his sword too tightly. He tried to relax his grip only to have it tighten again reflexively. The fear and uncertainty of his people rolled over him as a mental hum. He'd never known fear to loosen a Browan's mental control over their thoughts, but confronted with a dragon the likes of which none of them had seen and none knew how to defend against, their control slipped. He wondered if Arlana could feel their terror and confusion.

He wondered why Arlana didn't kill the beast.

Movement pulled Oric's full attention back to the dragon. Terror closed his throat as the creature stepped closer to the group then raised up on its hind legs to tower above them. It threw a cold shadow, blocking the sun, its head lost near the tops of the Pillars. Then the dragon let loose a bellow so loud Oric's hands flew to his ears without thought. Screams pulsed through the group, echoing the dragon's roar. Oric dropped his hands and drew his sword.

And found he could move no further.

The dragon dropped with amazing grace back to its forelegs, turned and moved off the path. Before his eyes, the creature shrank. With each step off the path, the dragon grew smaller, until at last its massive tail passed over some invisible line and shrank to a fraction of its size. It was like watching a circus performer's trick—a grown animal at one side of a hoop passes through the hoop to become a baby animal at the other side.

Oric would have dropped his sword if his body wasn't struck immobile. Between the Pillars moved a near perfect miniature of the copper-colored dragon. Its head was too big for the body and there was an awkwardness to its movements that hadn't been present in the larger dragon. Oric realized with a start that he really was looking at a baby and not simply a shrunken version of the dragon.

The baby sat just off the path, its wings sprawled out behind it to catch what little sun filtered through the shadows. It stared at them with what Oric was tempted to call curiosity, but it made no move to approach. The baby was still the size of a small barn.

The feel of a gentle touch on his arm washed life and movement back into his limbs. He caught his grip on his sword just before the sudden feel of its weight pulled it to the ground. Without resheathing it, he turned in the saddle to face Arlana. Fear, anger and curiosity made a volatile mix in his gut and several moments passed before he could force himself to speak. When he did, it was a harshly spat, "Explain!"

Arlana flinched and jerked her hand away from his arm. "She…she didn't intend harm."

Oric frowned but kept silent.

"She was trapped in the Pillars some time ago. Time is a strange thing here and it does strange things to the creatures that live here. As she is now," Arlana nodded to the still waiting baby dragon, "she has only a portion of the knowledge of her adult self. The baby is aware of not truly being a baby, has some of the awareness of her adult self, but the longer she lingers in that time phase, the more infantile her thinking patterns will become."

As if on cue, the dragon rose, folded its wings to its back and moved onto the path. A reverse of the earlier process brought back the adult dragon in increments. The Browans gasped and metal scrapped against metal as more than one sword was drawn. Oric threw back an order to hold and wait his command.

"Are you telling me, my lady," Oric kept his focus on the dragon as he spoke to Arlana, "that you have been communicating with that creature?"

"Yes. Dragons, after a certain age, possess an acute intellect and a very sophisticated communication system similar to our telepathy. Most magicians can sense the mental state of a dragon—feel their mood. Very few humans have the talent to talk with a dragon."

She paused so long Oric's attention was dragged back to her face.

Her gaze was turned inward, her expression distant. "What is it?" He managed to curb some of the harshness in his voice. He swallowed a curse when her blue-eyed gaze, darkened by a strange sadness, locked with his. He couldn't have pulled his gaze from her face at that moment if the dragon's open mouth was slashing down to swallow him whole.

"The Baroness of Georna once had a friend, a golden dragon named Hreedin. Everyone suspected that the two talked on some level, but Baroness Georna would never discuss it—even after Hreedin was killed." Arlana's expression moved further inward.

"Arlana?" Oric's fear had dissipated, but anger and tension still thrummed just beneath the surface. Only that distant expression on her beautiful face kept him from demanding more information.

She shook her head, half smiled and focused on him fully. "Sorry. I'm sure you're more concerned with the dragon facing us now. She won't give me her name because I'm a sorceress and that would give me power over her. But she's agreed to guide us through the Pillars."

"We don't need a guide," Oric snapped. "That is what the path is for."

"She says there's been a change. The path is no longer safe all the way through."

"What sort of change?" Suspicion and disbelief warred with caution. He couldn't afford to be dismissive of anything inside this place.

Arlana's gaze dropped to her mare's mane. "She wasn't specific except to say that some years ago—twenty as far as she can tell—everything inside the Pillars…shifted. Rearranged itself."

He knew without question she believed herself the cause of that shift. And she blamed herself for the trouble it would have caused other travelers. He ached to reach out and touch her, reassure her, pull her into his arms and never let her go. Instead, he asked, "Can she be trusted? The Pillars have been known to change the creatures trapped within them. If she knows of safe passage, why does she not leave?"

Arlana paused, then looked to the dragon. An agony of moments passed before she spoke aloud again.

"She says she was changed, trapped here when the Pillars were first altered. To leave would be death. But," Arlana met his gaze, "she means us no harm. Any magician of enough strength can sense a dragon's state of mind. She's not trying to deceive, and she doesn't intend any mischief. She's simply volunteered to help us."

"Why? What does she care?"

Arlana's gaze stayed locked to his as she said, "Because she knows who I am."

"How is that possible? The orb changed this place at its forming. She would have been trapped here before the prophesied one was linked with the orb."

"I don't know how she knows. She tried to explain. It has to do with the time shifts within this area, but I couldn't understand."

Oric looked at the dragon, frowning. He met the creature's purple and gold gaze and looked deep into an alien intelligence he couldn't begin to read or understand. "You will watch for traps if we follow her?"

"Of course. But I don't believe any traps we encounter will be of her doing."

He faced Arlana again and tried to harden himself to the strength and beauty of her. "Then we will gratefully follow her advice on movements through the Pillars. Please inform her of our gratitude for her help."

Arlana's smile hit him like a stomach punch. As she turned to face the dragon again, Oric relayed the change in plan to the rest of the company, emphasizing that they were not to deviate at all from the altered course. As he finished relaying the new orders, his mind settled back into contemplating the sorceress beside him. And he wondered just how much longer he'd be able to resist her pull.

*** 

The dragon told her to use the name Ryn'ah, as it was as good a name as any. Arlana obliged, more comfortable being able to refer to the magnificent creature leading them as something other than "the dragon". Ryn'ah proved a patient leader, to Arlana's relief. It wasn't exactly easy for their group to keep pace with the dragon's long step.

They left the trail only an hour after Ryn'ah took up the lead. At least, Arlana thought an hour had passed. Time within the Pillars was a strange and nebulous thing. Despite already traveling for what felt like the better part of a day, the sun still appeared directly above their heads. The implications of passing through these time shifts made Arlana's head ache.

*It is a paradox, is it not?*

Ryn'ah's deep mind voice startled Arlana. It sounded like the gong of large bass bells, felt as much as heard. The dragon's form of telepathic communication was like nothing Arlana had experienced before. Ryn'ah used words in a loose sense, blending them with images and emotional impressions. It wasn't remotely like speech and only vaguely like the mind-to-mind communication between humans.

Arlana smiled and raised a brow. *It's not the only paradox I deal with today, wise one.* Her own way of communicating with Ryn'ah was stilted and held none of the depth and nuance of dragon-speak. She was learning a new language, but it was as if she'd known this language before, a very long time ago and was now relearning it.

*You communicate well for a new one, sorceress. And time is a paradox even the bravest of philosophers must admit defeats them.*

*Wish you to learn what I know?*

*Oh yes, please.* Arlana accepted the offer enthusiastically. Anything to keep her mind from turning to the brooding warrior riding beside her.

*He understands time better than most, on an innate level,* Ryn'ah stated.

Arlana frowned. She wasn't entirely sure how to feel about the fact that Ryn'ah could read her thoughts so easily. She couldn't block the dragon or shield her mind the way she did with human telepaths. It was disconcerting to have Ryn'ah commenting on thoughts she considered private. But as no one else could speak with the dragon, it wasn't as if Ryn'ah would reveal any secrets.

*True,* the dragon said with a clearly implied sense of amusement. *And since you stayed his hand when he would have attacked me, your privacy I owe you at the least.*

Arlana chuckled aloud. *Thank you, wise one. I will trust your honor.*

*Wish you to understand time well, sorceress, you will take what I can teach and learn from the warrior.* There was a pointed pause. *I think you will need these understandings for great challenges you have to face and no small factor will time play.*

*Can you see the future, then?*

*Future time isn't set or solid to those traveling this direction. No one can see it for certain. Only glimpse possibilities. Though there is one...*

*One?* Arlana frowned.

*One of future and past times. He moves unlike we do through time. Ask him what he thinks of the future.*

Baroness Georna had once mentioned the penchant of dragons for riddles. Questions bubbled through Arlana's mind, questions she knew Ryn'ah could hear. But the dragon made no effort to explain.

With a sigh that was almost a groan, Arlana finally said, *Very well, wise one. Shall we begin my lessons on the paradox of time?*

# CHAPTER FIFTEEN

When the sun finally set, it was like it had been shot out of the sky, dropping abruptly beyond the horizon. One moment they rode through midday sunshine, the next midnight blackness. The group stopped in the sudden dark, and Arlana could feel their fear rising again. As time had passed, the group had relaxed somewhat, hesitantly trusting the dragon to lead them. With the sudden snuffing of light, tension reasserted itself.

*Will this last long?* Arlana asked Ryn'ah. She could just make out a faint coppery glow from the dragon's scaly hide.

*As we are at this point, if we do not move, you will watch a sunrise in what beyond this place would be half a night's time.*

"Arlana?"

Oric's voice coming from the darkness made her shiver, her skin growing instantly sensitive to his presence just to her left. She could only see his outline, dark against a lighter space between two of the Pillars, but her entire being was acutely aware of him.

"What does our guide have to say of this?"

She noted with a quiet sense of guilt and gratitude that he didn't attempt to speak with her mentally. "She says if we stay put, time will pass as if it's near midnight now. The sun will rise normally in roughly six hours."

"Can we camp here? Is it dangerous to spread out? We should rest, if our guide deems this a suitable spot."

Arlana heard a slight strain in Oric's voice—a tension that seemed to have nothing to do with their current predicament. He sounded distracted. She was afraid to question him, though. Instead, she conveyed his comments to Ryn'ah.

*I will a border show you*, the dragon said. *Within this border, you will be safe.*

A faint blue glow sprang up, forming a convoluted line outlining the area inside which it was safe to move. A collective gasp rose from the group. Arlana quickly explained the glow to Oric so he could translate to the worried Browans. While he passed on the information, Arlana murmured a quiet spell, rolling her hands around each other until a luminous white ball filled the area between her palms. With a gentle push, she sent the ball aloft to hover above them. Its white glow brightened until the entire area was awash in magician's light.

They set a hasty camp, no one venturing near the blue border. As a few small cooking fires sprang to life, Arlana set a protective shield around the encampment, just inside Ryn'ah's border. The dragon settled down at one end of the camp, her giant head resting on her folded forearms. To all who hazarded a glance, she appeared sound asleep.

Arlana hesitated, hovering between talking to Oric and talking more with Ryn'ah. She watched Oric moving around the camp, from fire to fire. He radiated calm assurance, spoke briefly with each group of soldiers and laid a strong hand on the shoulder of one. The soldiers seemed to relax in his wake, to settle into a quiet evening routine, losing much of the day's tension.

She smiled softly at the man responsible for this calming. He was so strong, so commanding and so very…human. She shivered as black eyes swam into her inner vision. Those eyes held little she could call human. And yet they enthralled her. There was passion, power, control and fury in those eyes. And there was pain. But none of it was human.

She didn't realize she was still staring at Oric until he glanced up and caught her gaze. His expression was distant at first, as if he were too deep in thought to notice where his gaze landed. Then emotion pushed aside the distraction. Hot emotions. Angry emotions. Her breath stuck in her throat and her heart hammered against her ribs.

She dropped her gaze, unable to face him. All she wanted was to go to him, to hold him and kiss him and tell him she was sorry. But her own fear and confusion kept her standing where she was, her gaze on the dirt at her feet. He couldn't understand, and she didn't think she could explain.

When she glanced up again, Oric was gone. She tried not to sigh and failed. Pressing a hand to her chest in an attempt to stop the ache there, Arlana moved toward her tent. She knew she needed to sleep, to be lucid to see their journey through. She was as responsible for the safety of their group as Oric. But she was afraid of what might come to her when she closed her eyes.

*Tonight he hears.*

The sound of the dragon's voice in her head startled Arlana and brought her to an abrupt stop. She'd been certain the dragon was asleep. *What?* Arlana changed directions to go stand near Ryn'ah's large head. *Who hears what?*

*The commander.* Ryn'ah's multifaceted eyes rolled open, then focused on Arlana. *The distraction. Tonight he hears.*

What Arlana thought passed for a dragon sigh blew through her mind and the bright eyes closed again.

*His senses he will trust now. Pillars time is no longer a problem.*

*What do you mean, 'he hears'? Hears what?* Arlana sat on the dry ground a respectful distance from Ryn'ah. The tangy smell of clean dirt wafted up to her.

*The other he hears. More often now too. Time is converging.*

Ryn'ah's eyes opened again, and Arlana felt a shiver of dread race over her shoulders.

*He must explain, sorceress. It is his gift and curse to know this thing, hear the approach. He doesn't understand it yet either. You are the key to solving his puzzle. But this is still a thing for you to learn. I cannot interfere.*

Arlana's brow furrowed. Frowning, she studied the unreadable eyes of the creature in front of her. *I don't understand you, wise one.* She sighed and dropped her gaze to her hands where they lay folded in her lap. *And just now, I doubt he'll wish to discuss much of anything with me.*

*Time will come when this will need discussing. Fortunately, the time is not the present moment.*

Arlana glanced up in time to watch the dragon's eyes close again.

*He will be ready to talk to you when to him you are ready to explain your other.*

Arlana gasped. *How do you...? You know?* Another dragon sigh blew softly through her mind.

*You should rest now, sorceress. We journey again soon. You will be tonight safe. From him. He cannot risk venturing here.*

With that, Arlana felt the dragon's mind withdraw.

She sat for a few more moments, staring at Ryn'ah's copper-orange face. After a day full of confusing lessons on time and its peculiarities, the dragon's last comments confused Arlana the most. She couldn't make sense of any of it. And the fact that the dragon knew her secret left her disconcerted and shaken.

Sleep, she decided. She needed sleep. Ryn'ah said she'd be free from dreams tonight. She could relax and not think about anything for a few hours. Then she'd be fine. As she rose to go to her tent, however, she found herself face-to-face with Oric. She knew when her heart started to dance and her stomach trembled that her hope for a few thoughtless hours of rest was in vain.

They stared at each other, an arm's length between them, neither rushing to speak. Oric hadn't sought her out like this since the night she'd forced him from her room. Arlana's pulse jumped as their gazes remained locked. She should say something. Anything. Her voice refused to work.

She was unreasonably grateful when he finally broke the silence.

"My lady. You should rest now. We depart at dawn."

His deep, quiet voice seeped hotly into her blood. "Yes." She didn't budge.

"Thank you for your intercession with our guide. I did not relish a fight with a dragon."

The barest hint of humor in his voice had her babbling before she could check her tongue. "My father killed a dragon once. Before I was born. He hadn't had a choice then, but he's always regretted it. My mother helped protect him. He'd have been killed otherwise. Dragons are very hard to kill, you see." Stop it, she told herself. He doesn't want to hear this. There were other things to say. Things that needed to be said. But nonsense continued to spill out. "My mentor, Merig, also helped. They built a special shield. It's the only way to defeat a dragon. They're difficult shields and require a lot of power. Though I wouldn't have hesitated to build one for you." She pressed her lips together, cutting off the ramble of words a statement too late.

The tiny smile that lifted his mouth tugged at her, willing her to take a step closer. She didn't move. Silence fell between them again, thick with all that was still unsaid.

Then Oric sucked in a deep breath. "You are all right, my lady? Your injuries of the other night…?"

"The bruises are gone now."

"I would have an explanation. As your protector, I should know if you are in some physical danger." He met her gaze without blinking.

"I…I don't think I can explain."

His mouth tightened, but he continued to hold her gaze. "Cannot or will not?" He raised a silencing hand when she opened her mouth. "Are you in physical danger, my lady?"

She didn't know how to answer. She doubted the black-eyed man would really hurt her. But she had no doubt he'd kill Oric. She feared that more than any danger to herself. "I'm not in any physical danger," she murmured. "You don't need to worry, Lord Commander."

He closed the space between them and clenched her shoulders before she realized he'd moved.

"I am worried, Arlana. How does a nightmare bruise the skin? How did we go from a passionate bed to this—because of a dream?"

His voice was quiet and intense, as harsh as his grip. She swallowed around the tangle of emotions clutching her throat.

"I dream of you," he said. "You haunt me whenever I close my eyes. You have been haunting me for a lifetime." His grip gentled and he began to stroke. "Perhaps dreams can hurt," he murmured as he dropped his mouth to hers.

She could do little more than gasp against his demand and his heat. Passion and pain flowed, devouring her. She returned his kiss without realizing what she was doing, desperate for the long-missed taste. Her hands fisted at his waist. With a heated curse, Oric wrapped his arms around her and walked her backward until she felt cold stone at her back. He savaged her mouth, her neck, drawing a low moan from her very soul. The leather and pine scent of him enveloped her.

"Arlana."

His voice was ragged and strained. His hard body pressed closer. She could feel his heart thumping madly, matching the frenzy of her own pulse. She wanted him so much. Her body as well as her mind ached to have him closer, for things to be as they were before…

Fear descended over her like a freezing rain. She pushed at his shoulders, forced him away despite his protesting grunt. Terror stole her breath and she covered her mouth with one trembling hand. What was she doing?

"I can't, Oric," she stammered, moving beyond his reach. "Goddess, I don't know what he'll do. I can't. If he finds out…" She turned and raced for the safety and solitude of her tent as tears blurred her vision.

***

Equal waves of rage and jealousy washed through Oric's system. Again. Two days later and he was still struggling to control an almost overwhelming edge of jealousy as one question repeated in his mind.

Who exactly was *he*?

For two days, Oric led his group, with the help of the dragon, on a convoluted path through the Pillars. He stopped their travels for a break every evening despite the position of the sun in the sky. His confidence in his sense of time had returned. Without fail, he knew what time of day it was, no matter his surroundings or what his external senses tried to tell him. It was one of the few comforts his turbulent mind could grasp each day.

Because for two days, Oric had barely been able to think beyond that one question. Who was he? Only the thinnest string of self-

185

control prevented him from demanding an answer to that question. He, whoever he was, could bruise Arlana in dreams. He had taken Arlana as surely as if he'd spirited her away. He was dangerous.

And may the gods help him, Oric wanted more than anything to destroy *him*.

The only thing keeping him sane was the knowledge that Arlana was more worried about his safety than her own. Oric didn't mind facing the danger of this mysterious man. In fact, a primitive part of him craved a confrontation. But jealousy or no, his primary duty was as First Protector. Even at the cost of his life, he had to protect Arlana. For the moment, it appeared this mysterious man wasn't out to hurt her…too much.

Strangely, Arlana's concern for his safety also gave Oric hope. Hope that he wouldn't have to spend the rest of his life near her, guarding her, without being able to hold her or talk with her or make love with her again. The fear of that life, being so close without being able to touch her, was nearly as strong as his jealousy.

Their last kiss only confirmed what he'd feared all along. She was in his blood and bones. He'd never be free of the memories of her skin against his, the feel of her in his arms, the jasmine scent that filled his nostrils when he was near her. He ached for her and a part of him reluctantly admitted that he always would.

He couldn't lose her to another man. Not now. Not ever.

He glanced up at the sun where it hung on the horizon. It had sat there all morning. He looked back at the dragon. Out of the corner of his eye, he glimpsed something moving through the Pillars alongside the group. He didn't bother turning to get a better look. They'd been flanked by shadows since entering the Pillars, and he'd yet to get a good look at the source of any of those mysterious movements. Since encountering the dragon, however, none of the shadows came too near, so he ignored them.

He shifted in his saddle, consciously not glancing to his right where Arlana rode, though it took a magnificent force of will. He'd given her space again, more for his own sanity than her comfort. He was afraid of what he might do, demand, even beg for if they were alone again.

Lost in thoughts of her, Oric failed to notice when the dragon stopped. Arlana's soft voice pulled him from his reverie. He looked up, blinked, then made the mistake of looking at her. Her eyes, still a deep ocean blue, were puffy and bruised. She looked pale and tired. And lovely. His breath caught with surprising force. Just looking at her did violent things to the ache already tugging at his chest. He sucked in a breath and asked, "Why have we stopped?"

Arlana hesitated and seemed to shake herself before answering. "Ryn'ah says we're about to pass through a dangerous part of the path. Once through, we'll only be an hour or so from the Pillars' edge."

His warrior instincts flowed back at the mention of danger. With effort, he pushed more personal thoughts aside. "Can she describe the dangers we will be facing?"

Arlana glanced away. In the silence, Oric took a moment to inform his soldiers of the reason for the halt. When he focused on her face again, she was frowning slightly. "What is it?"

Her full attention returned to him. "We'll have to pass through a section of altered time. Like the patch she stepped into when we first met."

Oric's brows furrowed. "When she appeared to grow younger?"

"Exactly. And like that, if we remain inside this patch for too long, our memories and minds will alter just as our physical appearance."

Oric looked back at the column of his soldiers, absorbing the news. Without turning to face her, he asked, "We will go through a patch of the past?"

"Yes."

"How far past?"

"Ryn'ah judges it to be about three years. We won't even be able to ride some of the younger horses."

He nodded, still keeping his gaze on the line of soldiers. After a moment, he asked, "How long will be too long?"

Her silence caught his attention and he faced her fully.

"Oric, the patch is maybe a mile long in actual length, but once inside, only Ryn'ah will be able to judge the distance properly. She's been teaching me. From outside, I can sense its length and breadth. But I can't guarantee I'll be able to do the same inside."

She paused, drew in a breath and held it for a heartbeat before letting it out in a whoosh of air. "Time is our problem here in more ways than one. If we move at a fast clip, we should be through in less than half an hour. Anything longer than that will be a danger. But, Oric, I won't know when half an hour has passed."

She met his gaze, the worry showing plainly in her eyes. And he knew she wasn't worried for herself. She was worried for the soldiers. He didn't even blink when he said, "I will know."

"But…Ryn'ah's told me you understand time, and you've proven well enough in the last two days that you can judge when real evening arrives. But this will be different. We haven't passed through a patch of the past yet. Even Ryn'ah can't judge time precisely when she's been aged backward. And even a few minutes too long inside could alter us."

"I will know," he said with absolute certainty. He had a guide he wasn't sure he could explain. But he was positive he would know. "If she can tell, I will need to know, to the day, how far back we are to go."

Arlana, still looking skeptical, nodded and her gaze moved inward.

The giant copper head of the dragon swung around a moment later, her giant gaze piercing Oric. He didn't flinch.

"She says, as close as she can tell, we'll go back three years and twenty-one days. As near as she can tell."

He nodded and began his mental calculations. When he'd finished, he smiled, more than pleased with the outcome. He'd have an even better guide than he'd hoped. Telepathically to Ferdinand, Oric explained the situation, trying for the moment to ignore Arlana's scrutiny. *I'll need you in the center, Ferdinand. You'll need to keep the group together and serve as translator between Arlana and myself.*

*Why? Your Karasnian is nearly as good as mine.*

*It wasn't three years ago,* Oric reminded him with a touch of irony. *We can't afford a miscommunication. Arlana will lead with the dragon. They'll be able to direct us quickly, but your skills will be needed to keep everyone from panicking.*

Oric toyed with the idea of lowering their mental barriers so the group could remain in constant mental contact, but he quickly dismissed the idea. There'd be too much going on in each of those minds, and even a fraction of that mental activity could cause chaos in the group.

He focused on Arlana again. "My lady, you and our gracious guide will lead, Ferdinand will move in the center, and I will take up the rear. Should I feel we are taking too long or coming near our danger limit, I will pass a mental message through Ferdinand to you." She opened her mouth to speak, but he hurried on. He'd explain later, if they survived. "You will have to send back regular messages, relaying distance to the end of the patch so I can judge the overall progress of the group."

She nodded but something in her expression had Oric frowning. "My lady, do not hesitate to leave when you reach the far side." Her eyes flashed, but he held her gaze. "Lady Arlana, you will not remain inside this patch of altered time any longer than it takes to get through it. Is that understood?" She looked away without answering. He moved his horse closer so only she would hear him. "If you are still inside the past time edge when Ferdinand reaches you, he will have orders to have you physically removed. We don't have time for argument. Your life and mind will be protected, whether you are pleased about it or not."

He moved away again, putting a safe measure of space between them. To Ferdinand, he said, *I'll be using the song as a guide for the time we're inside. No one is to stay in this past time longer than a half-hour.* He locked gazes with Ferdinand. *No one.*

The translator nodded.

# Chapter Sixteen



Arlana followed Ryn'ah into the time patch, trying not to be annoyed with Oric's command, without much success. It didn't matter that she knew he was right, that she couldn't risk staying inside the patch for longer than a half-hour. His attitude sparked off an irrational irritation. It sparked more than that, but Arlana wouldn't allow herself to think about the sensation skittering in her stomach. Anger was easier than facing her inner turmoil.

She passed the boundary of altered time expecting some sensation, some indication she'd stepped backward in time. But there was nothing. No feeling, no sign she was now three years younger physically. She glanced down at her figure, still the same, her dress, still the same. Then she caught a glimpse of her hair. It was a black so dark it was nearly blue. A shudder ran through her. She knew without looking her eyes were also black.

For most of her life, she'd shied away from colors that reminded her of him. She'd changed her hair and eye color to anything and everything but black. She had worn clothing that wouldn't remotely remind her of her nightmares. Something, some instinct, had always cautioned her against the man in her dreams, and her fear when trapped in that fog-filled world had always followed her out of the dream. But for years, she'd thought the dreams nothing more than that—dreams. Nightmares maybe, but not real.

And then, at seventeen, she'd decided the dreams might be more than just dreams. Her seventeenth year had been one of her loneliest. Two girls—daughters of Fordin nobles, one her own age and one a year older—had announced their betrothals at court. For the first time in her life, Arlana realized she'd probably never have what those girls had—a life mate. Every man she met was afraid of her power. Even if one were bold enough to ask for her hand, her family wouldn't agree to let her marry until her fate was revealed. She had a destiny. She was the prophesied one. Even if only her family and a few others knew. And at that moment, as she watched the two girls blushing and grinning at the prospect of their upcoming weddings, she'd hated her destiny more than at any other time in her life.

Arlana took a deep breath, trying to force down the rising memories of that awful period. But it was as if she was experiencing the emotions again for the first time. She ran a hand along Esmerelda's neck, trying to reassure herself. She was over that foolishness. She'd outgrown her girlish fantasies. A strand of black hair fluttered into her peripheral vision.

At seventeen, she'd toyed with the idea of running away again, but that had failed once when she was fourteen. Besides, running away wouldn't have done anything to alleviate her loneliness. Then another dream disrupted her sleep. And suddenly, Arlana had a life mate. Or so she'd told herself. The man in the dreams had always been with her, had always come to her. He sparked as much desire as he did fear. Perhaps he was her future, her fate. Perhaps that's why she dreamed about him. She wanted desperately to believe he was real, to believe he'd take her away from her isolation and loneliness. That he would love her.

She went so far as to change her appearance to suit him—black hair, black eyes, white clothing. Her parents thought it was another stage. Like her attempt at running away. She'd outgrow the obsession with black and white, they'd been sure. They had never known how deep her obsession went or how dangerous it could have been.

After a few months, when she'd hoped, prayed, begged for him to take her away from the life that was smothering her, when she had not a single dream of the mysterious man, she got angry. Then she felt foolish and convinced herself once more he was only part of a dream. Her hair and eye color returned to their ever-changing rainbow, her parents breathed a sigh of relief and Arlana felt more alone than she'd ever felt in her life.

The next time he did come to her in a dream, the underlying fear that had always permeated the experience was more intense. Something had changed for her. To this day, she wasn't sure what that something was. But from that moment on, she'd been plagued with the dual sensations of longing and terror that brought her out of the dreams in a cold sweat. And she'd never colored her hair or eyes black again.

Arlana had suppressed that memory for three years. She hadn't wanted to look too closely at what might have happened if he'd answered her prayers. Now, the thought racked her with a tremor that made Esmerelda dance restlessly.

But she wasn't seventeen now, not really. She was twenty and responsible for leading a group of people safely through the time patch. She didn't have time to think too deeply about the fear and anger and…disappointment the three-year-old memory stirred. She returned her attention to Ryn'ah, forcing herself to ignore the strands of black hair falling across her shoulders.

Her memories still tried to tell her all she'd experienced in the last three years didn't exist. Now she was the lonely young woman, desperate for someone, anyone to love. She forced aside those thoughts with effort, in favor of following the dragon only a few feet away. She couldn't wait to get away from the time patch.

*Arlana?* Ferdinand's mental voice was tentative and tinged with fear.

*Yes, Ferdinand.*

*Oric wishes me to tell you the entire group is now inside the altered time patch. Are you nearing the end?*

Arlana took a moment to ask Ryn'ah, though she found her ability to talk with the dragon almost as tentative as when they'd first spoken. Then she turned her attention back to Ferdinand. The mental form of communication that she'd grown used to over the last weeks also felt strange now. Not as strange as talking with Ryn'ah, but not as comfortable as before entering the time patch. *We're nearing the other side. Ryn'ah says it's only three of her lengths away.*

*Thank the gods.*

Ferdinand's relief made Arlana smile. She knew how he felt. She had an overwhelming desire to alter the black color of her hair, but knew it would be pointless. In just a few more moments, she'd leave this altered space and return to her dark blonde coloring. The memory of her desperate time would once again be pushed to the back of her mind.

Ryn'ah was just stepping through the other side of the time patch when Arlana heard the music. She pulled Esmerelda up just short of leaving the patch and motioned the soldiers following her to continue on as she scanned the surroundings. Two pillars to the north, Arlana thought she spotted a flicker of firelight. As she stared, she realized she was seeing the light of a bonfire. The music grew louder. She recognized the tune. With a giggle, she trotted Esmerelda toward the fairy dance.

Oric's attention was so focused on the hum only he could hear that Ferdinand's mental voice breaking in was like cold water being thrown on his face. It took him a moment to focus on responding to his translator and a moment longer to realize Ferdinand sounded panicked. *What is it?* he demanded, knowing his own mental voice carried a touch of panic as well.

*It's Arlana. She hasn't left the time patch. When I got to the far side, she wasn't there, but when I crossed she wasn't outside either. One of the men said he saw her riding north, just inside the edge of the patch.*

A feral growl rose in Oric's throat, causing his horse to dance. *Make sure the rest get out,* he told Ferdinand, already pushing his horse into a run. He moved up the side of the line of soldiers, throwing out a mental command to continue on, but his mind was on finding that damnable sorceress. If she was still alive, he was going to wring her neck.

He reached the edge of the time patch, reassured when he saw his soldiers collecting up on the other side around their dragon guide, then he turned north. He focused enough attention on the hum to know he only had another four minutes to get to her and get them both out before their minds started to revert to their past selves. He did not want to face a full-blown resurgence of the rages he'd kept safely to himself three years ago.

His duty, his inability to change his fate, and an almost constant and painful dream of a sorceress he hadn't met yet had kept him edgy and irritable for several months that year. The dreams had been so intensely erotic in nature he'd woken up hard and needy. But none of the women he had gone to for relief stirred even the remotest interest, nor had their ardent attempts to cool his blood worked. He still dreamed of Lady Arlana Von Fordin, knowing it was her even though he never saw her clearly. And he could never say exactly what happened in the dreams. He only knew that when he woke from one, he was painfully aroused and so angry about it he could have torn his room apart brick by brick.

Now that he knew what she looked like, had felt her beneath him, had tasted her, he could only imagine what kind of torment those dreams might manifest. And he didn't want to go through that again. His current dreams were bad enough.

He ruthlessly pushed aside the emotions stirred up by memories too close to the surface. Then he spotted Esmerelda. The mare stood to one side of a pillar, shifting restlessly, her eyes so wide the whites shone. He didn't stop, but raced around the pillar, only to pull his mount up short. The warhorse reared up onto his hind legs and began backing away despite Oric's commands to move forward. Rather than fight with his horse, he slid from the saddle and dropped his reins to the ground. The horse's training kept him in place, but only barely. Arlana's mare snorted and pawed at the ground.

But Oric's full attention was on the bonfire. And the black-haired minx swaying closer and closer to it. His heart caught in his throat and fear thrummed through him. For a second, he couldn't move, couldn't breathe. He knew without seeing her face the woman was Arlana, though he'd never seen her with black hair before. He'd know her in a crowded room if he were blind. His gaze flicked to the swirl of dancing fairies around the bonfire, then back to Arlana, panic licking at his nerve endings. May the gods help him. She was too far away.

And she was swaying steadily toward madness and death.

"Arlana!" He barely recognized his own voice as desperation ripped sound from his throat. He raced forward, terror pushing him.

The circle of fairies swirling around the bonfire sped up, their dance beginning to blur individual forms together. Over the crackling sounds of the fire, the eerie music permeating the air and the insistent hum in the back of his mind, he heard her giggle. It was a young girl's giggle, a sound he'd never heard from her before.

For just an instant, the carefree sound enchanted him. He staggered and felt himself drawn closer to the whirling fairies. He wanted beyond reason to sweep her into his arms and spin her into the circle of dancers. He wanted to lose himself in the music, in her. It would be so easy, so fun. She'd be his forever.

The fading hum in the back of his mind broke through the spell, reminding him of the time, the very little time he had left. He raced toward her again, ignoring the siren call of the dance. The closer he got, though, the more malevolent that song grew. Sound dug into his skull, stabbing him with bright shards of pain. He ignored it and continued forward.

When he reached her, she was only an arm's length from the now frantic swirl of dancers. Long, elegant limbs reached toward her, gossamer strands of material fluttered close, and just at the edge of his mental hearing ability, he heard their promises whispered into her hopeful mind.

The heat from the bonfire washed over him as he swept Arlana into his arms. He ignored her scream of shock, her panicked protests, her desperate attempt to climb over his shoulder to reach the fairy circle. He held her with all his strength against the heat of the fire and the stabbing pains lancing his brain and ran back to their horses. He threw her unceremoniously up onto his own horse, climbed up behind her and raced toward the edge of the time patch. He could hear the pounding hooves of her mare just behind him.

Her protests turned to desolate sobs, racking her body with tremors.

He held her closer but ignored the stuttering question she repeated over and over against his chest. "Why?" He raced through the edge of the time patch and into the midst of his soldiers just as the hum was fading, moments before he risked mental damage. As he passed through the time patch's edge, the sound at the back of his mind cut off abruptly.

Several soldiers raced forward to take the reins of his and Arlana's mounts while others helped him ease Arlana to the ground. Ferdinand held her while Oric dismounted then gently passed her pliant body back. The translator's blue eyes were huge.

*Is she all right, Oric? She must have been inside longer than the half-hour. What happened?*

Oric shook his head and cast him a look that said he would explain what he could later. He turned away from the group and carried Arlana toward the shade behind one pillar, far enough from his soldiers that he could speak freely, the solid rock of the pillar giving them privacy from prying eyes. He set her carefully to her feet, leaned her up against the stone and tilted her chin until he could see her eyes. They were no longer black. Neither was her hair. For reasons Oric couldn't begin to understand, that filled him with relief.

Her blue eyes were glazed, her focus turned inward, but as he watched, awareness flooded back. Another wave of relief washed over him, followed closely by the most unreasonable and intense anger he'd ever experienced. "What in the name of the gods did you think you were doing?" he shouted, unable to control his fury. "Do you know what you almost walked into? Do you have any idea what you almost did?"

Her eyes widened then narrowed as irritation sparking in the depths of blue-gray. "Shouting in my face isn't going to get you answers, Lord Commander," she hissed. "Besides, it was just a fairy ring!" She tried to straighten away, but the pillar at her back kept her from getting far.

He gripped her upper arms hard and locked gazes with her. "Nothing inside the Pillars is 'just' anything." His voice low, his teeth clenched so he wouldn't shout, he said, "The fairies within the Pillars have been changed the same way that everything else inside the Pillars has been, my lady. Stepping into that circle would have trapped you in a timeless place where madness would claim you. And then death." He wouldn't admit to her how close he'd come to following her into the madness, how close he'd been to carrying her into death. Admitting it to himself sent another flood of anger and fear through him so violent he trembled.

She turned her head to avoid his gaze. He shook her once. Her gaze snapped back to his, her anger lashing out, but beneath it he saw her dawning fear. He had to control the urge to shake her again, harder this time. His grip clenched convulsively on her arms and only relaxed when he saw her wince.

"How do you know?" Her chin came up, her mouth thinned to a hard line. "How can you know madness and death awaited me in that circle? Especially if it's a timeless place."

He growled low in his throat. "Travelers have lost companions to those very same fairy dances, never to see them again. If their bodies are found, it is often years after the disappearance, the bodies emaciated and withered. Destroyed, the healers say, by exhaustion." He stepped closer, pressing her up against the pillar with the length of his body. "There was often evidence of self-mutilation too, my lady sorceress. Would you have me condemn you to that?"

He watched with satisfaction as the muscles in her jaw clenched and unclenched. He wanted her to feel a fraction of the fear he'd felt— just a portion of the terror he'd experienced. If she understood, if she really knew the danger she'd faced, maybe it would lessen his guilt.

"And just how was I to know about this if you didn't warn me?"

Her voice trembled on the first word before steadying again. She all but spit the last word in his face.

"I presumed that when I warned you about the Pillars, you would assume everything you encountered a potential threat."

"Ryn'ah wasn't a threat."

"Our kind guide is the exception to the law of this place, Arlana. Do you have any idea what you risked?"

"I don't want another reminder of my responsibility to stay alive so that damned orb doesn't react to my death. Do you understand that, Lord Commander? I may have made a mistake—one I remind you I wouldn't have made if you'd warned me first—but isn't it your job to see to my safety? Well you've done your duty very well and no damage was done. So you can stop yelling at me now!" Her chest heaved, pressing her breasts hard against his chest, and her lower lip trembled.

"This has nothing to do with my duty," Oric growled, and then he kissed her. His need to reassure himself that she was whole and unharmed was so overwhelming he crushed her mouth beneath his. Then his kiss turned gentle, deep. He poured all of his fear into the kiss, all of his guilt and anguish. By the gods, he'd almost lost her. At that moment, he didn't give a damn that he'd have failed in his duty if she died. All he could think about was the blade shredding his heart at the mere thought of losing her forever. Of never seeing her, never hearing her voice, even when it crackled with anger.

He ran his hands up her shoulders, along her neck and finally cupped her face. She opened to him physically, though a part of him noted she still kept her mind closed. He didn't care. She was alive. She was safe. And she was returning his kiss.

He pulled his mouth from hers just long enough to ask, "Are you okay? Your mind…your memory…nothing is harmed?"

"No, nothing's harmed. I'm fine, Oric. I'm fine."

And then his mouth claimed hers again. Her arms wrapped around his waist, pulling him tight. His hands slid up into her hair, tightening, then relaxing to cup her head. He couldn't taste her enough.

"I'm sorry, Arlana. Gods, I'm so sorry." He murmured the apology against her lips, deepening his kiss when she would have spoken. He couldn't tell her why he was apologizing, but he had to say it. His instant of weakness, his moment of temptation by the fairy song, would haunt him for the rest of his life.

At last, he forced himself to break the kiss, but he couldn't bring himself to stop touching her. His hands ran over her face and through her hair as he searched her gaze. He caught a flicker of her vulnerability and her passion before she shifted her gaze to his shoulder. The hands encircling his waist relaxed then weakly tried to push him away.

"Don't. Please," he murmured, brushing a fingertip across her cheekbone. "Just a few minutes more. I need to reassure myself that you are all right."

"Oric…" Her voice hitched. "I'm fine. Really."

She met his gaze and the look there stole his breath.

"You risked your mind to save me. Not just your life but…but everything you are."

"I would risk all for you, Arlana. Not as First Protector to defend his mistress. But as a man. I would face madness and death and all the demons of the underworld to keep you safe."

She shook her head and raised her hand to close his mouth and silence his declaration.

He caught her fingers and settled her palm against his chest. "Understand this, fayria. I would face anything to protect you. Even this man who can bruise you in a dream."

"No," her voice was strained, "please don't say that. Oric, you can't face him. Promise me you won't. Please, promise me you won't ever…"

He kissed her lightly, quieting her pleas. "I can't promise you that." He heaved in a lungful of air. "Arlana, who is this man? Tell me. Is he a sorcerer? Are you afraid of him? Why don't you want me to face him?"

She opened her mouth, closed it again. Her forehead creased, lowering her light brows over narrowed eyes. She opened her mouth again, but all that came out was a gasp.

"I can't." She met his gaze and her eyes widened. "Oric, I can't. I… Before I thought it was just that I didn't know how to explain, but now… I've never talked… Never told anyone. And now, I'd tell you some things, but I can't. Physically."

Her eyes narrowed, her mouth pinched, and he watched as she strained against some invisible bond. She opened her mouth to force sound through but once again failed.

"Damn it."

"Arlana, is this his doing?" Oric tried to meet her gaze, but she was focused inward, her gaze settled firmly on his shoulder.

Finally, she shook her head and let out a frustrated breath. "I can't answer questions about him."

The anger building in her voice almost made him smile.

"He is responsible for this, isn't he?" Oric stated. She looked up, her eyes clearly showing her inability to answer and her frustration at this block. "Does it hurt you?"

"No. No I'm not being hurt. It's just…" The creases in her brow suddenly relaxed and her eyebrows inched higher.

He frowned.

"Ask me about him again," she said. "A yes or no question. Then ask me something I can answer, a question that has nothing to do with him directly. My answer to the second question will be the answer to the first."

This time he did smile. "You are a very bright woman, Arlana Von Fordin." He was rewarded by a faint flush coloring her cheeks. Rubbing a finger gently across one of her heated cheeks, he considered his next question. "Is he responsible for this block?" He paused then asked, "Do you like the color blue?"

She smiled and his heartbeat danced in his chest.

"Yes," she said firmly.

"Is he a sorcerer?" He cupped her cheek. "Do you like flowers?"

"Yes."

"Is he a powerful sorcerer? Do you like to dance?"

"Yes." She nodded.

"Does he only visit you in your dreams? Do you play an instrument?"

"No." Her lips pursed and she said, "I used to. Until very recently. But now the answer is no."

She paused and he nodded his understanding of the double meaning. "Does he threaten you? Have you a favorite song?"

"No. Not really. Maybe."

Her hesitation made him frown. "Are you afraid of him? Do you like the smell of rain?"

"Yes."

"Afraid for yourself? Do you eat many sweetmeats?"

"Sometimes, but not now."

"You are afraid for me? Do you sew?"

"Yes."

"He threatened me?" He lifted her chin when she tried to look away. "Is our dragon guide kind?"

"Yes."

"Why did he threaten me?" He breathed the question out on a whisper. But he didn't ask a second. She shook her head, her brows crinkling. She nodded to him to ask a question that would allow her to answer. Instead he asked, "Does he love you? Do you look forward to the summer?"

She swallowed hard. He watched the slow working of her throat before looking back into her wide eyes.

"Yes," she murmured.

He paused for a long time, watching her face, studying the confusion deep in her eyes. Something inside him constricted painfully, and he knew it would only take one word from her to seal his fate.

"Do you love him?" He hesitated, not sure he wanted to hear the answer. And then a question came to him that he needed answered more than any other question he'd asked, including the last one. Without thinking of the implications of her answer, he asked, "Do you think you could ever grow to love me?"

She sucked in a breath and stared. He knew in that instant he'd made a mistake. He'd been sure from the first that her answers to his second questions were as true as the answers to his first. She did like to dance, she liked the color blue, she liked the smell of rain and she used to eat too many sweetmeats. But he'd forgotten the double meanings of her answers when he'd asked his last question. Now, no matter what she said, it would shatter him. He started to tell her not to answer, opened his mouth to take back both questions when her quiet voice interrupted.

She looked deep in his eyes without blinking and whispered, "I don't know."

# CHAPTER SEVENTEEN



She'd lied to him. When she'd answered his last two questions, Arlana had lied to Oric. She hadn't been sure of it at the time. But now, riding across the grassy hills that separated the Pillars from the Timeless Forest, she knew without a doubt she'd lied.

Her answer to the first question was still an unresolved "I don't know". She didn't know. She'd spent her whole life with the black-eyed man—if only in dreams. She'd gone through periods of hating him, longing for him, relying on him. And he claimed to love her. He'd said the words. He claimed to be her destiny. But did she love this man she also feared?

She glanced at the back of Oric's head. He rode a few lengths ahead, deep in conversation with Ferdinand and Captain Voquz. She knew without a doubt now her answer to the second of his questions was yes. Yes, she could grow to love Oric, given the chance. The problem was, she didn't think she'd be given the chance.

He'd pulled back after she'd answered his final question. The look in his eyes made her want to cry even now with just the memory. He hadn't said anything else, merely nodded and returned to the group.

She'd followed, feeling desolate.

They'd ridden to the edge of the Pillars without any more trouble, and Arlana had said a long farewell to their guide. She even promised to return when she could to visit Ryn'ah. The dragon had given her the distinct impression of gratitude. Then another sensation had filtered through the dragon's mind-speak, but Ryn'ah blocked the impression before Arlana could interpret it. She still wasn't sure what had passed through Ryn'ah's mind in that instant. But she had other things to worry about at the moment. She'd ponder the dragon later.

Since leaving the Pillars, the mood of the group had improved. Riding without all the fear and tension infusing everyone was a relief. Unfortunately, it also gave her too much time to focus on Oric. And for the past several days, that's exactly what she'd done. He'd somehow managed to revert to a polite, distant attitude. No open hostility or chilly silences. No glares. He didn't even ignore her. In fact, he acted as if nothing had passed between them at all. And it hurt so much she wanted to scream. She'd almost rather he was angry. She'd prefer any emotion to the politely impersonal attitude he showed her now.

Tomorrow they'd enter the Timeless Forest. They'd reach Czanri a few days after leaving the forest. And she'd take up her long-awaited destiny. What would happen then? When Oric returned to his home, his life? Did he have other lovers? Would she have to see him with another woman on his arm? Goddess, that thought tore chunks out of her heart.

And yet, she couldn't promise him anything, couldn't promise him the future she'd glimpsed in his eyes. Not until she knew more about the black-eyed man and what he meant to her and her future. Until she could be sure Oric was safe from him, she couldn't dismiss him or his declaration of love. And there was still a part of her, a part she wished she could bury, that longed for the sorcerer in her dreams.

She knew she'd lose Oric. One way or the other, no matter her final decision on the mysterious man, Oric was pulling away. Distancing himself and his emotions. And there was nothing she could do about it, despite the selfish part of her willing to do or say almost anything to keep Oric near.

They camped that night within sight of the Timeless Forest. Arlana sat by a cooking fire, brooding. Since leaving the Pillars, she'd dreaded going to sleep each night. Yet the dreams still hadn't returned. She woke with a sense of relief that an unavoidable confrontation was once more delayed, but she went to bed each night tensely waiting for the inevitable. A small part of her longed for the confrontation. Maybe then she'd be able to decide, to understand her own feelings.

Maybe seeing the black-eyed man again would confirm he'd spoken the truth, and they were destined for one another.

But she woke the next morning from a dreamless sleep, nothing resolved. Only this time, she didn't wake up with a sense of relief. In fact, a knot of unease tightened her stomach. All morning, an itch at the back of her mind nagged and a whispered warning remained just beyond her hearing. The feeling grew stronger when they passed under the dark canopy of the Timeless Forest.

She stretched her senses, traced both the magical energies and the more mundane energies filling the forest. There was something out there, but she couldn't decide what she was feeling. Every time she tried to focus in on the anomaly, it skittered away like a kitchen rat. The harder she tried to pinpoint it, the more scattered and diffused it got.

She used so much energy trying to find this strangeness in the forest that even Oric's polite questions about the state of her health couldn't evoke more than a distracted grunt. For the first hour, she assumed the anomaly was the reason for her sense of foreboding. But the more she searched, the more she became convinced her sense of unease arose from a completely different source. The anomaly in the forest was something else, something less threatening but no less a puzzle. In fact, the anomaly was so distracting it almost overwhelmed her unease. Almost.

*Almost* saved her.

She watched them emerge from the surrounding forest seconds before a sound pierced her brain, screeching through the areas of her mind used for telepathy. It scorched her and doubled her over in pain so sharp she felt like her skull would split under the pressure. She dumped energy into the internal shields that held out the thoughts of others, reinforced them with a ward against intrusion. The sound stopped as abruptly as it started.

She slumped against Esmerelda's neck, her entire body aching from the mental attack. She couldn't muster enough energy to move but feared moving would hurt even if she had the strength. Nausea turned her stomach as her mare stomped out her unease. If she could just lift her head. But pain washed her vision with blackness at any hint of movement.

She could hear the high-pitched gibbering of dozens of voices, human voices, all around them. Beyond that, there was the sound of horse movement and harness gear rattling, and nothing else. No sound of soldiers fighting, no alarm sounded, nothing. The silence from her group was an ominous counterpoint to the fast-paced speech of their attackers. They'd looked like humans coming out of the woods, but Arlana couldn't force her memory to hold against the pain. Ragged-looking humans, she thought, as bodies moved in and out of her limited vision. Gaunt, almost skeletal-looking, with torn clothing. Images of sharp teeth and spears clashed in her abused mind. Faces swam together in front of her. The movement was too much. Bile rose in her throat at the constantly changing colors and shapes. She closed her eyes, forced the bile back down and tried to focus.

Then Esmerelda moved beneath her and the nausea rose beyond her control. She threw up what little she had in her stomach and passed out.

***

When Arlana woke, she was sitting on a soft mat of moss in the sun-dappled shade of a giant oak. She squinted against the sparks of light flittering through the parted curtain of her hair. Several moments passed before she realized there were other people around her. And that she was tied by rough rope to the oak. Slowly, she lifted her head. When the pain that had knocked her out didn't return, she ventured a look at her surroundings.

The oak she was tied to was at the edge of a small clearing, one of many ancient trees ringing the space. Just past the ring, Arlana thought she glimpsed a house, but her attention was too quickly diverted to pay it much attention. Like her, the Browan soldiers were tied with thick rope to the oaks circling the clearing. Each tree in the ring held as many as half a dozen soldiers tight against its base.

She scanned the bowed heads, searching frantically for Oric. He was tied against an oak directly opposite her, his head drooping, his black hair hanging over his face. But she didn't need to see his face to know him.

There were no other soldiers, unconscious or otherwise, tied to her tree, so Arlana murmured a single word and the rope that bound her loosened and crumbled to dust. Her heart hammered erratically as she slowly rose to her feet. She scanned the surrounding forest with eyes and magic senses. The anomaly she'd felt earlier was much stronger here, but she didn't have time to worry about it. All she could think of was getting to Oric and making sure he was all right. She could feel the presence of dozens of humans just outside the circle. The energy flowing into the ring of trees was heavy with menace and something else that scared Arlana more than their anger. She felt a wild insanity in all of them. An uncontrolled group of minds, all delusional, all gleefully full of anticipation. She didn't want to know what they were anticipating.

When they didn't move forward as she got to her feet, she started slowly across the ring. The emerald moss was spongy beneath her feet and a heady, earthy scent rose from the ground with each step she took. From the corner of her eye, she saw movements in the shadows beyond the trees, and she felt the first tentative touches of those insane minds. They probed at her barriers, tried to worm beneath her defenses. She added an extra layer of protection, but it was the only defensive move she made. She didn't know what they might do, what they were capable of, and she wasn't about to provoke another attack. She wasn't even sure if she could put up a shield to protect the group, as the attackers' weapon of choice was telepathy.

She could hear the constant chatter of their minds despite her own barriers. She'd never had trouble blocking out others before, but these minds were so erratic and chaotic the sheer volume of their mental noise squeaked through her shields. Thank the Goddess their conscious efforts couldn't defeat her protections. She wasn't sure her mind could take another of those mental attacks.

The thought had her heart skipping with fear. The Browan soldiers wouldn't have the same ability as she did to block out the chaos created by their attackers. Oric might be able to shield against it. But then, he was so strong he might be even more vulnerable to their attacks. She swallowed hard, the taste of her own bile still strong in her mouth, and continued carefully across the ring.

She reached the exact center before the attackers made a move to stop her.

The spears they carried into the ring were of no real physical threat. She put up a shield and their tentative pokes were bounced aside. But for all the chaos in their minds, they weren't stupid. One, a tall, lanky man with blond-brown hair to his waist, moved close to Oric and set a spear tip at his throat. Arlana gasped. The man grinned and pushed the spear a bit farther, drawing blood.

She met the man's gaze. A slight hand gesture and a few spoken words threw him across the circle, hitting high up on one of the oak trunks. He dropped to the ground with a thud and remained there, unmoving. The attack sent the group of forest people skittering away. The buzz of their mental attack battered her shields, but she ignored it. A second hand gesture sealed the slight wound at Oric's neck. Then she started toward him again.

Her show of strength scared the forest people for a moment, but their caution didn't last. They charged her personal shield, yelling wildly and swinging their sharpened spears. Her shield bounced them harmlessly away. They switched tactics and instead of attacking her directly, they attacked the other soldiers. As a distraction, it worked well. She diverted her attention from reaching Oric, stood in the center of the oak ring and summoned power. She knocked the attackers away from the soldiers with slight hand gestures and muttered words. She tried not to hurt them at first, but as they grew more manic, her retaliating strikes grew more violent. A dozen of the forest people lay bleeding just outside the ring. She hadn't been forced to kill any of them yet. But the longer they attacked the more vicious they got. She doubted she'd be able to fend them off for much longer without having to kill one. She pulled in power from the surrounding magics, careful not to incorporate any of the anomalous energy coming from just beyond the ring, and prepared for another wave of attacks.

All at once, the assault ended. The abrupt stillness rocked Arlana back on her heels. She whirled around, trying to guess their next move. Those still standing hovered around the edge of the circle. The mental attacks had stopped too. Even the chaotic humming of their uncontrolled minds had stilled somewhat.

She stretched out her senses, trying to find the source of their distraction. All she felt was the anomaly. She turned a slow circle until she spotted the cottage just beyond the edge of the clearing. The strange energy seemed to be radiating from the cottage. It was also the focus of all the forest dwellers. She took a step toward it, only to find a couple dozen spears pointed at her.

"You already know you can't touch me," she said in a calm, even voice, pitched low to command attention. "Yet you still threaten me. Why? Explain why you've brought us here." She had no idea if they'd understand her language. She doubted they could, but her intent was clear. If they didn't answer, she'd perform the language spell and ask them in Browan.

She waited while a mental hum like the sound of a wasp nest rose. Then one woman stepped forward. Her head was raised high, but her eyes were hidden behind stringy mounds of dark red hair. Like the others, she wore a ragged mix of old clothing. Unlike the others, around her neck hung a thick necklace of what looked like human and animal teeth. Her own teeth flashed gray against her dirty skin.

"We are his people. We await him. He requires sacrifices. You are they." The woman's voice was hoarse with disuse, but her speech was clear—and she spoke in understandable but heavily accented Karasnian.

Arlana kept her gaze fixed on the woman. She knew without having to see the bowed heads of the other forest people that this woman was important. "Who is he?"

"He is the Traveler. The timeless one. He speaks to us now. He demands sacrifice. You are they."

"I won't allow that, you know."

Another gray-toothed smile flashed out from between strands of matted hair. "You have no choice. No one escapes us. No one survives us." She turned to face the cottage, putting her back to Arlana. "He sings to us. He protects us. But he demands blood."

With that final word, the woman whirled around and threw her spear. Arlana raised a hand to deflect it, but before the gesture was complete, the spear fell harmlessly to the ground only a few feet from Oric. She sucked in a sharp breath. She hadn't stopped the spear. Her heart pounding, she looked up from the now harmless weapon.

And her world turned upside down.

She noticed the goblins pouring into the clearing, and a small but still functioning part of her mind registered them as GeMorin clan. Her parents had told her stories of the GeMorin and their part in her kidnapping when she was six months old. Their intelligence and warrior skills were only slightly less amazing than the deadly fangs they sported. But in that moment, she barely saw them.

All her attention was devoted to the black-eyed man who followed the GeMorin through a rectangular hole in the world, a gate from which no light escaped.

She remembered to breathe when her lungs screamed, and then her breath came in short pants. Goddess, it must be a dream. This had to be a dream! She tried to close her eyes and found she couldn't. She couldn't even look away. He held her gaze as easily as he'd always done. The danger that always surrounded him flowed toward her with his every step. And a little tingle of excitement raced through her blood.

He stopped an arm's length away and stared. Arlana could only stare back. She was vaguely aware of the rush of chaos around her, the high-pitched screams of the forest people, the guttural calls of the goblins. The melee lasted a few moments, then died away to silence. And still she couldn't look away from his ebony eyes.

When he smiled, her heart nearly burst from her chest and her breath whooshed out.

"My love."

His voice was the same—deep and rich, intoxicating and seductive, low and predatory.

"I am sorry for arriving late." His gaze flicked around the circle before latching onto hers again. "They didn't appear to be giving you much trouble, though."

"Are you the one?" She meant was he the one the forest people worshipped, the one that demanded blood sacrifice.

A sly smile lifted his lips. "Yes." He stepped closer. "But they worship someone else."

An expression passed over his face, startling her. It looked almost like fear. But he hid the emotion too quickly for her to be sure. He reached out, ran a hand down her hair, then cupped her cheek. Coherent thought scattered completely. She couldn't have moved if she tried.

*It is time, my love. We have much work to do and not much time left.*

His voice in her mind was like the caress of silk against hot skin.

He gestured to the black gate behind him. *Shall we go? I have a banquet laid out in your honor. You shall be introduced in my court this very night.*

She swallowed hard and shook her head. "I…I can't go with you." It took all of her willpower, more than she thought she had left, to look away from him and focus on the Browan soldiers. To her amazement, the GeMorin had almost all of them untied and most were rousing from their stupor. More than one held a hand to head. She could sympathize with the headaches they must have. Her gaze moved inexorably to Oric.

Two GeMorin soldiers held him by the arms in a standing position, but his head sagged. He was the only person still unconscious. "Why isn't he waking up?" Her voice hitched with a hint of panic.

*Perhaps he is weaker than the rest.*

She whirled to face the black-eyed man. "He is stronger," she hissed.

A slight snarl lifted his lips. *Then perhaps it is because he is stronger. More damage must have been done.*

Panic reared high at the pronouncement. She started to turn away, intent on going to Oric to see if she could help him, but a hand on her shoulder stopped her. His hold was light but insistent.

*He will recover. Does that ease your conscience? He will recover in a few hours' time and because you have asked it of me, he will live. For now.*

When she would have moved away, he tightened his grip on her shoulder. She looked back, into his eyes, and was lost again in their black depths.

*We do not have time for your pet, Arlana. We must leave here now.*

As he spoke, he began walking toward the black gate, taking her unresistingly with him. But her gaze turned back to Oric's bowed head.

*Wait. Please.* Speaking mind to mind with him was painful in its intensity. It was unlike anything she'd experienced in the past. Even with Oric. But the gesture of speaking into his mind stilled his movements and caught his full attention. She faced him. *I can't leave them. They need my help to get through this forest and safely home. Please.*

He stared for a silent moment. *Your loyalty to these small ones does you credit. You will make a fine and benevolent queen.* He gestured one of the GeMorin forward without taking his gaze from hers. "Escort the soldiers to the edge of the forest, GeNol. On your honor, ensure they reach the other side safely."

"Yes, Master."

The deep voice rumbled from Arlana's left. From the corner of her eye, she caught a glimpse of a large green-skinned arm with a blue tattoo around the heavily muscled biceps.

*Now, my love, are you satisfied?*

He flinched slightly as he asked his question. Arlana frowned.

*The GeMorin will guarantee their safety through the forest?* she said.

*Ask them yourself.*

She turned to face the large goblin beside her. He was easily as thick as two humans and stood an inch or two taller than her. Goblins didn't get that large—except for the GeMorin clan. The goblin had thick, long brown hair pulled back in a low tail, making his heavy brow ridges prominent. His lipless mouth was closed but the tips of his fangs still showed against the lower part of his mouth. He bowed his head when she focused on him and dropped to one knee. The gesture had her glancing back at the black-eyed man, but his expression was unreadable.

"GeNol," she said hesitantly, turning her attention back to the GeMorin. "Will you guarantee the safety of these soldiers until they've left the Timeless Forest?"

"Even as you command, my lady. As we are blood sworn to the master, so are we blood sworn to your service. Ask anything of us. We will die to accomplish the task."

Arlana's eyes widened with each sentence. She swallowed hard against the fear prickling her gut. "Why? I don't understand."

*Arlana.*

The sound of the black-eyed man's voice made her jump. She faced him and saw a strain in his features that belied his calm tone. Around her, she felt the strange eddies of magic, like grasping. The scars that characterized Browan magic were being pulled taut, tugging at…something.

*We must leave now.* The sorcerer's mental voice was still smooth and coaxing, but he could no longer hide the edge that crept into it. *GeNol will renew his vow, and I will explain its implications later. It is enough for you to know that your charges will be safe. Now come. It is time for you to see your new domain.*

*No. I can't leave until I know Oric will recover. I need to heal him.*

"There is not enough time!"

The barely contained violence in his voice made her flinch, but she held her ground. His anger damaged the sway he held over her and sparked her own anger. "I won't leave until I know he's recovered."

Their gazes clashed across the space separating them. She would never have dared defy him in her dreams. When he'd first appeared in the clearing, she hadn't thought she could defy him ever. But her fear for the people who'd been risking their lives to protect her far outweighed her fear for herself. And to protect Oric, she would risk anything. Even the sorcerer's wrath.

Without breaking eye contact, he gestured at the GeMorin holding Oric up. They started forward. Before Arlana knew their intent, they stepped through the black gate, taking Oric with them.

Her mouth dropped. "What are you doing?"

*If you will not leave without him, then your pet shall come with us. But I warn you, my love, he would have been safer left here. Beyond my easy reach.*

*No! Please, you can't.*

*If you would see him survive the hour, Arlana, you will come with me now.*

Her ability to stand against him fled. She had no choice now. Turning, she found Ferdinand in the group of terrified-looking soldiers and gestured him forward. "Ferdinand, go with the GeMorin. They'll see you safely to the other side of the forest."

"But, my lady…" Ferdinand's gaze jumped to the sorcerer and back. His eyes were so wide that the whites showed starkly against his dark skin. "What's happening? Where have they taken the Lord Commander?"

"I'll see to Oric's safety, Ferdinand. I'm depending on you to keep the group together and see them back to Czanri. The GeMorin will protect you through the forest." *But remain vigilant. Don't trust them any more than you must to survive the journey.*

*My lady, you must reach Czanri soon. The Guardian is expecting you. There is very little time left.*

*I'll be there as soon as I can. And I'll make sure Oric is returned safely. Do as I ask for now. Please. Everything will work out. Trust me.*

Ferdinand sucked in his lips and hesitated a moment longer, then he nodded his assent. Arlana could only hope she was telling him the truth. She hoped to prove worthy of his trust. When she glanced at the black-eyed sorcerer, she feared she might be hoping in vain.

He stretched his hand out to her, the gesture a challenge and a threat much more than a courtesy. She stared at the white of his palm for a heartbeat then placed her hand atop his. His grip closed like a trap. No longer resisting, Arlana let him lead her toward the black gate. And without looking back, she stepped into the darkness.

# CHAPTER EIGHTEEN

Catarin stood to one side of the shrine, in line with the highest of the Browan government and nobility. As Owen's consort, she held a political position envied by many of the lesser sorcerers within the empire. If they knew what she did, they wouldn't envy her the place.

She watched as the emperor motioned to the circle of sorcerers in the center of the shrine. One hundred and ninety-nine men and women stood in their white robes, heads bowed in concentration, a barely audible murmur rising from them toward the domed roof of the shrine. The unadorned white of the circle was a sharp contrast to the multicolored assembly surrounding them. The emperor himself was resplendent in robes of fuchsia and purple, orange and yellow. His jewelry glittered and glowed in the candlelight that brightened the white marble walls of the temple. His wreath of office sat prominently on his head, defying his political rivals to threaten him now. Now that he was creating the ultimate weapon. A weapon to control time.

He made another sweeping gesture, encompassing the entire shrine, and proclaimed, "Victory is upon us. With this weapon, we shall conquer Karasnia. We shall invade Bthak and beat back their barbarian hordes. We will ravish the Depnians. We will travel across the deserts and wastelands to conquer far-flung Palsaph and Glok. Our empire will spread across the known world. I will be as a god to them. And you will be my warrior disciples!" His heavy jowls shook with each thunderous pronouncement.

Catarin felt a shiver of foreboding course through her blood.

She turned her focus toward Owen, ignoring the shouts of victory and the clash of metal as swords met shields in applause. Owen stood at the top of the circle and just outside it, above the heads of the circle of sorcerers, on a golden dais. His white hair flowed around his shoulders, his lean face taut and his eyes slit nearly closed in concentration. Like the others, his white robe was unadorned. Nothing but his physical position distinguished him from the other sorcerers. Catarin swallowed back her fear and tried to send out as much positive energy as she could muster.

As the murmurs of the circle grew louder, the spectators fell silent. Catarin could feel the spell forming, coalescing. The magic in the air was sharp with the power the group wielded. This feeling of power being commanded, controlled was like a drug. A vibration built with the spell, striving toward the breaking point. The energy pulled them all along. The thrill of anticipation warred with the fear of what was being done.

Catarin tried to remain focused on Owen, tried to keep from losing herself in the building strength of the spell, but a feeling of being watched distracted her. She looked around the shrine, trying to find the source. Near the rear of the hall, like a beacon in the sea of radiant colors stood a stooped and wrinkled crone. Her brown homespun robe was so simple, her stance so innocuous, her bearing so humble, she should have looked like a beggar in the shrine. Instead she stood out as a queen among servants. She caught Catarin's gaze, her own eyes fathomless and bright. In that look Catarin glimpsed something almost familiar. The woman's lips lifted in an expression not quite a smile, and her gaze darted to the circle of sorcerers. When she looked back at Catarin, she held her gaze for an intense, overwhelming instant then bowed her head and left the shrine.

Taken aback, Catarin turned her attention to the circle, searching for what the old woman had tried to show her. Gavin, the only blood magician in the group, stood opposite her. His head was bowed, his white hair curtaining his face, but his eyes were raised and his gaze focused on her. When he caught her attention, his lips lifted in a smile so slight only she could have seen it.

Her breath caught, her heartbeat lurched, blood pounded in her temples. She turned back to Owen, frantic now. She had to warn him, had to tell him to stop. But before she could open her mouth, before she could take a second breath, she watched as chaos unfurled.

Just before the spell reached its peak, Gavin stepped into the center of the sorcerers, breaking the circle. He faced Owen. "You would be Guardian, Owen. When your power is but a pale shadow of what I can be, what I have become. I believe I'll take what should rightfully have been mine all along." He struck a magical blow that shook the walls of the shrine.

Before her horrified gaze, Owen deflected the blow, then moved to the center of the circle. The fight, had it happened at any other time, would of itself have terrified her, but she'd have been confident of Owen's ability to defend against Gavin. In the midst of the shrine, at the peak of a complicated spell, she was no longer so sure. Strain showed in the thin line of Owen's mouth and in the sweat that dripped across his long cheeks.

"You will take my place now, Owen!"

Gavin's voice came clearly to her despite the noise and turmoil around her. She spared little thought for the fact. At the head of the shrine, the emperor yelled orders. The spectators ran for cover. The sorcerers of the circle tried to close the gap Gavin had left, but she knew the effort was futile.

And then she felt the balance tip.

The spell, unstoppable now that it had gone this far, reached its peak and like an angry storm, exploded. A scream ripped from her dry throat, but she couldn't hear it. She collapsed to the ground under the force of the power unleashed. From behind the curtain of her hair, she saw one of the sorcerers from the circle break free and try to take up Owen's place, to control what was now out of control, to balance the spell. She struggled to her feet, stumbling toward the dais.

"No!" Her scream was lost in the thunder of the magical storm. "You must get back in the circle!" She forced her way toward the dais, had just reached its base when silence filled the shrine. Unnatural silence. She held her breath. Her head moved as if it belonged to someone else, turning toward Owen and Gavin. They both stood, eyes wide. Owen looked up to the man on the dais, then to her. His mouth opened, but he never got the chance to speak. Light and fire and pain exploded out across the room, blinding Catarin and sending glass shards of agony through her body. She thought she screamed again.

Her eyes still dazzled, she pulled herself up to the dais, and without thinking, reached out to take hold of the spell. It cost her dearly. But she pulled the threads taut, captured the chaos before it spread too far. Gasping under the weight of too much magic, she forced the power down into its boundaries. Her control slipped. She scrambled to regain her hold, fighting the power's violence. But she couldn't balance it, couldn't turn it around. It was wrong and rogue and all she could do was keep it contained.

She didn't know how long it took her to contain it. But when she finally looked up, she faced a man-sized ball of golden fire in the center of the shrine. It pulsed with anger and madness and the life forces of one hundred and ninety-seven sorcerers. She searched the bodies that circled it, hunting for one in particular. But Owen and Gavin had both vanished.

She felt a tear streak across her cheek.

And then the voices crashed into her mind.


Catarin came screaming out of her meditation. Two hundred years folded in on itself and it was as if she were reliving that horrible day over again. She panted, pressing a hand to her chest to ease the pain there. In the back of her mind, she felt the orb pulsing as she had felt it for the last two centuries.

Soon now. The prophesied one had to come soon. She was losing what little control she had over the orb. She wouldn't last much longer. Even the deep meditation wasn't working anymore. Instead of balance and strength, it brought her memories and pain too vivid to tolerate, further collapsing her control. She sucked in incense-scented air, allowed her posture to relax into the stiff pillow beneath her and prayed to the twin gods of mercy her son would return soon. And bring with him her release.

*Soon now*, she repeated to herself. *Soon.*

***

It took several minutes for Arlana's eyes to adjust to the surroundings once they'd stepped from the gate. Her stomach rolled and heaved. She focused on breathing steadily in and out to keep down the nausea.

*The discomfort will pass soon, my love. It's a side effect of traveling through a magical gate for the first time.*

She blinked, turning to face her escort. And realized she was standing in the room that had been the backdrop for all her dreams about this man. The white marble walls were lined with gold and the smell of sandalwood permeated the air. The area seemed as vast as it had in her dreams. The only thing missing was the fog. Her knees weakened. "Goddess." Her voice was a whispered echo beneath the vaulted ceiling. It had been real! All of it. From the beginning. "How?"

*I will explain everything soon, Arlana. For now, perhaps you would like a tour of your new domain?*

Arlana shook her head, turning full circle to take in the white room. Candles in mirror-backed sconces of gold lined the walls, but nothing else broke the white and gold marble. Ceiling, floor, walls were all the same. She found the room more disorienting than stepping through the gate. Looking back at the black-eyed man, she breathed, "I don't even know your name. For as long as I can remember, I've known you. Even when I didn't believe you were real, you were still there. And I don't even know your name."

He stepped closer, a slight smile on his full mouth. "Here I'm called Pgar."

She nodded, as if this solved some great mystery and now everything would be all right. "Pgar." His name sounded strange coming from her lips. "And where is here?"

"Here is atop a mountain range in the easternmost reaches of Bthak. This is my domain. Our kingdom."

She took a step back, panic washing through her. Our kingdom? For an instant, she couldn't think beyond the panic. She didn't want a kingdom. She didn't want a domain. She'd never wanted anything like that. But a kingdom shared with someone? Was that better? She wouldn't be alone.

She blinked and sucked in a deep breath. She needed to focus on something else, anything else. She couldn't face the future his words conjured. Not yet. She needed to think. Think about what? Some primitive part of her screamed out with the need to protest.

And then she remembered what had forced her here to begin with. "Oric. Where is he?" She spun around, but there was no one else in the room besides herself and Pgar.

Pgar snarled, a low growl rising from the back of his throat. It made the hairs on the back of her neck stand.

"He is being tended to in another part of the castle." He turned and stalked to the far end of the room. Despite his quiet tone, his voice reached her easily. "Do you realize what you do to me when you show this pet of yours such concern? Do you know how much it hurts me to see the caring in your eyes for a man that can never be to you as I can?"

Without knowing why, she felt the need to apologize. She took one step closer and whispered, "I'm sorry. But I can't stop caring about his wellbeing just like that."

Pgar's shoulders rose and fell, then straightened, and he turned once more to face her. When their gazes met, Arlana stopped breathing.

"It's hard for me to accept," he said. *But for the time being, I will have to.* "We won't talk about him now. Now, I will show you around your new home."

He moved toward her with such unerring grace she couldn't take her gaze off him. She felt very small beneath his stare, and very out of control.

He brushed his fingertips down her neck. She shuddered and closed her eyes.

"Come," he murmured. "There is much to see. I want to show you things beyond your imagination, my love." His fingers moved to her jaw, caressing, coaxing her gaze back to his. "I want to give you your dreams."

He leaned close, brushing her mouth gently with his lips. A shiver raced along her spine—an all too pleasant shiver.

"I've brought you here to give you the world, Arlana. I want you to be my queen. My wife." His breath caressed her cheek. "Together we will do things never done before. No power on Earth will rival ours." His hands dropped to her waist and pulled her close until their bodies pressed hard together.

Her breath came in short gasps. She knew she should push him away. But then she wasn't sure why exactly she should when his embrace felt so good, his caressing hands so tempting. She trembled and fell into the depths of his gaze.

"I will make you a goddess before the world, my love. Power beyond imagining will be ours." His lips dropped close to hers again, and he whispered, "We will rule the world, Arlana. Together."

Then he kissed her, wiping everything but Pgar from her mind.

***

Oric woke suddenly, bolting upward, only to drop back with a skull-splitting headache.

"Careful," a harsh, deep voice scolded from just beyond the sound of his pounding head. "You are not ready to move so much yet."

The words were Karasnian but the accent foreign. And when his brain focused enough for him to wonder about that, he realized it wasn't a Browan accent either.

"Where?" his voice croaked out. He swallowed, trying to wet his throat, but it didn't help.

"Drink this."

He felt the rim of a cool ceramic cup at his bottom lip. A sweet-tasting, cool liquid dribbled into his mouth and then was pulled away before he could satisfy his thirst.

"Too much of this cure would be worse than the original illness." The voice moved farther away. "The headache should be gone within the quarter hour, Lord Commander. Until then, I suggest you stay still and wait for my medicine to work."

"You…" Oric swallowed hard. The liquid had gone some way toward soothing his throat, but he still felt like he'd swallowed a dust cloth. "You know me?"

"Yes."

"Where am I? What happened?"

The silence stretched out so long that for a moment, Oric thought he'd been left alone. He cracked his eyes open. Fortunately for his screaming head, the room was dark, almost too dark to see. He could make out the shadow of a stone wall opposite him, and to his right the flicker of torchlight, but the ceiling over his head was in shadow. He pressed his hands against the mattress beneath him. It was made of rough sackcloth over what was probably the most comfortable straw he'd ever lain upon. A faint scent of fresh straw hung in the air, just beneath the more prominent stench of boiling herbs. He couldn't imagine the draught he'd just been given coming from the same concoction causing the stench. And if it hadn't, he didn't want to know what manner of brew would come from that smell.

When he turned his head, he could make out the dark shadow of a hunched figure just before a small brazier. The brazier cast only enough light to define the stranger's shape, but not enough to reveal any features. The only thing Oric could discern of the man was that he was probably the widest individual he'd ever come across. Easily the size of two men even seated, Oric wasn't sure he wanted to know what this man looked like standing.

As the silence continued, Oric thought maybe the man hadn't understood his Karasnian. He was about to ask again, when the stranger turned and light shone on his features. Oric couldn't stop his gasp. Despite the pain in his head, he lurched back on the bed and reached instinctively for his sword. The weapon wasn't there. He scrambled around the bed, frantically looking for a weapon and coming up with only straw. After a moment, he realized the stranger hadn't moved. Logic slowly seeped back. If the creature intended to kill him, he'd have done it already.

"What are you?" he demanded, his back pressed to the stone behind his small bed. He'd never seen anything like this creature with its green-tinted skin, heavy brow ridges and fangs. Fangs! He'd have guessed the creature a goblin but for those damned teeth.

"I am GeMorin, Lord Commander. And you are lucky you still live. Remember that."

The GeMorin rose. He wasn't as tall as Oric had feared, but he was wide and all the width was heavily muscled. The creature wore a cowled robe, a short leather kilt and nothing else. He was built like the strongest warrior Oric had ever seen. But the GeMorin's strength didn't bother him. Those fangs did.

"Where am I?" he asked again. The pain in his head was easing, but he didn't think he was capable of a fight just yet. So he'd collect information first.

"What is the last thing you remember?"

He thought back, the effort shooting a dart of pain through his brain. He ignored the ache and concentrated on remembering. The last thing he remembered… The last thing he remembered was riding through the Timeless Forest, brooding over Arlana, and then…then the sharpest skull-splitting pain he'd ever experienced. He sucked in a breath at the memory. It'd felt like someone had reached inside his head with a hot poker and torn chunks of his brain apart. He could remember thinking he had to reach Arlana just before he'd lost consciousness. He had a vague memory of rousing to the sound of thuds and screams. Then the song he'd been hearing all his life started, so close and so loud this time his damaged brain couldn't take it. He'd sunk back into blackness. The last was so blurred and faded in his memory, he wasn't sure if that part had been real or a delusion brought on by whatever had knocked him out. What was clear, however, was the sight of Arlana holding her head against the same pain that had lanced him.

"Lady Arlana? What of her?" Oric could feel panic rising to claw at his throat.

"The lady is fine. Fully recovered and with the master. She was able to defend herself better than you Browans."

"Defend against what?"

"The forest dwellers that attacked you. I assume the attack was telepathic? From what I can gather from GeNol and the master, the forest dwellers used their telepathic abilities as a weapon. A very useful weapon too, so it seems."

There was a faint hint of amusement in the otherwise dispassionate tone of the GeMorin.

Oric remembered now the legends of the people living in the Timeless Forest, driven insane when the orb came into being, their descendants raised to madness. It was known they were dangerous, completely mad, but very few survived an encounter with them to tell stories.

"Where am I now?" He knew without a doubt he was no longer in the forest.

"You're in Bthak."

Oric barely had time to choke on his surprise before the GeMorin continued.

"The master ordered you brought here when Lady Arlana refused to come until she'd seen you healed. He couldn't afford to stay in Browan long enough for you to be healed there. So you were brought here." The GeMorin smiled, revealing the deadly length of his fangs. "It left her ladyship with no choice but to follow. Very clever on the master's part."

Oric would have sworn the GeMorin was being sarcastic, but he couldn't begin to judge what a sarcastic GeMorin would sound like. "Who is this master of yours?"

The GeMorin snarled. "He is blood sworn master of my clan. Pgar is the name he uses here, but it is not his real name. He adopted it when he first appeared in Bthak so his country of origin wouldn't be easy to identify."

"You do not like this Pgar?" Oric was guessing, but the GeMorin's clipped tone was hard to misinterpret.

"I serve him. Our clan is blood sworn to him by our leader, GeNol. We can do no less than die for this oath. That is all you need know."

Oric nodded, letting the subject drop despite his curiosity. This creature might be an ally if he were dissatisfied with his master's rule, but only if Oric dealt with him carefully. "Pgar and Arlana are here then?" His heart hammered at the thought of Arlana with this man who claimed a blood oath from creatures such as the GeMorin. Pgar had to be the man she met in her dreams. Knowing the sorcerer's name gave his hatred a sharper focus.

"They are here. You will be brought to them before long. Lady Arlana insists on it. Though if I were you, I wouldn't wish to be so near Pgar. He despises you. I've only seen him lose his temper twice in the past. Both times it was over the mention of you."

Oric very nearly smiled. An inappropriate reaction given his circumstances. But knowing he could cause Pgar to lose control gave him a jolt of primitive satisfaction. "When will I be brought to them?

I must assure myself Lady Arlana is well."

"As I said, her ladyship is in good health. But as I understand you to be some sort of sworn guardian, I would not deny you the chance to see your oath through. You'll be brought to them this evening. Until then, rest Lord Commander. You will need all your strength for this encounter."

That said, the GeMorin turned to leave. Oric called out one last question before he reached the door. "What is your name, GeMorin?"

The creature turned, ducked his head in a quick sharp bow, and said, "I am GeJarn."

He turned and left the room without another word. Oric wasn't surprised to hear a lock falling into place behind him.

# CHAPTER NINETEEN

Oric woke without ever realizing he'd fallen asleep. It took him a few moments to identify what had brought him awake, then he remembered the sharp click of the lock opening on his door. He blinked up into the darkness, fighting fatigue to regain his equilibrium. "Something in that damned potion," he muttered as the door swung open.

He squinted against the sudden flare of light from a torch. With no little relief, he realized his headache was gone. Thank the gods! For a moment, he considered trying to reach Arlana telepathically, but innate wariness stopped him. He knew very little about the skills of this sorcerer, Pgar. He couldn't risk action until he'd gathered more information. Unfortunately, the GeMorin who carried the torch into his room wasn't GeJarn. The emotionless face and prominently displayed saber of the new GeMorin didn't give Oric much hope for gathering more information.

"Stand."

The creature's voice was impossibly deep, even more so than GeJarn's. Oric didn't move.

"I gave you an order, human!" The GeMorin's hand—a very wide, very thick hand—dropped to his saber.

Without breaking eye contact, Oric swung his legs over the side of the bed and slowly got to his feet. The GeMorin's eyes narrowed, but he grunted approval and nodded Oric toward the door. His hand remained on the hilt of his saber.

The dark corridors of black stone he was led through told Oric very little about where he was or even what time of day it was. He innately knew it was evening. He also knew, now that his head was clear, two days had passed since the forest people attacked. He'd lost two whole days in this place! Frustration and a hint of panic rose in his throat. He pushed it down and focused on his surroundings and collecting information.

He presumed he was underground, maybe in the bowels of some castle. The question was, where in Bthak? They passed a number of doors, all similar to the door of his room, all sealed. They walked up a few flights of stairs and down others, all looking much like the last. In fact, with every twist and turn, the surroundings seemed to remain exactly the same. A man of different talents would have been well and truly lost after the first dozen stairwells.

But Oric's innate sense of time came with an unerring sense of numbers and mathematical patterns. He was being led in a diminishing pattern that took him a level higher each circuit. So underground it was then. And by the hue and cut of the stone, he suspected they were in a mountainous region. A damp mossy scent permeated the air, adding to his impression of mountain terrain. Under the mossy scent, however, a coppery and frighteningly familiar stench oozed out of some of the doors. His nostrils flared each time they passed one such door. A warrior couldn't mistake the smell of blood.

The only sound was the ringing of his boots along the stone floors.

Even the GeMorin's steps were silent. But his oversensitive telepathic hearing picked up much more. Too much more. Pain, helplessness, torment and a sickening coat of resignation washed through the mental murmuring invading his mind. It made his stomach roll. Whatever went on behind those closed doors was too horrific to think about. He built up his mental shield even as he stomped down on his encroaching panic. The whine of torment quieted but didn't vanish completely from his subconscious.

Thank the gods none of the minds were familiar.

When the GeMorin guard stopped him in front of a set of wide brass doors unlike anything they'd passed before, Oric held his breath. One very familiar mind sneaked beneath his shield to reach him from behind that door. And as the doors swung open of their own accord, she was the first thing he saw, the only thing he saw for several precious minutes. Relief weakened his knees.

Her eyes, when they met his, were a lighter shade of blue than he'd ever seen, her hair only a shade darker than white. She wore a gown of black velvet edged with white fur around her wrists and the skirt hem. The neckline of the gown plunged low, displaying the deep creamy white valley between her breasts. The gown hugged her figure to just below her hips then flared wide. He'd never seen her in such a dress before. In fact, she'd had on gray leggings and an emerald tunic the day they'd been attacked in the forest. So the gown was a gift from the sorcerer.

Oric felt a growl rising in the back of his throat. Arlana should not be wearing anything given to her by that man. He knew it was a completely illogical reaction. It didn't matter. Possessiveness and protectiveness swamped him, warring with jealousy.

And again, a rising panic.

Because the crystal blue eyes in that beautiful, well-known

face were the eyes of a stranger. Cold enough to make him shiver, impersonal enough to make him want to weep. His only reaction, his best defense, was to wipe all emotion from his expression and pray the turmoil within didn't show.

He shifted his gaze, at last taking in the cavernous room. Black stone, polished to smooth perfection, covered the floor and walls. The vaulted ceilings were made of the same stone, but forms were carved into its surface, breaking its smooth finish. They were covered in shadows and too high up for Oric to see. When he stared, the shadows shifted and the carvings seemed to move. He looked away quickly from the disorienting sight.

To his right and left the seamless walls were lined with globes glowing white—the only source of light in the room. Opposite him, a huge throne sat atop a dais of red marble. The throne was also carved of black stone and polished smooth. Behind the throne, rising almost to the ceiling, was a statue carved of alabaster. White light from inside the stone made it glow subtly against its black backdrop. Oric's gaze traveled the length of the form's ornately carved gown, across a familiar curve of waist and breast, up to the face of a goddess.

"Arlana." He whispered the word as if in a temple. The face of the statue was undoubtedly hers. But the expression was as alien and remote as any of the temple gods at home. He didn't feel himself moving, yet he was drawn to the statue like a penitent to absolution. Before he noticed, he stood beneath the throne, his gaze riveted on the statue's face.

"It's amazing, isn't it?"

For an instant, Oric could have sworn the sultry voice came from the statue. He dragged his gaze away from the white glow to face the woman at his side. His breath caught in his throat. Though she faced him, her eyes were turned toward the statue. And those eyes were now as black as onyx. Her hair had also changed, now as white as the fur lining her gown.

When she turned her gaze to his, it was like staring at the statue come to life. He wasn't looking into the eyes of the woman he'd watched risk her life to save a little boy's, the woman he'd listened to fairy laughter with, the woman who'd stolen his heart. He was looking into the eyes of a power beyond his imagining, and it was all he could do not to drop to his knees before her.

The goddess smiled. "A remarkable likeness, don't you think, Oric?"

"Remarkable, my lady." He took some solace in hearing his voice come out steady. The coldness in Arlana's smile was more frightening than the horrors behind the doors in the corridors below.

"Pgar had it made for me." Her gaze shifted back to the statue. "He thought it fitting. And you?"

"My lady?"

"Do you find it fitting?"

Her black-eyed gaze returned to his face. He had to suppress a shiver. "If it pleases you, my lady, then it is fitting."

She stared for a long moment, her head cocked to one side like an inquisitive bird. Then she asked, "You are recovered, Oric?"

"Yes, my lady."

"GeJarn tells me you haven't eaten for the last few days. You must be hungry." With a negligent hand gesture, she waved to the center of the room.

Oric's gaze followed her hand. In the center of the throne room a giant golden table appeared, laden with every type of food imaginable. Fruits piled high on golden platters next to racks of beef and steaming plates of fish and fowl. Loaves of bread and bowls of stew vied for room with cups of wine and sweetmeats the likes of which he'd never seen. The golden table groaned under the weight of so much food. He stared at the feast she'd so casually created. His stomach gave away his hunger with a loud, insistent growl, but he didn't move.

"Eat," Arlana said, placing a hand on his shoulder.

A frisson of shock raced down his arm, and without thinking, he jerked away from the touch. Appalled that she would think he didn't want her to touch him, he faced her, his hunger forgotten. What he saw knocked the air from his lungs. He would have expected to find hurt in Arlana's eyes. What he saw instead was…nothing. No reaction, no emotion whatsoever. She didn't care if he jerked away from her touch any more than if he accepted it.

He realized then that the woman he'd known was gone. Tears welled in his eyes. He swallowed the lump in his throat and pushed down his pain. It wouldn't do either of them any good. He needed to stay alert, to learn as much as he could if he were to stay alive. He'd consider the bleakness of that life without her later. He swallowed hard again and turned his gaze to the floor.

"Why won't you eat, Oric? I know you're hungry."

"I'm not that hungry, my lady." He felt the power of her gaze on the side of his face but didn't look up. He could no longer face what he saw in those black eyes.

She was silent for so long Oric's nerves twitched. When she finally spoke, he nearly jumped.

"Perhaps you aren't fully recovered yet."

From the corner of his eye, he saw her make a slight hand gesture. A moment later, the GeMorin warrior who'd led him to the throne room entered through the brass doors.

"Bring GeJarn."

Her order was obeyed without question or hesitation.

She moved from his side, wandering slowly toward the table. "Pgar sends his apologies for not meeting with you in person just yet. I'm sure you'll meet him when you've recovered."

"I am quite well now, my lady. I assure you."

"No."

The surety of that statement brought his head up.

"I think it best if GeJarn attends you a few more days."

As if speaking his name called him, the GeMorin healer stepped into the room. "GeJarn."

She greeted the healer in that same neutral tone she'd used with Oric. Crossing the length of the throne room, she spoke in a low voice at the GeMorin's ear. The large creature was only Arlana's height, but he dwarfed her in width. GeJarn nodded when Arlana stepped back.

She smiled slightly, then said, "GeJarn will attend you until you've fully recovered, Oric. I've given orders that only he will attend you. For the time being. I must go now. But please, eat if you can before returning to your room."

She swept out the door without another glance, her gesture as dismissive as a queen's to a stable boy.

GeJarn moved a few steps into the room. His dark gaze fell on the food-laden table. "You must be hungry, Lord Commander. I suggest you eat some of that. She shows you mercy with the offering."

"She shows me misery with that table."

GeJarn looked at him through narrowed eyes. "I don't think you realize how great her mercy." The healer moved close to Oric and lowered his voice to a rumbling whisper. "Pgar has ordered you be fed only the barest of rations, enough to keep you alive but not enough to give you strength. She's broken his order by creating this table. And no one here disobeys the master's orders for fear of risking his wrath." GeJarn shook his head and said, "That's not true. No one here disobeys his orders—period."

Oric met the GeMorin's dark, serious gaze. "Has she endangered her life?"

"I doubt it. He wouldn't dare harm her. He needs her." GeJarn clamped his mouth shut.

Oric would have pushed for more information, but GeJarn turned away and headed toward the doors.

"Take some of that food while you can, Lord Commander. If you expect to…recover, you'll need all the strength you can get."

Despite his utter lack of appetite, Oric piled a plate with meat, bread, cheese and fruit. He knew the GeMorin was right. He needed his strength if he was going to face Pgar. And face him he would. Oric was still First Protector. If GeJarn's hints could be believed, he knew his duty to protect Arlana wasn't nearly over.

***

Another three days passed before Oric saw Arlana again, though he only knew that much time had passed because of his innate knowledge of time. He was kept in his room with only the occasional company of GeJarn to mark the day. Too restless to sleep much, what little sleep he got was often disrupted by the song. It grew in frequency and pitch, but it no longer hurt him the way it had after the forest people's attack. If his calculations were correct, as they'd always been, the song would reach its peak in exactly fifteen days.

The knowledge kept him edgy and impatient, though he couldn't say why. He didn't even know what would happen when it peaked, but that only made him edgier. Being kept in a hole with only a small brazier for light didn't help. Neither did the scent of blood that permeated the lower levels where he was held. The stench worked its way from his nostrils to a bad taste in the back of his mouth. A taste that lingered and disgusted. The mental sounds of torment surrounding him also lingered, worming their way beneath his defenses. He was almost grateful when the sound came because it drove away the anguished mental hum.

The time was good for one thing. After the first day, GeJarn started talking. Oric learned more than he'd hoped when his carefully worded questions got answers. Not nearly as much information as he wanted but enough so he knew what he faced.

He discovered they were indeed in a mountainous region of Bthak, north and east of Browan and a hard four weeks' ride from the border. He and Arlana had apparently been gated to the stronghold by some magical trick of Pgar's. His soldiers had been left behind with a GeMorin guard, honor-bound to see them safely to the edge of the Timeless Forest. With luck, Oric hoped they'd reach Czanri in a day or two. Though what they'd tell the Guardian, he couldn't imagine. Again, and not for the last time, he was tempted to use his telepathy. Not to speak with Arlana—he was almost certain she was Pgar's now—but to reach Ferdinand and the Guardian. He wasn't sure if he could communicate with them from this distance. But it was tempting to try. Only the information he got from GeJarn about Pgar stopped him.

Pgar was also telepathic. In fact, he'd made sure his servants and the GeMorin knew he could read their thoughts at his whim. It didn't seem to matter to most of the GeMorin. They were unerringly loyal to Pgar due to the blood oath sworn by their clan leader, GeNol.

"What about you?" he asked GeJarn three days after seeing Arlana. "Won't he know you're telling me things you shouldn't?"

GeJarn kept his gaze focused on the potion he was mixing over the brazier. He was silent for such a long time that Oric assumed he wouldn't answer.

Then quietly, he said, "He won't know. He can't read my mind."

"How is that possible?"

"I don't know. He assumes it's because I'm a healer and that somehow gives me special immunity. A natural block. He might be right. But I am GeMorin, blood sworn to his service. He has no reason to doubt my loyalty."

"He should, though. Shouldn't he?"

GeJarn didn't looked up. "Drink this potion when it cools. It will help restore your strength."

He rose and left the room without acknowledging Oric's question.

Several hours passed before GeJarn returned. Without preamble, he said, "Your question was an insult to my clan. To me. But as you spoke the truth, I am honor-bound to admit that you are right." GeJarn stared hard into Oric's eyes. "I give you knowledge that could get me killed, human. And it would be no easy death."

What GeJarn told him next showed Oric just how dangerous Pgar really was.

Pgar was a blood magician. He gained his power through the ritualistic letting of blood. And not just any blood. The blood of lucid, cognizant creatures. Their fear and terror and pain were all an essential part of the ceremony. Through their slow loss of life energy, a blood magician gained power, supplementing and strengthening his own.

And Pgar wasn't the only blood mage in the keep. He provided a type of sanctuary for other Bthak sorcerers wishing to pursue or already practicing blood magic. The citizens of Bthak, with unofficial permission from their governor princes, persecuted and often killed any person found studying blood magic. If they could. Blood mages were not known for being easy to kill.

Blood magic wasn't illegal in Bthak the way it was in Karasnia, Depnie and Browan—though it had only been illegal in Browan for the last two hundred years, at the Guardian's behest—but it wasn't condoned, either. The governor princes of each Bthak province were left to deal with blood magic in their own way, either allowing it or executing those who practiced the art. Most turned a blind eye.

Pgar had managed to carve out a small province of his own with the help of the GeMorin. He drew blood mages to him, increasing his power and keeping the other princes from rising up against him. GeJarn assured Oric this small province was just the beginning as far as Pgar was concerned. And Arlana was the key to more. How much more, even GeJarn didn't dare to guess.

"And you don't approve of the blood mages?" Oric asked after GeJarn had finished his story.

"No." GeJarn answered without any of his usual hesitation, his voice hardened and rough. "There is no honor in their way. And no honor in being associated with it."

Oric sat quietly, digesting that statement. GeJarn had told him some things about the GeMorin clan on the previous day. They were intensely honor-bound, willing to kill and die in the name of honor. The blood oath was their most sacred oath. They didn't give it lightly. It bound the entire clan, so their leader couldn't give the oath without permission of the entire clan. Once given, it couldn't be broken during the life of the clan leader except by the party to whom the oath had been sworn. GeJarn had hinted at another way the oath could be broken by the GeMorin, but hadn't gone into detail.

The blood oath to Pgar had been renewed by three different clan leaders. But if the GeMorin didn't consider blood magic an honorable way… "The rest of the clan doesn't agree with you, do they?"

GeJarn shook his head. "They consider it honorable to conquer a foe through might, to destroy a weaker enemy. In fact, it is acceptable to torture and kill those you have conquered if they so deserve. It is the one aspect of our culture with which I do not fully agree. Not where blood mages are concerned."

He stared at one of the stone walls, quiet and thoughtful. Oric opened his mouth to speak, but stopped when GeJarn spoke.

"I am bound by the blood oath, Lord Commander, so I do both myself and my clan a dishonor by even telling you this."

"Why was the blood oath sworn to begin with? What did Pgar do to gain your loyalty?"

"He saved our clan from extinction. It is a difficult debt to repay."

Oric couldn't pry any more information from the GeMorin healer that day. He asked a few more questions, but GeJarn refused to answer. He left Oric with another sweet-tasting potion and a mumbled good night.

The next day, Oric was called to the throne room again.

# CHAPTER TWENTY

Oric followed GeJarn through the brass doors into the throne room. When the doors closed without help, GeJarn stepped aside. This time, a man sat on the black stone throne. A man dressed in white, from his knee-high boots to his pristine velvet tunic, with black hair and the blackest eyes Oric had ever seen. Even seated, the man looked tall, though more slender in build than Oric. He didn't carry any obvious weapon, but death surrounded him like a mantle.

Oric stared at the figure on the throne. Pgar. His enemy. His rival.

They studied each other across the room for a long, silent moment. Oric became intensely aware of the state of his clothing, travel-worn and stained so even the brass rings accenting the vest were dull, of the rough scrub of beard on his unshaven chin, of the dirt and sweat clinging to his unbathed body and of how he compared to the spotless sorcerer. But such matters weren't what concerned warriors. And he recognized the man on the throne as a warrior.

Pgar smiled first. Oric's smile came out more like a snarl. The tension in the air was heavy and tangible, the silence loud. Oric stood at attention, his hands loose at his sides, his muscles relaxed and ready to move. He never took his gaze off Pgar, not even to search the room for Arlana.

Even before entering, he'd built up his mental shield, protecting his thoughts. He knew he'd succeeded when Pgar's eyes narrowed and his smile fell away. He couldn't actually feel Pgar testing his shield. But it was like walking into a supposedly empty room and knowing without a doubt someone was there. He knew the sorcerer had tried to read his mind and was surprised to find he couldn't. His smile widened.

"Lord Commander Oric," Pgar finally greeted with a mockingly gracious nod of his head.

"Pgar." He kept his voice carefully neutral.

Pgar rose from his throne and sauntered toward him. Oric didn't move. "Here, most address me as Prince Pgar. Or Master."

Oric remained silent, neither acknowledging nor refuting the statement, his gaze focused forward but his full attention on the sorcerer. Pgar stopped moving.

"This meeting has been a long time coming, Oric. We've a shared interest. It is time we reached an understanding on this issue."

Oric's gaze flicked to Pgar's, locked with his black eyes. "Yes. It is."

Pgar took a step closer. "Arlana is—"

"Glad to see you two getting to know one another."

The soft, feminine voice snapped both their heads around. Arlana stood just to the right of the throne. Her white hair was piled high on her head and decorated with pearls threaded by golden string. Her gown was white silk that hugged her body to the middle of her hips, then flared to a voluminous skirt. The skirt was overlaid with a train of fine gold mesh embedded with pearls. A thick torque of gold hugged the long white column of her throat. The similarity between her and the statue was breathtaking. Only the gold decorating her gown, neck and hair and the black of her eyes were different. She stood with one hand resting on the throne's armrest, staring at them with the impassive expression of the statue. When she moved, she embodied grace.

For a heartbeat, Oric couldn't think of anything but how beautiful and cold she looked. Then a memory rose, of Arlana standing in an inn room, her body silhouetted within a thin nightshift, her eyes eager, her hands urgent and hot. The memory sparked such a mixture of lust and longing, it nearly brought him to his knees. He'd rather face Pgar's full anger unleashed than the contrast between memory and the present. His heart felt like it was being ripped apart inside his chest.

To keep himself sane, he looked away, focusing on anything but her eyes. And waited.

Pgar finally broke the silence. "My love," he purred, "I didn't realize you'd be joining us for this meeting."

"Didn't you?" She tilted her head to one side. "Perhaps that's because you didn't tell me about it."

"My dear, a slight oversight. I assure you."

She smiled. "Of course." Stepping away from the throne, she swayed toward Pgar. "And what would you be discussing with my servant, Pgar?"

Oric's head snapped up. Pgar took two steps toward her and stopped. Arlana continued forward.

"Servant?" Pgar's tone was carefully neutral.

"The Lord Commander." She blinked and her brow creased. "He's still First Protector. Are you not, Lord Commander?"

"Yes." Squeezing the single word out hurt Oric's throat.

"And isn't it your duty to protect me? With your life, if necessary?"

Her voice was so cool, so assured, so regal he barely recognized it. He still couldn't meet her gaze when he said, "Yes."

"So you're loyal to me?"

"Yes," he ground out between clenched teeth, silently damning his duty for what it forced him to admit to now.

"There. You see, Pgar?" She sounded quite pleased. "He's mine. Loyal only to me. What more could one ask of a slave?"

Oric's temper snapped. That was it! Angry words of denial and accusation were on the tip of his tongue when he felt a very gentle touch on his mental shield. Not an attempt to enter his thoughts, not even a very strong nudge. It was like the caress of a breeze barely strong enough to move a feather. But it was a familiar touch.

He forced himself to look up, into her eyes. The passive, carved expression never changed, but something in her eyes, hidden inside the black depths and revealed only to him, shifted and moved. And something very like pleading was revealed for a brief instant. The flash of emotion vanished quickly.

Only a supreme act of will prevented a silly grin from lighting his face. He had to glance away before he started to laugh with relief. He acknowledged the message with the barest of nods before turning his gaze to the ground. He'd follow her lead and do as she wished because beneath the mask of a goddess, she was still Arlana, still the woman he loved.

She returned her attention to Pgar. Oric could feel the sorcerer's stare, but he kept his gaze averted until he was sure he could control his expression.

"He's your slave now, my sweet?" Pgar's voice was soft with suspicion.

"Didn't you hear him? Of course he's my slave. A very fitting slave for a goddess, isn't he?"

"Is he?"

Pgar stepped closer. Oric didn't move. He kept his gaze focused forward even when Pgar began pacing around him.

"Are you, Lord Commander? Are you the lady's slave?"

After only a brief hesitation, he faced Arlana and dropped to his knees. He made a show of forcing the words out. "I am your faithful servant, my lady. For my life or as long as you will have me."

Pgar's eyes widened. "You've enchanted him!" He threw the words at Arlana.

She laughed. "Don't be silly. You can see for yourself there aren't coercion spells on him. He's bound by duty. Duty makes him my slave."

From the corner of his eye, Oric watched Pgar loosen his stance and school his features back to the charming expression he'd worn when she first caught their attention.

"But of course he would be loyal to you, my goddess," Pgar said. "Who would not?" He sauntered toward her. "Your radiance pales the very sun." He stopped before her and ran a caressing finger across her jaw.

Oric thought his own jaw would break from the pressure of controlling his reaction to the sorcerer's hand on her. He rose slowly to his feet, carefully keeping his hands open and at his sides. They fisted once, almost beyond his control, then loosened. He couldn't afford to force a fight with Pgar in a fit of jealous rage and ruin whatever plan Arlana had.

His fury wasn't helped by the soft smile she gave the sorcerer or the way she rubbed her cheek against his palm. Doubt crept in past his relief, sneaking in with the jealousy. Had he imagined the soft mental touch, the flash of pleading in her eyes? Was he fooling himself into believing the real Arlana still lived beneath that statue's mask?

When Pgar leaned forward and brushed a kiss against her mouth, Oric had to bite the inside of his cheek to keep from howling in rage. His hands clenched, nails biting into flesh, and he couldn't relax them until the kiss ended. Arlana was first to break contact and move away. Pgar watched her walk toward the throne, his gaze drinking in her curves, lingering on her bottom. As if sensing his gaze, Arlana's hips swayed more, causing the gold mesh train to tinkle.

Oric swallowed and tasted blood. He wasn't sure how much more of this he could take before either attacking Pgar or going insane. In all likelihood, both of those things would happen at once.

Arlana reached a spot just below the throne and turned. Pgar followed her path, taking slow, measured steps.

"Doesn't it seem a strange thing though," the sorcerer said, "for an all-powerful sorceress to possess a bodyguard? He can hardly do more to protect you then you can do for yourself. What use will he be?"

She pursed her lips, appeared to consider this question seriously. "I think it's appropriate that a queen has a bodyguard. Even if only for show. He's big and strong. I'm sure just looking at him would divert most anyone interested in attacking me. Then I could conserve my energy for more important matters."

"But my dear, that's what the GeMorin are for. They would do more to protect you than one human could. I think you should give up this slave. I'm sure I can find a better use for him."

"No."

She said it so simply and so absolutely that Pgar stopped moving toward her. "No?"

"No. I want to keep him. He's mine."

"But he serves no function, pet."

Arlana's gaze flicked to Oric, then back to Pgar. She blinked once in a slow and seductive way before turning to stare up at her statue. "Pgar, for days now…well, perhaps for most of my life, you've been telling me I'm to be a goddess. My power sets me above all else. And together we'll rule the world. I have one question." She looked over her shoulder. "If I'm so powerful," she turned around, locked his gaze to hers, and sat on his throne, "then why would I need you either… *pet*?"

And suddenly, Arlana's gown was no longer white, but the deepest ebony. The stones encrusted in her hair and on the gown's train were onyx, all the gold now turned to platinum. Her hair remained white, her eyes black. Except for her eyes and skin color, she was now the complete opposite to Pgar, her black to his white, her white to his black.

The change, the position on the throne and the statement had an impact—on both men. Pgar's eyes flared, his hands clenched and any color he'd had drained from his face. Oric simply stared, too stunned by her boldness to do more. The very air in the room felt charged, like the atmosphere before a thunderstorm. The hair on Oric's arms rose.

He sensed that Arlana was engaged in a silent struggle with Pgar. They were dueling on a level he couldn't see. Arlana never lost the passive expression, never appeared ruffled in the least. She simply stared at the sorcerer. And though he couldn't exactly understand or see the struggle, Oric was positive he felt it end.

Pgar's color came back, his fists slowly relaxed and his calm smile struggled back into place. "My love. You are a goddess. Powerful beyond all others. Powerful enough to rule the world. But you are still very young. You lack the wisdom I've gained during the nearly three hundred years of my life. A goddess can hardly rule without wisdom. I would be your teacher, your mentor. I'd guide you and help to make you untouchable by others. Men will fall to their knees before you."

As he said this last, he turned to Oric and with a smile only Oric could see, he flicked his wrist and brought Oric to his knees.

The jarring, unexpected drop knocked the air from his lungs. He tried to struggle to his feet again and failed, held to the ground by

Pgar's unseen hand. He snarled up at the sorcerer but stayed helplessly on his knees.

Pgar's smile widened. "You see, Arlana. All men will bow before you." He turned back to her. "Because of me. Because of what I can give you that no other can."

Her gaze moved over Oric and then back to Pgar, assessing but unaffected. She made a negligent hand gesture in Oric's direction and the pressure holding him to his knees lifted. He almost fell forward with the release that came as suddenly as the hold. He rose to his feet slowly, careful to keep his thoughts out of his expression. He didn't like being the focus of their power struggle, but now was hardly the time to mention it.

"Don't play with my slave, dear," she chided. "It's rude."

"So you're determined to keep him?"

Pgar sounded almost resigned. Almost.

"Yes."

"And if I object?"

"What is there to object to? I want him—"

"That is exactly what I object to!" he roared.

Arlana flinched, the first sign Oric had seen of any obvious human emotion in her. And though it quieted some of his worries, as a tactician he knew it had been a dangerous reaction. A change in Pgar's manner proved he'd seen the flinch as well.

"I think I will have to insist on this point, love." Pgar's voice smoothed over the echo of his roar. "If I'm to give you the ultimate prize, if I'm to teach you and counsel you to becoming the greatest power the world has ever known, if I'm to be your husband and share eternity with you, then I must demand you turn your slave over to me." He stalked toward her and his voice dropped to a quiet purr. "Arlana, he has hurt you as I never would. He's brought you nothing but pain. You'll thank me for ridding your life of this man."

Arlana remained silent, her features a stubborn mask.

Pgar smiled. "My love, so like a petulant child. I do adore you. But you still have so much to learn, so much you don't understand. Trust me in this. I've promised you everything. The least you can give me is a little trust." He closed the space between them, cupped her jaw and brushed a kiss over her lips.

Oric barely had a chance to flex his fists when pain seared through him, knocking him to his knees. It felt like a thousand daggers plunged into him at once. A scream tore from his throat. From his peripheral vision, he saw GeJarn kneel down beside him. In the next instant, GeJarn flew through the air to slam into a wall. He fell unmoving to the floor.

And then the pain struck again, racking Oric's body until even screaming was impossible. He curled into himself, hoping either unconsciousness or death would come soon.

He hoped in vain.

# CHAPTER TWENTY-ONE

The second she saw Oric fall, Arlana leapt from the throne. She didn't get more than two steps before coming up against the steel of Pgar's arm around her waist.

"Don't," he hissed into her ear.

Her heart skipped as she watched him absently fling GeJarn from Oric's side with a flick of his hand. A small gasp was the only sound she could force through her dry throat.

"I understand you still feel compassion for these lesser creatures. It will go away eventually. For your sake, I'll kill him quickly, though it will be a terrible waste of energy. But Arlana, I've worked to have you with me since before you were born. I have gone through more for you than any man should. I will not have you betray me now. Not with him. Not with anyone."

"Since before I was born?" She struggled out of his hold. "What do you mean?"

"I mean I have been planning for your coming for a long time. When the signs indicated you'd be born in Karasnia, I sent a prince dreams that would have made him mine when he came to the throne.

A waste of energy in the end. Your king's son was a fool. So I sent the GeMorin to watch over you after you were born. And I tried to bring you to me. It would have been easier to begin your training while you were still a child. But I was thwarted again. Since then, I've come to you personally, been yours, learned your desires, given you my devotion. And now it's finally time. We will be together always. We will rule the world."

"I don't believe…" Her protest was cut off by a low moan from across the room, reminding her Oric was still alive, but only barely. She extended her power, traced the spell Pgar had cast and saw the blood and horror that had gone into creating the power in it. The spell was complex, torturing as it killed, and Arlana was so desperate to break it she couldn't think clearly.

Pgar smiled almost gently as he said, "I underestimated you once, my love. I swore I wouldn't do it again."

"What are you saying?" Another moan drew her attention. "Please. Please stop hurting him." Her heart hammered with fear so intense it threatened to overwhelm her thinking. She dropped to her knees at Pgar's feet, putting the panic and terror simmering in her into her eyes when she looked up. Beneath it, she forced her anxious mind to study the spell. Concentrate. Tease out its elements. Focus. Hunt for its key. "Please," she begged again.

Pgar rested a finger on her temple and stroked small circles. He didn't smile. "I find I like this part of you, Arlana. Pleading with me on your knees. It pleases me."

"Will you stop hurting him? I'll do as you like. Anything. Just please don't hurt him anymore." She knew what his intentions were, as she'd known since shortly after arriving. He'd kill Oric no matter what she said or did. He wanted her crushed. He wanted her at his mercy. She'd overplayed her hand when she'd asked what use he was to her. Now he would prove his power. She read his intentions as if they were her own. Fortunately, he could no longer read her intentions so clearly.

Concentrate. Find the key. Focus. Find the flaw.

He sighed, a resigned sound. "Arlana. He stands between you and me and eternity. I know this will hurt you, but trust me when I say it's for the best. How can a goddess rule when her emotions cloud her judgment?"

"What of mercy and compassion, my lord? Shouldn't a goddess possess these traits?" Breathe. Focus. Tease out the paths.

He cupped her cheek and lifted her head higher until their gazes locked. "There are other traits more important. Today you shall learn of these. With time, you shall acquire them."

"What are they? What will his death teach me?" Almost there. Arlana felt her way along the tender threads of the spell, knowing she was close, very close to the key—the flaw. Anxiety clutched her stomach. Panic almost swamped her again. She slowed down, focusing her thoughts. This wasn't something she could rush, but Goddess, she wanted to hurry. A low sound from Oric—not even loud enough to be a moan—reached her, pushed her to work faster. She took a breath and held it. Focus. Concentrate. Almost there.

"His death will teach you pain. More pain than you could ever have known before. And that pain will give you strength, harden your soul to creatures less than you. You'll learn that pain can give enormous power. And the strength you gain through your pain will give you the will you need to be invincible. You'll grow to appreciate pain, my love. It will become a very close friend." Pgar spoke in a near monotone, his gaze turned inward to his own thoughts. He blinked, focused on the room again, and his gaze went to Oric. He raised a hand.

Arlana felt the power building and knew he was poised to strike the killing blow. The currents of magic made the fine hairs on the back of her neck stand. Pinpricks of awareness danced painfully along her skin. Concentrate, focus, almost there, nearly got it, breathe, focus, center, concentrate.

"I do this for you, Arlana," he murmured as he gathered power to his spell. "Everything I've done for years has been for you."

Her head snapped around to Oric. Their gazes locked. Pain and regret filled his blue eyes, and something else that caught her breath. She felt Pgar's spell peak, felt him cast it outward.

The sound of his magical strike rebounding off her shield screamed through the room, echoing along the walls and high ceiling. Light and pressure filled the room, sucking away air until she thought her ears might burst. Then the light winked out and a rush of air swept through the chamber. The explosion that followed shook the room and rumbled through her bones. Fine dust trickled over them, bringing with it the scent of scorched earth and the coppery tang of spilled blood.

In the shocked silence that followed, Arlana shattered the pain spell binding Oric.

She took a deep, slow breath. Her heartbeat raced and the rapid rush of her pulse sounded in her ears. She closed her eyes for a moment, took another deep breath, and got to her feet. When her knees held her weight, she sighed. Surprisingly, her hands were steady and her heartbeat was easing to its natural rhythm. She squared her shoulders. "Pgar, you said you underestimated me once before. Was it when you tried to kidnap me when I was a baby?"

"Impossible. Impossible!" he roared.

She shook her head and crossed the room to Oric. She didn't have to see his eyes widen or the warning "O" of his lips to know Pgar's attack was coming. His angry blast of power dissipated harmlessly around her personal shield. She didn't even hesitate as she closed the space between herself and Oric.

"From the beginning of my training, when I was very young, I was taught how to defend myself. Particularly, how to defend myself against magic." When she reached Oric's side, she offered him a hand. With effort, she helped him to his feet and steadied him with a hand on his chest, letting him lean on her.

Finally, she turned to face Pgar. The sorcerer's eyes blazed black heat. She could almost feel the air sizzle. He built his power for another strike but held back, studying her, looking for an opening in her defenses. She could sense him trying to get around her to Oric. He didn't want her dead, even now. He wanted her to suffer for her rebellion. And he wanted Oric eliminated—in the most painful way possible.

"The second thing I learned," she continued in a quiet voice, "was how to protect others. You're responsible for the first lessons I received, even if you weren't the one to teach me. Because of my kidnapping, the first few years of my training were devoted almost exclusively to defense and protection spells. So you see, you did shape me. I'm what I am today largely because of you. Ironic, isn't it? Should I thank you, do you think?"

Pgar took one lurching step forward. "You will not defy me now! I've worked too long. I've given you everything you could wish, offered you the world. You belong to me!"

She shook her head and lifted a hand to deflect his next magical attack. His control teetered along the slippery ledge of his rage. "I belong to destiny, Pgar," she murmured. Then louder, "I am destiny. No one can own destiny. And no one can control it."

"You think to leave? You think you'll simply take your pet and go? How? You barely know where you are. And you won't get past my GeMorin without my orders." He stalked toward her as he spoke, closing the distance with measured steps. He froze when he came up against an invisible barrier. When he stretched out his hands to touch it, it burst into flames.

She ignored his snarl. Oric stiffened beside her, and she glanced over her shoulder to see GeJarn taking the bulk of Oric's weight. When she met the healer's dark gaze, he stared for a long, silent moment. Then he bowed his head. She returned his nod with a slight smile and faced Pgar again.

He was studying her barrier, but everywhere he touched, flames leapt out. As she spoke, his gaze burrowed into her. "I'll leave the way we arrived," she told him. "Oric, GeJarn and I will gate away from here to a place I know you won't follow. A place you can't follow."

"Impossible."

"I studied the gate you used to bring us here. The gate you've used to come to me before. You've made me a gate focus and yourself the harmonizing focus. A good idea. Almost impossible to disrupt such a gate. And without another harmonizing focus, I couldn't possibly gate away without you disrupting the spell. But I do have another harmonizing focus, Pgar. One that has been with me since I was born."

His eyes widened. "No."

"Yes. And you can't disrupt the gate without bringing it down upon you. And you can't follow or it will pull you in." She closed her eyes and began reciting the spell, sending her power out to the orb. It pulsed in recognition. She heard Pgar's howl of denial, the sound of fire roaring to life, but she ignored it all as she constructed the gate.

A small square of the wall to her left began to glow, at first black, then lightening to purple. Slowly, the square elongated, taking on the shape of a door. As it grew, the color continued to lighten and the glowing within pulsed. A deep rumble started at the edge of her hearing, a sound felt as well as heard. The room trembled. When the door reached a length tall enough for Oric and wide enough for GeJarn, it stopped growing. It was now the color of lavender with shards of blue and pink scattered over the surface like an opal. Then the glow brightened, the color shifted. With a blinding flash, the gate changed to a deep golden glow. The rumbling stopped. Through the gate, just past its golden light, Arlana could see a bright, deep green room.

She turned back to Pgar. His skin had paled to near the color of his tunic. He no longer tried to move beyond her fire barrier. He stared in horror at the gate and the room just beyond it. "You can't do this, Arlana. We are meant to be together. I love you. After all I've done for you—"

"You've done what you've done for yourself, Pgar. For power. For glory. But never for me. You don't know anything about love. I won't be your pawn anymore." She faced Oric and GeJarn, turning her back to Pgar. "GeJarn," she murmured, "are you sure about this?"

"I have nowhere else to go now, my lady. I would continue to serve you so I do not deface the blood oath of my clan entirely."

Arlana nodded her understanding, then gestured the GeMorin and Oric toward the gate. They stood before it, staring into it for several moments. Then GeJarn stepped away from Oric, sucked in a deep breath and passed into the gate. Oric, hand braced against the wall beside the gate to keep his balance, looked back.

He held out his free hand. "I'm not going without you."

Arlana's heart thumped and her stomach danced at the look in his eyes. That same something was still there, only now it wasn't clouded by agony. She walked to the gate and took his hand.

"Arlana!"

Her head snapped around at Pgar's bellow. The look in his eyes sent a shiver up her spine.

"This is not done between us," he growled, but he moved backward, away from her barrier, away from the gate. "We are not done yet."

"Pgar, you say you offered me everything. The world. The existence of a goddess. Unimaginable power. You say you learned my desires, but you never understood them even after all these years. You underestimated me again, Pgar. Or maybe this time it was an overestimation. Because the one thing you offered me was the one thing I didn't want and have never wanted—power. That was your biggest mistake."

She turned her back on the sorcerer for the last time, squeezed Oric's hand and, together, they stepped into the golden light.

# Chapter Twenty-Two

Arlana stumbled through the gate with Oric leaning heavily on her. The first thing she saw when they emerged was a contingent of twelve guards surrounding GeJarn, their swords pointed at the GeMorin's chest. He stood perfectly still, hands open and in plain view, waiting patiently.

"Don't hurt him," Arlana called. "He's with us."

"And who is 'us'?"

The deep, feminine voice came from somewhere behind Arlana.

"Guardian, it's me," Oric said, straightening. "And Lady Sorceress Arlana Von Fordin." He stood without help, wobbling only slightly, and gave the soldiers an order in Browan. All twelve swords returned to their scabbards, but the soldiers remained in a half circle around the GeMorin.

As Oric gave his orders, Arlana closed the gate. When its white-gold glow vanished, the entire chamber came into full view. Just beyond where the gate had been sat a small white stone pillar topped by a stand of gold rope woven in an intricate design. On the stand, roughly the same size as a small dog, sat an irregularly shaped globe pulsing golden light.

The orb.

Just to the right of the orb stood a woman who could only be the Guardian. She was small and delicate-looking with white hair that hung nearly to her ankles and eyes a pale, clear blue. She wore a very simple full-length white robe cinched at the waist by a thick gold and green girdle. For all that she was tiny, the woman radiated command and strength. Her hands were clasped loosely in front of her. She wore no jewelry or ornaments of any kind. She looked remarkably plain for a Browan. And yet there was a beauty about her, a calm elegance too refined for jewelry. There was also a sorrow in her eyes that hurt to look at.

Arlana and the woman stared at each other silently for a long time. Then the Guardian smiled and bowed her head.

"I am the Guardian of the Orb, high priestess of the temple of Ramisha, the goddess of prophecy, Lady of Tzenro, Chatelaine of the Six Rings and Senator of Czanri. But you may call me Catarin."

Arlana smiled and bowed her head in turn. "I am honored, Lady Catarin."

"No, it is I who am honored by your presence, child of the prophecy. I have been waiting more than two hundred years to meet you."

Catarin's Karasnian was heavily accented—evidence she'd learned it without the help of a spell. For some reason, that made Arlana take a closer look. Her hands were clasped more tightly than Arlana had first thought, a light sheen of sweat covered her forehead and a shudder, almost but not quite controlled, shook her small shoulders.

Arlana gasped. "Goddess! The gating… Guardian, it didn't cause the orb to…to react, did it?"

Catarin smiled. "No more than it usually does where you are concerned." She waved away Arlana's concern. *This struggle has been going on between myself and the orb for a long time, child of the prophecy. We will discuss it later. After you have settled in. There is much to discuss. And much to do.*

Arlana nodded, but reluctantly. Catarin didn't look well, now that Arlana's attention was called to the signs. She hadn't even stopped to think what sort of reaction the orb would have to the gating. She should have thought, should have at least considered the possibilities.

The sound of Oric's strained voice washed away her worries about Catarin.

"Guardian, if you will excuse me, I am afraid our journey has…" His voice faded away.

Arlana turned in time to catch him as he stumbled forward. His size almost brought them both to the ground. GeJarn disentangled himself from the soldiers, moving with studied calm so as not to alarm them, and took Oric's weight.

"Forgive me, Guardian." Oric's voice was harsh and roughened. "The past few hours have taken their toll."

He was silent a moment but still looking at Catarin, so Arlana presumed they were speaking mentally. She waited, studying the Guardian. The woman was still pale and the sweat still beaded on her forehead, but her hands weren't clenched so tightly anymore.

"Lady Arlana," Catarin said aloud, "my guards will show you to a suite of rooms readied for you. When you have rested, send word and we will meet."

"But, Oric?"

Catarin's eyes narrowed. "He will be seen to by the healer. A room is also being arranged for your GeMorin friend."

"Thank you for your kindness, Guardian. I'll rest after I've seen to Oric's injuries." When Catarin's brow creased, Arlana said, "I'm a magic healer. And I broke the spell that caused his injuries. I'm best qualified to heal him."

"Very well." The Guardian's brow smoothed, but the corners of her blue eyes creased. "At your pleasure, Lady Sorceress." She bowed her head and motioned to the guards.

They were led from the orb chamber into a series of tall corridors topped with long, narrow skylights. The walls were various colors and textures of stone and metal, the carpets jeweled shades in complicated patterns, the wall sconces made of intricately folded and twisted ropes of gold and the candles marbled in a wide range of colors. It was dazzling. But it was nothing to the clothes of the courtiers and servants moving through the corridors. Arlana had thought the soldiers and inn owners dressed with eclectic enthusiasm until she saw the people of Czanri.

From what little she could gather from the one guard who spoke Karasnian, the corridors they were being led through connected several of the main buildings of central Czanri, including the senate, the Orb Temple, the shrines of two primary gods of Czanri and the former palace of the emperor—now used as the residence of the Guardian and her family as well as accommodations for visiting dignitaries from other parts of Browan.

They were taken to the door of Oric's rooms. In Browan, one guard told Oric they'd send for the healer and Ferdinand. After Oric translated, she asked him to tell the guards not to bother with the healer. She pushed through the door, holding it open as GeJarn half walked, half carried Oric inside. They'd just made it into Oric's sleeping chambers and within a few feet of his bed when he passed out. GeJarn carried him the rest of the way. Despite his considerable bulk and slight height advantage, the GeMorin carried Oric with no more trouble than he would a child.

Once Oric was laid out on the simple mattress covered by purple and maroon silk blankets, Arlana forgot about everything but healing him. Pgar's spell had done a lot more damage than Oric had let on. The healing would take time. Arlana brushed a hand across his sweat-dampened brow. "Rest, my love," she murmured close to his ear so neither the remaining guards nor GeJarn would hear. "I'll fix everything. You'll be restored to full strength soon." She kissed his cheek, closed her eyes and began the healing.

***

Arlana was called to the Guardian two days later. Oric still slept, still healed. GeJarn had taken it upon himself to sit vigil at Oric's bedside. "As a warrior of honor deserves." The GeMorin had remained mostly silent since they reached Czanri. He refused to talk about what had happened at Pgar's castle. She could only imagine what it must be like, cut off from his clan, his beliefs, dishonored in his own eyes and trapped in this place with no real way back. She, at least, knew she could go home again—someday.

Pushing aside her concern for the healer who had done so much to help her during their time in Pgar's realm, Arlana prepared to face the Guardian and her undoubtedly endless list of questions. She had a few questions of her own.

A guard escorted her to the orb temple and left her alone in the room with the orb. She wondered at that, but only briefly as she began to study it.

The lines of damage to the magics of Browan did indeed radiate from the orb. It was larger than she'd expected and more irregularly shaped. What, she knew instinctively, should have been a perfectly spherical object was warped, like unrestricted candle wax, distorted to only a vaguely spherical shape. And the distortion kept shifting, the shape changing and rearranging itself like clay beneath a child's hands. She moved closer, looking deeper into the product of a very complex spell, hunting for the source of the distortion. The closer she moved to the sphere, the more she opened to it. The more she opened to it, the more it moved, taking on a regular shape.

She was just preparing to delve a level deeper when a small gasp caught her attention.

"How have you done that?"

Arlana faced the Guardian. "Done what?"

"It is more stable than it has ever been before. How are you doing it? I cannot even sense your spell."

"I'm not doing anything, Guardian. I've opened to it to study it, but that's all."

Catarin's eyes narrowed. "Then…?" She shook her head. "Perhaps if we begin at the beginning, it will become apparent. Would you like something to drink or eat before we begin?"

Arlana declined absently, her attention drawn again to the orb. She closed herself off from it—as much as was possible—and the distortion returned. "That's the struggle between you and the orb, isn't it?" Arlana asked quietly. "You don't have complete control over it."

"No. I never have."

Arlana faced the tiny woman again.

"I was never intended to be the Guardian." She walked toward Arlana and the orb. "I was never even meant to be part of the spell. I wasn't strong enough." She whispered the last comment.

"You were there? When it was formed?"

Catarin nodded. "It was to be a great accomplishment—the greatest feat ever achieved by any magicians ever. It was to bring glory to the empire and be an invincible weapon in the wars. The emperor was near to bursting with excitement over his impending conquests. Then it all went wrong."

"What was it intended to do? What sort of weapon would it have been?"

Catarin's sad gaze focused on Arlana. "It was meant to control time."

Two hours later, Arlana was still astounded by the sheer arrogance it had taken to attempt what the Browan sorcerers had attempted over two centuries earlier. She wouldn't have tried it, and she, of all people, might have been capable of success. But she would never have considered controlling time on such a grand scale. Even if she could have found one hundred and ninety-nine other sorcerers willing to give up their physical existence to the spell.

"Didn't you stop to consider the consequences?" she asked Catarin, not for the first time during the telling of the story. One hundred and ninety-nine men and women of great power all concentrating on a single spell, led by one sorcerer who would ultimately control the creation and, with it, time. But the implications of controlling time… It was more baffling even than her conversations with Ryn'ah about time, and the dragon had done a thorough job of baffling her.

"The consequences of the spell itself, or the consequences of the spell going wrong?" Catarin's voice had taken on a monotone as she told her story. It was only now beginning to reanimate.

"Both!" Arlana paced across the room, away from the orb, then paced back. "You admit there was a sorcerer involved that you didn't trust—"

"Gavin."

"And yet, you still went along with it."

"It was not my choice. I had no say in the matter. I was not to be part of the spell. I wasn't strong enough."

"But surely you could have talked to your mentor—Owen. Surely you could have convinced him to see reason."

"Owen was a great man. A powerful sorcerer. There was no other I would have trusted with the power he would have once the spell was complete. He would have made a splendid Guardian."

Catarin's defense of her mentor nudged Arlana to look closer at the woman. She caught the look in her eyes before Catarin could disguise it. "You were lovers, you and Owen."

"We would have been life-mated."

"I'm sorry." Until recently, Arlana could only imagine what it might feel like to lose a lover to death. Now the emotion felt too near, too immediate. It had almost happened. Her mind skittered away from the thought. Instead, she focused on the reason for this conversation, the reason she'd been born—the orb and the failure of the spell to finish it. "Didn't Owen suspect Gavin would try to usurp his position? If you didn't trust him, why did Owen?"

"Gavin was tied into his position in the spell weeks before the ceremony in the temple. The ceremony was merely the final part and was more for the emperor's sake than the sake of the casting. Gavin should not have been able to break from his particular part in the spell by the final ceremony. I think that's why Owen did not worry much about him."

"You were worried, though. What did you think he'd do?"

"Until a specific moment during the final ceremony, it was still possible for a sorcerer to pull out, to refuse to complete the spell, or for the Guardian to stop it. I was afraid Gavin would pull out of the spell, causing it to fail. The failure would have damaged Owen's reputation in the emperor's eyes. Gavin was next only to Owen in the emperor's favor. If Owen had been disgraced, Gavin would almost surely have been named the Guardian when the spell was attempted a second time."

"Then why didn't he just do that? Why in the name of the Goddess would he risk the disaster that happened by trying to usurp Owen during the spell?" Arlana threw her hands in the air.

Catarin glanced down at her hands where they were clasped on her lap. She sat in a high-backed chair near the orb while Arlana, too frustrated to sit for more than a second, paced around the room.

The Guardian didn't look up when she said, "None of the others would have gone through with the spell if Gavin was named Guardian. No one else wanted him to have so much power and control either. I suspect that was the reason Owen was named to begin with. The emperor was greedy, but he was not an imbecile."

"Yet you were still afraid that if Owen was disgraced, Gavin would have an opportunity to cast this spell in the role of Guardian?"

"Yes. Gavin could be very…persuasive when he chose. I didn't trust the resolve of the others to stand against him if Owen was ousted. I never guessed he would try to disrupt the spell as he did."

"Obviously." Arlana faced the orb, unconsciously opening herself to it so its shape became more regular again. Her mind centered on the story she'd been told. A greedy emperor bent on destroying his enemies utterly. A group of powerful mages willing to sacrifice their physical forms to gain the power inherent in controlling time. A blood sorcerer so hungry for power, he ruined the spell. "The man who foretold my birth as the answer to the orb problem…who was he in all of this?"

"Derek? He was one of the one hundred and ninety-nine. He should not have left the circle to take control. It is one of the things that threw the balance of the spell so far off. But without a Guardian, the orb would have been uncontrollable upon creation. He was trying to prevent a greater catastrophe than what actually happened. I can't blame him for the result. I blame Gavin and his greed."

"Why did Owen leave his place?"

"I don't know. I didn't have time to ask." Her voice dropped low. She took a deep breath and said, "I suppose he thought it the only way to meet Gavin's challenge. It all happened so fast. I still dream about it. Sometimes during meditation, I experience the day, the sights and sounds so vivid and real it's like I am there all over again. And yet after all these years, it still isn't entirely clear."

"The telepathy among Browans was directly related to the orb's creation. Would this have happened if the spell had succeeded?"

"It was not supposed to, no. I'm not even sure why it caused the reaction. I do know the time paradoxes throughout our country are due to the failure of the orb spell. And the mind-speak opened up just after I took control of the orb."

"That must have been difficult for you."

"It should have been impossible. I was not prepared. I was not strong enough. I have only barely held the orb in check for these centuries. It is…draining."

"Why did the damage stop at the border? Why didn't some of the scarring lash out into Karasnia? Or Bthak, for that matter?"

"I attempted to pull it under control before it spread far. I can only assume I succeeded in time to keep it within our borders. I'm not sure how that was possible."

Catarin shook her head and looked up, her gaze showing a frustration Arlana could well appreciate.

"There is much I do not understand about the results of the failure, Lady Sorceress. And after…there was no one left for me to ask. With Owen and Gavin killed and Derek following them so closely, with all the other most powerful sorcerers having become part of the orb itself, the only hope I've ever had was Derek's last coherent words about you." Her gaze flicked to the orb. "And I can see now my hope was not misplaced. Your presence agrees with it, I think."

Her comment and the slight smile touching her lips made Arlana focus on the orb. It was only slightly irregular now. Nothing like the melted wax shape it resembled before. And it seemed more compact than it had before she opened to it. "Tell me about its reaction when I was born." She whispered the request, afraid to hear this part of the story.

Catarin was quiet for a while. Then in a murmur, she started. "We…I should have expected it. Prepared for it. The signs were there. We knew you were to be born and soon." She took a deep breath. "About forty-five years ago, I had a vision. Prophecy, in a small way, is part of my skill. In this vision, I foresaw your coming. And I foresaw the need for me to have children. Two. I was even granted the image of the men their fathers should be. One was a scholar at the university, the other a traveling bard—both were men who did not mind being released from the responsibilities of fatherhood. Ramisha was less… obscure than normal in this vision. The images were easy to interpret. At least, I thought they were easy to read. I gave birth to a daughter first. Her name was Hilda."

"Oric's older sister."

"Yes. She was a gifted sorceress, her talent obvious from birth. She was to be stronger than me eventually. She would have been the strongest sorceress born in Browan since the creation of the orb. She was my pupil. With her strength, I was able to control the orb better than ever before. She would have been my successor had I been unable to survive until your arrival."

"Why wouldn't you have survived?"

Catarin met Arlana's gaze. "There are many things that could happen, Lady Arlana. Some the result of politics. Some simply biological. Holding the orb under control has taken its toll on me.

Giving birth to two children while maintaining control of the orb was tricky. I did not trust my body to hold out for many years longer. But none of that matters now that you are here. In time, we will be able to transfer control of the orb to you, and I…I will be able to rest for the fist time in two centuries."

She looked down at her hands. "I gave birth to Oric about fourteen years after Hilda. I…I did not have much energy left to raise him. Tutors, nurses and Hilda raised him. He showed an aptitude for mathematics at a very young age. And music. He loved music." She trailed off, falling silent.

"Catarin?"

The Guardian shook herself and blinked. "From a very young age, Oric also heard a…a sound. He calls it a song most of the time. Or the noise. He was only five when he discovered there was a pattern to it." She smiled. "He was very proud of his discovery.

"During this time, Hilda was being trained in the arts of diplomacy, learning Karasnian, studying martial skills and tactics, studying to be First Protector. I had just assumed… I'd thought the visions pointed clearly to Hilda as First Protector as well as my aide in controlling the orb. It made sense, really. Then you were born.

"We knew the time was soon, but we were still caught unprepared. Hilda and I were in the middle of a training session with the orb. She had just taken primary control for the first time—not complete control, but she was deeply tied to it at the moment of your birth. She was not protected against an orb surge as I habitually was. It was my fault, you see. She was killed because I did not think she would require the extra expenditure of power on protections. I was there to support her. And the orb had never…reacted as it did at your birth. Not since its forming. So she wasn't prepared and it was my failure to…" Catarin closed her eyes and sucked in a ragged breath. She held it for a heartbeat then let it out slowly.

"Guardian," Arlana murmured, "don't. You couldn't have known." Arlana looked away from the woman's grief and focused again on the orb. One more person's life she'd devastated. Just by being born.

"I should have known. But it is of no consequence now. Hilda was killed and the truth of my vision came to me as I wrested back control of the orb. Oric was to be First Protector. It was his position from the start. His duty. His music lessons came to an end, and his instruction in diplomacy and martial skills began that very day. He has become a very good First Protector." She paused, then stood and began pacing around the orb. "He still hears the song. He has plotted its pattern, knows when it will recur down to the second. According to his calculations, the song is going to reach a peak very soon." *Neither of us knows what it is, Lady Arlana. We do not have any idea what it portends. But we think you are part of it.*

Arlana glanced at Catarin, her words echoing in her mind. Then another voice… No. Voices. Voices spoke into her mind. They were faint and disjointed, almost a whisper. *He is coming. He is coming.* The phrase repeated until the voices faded away.

"Did you hear that?" Arlana demanded.

Catarin's eyes narrowed. "Hear what?"

"Those voices. They said, 'He is coming'."

"What voices? Who is he? Lady Arlana, I heard nothing. The orb pulsed very slightly, but…"

Catarin fell silent when Arlana spun to face her fully. "The orb pulsed? When? Just now?"

"Yes."

Arlana's gaze flew to the orb. "Is it possible?" She looked back at Catarin, horrified by the idea. "Could they still be conscious in there?" Arlana's stomach rolled. It couldn't be. She stared at the orb.

A shudder raced across her body. What if it were possible?

"Who?" Catarin's gaze shifted between Arlana and the orb.

After a moment's hesitation, she met the Guardian's quizzical gaze and said, "The sorcerers."

# Chapter Twenty-Three

❧

Oric woke to the scent of Arlana and the face of GeJarn. Not a pleasant contrast. Grimacing, he sat up in bed, greeting the GeMorin with a grunt. GeJarn grunted back, and Oric almost smiled. He looked around, taking in the familiar surroundings of his room. He could barely remember reaching his chambers.

"She healed you."

GeJarn's harsh voice startled Oric. "What?"

"Lady Arlana. She healed you. Pgar caused you a lot of damage. You were lucky to survive. But she seems to think you will recover now."

"Where is the lady?" Oric tried to keep the anticipation from his voice but knew he'd failed when GeJarn's mouth turned up in a suspiciously amused expression.

"She was called to the Guardian several hours ago. I have not heard from her since. She said she would return here when they were finished."

"So you volunteered to watch over me until then?" Oric swung his legs over the side of the bed, amazed at how good he felt. No aches, no pains, no lingering bruises. Even the memories of the intensity of the pain he'd endured were fragmented and faint. And he was starved.

"How are you feeling?" GeJarn asked, ignoring Oric's question.

"I feel great. Hungry. But healed. How long have I been unconscious?"

"Two days. Lady Arlana thought it might be more. It is good you are awake."

GeJarn rose from a chair set against a wall in the corner of the room. He rolled his shoulders, then scooped his cloak off the back of the chair and tossed it over his arm. He was still dressed in only a leather kilt. In the bright sunshine filling Oric's room, the GeMorin looked massive and dangerous and completely out of place.

"I will have food brought to you," the GeMorin said. "Then, if you are well enough, I will leave you for a time. I require sleep."

Oric looked closer at the healer. "When did you sleep last?"

GeJarn turned and headed from the room. Over his shoulder, he said, "Tell Lady Arlana to send for me if she has need. I will be in the rooms I have been given."

Oric growled at the silence left behind. The GeMorin healer could be as irritating as a pet *chok-kee* bird. He eased to his feet and wandered to his washbasin. He cleaned and shaved, feeling almost human again as the layers of sweat and grime were scraped away.

As he lathered soap on his cheeks, he wondered if it would be wise to try reaching Arlana. She'd want to know he was awake, wouldn't she? He could almost see her smile. The thought caused him to nick his jaw with the razor. He concentrated on finishing the job at hand, then considered contacting her again. But if she was talking with the Guardian, they might not want to be disturbed.

He debated for nearly an hour, his need to see her intensifying with each passing minute. Despite the anxious feeling in his gut, he devoured the food brought to him, then wandered his rooms, irritated by his inability to decide whether or not to contact her. The indecision mixed sourly with his intense desire to see her. He was acting like a lovestruck youth.

With an impatient curse, he went to his music trunk, recovered his long neglected pipes and walked outside to the small garden behind his rooms. The familiar riot of colorful blossoms and many shades of green and blue foliage that covered the small area greeted him. He walked through the heavy perfume of flowers to the low white stone balustrade that surrounded his balcony.

From this height, he had a spectacular view of the eastern part of Czanri. He took in the familiar spires and domes, the glint of brass, copper and gold, the geometric patterns of colored stone and marble that made up the buildings of the city. Just to the north, he could see part of one of the massive walls of the temple of Gormovich, god of war. To the south, the market square bustled with activity and the slow-moving water of the Rain River twisted through the city.

Home.

So much had changed since the last time he'd looked out over the city. The familiar now felt distant. He rested one hip against the balustrade and took a deep breath. Barely, just at the edge of his senses, he caught a faint scent of jasmine. He swung around, searching the balcony for her. Then he saw the vine twisting up a wooden lattice at one side of the garden, its white flowers mocking him with their subtle scent. That vine, for reasons neither he nor the gardener had been able to guess at, had never bloomed—until now. He'd almost forgotten it was jasmine.

He hissed out a disgusted breath. He was getting worse. Maybe he was still sick. He turned back to the view of the city and knew the way he was feeling had nothing to do with his health and everything to do with Arlana. Now that they were finally in Czanri, he had no idea what would happen next. What he did know was that he was in love with her and even dying for her seemed a simple thing compared to that.

He rested a hip on the balustrade again, raised his pipes to his lips and began to play for the first time in over a year. At first, the notes were harsh and disjointed. But before long, as his fingers loosened and his lips remembered, his natural skill turned the song to something more than mere pipe music. The balcony vibrated with longing and the bittersweet echo of uneasy love. He lost himself in the sound, the feel of music. It had been so long since he'd allowed himself the luxury that it swamped him with its power.

When he finished the song, he dropped his hands and the pipes to his lap, his gaze still turned to the city.

"That was beautiful."

The sound of her voice made his heart hammer. He'd been so engrossed in the music, he hadn't heard her approach. He closed his eyes and took a deep breath before turning to face her.

Gods but she was beautiful. Her hair and eyes were, at last, their natural colors—pure white and crystal blue. She was wearing a simple black robe cinched at the waist by a gold rope belt, the uniform of her position as a sorceress in Karasnia. She hovered near the stained glass doors which led from his rooms into the garden, her hands clasped in front of her, looking almost as unsure as he felt.

He stood and bowed in the Karasnian style. "My lady. I did not hear you come out." His voice shook a little, so he stopped talking.

"I didn't want to interrupt. You're very good."

"Thank you." He smiled, then smiled more when she blushed and looked away.

"You're feeling better?"

"Perfect. Thank you for healing me."

Her gaze flashed back to his. "I had to. It was my fault you were hu—"

He shook his head, cutting her off. "No. It was Pgar's fault. You did everything in your power to save me. I understand that."

"I wanted to explain. About the way I was to you when we first met again in Pgar's castle."

He tried to shake away her explanations again, but she raised a hand.

"I have to explain. You need to understand. I knew, not long after we arrived, what he wanted from me. I knew what he was. I knew…I knew a lot more than he wanted me to know. The bond between us, the connection he forged when I was too young to notice, it links us… links us in ways even he didn't anticipate. For years he's been able to see and feel my inner emotions. To know most of what I was thinking. Until I found the line connecting us, I didn't know that was how he understood what he did about me. We'd never been together, so close together for so long before he came to get me.

"I was in his company for only a few hours before I sensed the bond. And once I found it, I learned how to use it. But my thoughts were still his to read for days. I… It took time to learn how to let through only what I wanted him to know. When I first had you brought to me, I hadn't perfected the skill yet. The act was for his benefit as much as yours."

"Mine?"

"I wanted you to be angry. I needed you… I didn't want him to see anything in your eyes but hate for me. I thought you'd be safer that way. I made sure GeJarn looked out for you, though. I didn't trust any of the other GeMorin, despite their oath to me. They'd made the oath to Pgar first."

"I did not hate you after that scene, you know."

She sucked in a deep breath, her lips trembling as she released it.

"I could not hate you, Arlana. I thought I'd lost you to him. And it almost killed me. Death would have been easier to accept. But I could not hate you. Ever."

"Oric…" She closed her eyes and a single tear slid down her cheek. "I was so afraid for you. He wanted to use you as a sacrifice. I only know a little about the way a blood sorcerer sacrifices victims—from Vic and Jacob and from Pgar himself—but the idea that he might do that to you terrified me. I would have done anything to prevent it."

"You did. But I would have faced it to save you."

A choked sob broke from her. She pressed a hand to her mouth, but tears flowed freely down her cheeks. "I'm so sorry, Oric," she whispered between ragged breaths. "For everything. For my confusion in the Pillars. For my deception. For the pain and trouble Pgar brought you. For…"

He crossed the garden in three strides, his pipes left forgotten on the balustrade, and pulled her into his arms. For the first time in weeks, he felt right. "You have nothing to be sorry for. You did what you had to. And I love you all the more for it."

"W-what?" she stuttered, her blue eyes flaring.

He smiled, let go of his fears and said, "I love you, Arlana." *I have loved you for a very long time.* He brushed a tear from her cheek. *And I suspect I will continue to love you for a very long time into the future.*

*Can you tell the future, Oric? Can you see what will happen to us?*

*All that matters is we're together when we face that future.* He lowered his lips to hers, tasted her, caressed the smooth skin of her cheeks with his mouth, and then he kissed her, deep and long. He poured out his emotions, his hopes and fears. He hugged her tight, afraid that if he let her go, he'd never feel this right again.

All that had come before, everything that had happened since the long ago night when she'd forced him out of her inn room fell away, leaving behind only passion. And desperation. He kissed her mouth, her face, her neck. He couldn't taste enough of her, breathe in enough of her scent. He lifted her into his arms, drinking in her gasp at the sudden movement, and carried her to his bedchamber, barely thinking beyond getting inside her.

But he needed more from her than just sex and lust. So when he laid her on his bed, he slowed down. Despite her best efforts to hurry him, he took his time undressing her, lingering over each new inch of exposed flesh. He kissed her shoulder, drew a warm, wet line from her neck to her breast with his tongue and suckled her nipple until she writhed beneath him.

He opened his mind to her. Demanded the same of her. And when she did, he was overwhelmed. Again. He remained perfectly still for several heartbeats, absorbing everything she gave him, letting her feel everything she did to him. Then he kissed her, their tongues clashing—a physical anchor in a tumultuous emotional storm.

*By the gods but you taste good, Arlana,* he breathed into her mind and reveled in her shudders. *I have dreamed of you for weeks. Wanted to touch you here.* He cupped her breast and squeezed. *And here.* His hand slid along her stomach, stopping only when he felt her muscles bunch and quiver. *I've longed to taste you again.* His mouth moved to her throat. *I have been going out of my mind wanting you, fayria.* Her reaction to his use of the pet name made him groan.

He moved away long enough to rip off his own clothing, then he was next to her again, soaking in her heat and passion. *Do you want me, fayria?* He murmured the question in her mind as his hand glided over her hip.

*Yes.*

He slid his hand to the inside of her thigh and stroked the soft flesh.

*Can you feel how much I want you?*

*Yes.*

She gripped the bedcovers when his hand moved higher on her thigh. He leaned down, lapped one nipple with his tongue teasingly as he moved between her thighs to cup her wet heat. She moaned, and Oric's erection jerked in response. He covered her mouth with his at the same time as his finger plunged into her heat. Her muscles contracted. He felt the knife's edge she balanced on, knew she didn't want to go over just yet. But his own control was quickly dissolving.

Later he'd slow down, he promised himself as he settled between her thighs. Later he'd make love to her lingeringly, gently. For now, he had to be inside her or he knew it would kill him.

*Oric, I can't wait much longer. Please.*

Her quiet plea was more than he could take. He plunged deeply into her. She was so tight, so warm his control almost shattered. He groaned and began to move. *I love you, Arlana.* He sped his rhythm to match her breathing, lost himself in the joining of their minds and bodies. When she peaked, he followed in an explosion that seared his soul.

As his breathing slowed, he braced himself up on his elbows to study her. Her cheeks were flushed, her eyes closed, her hair a tangle of white around her face. He traced the line of her jaw with one finger. Her eyes fluttered open and she smiled.

"I must apologize, fayria," he told her as he leaned down to kiss her swollen lips.

"For what?"

Her eyes widened so much he almost laughed. "I wanted to make love to you slowly. I wanted this to last a little longer."

"It lasted long enough. I don't think I could have taken much more. Besides, do I look like I'm complaining?"

He did chuckle then. "Next time, I will take my time."

"Mmm. Okay."

Her eyes drifted shut again and a small smile played around her lips. He watched her, content just to have her near, to know he could touch her freely. He was still studying her relaxed features when her eyes opened again.

"That didn't…" She sucked in her lips, looked away for a moment before focusing on his chin. "That didn't tax you too much, did it?"

He choked on a sudden burst of laughter. *Tax me too much? In what way, fayria?* She squirmed beneath him, a delicious sensation that started his body humming again.

"I just meant…well…you've only just recovered and you were badly injured, and I don't want you to do anything that might compromise your health, and that was, well, that was a bit more…energetic than I'd normally recommend for someone in your condition… Oh. I mean, not that condition, because what we did was sort of a necessary end to that condition, I meant more your health and well…" She frowned, and when he started to chuckle, her bottom lip thrust out. "Damn it, Oric, you know what I mean."

He laughed so hard he had to roll to the side to keep from collapsing on top of her again. She reached around and slapped his chest, sighing with frustration, which only made him laugh more. When he thought he could control himself, he cupped her cheek. She tried not to look at him, tried to keep frowning, but when he forced her gaze to his, her smile broke through. *I knew what you meant, love. And I appreciate your concern. But it would have been far worse for my health if I had waited any longer to make love to you.*

"Well, so long as you're sure."

"I am sure." He leaned over to kiss the tip of her nose, then he moved to the curve of her cheek and across to the tender skin beneath her earlobe. He was rewarded by her small gasp. "Mmm. Do you know how good you smell, fayria? Do you have any idea how good your skin tastes?"

*Actually, I have a pretty good idea.* She opened her mind to him enough that he could feel her response to his tender ministrations. *When your mind is open to me, I can taste my own skin on your lips. Feel what I feel like against your hands. I've never imagined anything so erotic before, Oric.*

*It is the same for me, love.* He closed his mouth over hers, delighted in her surprise as he made good on his promise to make love to her slowly the next time.

***

The sun had long set by the time they dragged themselves out of bed for a meal. Oric had food brought up to his rooms, and they ate out on the balcony, blanketed in warm flower-scented air. Arlana could hardly look away from him long enough to eat. She was so happy at that moment she thought she might burst. It had to be a dream. But if it was, she didn't want to wake. She hated to bring up her conversation with the Guardian and the many revelations it had brought. She didn't want to break the sensual spell he'd wrapped her in.

He loved her. Just thinking about his declaration made her heart beat faster. Lord Commander Oric of Myseen of Czanri, First Protector to the Prophesied One, loved her. Not her magic, not the wealth and power she could bring him, but her. He'd left all of his feelings open to her as they'd made love and the strength and simplicity of his devotion staggered her still.

Oric's love and his lovemaking had gone a long way to healing her wounds after the ordeal with Pgar. She tried not to think about those dark days too much, or the repercussions that would come from her defying the sorcerer. She had no doubt he'd try to make good on his promise to finish what they'd started. But she was too happy to want to talk or even think about any of that.

She breathed in the heavy scent of flowers and tore her gaze from Oric long enough to study his garden. It was a beautiful mix of colorful flowers and foliage, almost wild looking but for a few stone paths and a patch of cropped grass. The view beyond the balcony was magnificent. Czanri was a beautiful and exotic city. She could see why Ferdinand loved it. She'd seen little of the translator in her first few days here. Her time had been fully occupied with healing Oric. But he was ready to resume his post as her translator when she called. And she found it reassuring to have another friend here.

"What are you thinking?" Oric asked.

She blinked and pulled her thoughts back to the garden. "I was thinking how beautiful Czanri is. I can see now why Ferdinand likes it so much."

Oric smiled. "He likes it for its excitement and intrigue, not for its beauty."

"Well, I like it for its beauty. Maybe, when there's time, you could show me around? I haven't left the central buildings since arriving."

"Of course. We can go tomorrow morning if you like."

She thought a bit before nodding. "Okay. That would be nice."

"Did you have other plans?"

He popped a grape into his mouth, but the casual action belied the slight tension in his shoulders.

"I still have a lot to discuss with the Guardian. But we hadn't planned on meeting until tomorrow afternoon."

"Of course." He fell silent, focusing on the food laid out across the quilt on which they sat.

She sighed. "I wish…" He looked up. *I wish I was nothing more than a bookbinder, and you were nothing more than a bard.*

He cupped her cheek. *Sometimes I wish the same thing, fayria. But it is not to be.* "Tell me about your talk with the Guardian. Did you get the answers you were looking for?"

"Some." She picked up a chunk of bread and kneaded the soft center between her fingers. "She told me about you and about Hilda." She looked up to watch his reaction as she spoke. He merely nodded, then motioned for her to continue. "It doesn't bother you that she told me about your sister?"

"No. You would have heard more about her eventually. It was right that the Guardian explained."

"Do you miss her?"

He shrugged. "She was like a mother to me more than a sister. I miss her. But it's been twenty years. I have had time to adjust."

She nodded and looked back at the mush of bread between her fingers.

"What else did you talk about?"

"She told me the story of the orb's forming. How it was a blood sorcerer named Gavin who caused the disruption in the spell." She looked up. "Strange, isn't it? Two blood sorcerers after the same thing…" She shook her head and frowned.

"What is it?"

"The Guardian is sure Gavin was killed when the spell went wrong, but… When Pgar came for me, in the Timeless Forest, there was a… I don't know how to describe it other than as a pulling sensation."

"Pulling at you?"

"No, at him. After a time, I knew it was the orb pulling. That was why he was desperate to leave Browan, and why he didn't follow us when I gated into the orb chamber. The orb pulls at him. And he's afraid of it. But there's no reason for his fear or for the orb to pull at him unless he was tied to the original spell."

"The orb does not…pull at you?"

"Well, yes it does, in a way. It draws me. And I suppose there's no doubting I'm tied to it, despite not even being born when it was formed. But… What I felt from Pgar wasn't just this gentle tugging sensation I feel the closer I get to the orb. It was much stronger and there is real fear in Pgar when it comes to getting close to the orb."

"You think he's this Gavin?"

"Only Catarin would be able to say for sure. But I'm starting to suspect that's why he won't venture into Browan for long."

"He thought you would somehow be able to stop this pulling from the orb, then? Otherwise, he would not be able to have you and the power of the orb in his presence, and then what would be the use controlling you?"

She tried not to flinch under his too accurate judgment of Pgar's use for her. "I don't know. Maybe he thought I'd stabilize it to the point that it would no longer draw him. Maybe he thought it would absorb me and leave him free to wrest control of it from Catarin. It's a part of his plans he hid too deeply from me. And I don't dare try to use the link between us now to find out."

"You are still linked to him, then?"

She nodded. "I'm not sure what breaking the link would do. I've closed it off. He can't easily get to me now. But likewise, I can't easily get to him." She met the uncertainty in his gaze. "As soon as I can find a safe way to break the link, I will. I no more want to be tied to him now than I want to be tied to the orb."

His lips lifted, just a little, and she knew she'd quieted his fears. She reached across and gripped his hand, squeezing. *Always remember I chose you, Oric. I made the choice freely and continue to do so. He doesn't have a hold on me anymore.*

Oric leaned forward and captured her lips, his free hand tunneling into her hair, pulling her head closer. *Thank you for that, fayria.*

He sat back, but not before caressing her jaw with his fingertips.

She grinned, flustered under the intensity in his gaze. "Anyway," she made of show of cutting a chunk of cheese from the round, "I may be all wrong about Pgar. It may be a coincidence that he's also a blood sorcerer. I'll talk to the Guardian about it tomorrow." She stuffed the chunk of cheese in her mouth in an attempt to keep from babbling. Oric's knowing smile made her want to blush and thump him all at the same time. She settled for frowning.

"What else did you and the Guardian discuss?"

He took a slice of peach between his lips and sucked on it, meeting her gaze with all the innocence of a mountain lion on the hunt.

She swallowed a gulp of sweet Myseen ice wine and blurted, "She told me about this song you've been hearing all your life."

He bit into the peach slice. "Mmm. I suppose you had to hear of that eventually too, though I would have preferred to be the one to discuss it with you."

"You can now. I'd like to know more. She didn't say very much except that you've figured out its pattern and the pattern is reaching a peak. Soon."

"Very soon." He nodded and popped the other half of the peach slice into his mouth.

"How soon?"

"Within the week."

"Goddess, that is soon! And you don't know what it means?"

"No."

Arlana frowned. "It's a mystery that needs solving soon though, don't you think?"

"Yes. And if you have any ideas, I would be more than happy to hear them, my lady."

Her brow furrowed in deep thought, but no inspiration struck. She shrugged. "I don't know. Perhaps once the Guardian and I have talked more. Or maybe the orb will be able to explain."

"The orb? How in the name of the gods could the orb explain anything?"

"It spoke to me today." She tried to hide her uneasiness, but her brow furrowed with her concern.

"It what?"

"It spoke. In Karasnian, though I can't imagine how disembodied two-hundred-year-old sorcerers could have learned my language. Maybe they've picked it up from Catarin."

"What do you mean, it spoke to you, Arlana? The orb has never spoken to anyone. Not even the Guardian. Do you not think if it were possible, it would have communicated with her long ago?"

"We talked about that a lot too. She seems to think because I'm a stronger telepath than she is they're able to reach me where they couldn't reach her." If she kept talking about the mechanics of the orb talking, she could almost forget the horror she'd felt upon realizing all those minds were trapped in it. When Catarin had told her about the spell and what it required the one hundred and ninety-nine sorcerers to give up, she hadn't really considered the implications of that choice. She reminded herself again that they'd freely chosen to give up their physical bodies to the creation of the orb. It probably wasn't accurate to think of them as individual beings anymore anyway. And they probably didn't perceive themselves as trapped. At least, she hoped they didn't.

Oric rocked backward, his breath coming out in a loud whoosh. *Amazing. But... If strong telepathy is required, why did it never speak to me? I have spent more time around the orb in the last twenty years than any other besides the Guardian and her personal guard.*

*Maybe they didn't have a reason before. Maybe it's because of my tie to the orb.* "We should try it." Suddenly, the idea of all they might discover from the orb flooded her in curiosity, washing away most of her hesitance and unease. She sat straighter. "You should come to the orb chamber with me tomorrow and see if you can reach them. The voices aren't very strong. It seemed to take a great deal of effort for them to come together enough to form coherent words. But maybe if I'm stabilizing it, they'll be able to speak more easily."

"I'm not sure the Guardian would approve such an experiment."

"She doesn't really have a say in the matter now, Oric. Eventually, I'll take over control of the orb, whether I like it or not." *In the meantime, I intend to learn as much about it as possible. I won't spend the next several centuries subservient to that thing the way your mother is.*

His eyes flashed. *Subserviency? You would be one of the few to claim so of the Guardian.*

*Because I know what others can't see. It would cause chaos if others knew she barely maintains control of that thing. She's only barely had control of it since it was formed.*

He looked about to disagree, then stopped.

After a short silence, he nodded. *I knew her control was waning. I never guessed it was so tentative as to have made her a slave. You are right. And to that end, we should not discuss this weakness either. Until you have taken up her role, it is best for the people to believe the Guardian fully in control.*

*Agreed.* She took a deep breath. "So, you will come to the orb with me tomorrow then?"

"Yes."

She smiled.

"Did you discuss anything more?"

"I think what we covered was quite enough for one day, Lord Commander."

"As my lady says."

He ducked his head in a mock bow that made her giggle. She took another sip of wine. "Do you know where GeJarn disappeared to? He's kept vigil at your bedside since we arrived. I've barely been able to get him to sleep. And he's refused to leave your chambers."

"Really? He didn't say. When I woke, he told me where you'd gone and after his usually gruff conversation, he left. He's been given chambers?"

"Yes, but I'm not sure he knows where they are. He never went to them before this."

"I'm sure a guard gave him directions. Most of the guards in the residence speak at least a little Karasnian."

"Because of me?"

"Because of you."

"Do you think we should check on GeJarn? I mean, this must be very hard. Being ostracized from his clan."

"He is also a warrior, fayria. I think it best if we give him time alone to…adjust. I'll search him out tomorrow before we leave for the city."

She nodded. "Okay. If you think he'll be all right."

Oric smiled and traced his fingertips along the point of her chin. "You are very tenderhearted for an all-powerful sorceress."

"No, I'm not." She tried to pout, but the gesture lost its impact when his fingers moved to caress her lower lip. She sighed instead.

"You are, fayria." *And it is one of the many things that I love about you.*

She leaned forward and kissed him, humming her pleasure into his mind. *Play something for me, Oric. On your pipes. Play me a song.*

He eased back enough to meet her gaze. "As my lady wishes."

# CHAPTER TWENTY-FOUR

Arlana rose slowly out of sleep the next morning to the feel of Oric caressing her. At first, it was a vague and lazy sensation following her to full wakefulness. Then it was something more. His hand traveled over her shoulder and down her chest to cup one breast. He lingered there, toying with one nipple, then moved to her other breast. Her breathing sped. His hand moved to her stomach, gently teasing her skin. She kept her eyes closed, even when she realized he knew she was awake, and concentrated on the feel of his hand.

His touch moved over her stomach, teased her navel then slid to her hip. He caressed her hip, his fingers moving just close enough to make her breathing hitch. Then he moved down her thigh. The bed shifted under his movement. And his mouth followed his hands.

"Mmm." The murmur broke from her without thought. His chuckle brushed warm against the heated skin of her inner thigh.

*Good morning.*

His voice whispered into her mind, as seductively as his lips slid over her legs, up her legs. She was panting by the time he moved her thighs apart and settled between them. She still didn't open her eyes.

She did open her mind.

When his lips touched her heat at the same moment as his mind opened to her, she cried out both mentally and physically. The pleasure-pain that broke through her body with each lap of his tongue, each caress of his mind, was acute and breath-stealing. *Oric!* His name was the only coherent word she could form under his onslaught. When he pushed her over the edge, when her body jerked with release, even forming his name was beyond her.

He moved back up the bed, covering her body with his, his chest hair tormenting her too-sensitive nipples. She sighed and opened her eyes. His grin looked entirely too smug and satisfied. She had the overwhelming urge to wipe that look off his face. But first she had to find the energy.

"You look very beautiful, flushed from excitement first thing in the morning, fayria." He cupped her cheek, his thumb caressing a pattern designed to tease as much as soothe.

She smiled, unable to stop it, and turned her head to kiss his palm. The taste of him filled her mouth, his scent filled her nostrils, mixing erotically with her own scent. She reached up and held his hand as she kissed her way to his fingertips. When she gently sucked on the very tip of one finger, he hissed in a sharp breath. Arlana smiled and pulled more of his finger into her mouth, using her tongue and lips to savor his salty flavor. *Mmm. You taste good, Oric.* She whispered the words into his mind, knowing he liked it, and was rewarded by the shudder that racked his body.

"Arlana."

The smugness in his voice was now strain. She could feel his excitement in his mind, pressed against her thigh, and she felt the pleasure she gave him. The knowledge was like the sweetest of wines, the richest chocolate. And she wanted more.

He tried to pull his hand away, but she protested. "I want to kiss you, Oric." He leaned his head down to her, kissed her on the lips, and she responded, but in his mind she said, *I want to kiss you the way you kiss me. All over. I want to taste every part of you. May I?*

He groaned and pulled his lips away from hers so he could meet her gaze. He smiled. *At my lady's pleasure.*

The murmur was both erotic and challenging. He rolled onto his back, propped his hands behind his head and stared up at her with a wicked glint in his blue, blue eyes. Arlana licked her lips. She started kissing at his throat, nuzzling against his rich, masculine smell. Then she moved lower, across his shoulders, to the hard wall of muscles on his chest. She sucked at his nipples until both were erect and his breathing had quickened.

Using the connection between them, she sought out the places that gave him the most pleasure, knowing when she did something that excited him, despite his outward silence. She wallowed in the taste and feel of him even as she soared with pleasure to know she was making him feel the way he made her feel. She didn't have to hear his groan or feel his body tense when her lips dropped to the tip of his erection to know how much he wanted her mouth there and how desperate he was to maintain control. She whispered into his mind as she explored the length of him with her tongue. His fingers buried into her hair and his body strained against the opposing need for release and control.

*Arlana.*

*Hmm?* She ignored the plea in his voice, too caught up in the silky texture of his most sensitive skin.

"Enough!"

The bellow was ripped from his throat, sounding raw and hungry. He reached down, gripped her shoulders and pulled her up so they were nose to nose and she was straddling his hips.

*You drive me mad, Arlana.* And he plunged upward into her.

She cried out at the exquisite feel of him buried fully inside her. Then he gently lifted her hips and brought them down again. Arlana groaned, long and low in her throat. *Oric.*

*Move for me, fayria.*

He guided her hips, teaching her the rhythm, and Arlana gladly danced. Her long hair hung around her shoulders, curtaining his face, filling the space between them with the scent of jasmine and sex.

*Gods, but I love you, Arlana.*

It was the last thing he managed to say in Karasnian.

He continued to murmur into her mind, Browan words she didn't understand, but she could feel the meaning. They danced until neither could form a coherent word, either mentally or aloud. And when they reached the peak of release, they tumbled over together.

Arlana sprawled across Oric's chest for a long time before the world settled and became solid again. She breathed in heavily and sighed. *Good morning*, she murmured into his mind when she remembered how to form words again.

He chuckled and caressed the back of her head with one hand, stroking over her tangled hair. "Yes," he whispered against the top of her head, "it is, isn't it?"

Later, when they were both able to stand, they climbed out of bed, washed and dressed. Oric studied her as she slipped into her black robe, a frown creasing his brow.

"What's wrong?" she asked, cinching the robe around her waist.

"Will you wear the robe into the city today?"

She looked down at the outfit that proclaimed her a sorceress in her own country. "Yes, I thought… I hadn't planned…"

He smiled as he crossed the room. "You'll be quite conspicuous.

Though, it would be very difficult for you to be inconspicuous in anything you wore, my love."

"Because I'm a foreigner here?"

"Because you are far too beautiful."

"You're the only one who thinks I'm beautiful."

He shook his head. "No. I am not. But it's true that merely being a foreigner in Czanri will make you stand out. And because everyone knows who and what I am, they will know who and what you are."

"Maybe if I wore Browan clothing—"

"They would still recognize you. I am sure word has spread throughout the city that you are here. Even Browan clothing would not be enough of a disguise. Especially when you speak."

Arlana frowned. She'd forgotten her language would give her away no matter what she wore. Even changing her hair and eye color would do her little good. And she couldn't use Browan without offending the Browans. She sighed. "I'll still wear something else," she said. "Something that will draw less attention."

He looked long into her eyes, a frown continuing to crease his forehead. She could see he was debating something so waited quietly for him to speak.

"May I request you wear something specific?"

"Of course. What?"

"Your wrist scabbard and knife."

Arlana tilted her head to one side. "Why?"

"Do not forget, fayria, the Mokrez are still determined to murder you. They are strong in this city. I will request GeJarn also comes with us as added protection."

"Why not bring an entire contingent of guards as well?" Arlana couldn't keep the disappointment and hurt from her voice. She'd hoped to spend time alone with Oric. She hadn't anticipated a trip into the city turning into an ordeal.

"I think the GeMorin and I will be sufficient guard."

"Then why wear the knife?"

He laid a tender hand on her shoulder. "Because no one would suspect a sorceress of your power to have need of a physical weapon. And any surprises we can bring to a conflict will work to our benefit."

Reluctantly, she agreed. Vic had always told her the same thing. That was why Vic had taught her to use a knife in the first place. "Okay. For you, I'll wear the knife. And I'll be happy to have GeJarn along, if he agrees. Though he'll make any sort of anonymity impossible." She smiled, giving in to the inevitable. She'd never be a normal person, simply wandering the streets of a foreign city with her lover. It was time she accepted that. She touched Oric's cheek with her fingertips. "I'd still like to buy some Browan clothing while we're seeing the sights."

Oric smiled too and kissed her tenderly. "Anything you wish, my love."

***

Czanri proved no less exotic from the ground than it had from Oric's balcony. Arlana gazed in awe at the magnificent architecture of the city—temples to every god in the Browan pantheon, a university the size of a small town, squares that dwarfed anything in Fordin, gardens of multicolored and complex beauty, not to mention the houses, shops and assorted businesses lining the stone-paved streets. Geometric patterns of stonework and highlights of various metals gave the buildings a beauty and brilliance that outshone the Browan inns she had, at first, thought the most beautiful creations she'd ever seen.

She smiled often and found herself able to forget the stares and nods of acknowledgment from many of the people they passed. With the rather intimidating presence of the GeMorin at her side, no one approached them for most of the morning and she was free to enjoy the tour. She was contemplating a Browan woman's magnificent attire, thinking she'd ask Oric to direct her to a dress shop, when the first stranger approached.

The man was in his advancing years, but appeared physically fit and was dressed lavishly. After a few hours on the streets of Czanri, Arlana recognized the show of wealth in his clothing and jewelry. His hair, short-cropped beard and mustache were silver and his eyes were the usual Browan blue. It occurred to Arlana for the first time that perhaps the blue eyes of everyone in Browan had to do with the orb. She wasn't given time to digest the thought before the stranger started talking.

There was a resonance to his voice, a power evident even though she couldn't understand his words, and she suspected he was a great orator. Oric returned the man's greeting in Browan then turned to her. His face had taken on the unreadable expression he wore to hide his thoughts. She frowned a little as he spoke.

"Lady Arlana Von Fordin, I would like you to meet Senator Petrov of Browan of Czanri of Tschec. Senator, Lady Arlana Von Fordin."

Unlike the other Browans she'd met, the senator didn't drop to his knees and bow. He inclined his head—a small nod of acknowledgement—and smiled. The look didn't reach his eyes. Arlana curtsied without taking her gaze off the senator's face. "A pleasure, Senator."

"The pleasure is mine, my lady." Petrov spoke in Karasnian, his accent heavy but discernable. "The people of Browan have awaited you for a long while."

"And they have been most welcoming."

He nodded again, his smile remaining firmly in place. His attitude reminded Arlana of some of the courtiers at both Fordin castle and the royal castle in Dareelia. The false charm made her skin crawl. She had the feeling the senator was making no effort to hide his true feeling—the smile was for the common people watching the exchange.

"I felt I should bring you greetings from the senate personally, my lady. I do hope we will have the opportunity to…discuss matters of state some time soon."

She forced herself not to frown at the comment. She didn't trust her voice, so she simply inclined her head.

"Now, I will let you finish your tour."

He spoke to Oric for a minute in Browan. Then he bowed and left, but not before she caught his assessing glance.

"What did he say?" she and GeJarn asked simultaneously.

"He spoke of politics and things better left for the council chamber. He wished me to ask the Guardian for a meeting. Soon. One also attended by Lady Arlana."

The clipped tone of Oric's voice revealed quite plainly what he thought of Senator Petrov. "You don't like him," she said.

*No. I do not. His ideas and rhetoric are a danger to the country. In my opinion.*

Arlana stared off in the direction Petrov had taken. The crowds had filled in behind him so he was no longer visible. She pursed her lips, thinking that soon she was going to have to talk to the Guardian about more than just the orb. A movement at the corner of her eye caught her attention. A flash of black, so solid and plain it couldn't have been a Browan. She turned in a half-circle but couldn't find the source of the movement. No one near them was dressed in simple black. For an instant, thoughts of Pgar surfaced and she had to suppress the desire to run. He wouldn't be here, couldn't be here without her knowing. The orb would react. She would feel him.

But then what…

*Arlana?*

Oric's concern brought her full attention back. "I'm sorry. I just thought I saw something." She blinked and suddenly remembered. "Whypp!" She meet Oric's gaze. "I completely forgot. There's been so much…" She shook her head. "What ever happened to him?"

Oric's brow furrowed. She watched as his gaze turned inward and recognized that he was listening.

"I do not hear him anymore. Either he has perfected the mind tricks I taught him or he has left the country."

"Do you think he'd have left? After all the trouble he went through to follow?"

"No."

He sounded disappointed but resigned.

"I believe he has perfected the skill of concealing his thoughts. Perhaps I should not have taught him."

"You said yourself his thoughts weren't pleasant enough to want to overhear."

He grunted in agreement but still didn't look happy.

"Is this Whypp someone I should know about?" GeJarn asked.

"He's…He's someone a friend sent to watch over me. He's from my country."

"He's an assassin," Oric stated.

GeJarn looked at Arlana. "You have many people trying to protect you, my lady. But is an assassin really the most practical of bodyguards?"

"His boss owed a friend of mine a favor. I think. Anyway, I trust he won't hurt me or anyone near me, so I don't think we need to worry about him. Too much." She pursed her lips. "I'm worried that we haven't heard from him in so long. I hope he's all right."

"You worry about an assassin, Lady?" GeJarn's brow ridges rose. "You are truly a strange one. I have never met someone of your power so concerned with the welfare of others."

The look of surprise on the GeMorin's face made Arlana smile. His not quite compliment made her cheeks heat. "Enough of assassins and senators for the moment," she said to lighten the mood. "It's too fine a morning, and I want to buy a new dress."

GeJarn's expression could almost be called a smile.

Oric chuckled and took her arm. "Then my lady must have a new dress."

The heat of his touch traveled up her arm and spread over her body, warming her to the center of her being.

# CHAPTER TWENTY-FIVE

Arlana and her companions had barely returned to the complex when she was summoned to the Guardian. "So much for lunch together," she sighed. As GeJarn was still with them and the servant sent to escort her to the Guardian watched closely, Arlana did no more than thank Oric for the day out. What she wanted to do was mold her lips to his. Unintentionally, her gaze dropped to his mouth. It curved in a smile that melted her knees.

"Summon me after you have spoken to the Guardian," he said. "If she agrees, we will try your experiment."

Arlana nodded and followed the servant reluctantly. She'd have preferred spending the rest of the day with Oric. Even GeJarn, for all his brooding presence, had proved remarkably good company. His sense of humor was a bit skewed, in her opinion, but intact, despite all he'd been through. The nervous looks cast his way by the Czanri citizens seemed to have gone unnoticed by the healer. And once or twice, she caught him enjoying the new scenery. At those moments, when their gazes met, the haunted look he'd carried since coming to Czanri seemed to vanish and for an instant, he looked content with his decision.

Her thoughts turned inevitably to Oric as she walked the lengthy corridors to the orb chamber. He made her feel free to be herself, to do and say exactly what she wanted without fear. Someday, she promised herself, they'd be able to spend more time alone together. The thought made her stomach dance.

When she reached the orb chamber, she tried pushing thoughts of Oric aside. She and the Guardian had more to discuss, and she had a lot to learn about the orb. She couldn't afford to get distracted. But she still found herself grinning like a fool.

As she crossed the large room, unable to control her smile or her imagination, the Guardian looked up from the orb. The older woman blinked and frowned. Arlana grimaced and felt heat flare across her cheeks for no good reason except that Catarin was Oric's mother, and she'd just been having some very erotic thoughts about the woman's son. She could only hope none of those thoughts had leaked out for Catarin to hear telepathically.

Fortunately, whatever Catarin might have been frowning about she kept to herself. Arlana wasn't prepared to discuss her relationship with Oric with his mother. Not yet. She was still getting used to it herself.

He loved her. The thought made her want to shout in joy, but because Catarin was watching so closely, she smiled in greeting. "Good day," she said, much too brightly.

"Lady Sorceress," Catarin said. "I hope you enjoyed your morning."

"Oh yes! You have a lovely city. I imagine it will be some time before I've managed to see it all."

"Oric tells me you met Senator Petrov while you were out."

Arlana gasped and stared at the Guardian.

She smiled. "I asked the First Protector to tell me of your day before you arrived. He is such a strong telepath it is easy to communicate with him anywhere inside the complex."

Arlana nodded, feeling silly for not having realized. "Senator Petrov was actually the only person to come up and introduce himself."

"Quite rude of him. I apologize."

"Rude?"

"It is not our custom to be so…forward. He should have waited until you were formally introduced to the senate by me. And then he should have awaited your pleasure for a personal introduction."

"I see." Arlana frowned. "I still have a lot to learn about your customs, Guardian. Perhaps I should talk with Ferdinand this evening."

"He would be a very useful person to consult on such matters. I will have him sent to you when we are finished here."

"When will I be formally introduced to the senate?"

"Tomorrow."

"So soon." The world seemed to be moving faster just when Arlana wanted it to slow down.

"We have much to do before then, my lady. Shall we get to work?"

"Of course." Arlana smiled weakly and threw herself into the lesson.

***

They'd been working for several hours before Arlana brought up the possibility that Oric might be able to hear the orb voices too. She hadn't heard the voices again, but then she hadn't been trying. She ignored her reasons for avoiding the effort.

Catarin frowned at her suggestion. "He has never heard the orb speak before. He is not tied to it as you are. I doubt he would be able to hear them."

"Isn't it worth a try, though? I think he may be a stronger telepath than I am. Maybe he could reach them again."

"I…"

Catarin's hesitation baffled Arlana. Her reluctance to allow Oric to try communicating with the orb seemed groundless. "What's wrong, Guardian? Why don't you want him to try?"

Catarin raised her head. "I would prefer to keep the workings of the orb between you and me, lady. For the moment, I think it best my son know as little as possible about the orb."

"I don't understand."

"For now, I do not wish to involve him in this. He has enough to do already."

Arlana shrugged. Despite what she'd said to Oric the night before, she still felt compelled to respect the Guardian's wishes in relation to the orb. If the woman wanted to keep her son away from the orb for the moment, then she would respect her choice. For now.

"Have you tried to communicate with them again?" Catarin asked.

"No." She hoped the older woman didn't notice her guilty flinch.

"Perhaps you should. From what you describe, the message must have been important. Perhaps they will be able to tell you who it is that is coming."

Uneasiness crept through her belly. Despite her desire to communicate with and question the orb, the idea of so many minds trapped for more than two hundred years still disturbed her. Her horror at the idea had eased over the last day. She'd been able to concentrate on the wealth of knowledge they could gain by communicating with the orb. Only now, when faced with the reality of actually talking to the orb sorcerers, did she acknowledge she'd been avoiding opening herself to them. But if she was willing to ask Oric to attempt communicating with the orb, then she should be willing to undergo the process herself. *If* she could communicate with it again.

She straightened her shoulders, took a deep breath and nodded. Turning her full attention to the orb, she opened herself to it, delving deep into the heart of the creation. She watched as it pulsed and changed and shifted, watched it grow more regular in shape. Instinct told her the more balanced the orb was, the easier it would be to communicate with it. She allowed it to use her strength to align itself. It never formed a perfect sphere, but her power got it closer. When she felt it almost balanced, she closed her eyes and sent out a greeting.

The feeling of urgency was sudden and overwhelming. She gasped as the need to hurry and accomplish something washed through her. But accomplish what? *Please, tell me. I don't understand.*

The voices rose up out of the tumultuous urgency, still disjointed, but growing stronger as she held the orb as constant as she could.

*He is coming. He is coming.*

*Who? Who is coming?*

*The traveler. The timeless one. The traveler. He is coming. Soon. Must meet him. Must meet him.*

"The traveler?" She groped for more from the voices, but they faded, losing the cohesion she'd managed to give them briefly. With a sigh, she let them go and pulled herself away from the orb. "The traveler," she murmured again as she opened her eyes. Something about that struck a memory, if she could just catch it…

"They spoke to you." Catarin's voice was quiet with awe.

"They said the traveler is coming. And I must meet him. But that's all I could get."

"Who is the traveler? That makes as little sense to me as their original message."

Arlana shook her head, more to jog her memory than to respond to Catarin. "The traveler. The traveler. I've heard that before."

Her thoughts were interrupted by a knock at the door. The Guardian gave a disgusted grunt as her gaze turned inward. After a moment, she sighed. Turning to Arlana, she said, "I am sorry, Lady, but I am afraid

I will have to end our study for the moment. It seems I am urgently needed elsewhere."

"Can I help?"

She smiled. "You know," she said, "most people do not think to offer me help. They assume I do not need it." With that, she left the orb chamber.


As Arlana walked back to her rooms, she reached out to Oric. His mental reply was immediate. *The Guardian was called away*, she told him, *so I'm going to meet with Ferdinand for a few hours. I've discovered there's a lot more about your customs I should learn.*

*I would be happy to assist you in your lessons, my lady.*

The undercurrent in his thoughts made it clear he was not thinking about the same sorts of lessons she intended to get from Ferdinand. Her stomach did a tight little dance. *Later. For now, I think it best if Ferdinand helps me. You'd distract me too much.* His mental chuckle made her pulse jump.

*Did you discuss my trying to communicate with the orb with the Guardian?*

*Yes. For now she'd prefer if you weren't involved.*

*And you have chosen to heed her wishes in this?*

She wasn't certain, but she could swear he was pleased by the idea. *Yes. I was able to communicate a little with the orb today, so I can probably manage without your help for a while. But I still want you to try one day soon.*

*Of course. Will you dine with me? After you and Ferdinand have finished?*

Arlana grinned. *Yes. I'll let you know when we're done.*

*Arlana? What did the orb say to you?*

*They said the traveler was coming. And I had to meet him. Soon.*

*Do you understand the message?*

*No.*

She felt him acknowledge the point wordlessly.

After a few minutes, he said, *I will see you later this evening, fayria.*

*As soon as I can.* The mental caress he sent her made her shiver.

***

They'd only been asleep for a couple of hours when the summons came. Oric sat up in bed, the sudden voice in his mind bringing him fully awake in an instant. He shook Arlana's shoulder, waking her as he spoke to one of the Guardian's personal guard.

*She requests the presence of the prophesied one immediately, Lord Commander. A matter of great urgency. But the Lady Sorceress is not in her rooms.* Panic colored the guard's thoughts.

*I'll locate Lady Arlana and escort her to the Guardian's chambers.* Oric didn't feel the need to tell the guard that locating Arlana was a matter of turning his head to face her.

*The Guardian has requested she come to the orb chamber.* There was still uncertainty in the woman's mind.

Oric tried to infuse his own thoughts with as much confidence and command as he could muster at such a late hour. After such an active evening. He smiled slightly as he said, *Lady Arlana will be brought to the orb chamber shortly.* Then he cut contact. He turned to Arlana, frowning in thought until he set eyes on her.

Her hair was in disarray, her eyes narrowed and heavy with sleep, her bottom lip stuck out in a slight pout at being awoken, her lips were still slightly swollen from their lovemaking hours earlier and the blanket had pooled in her lap to reveal the beauty of her naked torso. For a moment, Oric forgot about the summons, too enchanted by the mere sight of her. He could hardly believe she was his. He kept expecting to wake up and find he'd been dreaming that she cared for him and came to his bed so willingly.

She tilted her head to one side and her frown deepened. "Why did you wake me?" Her voice was husky with sleep.

"I just received word that the Guardian wishes to see you. They could not find you in your chambers and woke me to see if I could locate you." He grinned as a blush crept across her cheeks. The only light in the room came from the light of the city seeping in through his window, but it was enough to see her color rising.

"Did you tell them I was here?"

He shook his head. "Where you spend your nights is a private matter. As long as I am able to reach you when need be, there is no reason for others to be privy to your choice of bedmates."

Her eyes gleamed with mischief. "So, as long as you know where to find me then? I suppose that's easy enough when I'm next to you."

"A place I hope you shall be often, fayria." He stroked her cheek, unable to resist the urge to touch her. What he really wanted to do was kiss her, but the summons had been urgent. He knew if he started to kiss her now, he wouldn't stop until he'd finished making love to her again, thoroughly. "Get dressed," he said, climbing out of bed and away from temptation. "The messenger said it was a matter of great urgency."

Without another word, Arlana climbed out of bed. As he pulled on his trousers, he noticed out of the corner of his eye that she strapped on her wrist sheath while dressing. The action made him smile. It pleased him a great deal to see she took his advice and wasn't going to take chances with her life.

"What are you smiling at?" She stood with hands on hips, her eyes narrowed.

He tugged his tunic over his head. "I am smiling because I am looking forward to getting you out of your clothes for a second time tonight."

Her eyes widened, then she grinned. *I can't wait.* "But what in the name of the Goddess could the Guardian want at this hour? Is she prone to late-night councils?"

*No, fayria. She isn't. I do not know what this is about.* He crossed to her and rested his hands on her shoulders. "Perhaps it is nothing."

*She spoke with the senate during the afternoon. Could it have something to do with that?*

Oric's jaw tightened. The relationship between the Guardian and the senate was…strained at best. It was likely this summons had to do with Arlana's introduction to the senate in the morning. "I don't know. We shall see." He squeezed her shoulders once, then took her arm and led her to the orb chamber.

The corridors held the usual contingent of soldiers and guards until they reached the area just outside the doors to orb chamber. No one stood outside where normally four of the Guardian's personal guards stood vigil. Oric frowned. *Arlana, how many people do you sense inside that room?*

She cast him a curious glance, then her gaze turned inward. *Six people.* Her frown deepened. *But I can't tell who they are. There's something…interfering.*

His hand fell to the hilt of his sword. He opened his mind, trying to hear the thoughts of those in the chamber. Nothing. He didn't dare try to contact the Guardian directly. *Be prepared for anything, Arlana.* Then he pushed open the doors.

Inside, the Guardian stood to the right of the orb, her face an emotionless mask. Behind her stood Senator Petrov. "Come in," he said. "Close the door."

Cautiously, Oric and Arlana entered the room, and he closed the door. He stood at Arlana's side and scanned the room. The four guards lay in an unconscious heap against the wall to his left, but they were the only other people in the room. His gaze moved back to the Guardian at the same moment as Arlana gasped. Senator Petrov stood with a knife to the Guardian's neck.

"What the hell's going on here, Petrov?" Oric boomed. He spoke in Browan, forgetting for a moment that Arlana wouldn't understand. He switched back to Karasnian for her sake. "You dare threaten the Guardian? Do you know what you do?"

Petrov raised one eyebrow. "Of course I know what I do, Lord Commander. Or I would not do it. I know more than the Guardian ever wanted me to, in fact." His gaze shifted to Arlana. "Do not try to use your magic to save her, Lady Sorceress." He moved to one side and motioned with his free hand to a bronze charm hung on a chain around his neck. "This protects me from a magician's spells. Even yours. While I am this close to Catarin, your powers won't affect her, either."

Oric started. He'd never heard of a charm that could block magic as powerful as Arlana's. Did she know this was possible? And if she did, why hadn't she warned him?

"Guardian? Are you injured?"

Arlana's voice sounded calm and steady. Oric couldn't risk glancing at her, but her even tone reassured him. Maybe Petrov was bluffing about the charm.

"I am fine for the moment, my lady. I would you had not heeded this particular summons."

An ironic smile played at his mother's lips.

"It wouldn't matter if she were here or not," Petrov barked. "But I thought it only fair she sees the face of the man who will soon be emperor of Browan."

"You will not be made emperor for this treason, Petrov. You will be executed."

"No, Guardian. You will be the one to die, and when you die, she will be forced to wrest control of the orb before she is prepared. It will leave her as weak as you. And eliminate a threat to the senate. To me."

"I wouldn't be so sure of that," Catarin said, her expression passive.

"Ah, Catarin. I know what you did not want us to know. You are weak. Your control of the orb is tentative. Oh, it took time to find out, of course. But I know now how close you are to losing control." He shifted the dagger lower, resting it near the base of the Guardian's throat. "I had thought killing the prophesied one the best option, but I have recently received information that has forced a change of heart." He smiled at Oric and Arlana.

Oric's gaze narrowed. "You head Mokrez." He wasn't asking. "You realize that if you had succeeded in killing Lady Arlana, it would have destroyed us all."

He shrugged. "Truthfully, Lord Commander, I doubt it. But once I learned of the possibility, I did rethink my plan. Just in case."

"Does your group know this?" Oric moved a few slow steps to the left.

"Stay where you are, Lord Commander," Petrov warned, the knife at the Guardian's throat pressing harder against her skin. "Until I tell you to move. And no, my group does not know this plan because there is no need for them to know. Mokrez was a tool. Fanatics. Too unstable to suit my needs for long. They have served their purpose, but now I have no more use for them."

Oric opened his mind and tried to speak to Arlana quietly.

Petrov shook his head. "I wouldn't try that, Lord Commander. I am strong enough to hear when you try to speak with the lady even if I am not strong enough to overhear. If you try it, I will make sure the

Guardian dies slowly and painfully. It is not the way a son would wish to see his mother die. Is it?"

Oric ground his teeth together, refusing to respond to the barb. But he didn't try to speak with Arlana telepathically again.

Petrov smiled and nodded. His gaze moved to stare at the side of the Guardian's face. "You should have chosen me as your consort, Catarin. I would have given you a stronger son. And the situation might never have come to this." He sighed. "But what is done is done. The gods have their ways."

"This is not the way of the gods, Petrov." The Guardian's gaze shifted to the group of unconscious guards. "This is your way. For your own glory. Your own power. I've seen men follow that way before, and it has always failed."

Her gaze flicked to Oric then back to the group of guards. He suspected she was trying to tell him something, but he didn't understand. He couldn't look at the guards without taking his eyes off Petrov, and he wasn't about to do that.

Petrov growled. "It is more than that! Lady Arlana must not be allowed to have full control of the orb. We would be helpless before her. Her slaves. I will not allow that. I will not stand for it!" His voice rose until it boomed off the chamber walls.

Oric saw, not for the first time, the light of something unhealthy in Petrov's gaze. He wasn't mad. But he was so ambitious it moved him in ways very close to insanity—his need for power was so great it engulfed him.

"I would not rule you," Arlana said quietly.

Oric noticed she'd also taken a few steps to the side, opposite him. He could see her better in his peripheral vision now.

"I wouldn't make you helpless."

Petrov snorted. "I do not believe you, Lady Sorceress. There are many people who do not believe that. Some claim you are our savior, but I disagree. You are no savior to us. Your coming marks our enslavement."

Arlana shook her head, but Petrov cut off her comment with a slash of his free hand.

"No! I will not hear more of this. The senate is too weak to stand against the Guardian. They would not hear me when I said you brought our doom. But many of them feel as I do. They just don't have the courage to take action. When I give them freedom from your rule, they will give me the title of emperor." He smiled. "We were a great country once. An empire on the verge of triumph. We shall be again."

"I will not stand by and allow you to kill the Guardian," Oric said quietly. He'd taken a few more steps to the left while Petrov's attention was focused on Arlana.

"You have no choice, Lord Commander."

Oric felt the movement of air currents behind him too late to react. The feel of steel against his throat kept him still. His hand flexed on the grip of his sword but a low voice stopped him.

"I wouldn't, Lord Commander. Move your hands out in front of you."

The knife at his throat pressed harder, so Oric did as he was told, frowning at the familiarity of the voice. He watched as his sword was drawn from its scabbard and tossed uselessly across the floor. He realized suddenly what the Guardian had been trying to tell him with her gaze.

"I would not try to defend the Lord Commander with magic either, Lady Sorceress," Petrov said.

Oric's gaze flashed to Arlana. Her eyes were wide and horror filled her expression.

"As you can see, my new acquaintance also wears a ward."

"Whypp?" Her voice was breathless, only just above a whisper.

At hearing the name of the assassin, rage and helplessness swamped Oric. He cursed low and with a great deal of feeling, but what he wanted to do was roar with the implications of his own failure. He'd placed Arlana in grave danger by not listening to his instincts where the assassin was concerned, and now he was helpless to prevent the scene playing out in front of him. He was so overwhelmed by impotence and rage he almost didn't hear Arlana murmur, "Why?"

Petrov answered for the assassin. "I found him not far outside the city, still struggling to contain his thoughts. I'd heard enough to know who he was, though, and why he was here."

"He was sent to look after me," Arlana choked.

Oric took in her shattered expression and cursed himself more viciously.

Petrov snorted. "He is a paid killer, Lady Sorceress. His loyalty falls with the coin."

"He's right, Arlana," Whypp's said matter-of-factly. "But so are you. I refused his first offer—a contract to kill you."

The dagger at Oric's throat shifted so that the sharp edge no longer pressed against his skin.

"The Lord Commander, on the other hand, isn't on my list of people not to kill. Neither is this Guardian. So long as you're not killed, I've done my job. And I couldn't refuse the senator's generous offer."

"Whypp, you can't! Please," Arlana begged.

Oric felt the assassin shrug.

"I've already been paid," he said.

"I knew the Lord Commander would join us when I had the summons sent to him," Petrov said.

Oric's gaze flicked to the senator. Petrov's smile made his stomach turn.

"I knew it most likely she would be in your bed, Lord Commander. My new assassin friend was a wealth of information about the… tension between you two." Petrov's gaze moved back to Arlana. "If you wish to see your lover survive this, Lady Sorceress, you will not attempt to interfere."

"You'll let him live if I don't prevent you from killing the Guardian?"

"Of course."

The false sincerity in the man's voice made Oric snarl. "Don't listen to him, Arlana. He will kill me either way."

Arlana's wide-eyed gaze came back to his, then focused on the man behind him.

"Is this true, Whypp? Will you kill Oric no matter what happens?"

"No. I've been paid to keep him quiet and harmless."

Oric watched Arlana's eyes narrow.

"Whypp, if you harm him, I won't let it go."

"You can't use magic while I've got this thing around my neck, Arlana."

Whypp's voice was low, his easygoing manner gone. He pushed Oric forward a step, moving the dagger from his throat to poke him in the back.

"Do as the senator says and I'll let the Lord Commander live. But don't try to threaten me."

"I won't allow it, Whypp." Arlana shifted so both the senator and the assassin were in her line of sight.

Petrov laughed. "You have no choice, my lady." He stepped to the right side of the Guardian, putting Catarin between himself and the orb. He held the dagger in his left hand, its point rested at the hollow of her throat. "You will be too busy trying to control the orb."

"Don't do this, Petrov," Arlana warned, her voice leeched of emotion.

Oric's gaze snapped to her face.

"You underestimate me if you think I won't punish you for this," she said.

Petrov snarled. "I think not, Lady Arlana. If I were you, I would worry more about the orb and the damage it will do if you don't control it." He shifted and raised his dagger.

Behind him, Oric felt Whypp move as well, felt the dagger at his own back slide upward. Without warning, Oric was dropped to his knees by a sharp kick to the back of his leg. Whypp jerked Oric's head backward with a painful grip in his hair, and the knife once again bit into his neck. The skin along his throat crawled in anticipation of the assassin's strike. He looked up to see Arlana staring at the assassin, her expression blank, her eyes unreadable.

"Vic warned you about trusting assassins," Whypp said over the top of Oric's head. "She always was good at reading a situation."

Arlana's eyes narrowed.

From the corner of his eye, Oric caught a glint of light off Petrov's knife. "Goodbye, Catarin," the senator murmured, and his dagger plunged down toward her throat.

# CHAPTER TWENTY-SIX

Arlana acted without thinking, just as she'd been taught. Everything around her slowed to crystal clarity, yet the moment came and went within the blink of an eye. It took several breaths for her to recognize the reality of what she was seeing, a moment later to realize what she'd done. She stared at the hilt of her knife protruding from Petrov's throat, then her gaze shifted to the second knife embedded in his chest. The senator sprawled on the floor of the chamber, shock etched in his death mask, his blood pooling on the green marble.

The magical ward around the senator's neck hung to one side, just above the blood. Petrov had been wrong. She could have eventually gotten around the ward. She was probably the only magician who could have, given its strength. With enough time, she would have been able to use her magic against him. In the presence of the orb, though, with the scarred magics at their most complex and twisted, safely pulling in the necessary energy she needed to break through the ward would have taken her longer than Catarin had. So she'd used the only other option available.

She'd never taken a life before. Not that she could remember. Though she'd been the cause of any number of deaths in her lifetime, she'd never personally, consciously killed another human. Vic had warned her about the guilt and remorse she might feel if she were forced to this action. "If you've done it because you had to, Arlana, remember the act was necessary when you look at the body. Don't regret it if someone else forced you to it, if it was to protect your life or a life in your care."

Arlana looked into the dead face of Petrov and thought of his greed, his anger, his fanaticism and his ambition. She thought of what it would have meant to Browan if he'd succeeded in his ambitions to become emperor. He would have killed Catarin without remorse. He would have left Arlana damaged if he could. And he would probably have killed Oric. In the end, he would have tried to use the orb to his benefit, no matter the political rhetoric he spouted. She looked closely at his dead eyes. Her guilt was a pale and weak thing. There was no regret in her.

She took a deep breath and met Catarin's wide-eyed gaze. "The orb is still under control?"

Catarin nodded, but didn't speak.

"Good." There was a thin line of blood along Catarin's throat where Petrov's knife had cut, but otherwise the Guardian appeared uninjured.

She turned to Oric, who was also staring at the dead body of the senator. He was still on his knees but no longer held in Whypp's grip. Her gaze rose to the assassin. The guard's uniform he wore hung loosely on his thin frame, giving him an awkward and almost endearing look now that he wasn't holding a knife to Oric's throat. It was a relief to know that if she had failed in her aim, he wouldn't have. He smiled when she met his gaze.

"Good shot, my lady. Vic taught you well." He winked, then walked silently from the room.

Oric made a move to stop him, but she shook her head. "Let him go."

He faced her, his expression unreadable. She frowned and took a step toward him. "Are you hurt? Whypp didn't…?"

Oric got to his feet and closed the space between them, pulling her into his arms so quickly it stole her breath.

*I am uninjured.* He ran his hands over her back, her shoulders, cupped her face in his palms. *The orb?*

*Still under the Guardian's control.*

He brushed his lips lightly over hers, then pulled back. *The charms Petrov and Whypp had—did they really block your magic?*

*Yes, but I could have gotten through it eventually.*

His hands dropped from her face and he frowned. *Did you know such a thing existed?*

She nodded. More than anything, she wanted to fall into his arms but this wasn't the time or place. And he deserved an answer. *They're extraordinarily rare because they cost the maker every ounce of power they have. To make one to block my magic, even for a little while, would force a powerful sorcerer to drain all his magic irrevocably. I've never heard of anyone who would do that, no matter the payment. To have found two sorcerers willing to make that sacrifice…* She shook her head. *I wouldn't have thought it possible.*

*Why didn't you tell me this before?*

She shrugged. *I didn't expect it.*

He was silent a moment, studying her. *We will talk more later.* He moved toward Catarin who was staring at them, a frown etching deep lines in her brow.

"Guardian, you are injured," he said. "I will send for the healer…"

"It's nothing." Catarin's hand came up to her throat. She winced as her fingers brushed the cut. "We must call an emergency session of the senate at once. Lord Commander, see to reinforcing the guards in the complex. Hunt down any persons of known loyalty to Petrov. He had a spy among my guard. Find her."

He gave a sharp nod and turned back toward the door. As he passed Arlana, he reached out to cup her cheek. *Stay with the Guardian. She will need your support when she goes before the senate. I will join you when I can.*

She grasped his hand before he could move away. *Are you sure you're all right?* There was a hesitance, a distance in his mental voice that belied the affectionate caress of his hands.

*I am angry with myself, Arlana.*

*But why? You couldn't—*

*We will discuss it later. There are things to be done now.*

Just as he moved beyond the length of her reach, Arlana felt the orb pulse. Oric stopped, one hand on the chamber door, the other rising to his temple. *Oric? Did you feel that?*

He turned to face her, his brows drawn together. *Feel what?*

*The orb pulsed and you reacted.*

He walked back toward her, his frown deepening. *I did not feel the orb pulse, Arlana. The song my mother told you about, the sound I hear in ever increasing increments, just began again. But it is at the appropriate time. I was expecting it. It had nothing to do with the orb.*

"But…" The orb pulsed again, stronger this time. So strong it brought a gasp from Catarin. Arlana's head whipped around to see the Guardian standing with her hands braced against the column on which the orb sat. The orb itself was turning and shifting, its shape growing more irregular with increasing speed. Arlana opened herself to it, focused on augmenting the Guardian's control to stabilize it. She wasn't even trying to hear the voices when they rose up to scream in her mind. The screech dropped her to her knees. Her hands flew to her head, fighting to push the voices out. They refused to quiet.

*He is coming. He is coming. Time is almost out. He is coming. Must meet him. The traveler is coming. Hurry. Must meet him. The traveler. No time left. Hurry!*

Over their insistent wail, Arlana thought she heard someone scream and realized belatedly it was her. And then as suddenly as they'd started, the voices stopped. No fading away this time, no lingering sound. The voices were just abruptly cut off. A gentle grip pulled her hands away from her head. She looked up to see Oric kneeling at her side.

"Are you all right now?"

She swallowed, tried to nod, but the movement made her head rage in protest. "I'm fine," she muttered. "What…? Did you hear them?"

"Yes. They are still trying to be heard, but I've put up a block to protect you. Has communication with the orb hurt you like this before?"

"No. Never. How are you blocking them?"

"They are using telepathy. No magic involved. I've simply reinforced your own protections. If you try, you'll still be able to hear them through the shields, but I think it best if you do not just yet. They focused the full force of their efforts on you, and you were wide open when they started. Luckily, although I could hear them, I was not affected by the attack."

"I don't think they meant it as an attack, Oric. They're desperate. But I still don't understand."

"Whether they meant it as an attack or not, it had the same effect, just like the attack of the people in the Timeless Forest. Fortunately, I was not hit this time, so I could help you."

The mention of the forest people made Arlana frown. Slowly she rose to her feet with Oric's help. Something about the forest people teased at her, coaxing a memory. Then, suddenly it hit her. Her breath rushed out in a whoosh. "Oric, the forest people. When I woke up in the ring of oak, the leader or whoever she was mentioned the traveler. She said he was the one that required sacrifice." Her heart danced a jig against her ribcage. She watched as Oric's gaze narrowed, then widened.

"The orb sorcerers said the man you're to meet is the traveler."

She nodded, though he hadn't asked a question. "You've said the song you hear is reaching a peak soon. You heard it just as the orb pulsed and the orb sorcerers spoke. Are they connected, do you think?"

He was quiet for a few minutes, his gaze turned inward. Then slowly he nodded. "Maybe. While we were being held in the forest, as I was returning to consciousness, I heard the song again. But it was louder, stronger than I'd ever heard it. It was too powerful for my raw mind at that moment, so I blacked out again."

"The sound knocked you out? While we were in the oak ring, or before?"

"While. I was sitting, not being carried, my back to a tree when I started to recover from the initial attack."

"When the forest people mentioned the traveler, their attack on me and the soldiers had just stopped and they were all focusing on a cottage just beyond the clearing. I'd been feeling anomalous energy coming from that cottage since waking up… No, actually, since entering the forest." Arlana paced away from him, her hands fisting and relaxing as she thought. "So the cottage is the where."

"You are sure?"

"Yes. It feels right. And the traveler is the who—though it's anyone's guess who he *actually* is. The when must be the peak to your song. Which is soon enough for the orb sorcerers to be panicking, isn't it?"

"The peak will happen tomorrow morning. If it is the time, and we are to reach the Timeless Forest before then, I can understand their panic. Arlana, it will be a hard ride to reach the cottage before the peak. That is, if we can still find the cottage. Neither you nor I left the forest…conventionally. We'll have to take a small guard—some of the original group so they can lead us there. But it may still take longer to reach the cottage than we have."

"Then we'll have to get there another way."

"One of those gates you used to bring us here?"

She nodded.

"No!"

Both Oric and Arlana's heads snapped around at the sudden but strong declaration from Catarin.

"I cannot allow you to gate, my lady. It is too easy to disrupt. And Petrov acquired his magic blocks from someone. He may have sympathetic sorcerers willing to disrupt your gate."

"The ones who provided the blocks wouldn't have enough power to disrupt a sneeze anymore," Arlana said.

"But what if they are not the only sorcerers he worked with?"

Arlana's gaze flicked to the dead man still sprawled on the floor. "If no one knows I'm the one gating, then there'd be no reason to disrupt it."

"You are too powerful, prophesied one. The energy it would take to build a gate big enough for a contingent of soldiers would give you away."

"We won't be taking a contingent of guards. I can build a gate small enough to accommodate a handful of people without the power signature giving me away. By the time anyone realizes I've created the gate, we'll be through."

"And who do you propose to take with you, my lady? You will need some protection."

"I will accompany her, of course," Oric said. "And I believe GeJarn would be suitable to the situation."

Arlana smiled. "Exactly what I was thinking. And you, Guardian. You must accompany me because we'll be taking the orb."

Catarin's eyes widened. "My lady—"

"This has to be done, Guardian. I feel it. We have to meet the traveler at that cottage with the orb at the time of the song's peak." She dropped her gaze, ignoring Catarin's pale shock. She fisted her hands again. "The only problem is, how? How will we meet him? Does he hear Oric's song too? Was he creating the anomaly at the cottage? Is it a type of spell I've never seen before? There wasn't a person in the cottage when the forest people said he spoke…" She looked up at Oric. "They must have been hearing the song too. That must be what they meant when they said he spoke to them."

"They also said he required blood sacrifice, Arlana. They are insane, the ancestors of those driven so at the creation of the orb by the sudden opening of our minds to telepathy. They are the descendants of those who could never learn to control their minds."

"But that may be the very reason they hear it, Oric, because they can't block out other mental noise. And because they live so near the cottage."

"And the part about blood sacrifice?" Oric's stare was intent.

She shrugged. "Probably just a product of their insanity. But even if it's true, the orb sorcerers still want me to meet him. They're desperate for me to meet him. I have to take the chance."

Oric sucked in a deep breath and let it out slowly between his teeth. He nodded reluctantly.

"I still don't know how to meet the traveler, though." She sighed and began pacing again. "It can't be as simple as walking into the cottage. He wasn't there when the forest people claimed to hear him. And the anomaly didn't feel like a shield or even a spell of illusion. It didn't feel like a spell at all." She brought her fingers to her temples, rubbing small circles. "Oric, is there anything about this song you haven't told me? Anything that might help?"

"I have told you all I know of it, Arlana."

"It must have to do with the song." Her brow creased. "How is it cycling down? Why is there a specific time when we have to meet the traveler? Is it to do with the orb…some property of the orb that makes the timing of this meeting important?"

"I would not risk asking the orb again." Oric took a step closer when she hesitated. "Arlana, they're still screaming. Do not risk it. I doubt they could be coherent enough to explain anyway."

Reluctantly, she nodded. "They did say he was coming. That implies he isn't at the cottage yet. So he'll arrive there when your song peaks. Maybe he hears it too and is traveling to reach the cottage at the same time." Her head snapped up. "Time. Traveling. Something Ryn'ah said…" She faced Oric. "The dragon said you understand time better than others."

"Yes. Well, I feel time exactly. Understand it?" He shrugged. "Who understands time?"

"She also said something like that. Actually, she said no one can… see…the future." Arlana's heart started to pound. "She said there was someone, a man who didn't move through time like the rest of us. She said I should ask him what he thought of the future." For a moment, all she could do was murmur, "Goddess."

"Are you saying this traveler is coming from the future?" Catarin sounded both incredulous and stunned. There was the barest hint of fear in her voice as well.

"The orb was designed to control time, wasn't it?"

Catarin nodded.

"I think the traveler is moving backward through time." Intuition and conjecture came together, crystallizing her thoughts. It was as if someone whispered the answer in her ear, and she saw it all with perfect clarity. "The peak of Oric's song, the time the orb sorcerers are desperate for us to meet, is the moment the traveler's backward movement through time will meet our forward movement. For an instant, we'll both be in the same time."

"And then?"

Oric's deep voice drew her gaze. "Then we'll pass and he'll be gone."

He held her gaze for several moments, then said, "The orb has fallen silent. They are no longer screaming."

Arlana knew then she was right.

"What will you do, my lady?" Catarin spoke in a whisper, as if the orb's silence and the revelations merited hushed tones.

"I'll stop that instant of time." She knew it was what she had to do, and that she sounded matter-of-fact about doing it. But her heart was tumbling inside her chest. She had no idea how to stop time, or even if she could.

*Ask the orb now, Arlana.*

Oric's voice soothed across her mind, calming her fear and panic. She met his gaze, surprised he understood, but enormously grateful.

*They have calmed. Perhaps now you will be able to get an explanation from them. If the orb was built to control time, then the sorcerers should know how to use it to that end.*

She nodded and smiled. *Thank you, Oric.*

His expression never changed, but his mind caressed hers gently.

She closed her eyes for a brief moment, savoring the caress. Then she turned to Catarin. "Guardian, do you understand how to use the orb to control time?"

Catarin shook her head. "It cannot be done safely while the orb is still so unstable. That is why it has never been done before."

*If I can stabilize it, will you help me learn?* She directed her question to both Catarin and the orb. Catarin's response was hesitant, the orb's enthusiastic. Both agreed to help.

"We still have a spy, a dead senator and the senate to deal with," Oric said. "I will see to Petrov, the guards and tracking down the spy while you two work. Arlana, I shall send GeJarn here to guard you both. I cannot trust the Guardian's soldiers yet. I will also tell him to be prepared to leave when you are ready."

"Thank you, Oric." She hesitated, then went to Petrov's body and pulled the amulet over his head. She studied it, teasing out the spell. It wasn't specific to a person. It would block no matter who wore it. Which meant the sorcerer who'd created it hadn't had enough power left when he was done to specify who the ward protected. She wondered what Petrov had done to convince the maker of the charm to go through with such a sacrifice.

Too late to ask the senator now. But there was no point in letting the sacrifice go to waste. She rubbed off the blood splattering the charm on Petrov's tunic, then carried it to Oric. "Wear this when we go." She slipped it over his bowed head. *And Oric—find Whypp. I'd like him to go with us.* She felt his mental protest even before his head snapped up, eyes flashing. She touched his cheek. *He didn't betray us. His knife would have killed Petrov even if mine had missed. He was playing a part to keep his intent from Petrov. You can understand that, can't you?*

She felt his acceptance come reluctantly with her subtle reminder that she'd had to do the same thing not so long ago to save his life.

After a moment, his mouth twisted into a half-smile. *You are right. And an assassin would be a useful person to have on hand in the forest.* He touched the amulet where it hung against his chest. *It seems, fayria, that just when we are able to settle into something of a normal existence, our fates conspire to interfere. Will we ever be able to live for more than a few days without fate interrupting?*

*Perhaps the traveler will know.*

He leaned in and kissed her, a soft touch of lips so tender it made her heart hurt.

*Contact me when you are ready. I will take care of the other complications.* His gaze flicked to Petrov. *I will have my men take care of the body for now. I think it best if we do not go before the senate with this until after we've met with the traveler.*

*If you think so. You understand the political situation better than I do.*

*I will contact a few of the senators whom I can trust and arrange for them to stall the senate.*

She nodded and leaned in to kiss him again. Her sigh was deep and weary as she watched him leave the chamber.

# CHAPTER TWENTY-SEVEN

Arlana studied with the Guardian and the orb for hours. The sun kissed the edges of the windows opening into the orb chamber before Arlana allowed herself to sit back and take a breath. She rubbed a hand over her eyes, trying unsuccessfully to knead away the grit. She needed sleep before she tried to gate. Both that spell and the complicated spell used to stop a specific instant of time were going to take an incredible amount of power. And pulling in the necessary power in the presence of the orb was more difficult and would take more time and concentration. No matter how much power she pulled in, no matter that she'd never reached her limits in power before, the human body could only take so much before it had to shut down. She could push herself farther than most humans, probably farther than any human. But it didn't make her invulnerable to exhaustion. And the spell to stop time—a very specific instant of time—was going to test her abilities farther than she'd ever tested them before.

She filled her lungs, let her head drop back and fought a surge of fear. Since she'd realized what would be required of her, she'd experienced more than one moment of panic. What if she couldn't do this? No one had ever done it before. Despite everything, what if, in the end, she wasn't strong enough? How would the orb react? The orb sorcerers wouldn't tell her why she had to meet with the traveler. They just kept repeating that she had to be there.

This was her destiny. At least, it seemed like this was her purpose for being. The orb seemed to think so. That long-ago mage who'd died trying to keep the orb spell under control when it had already gone too far, he believed she was destined for this moment. But why? And what if she failed?

Goddess, what if she failed?

"Arlana?"

Catarin's quiet voice pulled her head up. The Guardian was seated across from her in one of the chairs Oric had had brought in for them after Petrov's body had been removed. When Arlana's gaze settled on her, Catarin stood and began to pace a small circle around the orb. Arlana frowned. "Is there something wrong, Guardian?"

She didn't answer at first, but continued pacing for several minutes, her forehead creased with her frown. "My lady," she started, then fell silent again. Then she stopped pacing and faced Arlana. "Prophesied one, I am beginning to suspect the reason for this meeting. The orb is missing two sorcerers to balance it—and a proper Guardian. I am beginning to believe that you and I and the traveler are to come together to balance the orb. To control it…contain it," she shook her head, "and maybe even to use it."

Arlana sat straighter in her seat. It was as if the Guardian had been reading her mind, answering the very question she'd been asking herself. Why? She knew Catarin wouldn't really read her mind—she wasn't strong enough, even if she decided to try. So they'd been worrying over the same problem. Hearing an explanation was something of a relief. She thought about it, following Catarin's logic, and nodded at the possibility. Though it was good to have an explanation of some kind, this particular answer didn't make her feel much better about her existence. All the centuries of prophecy to foretell her coming so she could balance this human creation? It was obviously going to take someone of her power to do it. Three sorcerers who'd been tied to the spell were dead, and it would be impossible for a less powerful mage to link a new three to the orb to balance it, especially three who hadn't been part of the original spell. The orb was dangerous without the balance. So her birth, her power, was in a sense saving Browan, if not the world.

She still didn't feel any better. With a sigh, she said, "You understand the orb and its peculiarities better than I do, Guardian. I trust your suspicions over mine." She frowned. "Though why the traveler, and not some other powerful magician?"

Catarin shook her head. "Maybe it is because he travels backward through time and understands something of time that he will be able to take up a part of the orb." She wet her lips, dropped her gaze to the floor and started pacing again. "I brought this up for a reason, my lady, but I don't know how to broach my real purpose without offending you."

"Offend me? What could you say that would offend me?"

"I want you to release Oric from his responsibilities as the First Protector. You are the only one who can do this. I ask that you do so when…if we return from meeting with the traveler."

"Why?"

Catarin stopped pacing and faced her, meeting her gaze steadily. "My son does not deserve to have you toy with him."

Arlana's mouth dropped open. A full minute passed before she could think of a response. But when she started to speak, the Guardian cut her off with a hand gesture.

"After seeing you together tonight, it is perfectly clear he is in love with you. It is unfair to him. He has been duty-bound to be First Protector since his sister's death. He takes that duty very seriously. Feelings for you will only blur his ability to perform that duty."

"You didn't say he was unfit to be First Protector, so I should release him from his duty. You said he didn't deserve to have me toy with him. What makes you think I'm toying with him?"

"You can never commit to a relationship. Even if you want to, you will never be allowed because your duty, your destiny will come first. It must be so. The fate of the world is in your hands." She made a disgusted grunt and returned to pacing. "All Oric has ever wanted was to be a musician and lead a normal life. He doesn't realize I know this, but it has been obvious from the beginning. Not only was I forced to take away his dreams, I was…unable to be a suitable mother to him as he grew up. This does not mean I do not love my son, nor that I wish anything but his happiness."

"And you don't think I can make him happy?" Arlana's voice lost all emotion. She rose from her seat and faced Catarin, forcing the woman to stop her pacing and look at her. Her words bit deeper, more painfully than Arlana thought possible. After all she'd been through with Oric, the idea of being without him was intolerable.

"I think you will never be able to give him what he wants, what he has always wanted. And what he deserves. A normal life. You will always be tied to your destiny. Your life will never be ordinary or quiet. Would you condemn him to that as well? For the sake of your own…gratification?"

"Gratification?" Arlana's voice rose. "How dare you presume I'd use Oric that way. After everything we've been through in the last few months. My feelings for Oric are not based on simple gratification."

Catarin stared unflinching into her eyes. "Do you love him?"

Arlana blinked.

"Do you love him?"

"What if I do?" she breathed.

"If you love him, if you feel anything for him at all, then release him. Send him to Myseen to live out the life he always wanted. Free him to marry an ordinary woman who can give him a family. And peace."

Arlana turned away from Catarin's steady gaze and heartrending words. Her chest was so tight it was hard to breathe. How could she let Oric go now? They'd just found each other. She finally had someone to turn to, someone who didn't want to use her for her power, someone who wasn't afraid of her power. Someone who loved her for who she was beyond the prophecy. Was it selfish to want that love, to need that companionship? To let him go now would tear her soul out bit by bit until she was no more than an empty shell existing to please an unfeeling fate. She loved Oric.

She loved him more than her own life.

Arlana closed her eyes. She loved him. And because she did, because she knew Catarin was right about the life he'd always wanted, how could she do anything but let him go? Her throat closed and her hands trembled. A single tear slid over her cheek before she swiped it away. Goddess, she wasn't strong enough for this. Everyone thought she was so powerful, but she wasn't strong enough for this. She tried swallowing around the thickening of her throat.

A gentle touch on her arm made her jump. She shrugged off the Guardian's hand and stalked a few steps away.

"My lady, I do this for love of my son. I was never able to show him my love before. But I…we can give him this. It is not too late for him." Her voice dropped to a whisper. "I know what it is to lose someone you love. I know it can shatter you. But you will survive it."

Arlana shook her head, sure she wouldn't.

"Arlana, for love of him, let him go. Give him a chance at real happiness."

The tears streaked unchecked down her face now. "I…I can't…" she stuttered. She sucked in a breath and tried to steady her voice and control the tears. "What if he refuses? What if he insists on staying?"

"He must obey you if you terminate his duty as First Protector. He must abide by your will in this matter. And after that, when he is no longer duty-bound to stay here, he will leave."

"How do you know?"

"I know my son. I know him better than he thinks I do."

Arlana took in another shaky breath and released it slowly through pursed lips. She scrubbed the tears from her face and continued to breathe slowly. When she felt like she had some semblance of control over her expression, she faced Catarin. "I have to think about this. I…" She bit her bottom lip hard to hold back her fresh surge of tears. "I don't want him to be…doomed to my life either." She held Catarin's gaze for a second before she swung away and walked stiffly toward the door. "I have to rest now. Send word when the preparations for our journey are complete." She cursed under her breath as a hiccup jerked from her.

"What will you do, Arlana?" Catarin's voice was unyielding.

"What I've always done." She paused with her hand on the door latch. "I'll do what I have to do." She pulled the door open and walked out, passing GeJarn without a word. She just made it to her rooms before her control broke and the sobs tore free.

***

Arlana was standing over a saddlebag, trying to remember what she was supposed to be doing with it, when she felt him come into the

336

room. She didn't have to turn around to know it was Oric. His hands dropped gently onto her shoulders and her entire body tensed. For just an instant, tears trembled, but she blinked them back and took a step away from his touch. She couldn't face him.

"Arlana? Are you all right?"

The soft question shattered her. She sucked in a breath. "Your… The Guardian thinks she knows why we're to meet the traveler. She thinks the three of us, using my power to fix the spell, will balance the orb. We'll replace the three magicians that died while the orb was being formed. Do you understand what that means?"

"I believe it means the orb will no longer be in danger of getting out of control."

She shook her head. "No, I mean do you understand what this means for me, for my life?"

*You don't mean you will have to lose your physical existence?*

The sharp note of fear in his mind made her flinch. "No." His relief washed over her. He was so open to her now, and she to him. She couldn't be near him without feeling his thoughts. It was more than she could bear. She built up a layer of mental barriers against him.

*Arlana?*

She held up a hand, stilling his question. How could she explain that it was killing her to feel how much he cared? "I won't lose my physical existence, Oric. But neither will it be mine to do with as I please. Do you understand? I'll be irrevocably tied to the orb forever. For as long as I live anyway. I'll never be free of it."

She felt the heat of his body just behind her and heard the soft jingle of the copper rings decorating his vest as he moved closer. The familiar scent of pinewood and musk swirled around her.

"I do not see this is much of a change, fayria. We have always known your life was tied to the orb."

"Oh, Oric." She sighed and pressed her palms against her stomach in a vain attempt to hold in the emotions threatening to break free of her control. "Can't you see? There's no hope now. Not even the chance that I can ever lead a normal life. I suppose I've always known. But a part of me has hoped…" She moved away from him again, toward the window. A soft breeze pulled in the scent of fresh summer flowers blooming on the balcony just outside her bedroom. She stared at the sunlight glinting off brass and gold rooftops, and her mind slid back to her fourteenth year.

"Once, when I was about fourteen, I ran away from home." She let her mind drift to the elation she'd felt, the freedom. "For three whole weeks, I was just me. No prophesies, no expectations—just me. I went into the woods north of Fordin. I kept myself shielded so my mother and Merig couldn't track me. I took a horse and a week's supply of travel rations, and I didn't look back. I'd realized with sharp clarity that year that I'd never have what others my age had. I'd never be able to have a normal life, a family of my own. So I ran away. I didn't want to be a child of destiny. I didn't want anything to do with my fate."

She listened to the sound of bells ringing from a nearby temple and smiled. "That was the best three weeks of my life. I wandered for most of the first week. Camping, hunting when I needed more food, riding whatever trail I happened upon, just existing from day to day. Then some time during the second week, I came across a cabin. It was small and tattered-looking, but a little line of gray smoke rose from the chimney and a heavenly smell of baking bread wafted out of the open door." Arlana closed her eyes. She could almost smell the bread and the musk of wood smoke again. The air had been damp and cool, the sky threatening rain most of the day. The sight of that little line of smoke and the scent of baking bread promised such comfort she couldn't have turned away if she'd wanted to.

"I knocked on the door, peeked inside, and was greeted by the happiest face I'd ever seen. She was a hundred years old if she was a day, her face so lined it was hard to tell her eyes from her mouth, but for the twinkle in one and the smile on the other. She looked up as if expecting me and said, 'Well, come on in. The bread's almost ready.' I ended up staying with her for almost two weeks."

"You stayed?"

Arlana smiled, letting the memory of that time ease her heart. "Yes. I didn't even think about it. As soon as I stepped through the door it was as if that was where I'd been going all along. She had a cot made up for me in one corner of the room. I helped her gather firewood and brought back fresh meat. She talked and told stories and made me laugh. I felt…I felt at ease for the first time in years. I felt like myself."

She turned away from the window and faced Oric without being able to meet his gaze. "After two weeks of this happiness, she woke me up one morning with my saddlebag packed. She said, 'It's time for you to go home now, Arlana. Your parents will be worried.' I tried to protest. I didn't want to go anywhere. I told her I'd send word to them, let them know I was okay. As long as I could stay. She smiled and shook her head, and I knew she was right. I couldn't stay. It wasn't my place. There were other things I had to do. I can still remember the look in her eyes when I realized this. I swear she must have read my mind.

"In the end, I left the cottage with a lighter heart. Despite not wanting to leave, I felt refreshed, like I could face whatever destiny would hand me. By the time I got home, I'd come to face my fate, to accept that my life would be dictated by a force beyond my control." She looked up then and met his gaze. "But I've never forgotten what it was like to be free, to lead a normal life. If I could have that again, I would."

Oric's smile was gentle and understanding. He took two steps closer, but she raised a hand to stop him.

He hesitated, eyes narrowing. "I understand, fayria. I would have the same, were it possible."

She choked on his quiet admission. All the pain she'd pushed behind memories burst through and a single tear escaped down her face. "That's just it, Oric," she murmured, forcing speech through her tight throat. "You *can* have freedom. You *can* have a normal life." She straightened her shoulders and firmed her voice. "When we've meet with the traveler and this situation with the orb is finished, you'll be released from your duty as First Protector."

"What?" His expression cleared of emotion as he stared.

"I'm releasing you, Oric. Your duty as First Protector is over. You're free."

He shook his head. "You cannot release me."

The lack of emotion in his face scared her and made her hurt more than if she could see what he was feeling. "Yes. I can. The Guardian told me I'm the only one who can."

"The Guardian told you? Was this her idea?"

"It doesn't matter. You've always wanted a normal life. We both know that. As long as you're duty-bound to me as First Protector, you'll never be able to have the freedom we both want."

"And what about us? I am more than just your First Protector now, Arlana." His voice dropped to a menacing whisper.

"I've just told you, Oric. I can't ever have a normal life. We can't have a normal life together. I'll always be bound by my duty and destiny. It doesn't have to be the same for you." Her voice broke on the last word. She bit back the sudden sob and pressed a hand to her lips.

He reached her before she had a chance to regain her control, his grip on her shoulders unyielding.

"You do not want to do this, Arlana. Any more than I want you to do it. I will not be released from you so easily."

"Oric, please. Don't make this any harder than it is. You're better off leaving here, leaving me. This is the only way I can give you what you've always wanted."

"What I want," he said, very quietly, his mouth dropped close enough to her face for his breath to brush her cheeks, "what I have wanted for a very long time now, is you."

She shook her head. "Staying with me will rob you of your chance at freedom. And sooner or later, you'll resent me for forcing you into my destiny."

"I have been forced into your destiny from the moment you were born. For most of my life, I did resent you. Then I met you. And I knew what I wanted in life. The way I felt about my own fate would never be the same."

"No. You say that now. But even after we met, I knew you didn't want the duty that bound you to my life. I care too much about you to force that on you now."

His arms dropped to his sides. The sudden loss of contact rocked Arlana on her heels. She took advantage of the moment and moved across the room to get beyond the heated feel of his body too near hers.

"Care for me?"

She whirled to face the quiet anger in his voice. His eyes were blue fire in a face gone stony.

"Is that all, Arlana? You care for me? So you will turn me away, despite what I may want. Is that how you show your feelings?"

"Do you think I want to do this?" she screamed, her control in tatters. "This is the hardest thing I've ever had to do! And you mock me for it?"

"If it is so hard, then don't do it. If you really care for me, you will not try to push me out of your life again."

"It's because I care for you that I do this. I can't doom you to my fate, Oric. Not when I know you'll hate me for it one day. I'd rather have your anger now than to have you despise me later."

"And you think I will not despise you for this?"

Her bottom lip began to tremble. "I do this for you," she whispered. "One of us should be free to live as we would choose and not as fate would choose for us. If you have to hate me now, you'll be grateful to me later. When you realize how close you came to being trapped, you'll thank me for this."

"Thank you? You think I should thank you for ripping my heart out and tearing it into pieces? You think I will be grateful for the void you will leave in me by doing this? You could not care for me and do this, Arlana."

"I do care for you!"

He was on her too fast for her to move away. "Do you?" *Do you really?*

His fingers dug into her biceps, but she flinched away from his angry words more than his grip. "How can you even ask that?"

*Because I am not seeing the actions of a woman who cares for a man. You send me away and call that compassion?*

The pain and anger and confusion in his mental voice raked across her soul.

"I love you," she whispered, meeting his gaze and facing his anger. "I love you so much." His grip began to relax and the hard lines in his face softened. She looked deep into those blue, blue eyes and felt a part of her die. "I love you so much I have to let you go. Because I love you. I release you of your duty as First Protector, Lord Commander

Oric of Czanri of Myseen of Browan. After we've met the traveler, you'll be free to go where you will. Your duty to me fulfilled."

She stepped away, straightened her shoulders and stared at the wall just beyond him.

"You will not change your mind?"

He said it as more a statement than a question. She couldn't answer past the lump in her throat so she let her silence answer for her.

The silence dragged on and on. Then Oric turned and left the room, calling over his shoulder, "The Guardian says all is ready for the journey. We will meet in the orb chamber in one hour. I suggest you finish your packing, my lady."

Arlana hoped the sound of her sob was hidden beneath the slamming of her door.

# Chapter Twenty-Eight

Tᴴʜᴇ clearing was exactly as she remembered it. The circle of oak trees, the strange anomalous energy coming from the direction of the cottage. Except this time, there were no soldiers for her to defend, no insane forest people trying to kill them all. No Pgar.

She left her small group to wander closer to the cottage, getting a better look at it than she'd been able to the last time. It was ordinary enough, made of ivy-covered stones, the roof thatched, the front door a solid-looking oak. Two uncovered windows peered out the front of the house, but they were too dark to give a view of the inside of the cottage. Against the wall, to one side of the door, sat a pile of wood for a fire. On the other side was a deep, wide wooden barrel for collecting rainwater. A single step led up to the door.

Arlana took a deep breath, tasting the mossy, earthy scent of the place on the back of her tongue. She could feel the gaze of her companions and turned to look at them over her shoulder. The GeMorin and the assassin both stood wary, their gazes scanning the forest in opposite directions before returning to her. The two had formed a strange bond on first meeting and had almost immediately fallen into acting as a team. The process of working with another seemed to ease some of GeJarn's solemn mood. Working to protect her did even more. She would have smiled but for the other two people standing in the middle of the oak ring.

The Guardian stood tense and clutched at the orb. Her eyes were huge, her face pale and sweat-dappled. The effort it took Arlana to build a gate of controlled strength without using a focus of any kind had caused a reaction in the orb. Catarin had used much of her strength to hold it under control. Now that they were so near the cottage, Arlana could feel the orb churning with anticipation. It pulsed and spun more irregularly than she'd seen it before. The strain it put on the Guardian wasn't helping their situation, but she didn't know how to get this across. If she opened her mind up to the orb, even a little, as she had just after arriving in the oak circle, the sorcerers yelled out an incomprehensible litany, too garbled and disjointed to be deciphered. She'd given up trying. Instead, Catarin had insisted she could hold the orb for now and Arlana should concentrate on the task ahead.

She still wasn't sure if that had been the right decision. As she watched Catarin struggling with the orb, she let just enough power twist out to touch the surface of it. It grabbed at her in response, but she held back, keeping its clutching at bay like she would have an overeager puppy looking for a treat. She used the tentative touch to augment Catarin's power, to stabilize the orb a bit more. The older woman nodded gratefully.

Only then did Arlana allow herself a moment to look at Oric. The First Protector stood silent and emotionless, his hand resting on the hilt of his sword. He wouldn't remember this place the way she did, wouldn't know the fear she felt just standing in this spot, knowing his life had been in her hands. She wondered if he felt the power coming from the cottage. Would he sense the same strangeness she did? Did he understand it any better? Goddess, but she wanted to talk to him. About the cottage, about her fears that she would fail. Her gaze glanced across his, and she turned away. She'd given up the right to turn to him for comfort. She knew she could never turn to him again, for anything. It was the right decision. The only thing to do. For him. Because she loved him.

Logic didn't make her ache less, though.

She forced her mind back to the cottage. She had a destiny to face. And when that was over… She'd concern herself with the rest of her life if she survived this.

Her back stiff, she walked to the cottage and pushed open the door. There was nothing but a table inside. A huge wooden table with dust thick enough to look like a blanket covering it. The huge hearth to the left of the room was empty, even of ashes. The back windows, looking out into the deeper quiet of the forest, were covered in a thin veil of dust. As Arlana looked around, she noticed a long shelf on the wall near the door, empty and dust-covered as well. There wasn't even a chair or bench. The cottage was made up of one large room. The area to the right was lowered and guttered for bringing cattle or horses inside during the winter, but there were no remaining bits of straw or hay in the room.

She looked up to the rafters, studied the back door. Nothing hinted that anyone had ever lived here. The strangest part was that no animals had moved in to take up the space. No nests hugged the rafters, no rodents skittered along the floor. There weren't even any bugs. The place looked as deserted and empty as any dwelling Arlana had ever seen.

And the feel of anomalous power was at its strongest here. It made the hair on her arms stand up. Yet she wasn't afraid. The brush of energy was more irritating than frightening. She sucked in a breath of dusty air and noticed at once the lack of mold or moss. No moisture seemed to have permeated the house. Another strange thing about the place. It was too dry and too empty to feel real.

The irritating rub of power against her skin finally drove her out of the cottage and back into the oak grove. Just beyond the ring of trees, GeJarn and Whypp had begun setting up a small camp. They were talking in quiet voices, seemingly undisturbed by the strange energy of the place. Catarin still stood in the center of the ring, clutching the orb, but her skin was no longer so waxy looking, her eyes no longer so panicky and drawn.

"Are you all right, Guardian?" Arlana asked in a quiet voice when she joined Catarin.

"I am managing. Thank you for your help earlier. It is…it is much harder to control here. It is reacting to the power coming from the cottage."

"I'll try to keep helping, but I'm going to need as much power and focus as I can manage to complete the spell. I won't be able to divert much attention to balancing the orb in a few hours." With the orb so near, it would take her most of the night just to safely pull in the necessary power for the spell.

"Of course. Do what you must."

Arlana frowned, turning to watch GeJarn and Whypp. "I think I'd better be alone for a few hours. I need to focus." She faced Catarin and tried a smile. "Will you let them know I'm not to be disturbed?"

She didn't need to specify who "they" were. Catarin nodded. Before she could move away, though, Catarin laid a gentle hand on her arm.

"You have done the right thing, my lady."

Arlana frowned. When Catarin flicked her gaze to Oric, where he hovered just at the edge of the oak ring, she understood. Her nod was curt. She walked away before the Guardian could see the tears pooling in her eyes. Outside the oak ring, Arlana wandered deeper into the woods. She extended her senses, looking for the forest people. They weren't anywhere near the campsite. With luck, they'd stay away until she'd completed her task.

She worked her way through a thick patch of trees until she found a convenient fallen log to sit on. She needed to think, needed to clear her mind. She'd done well to focus on the gating that morning. It had taken all her concentration and willpower to force down feelings and inner turmoil to gate them here safely. She'd need even more concentration to stop time. And she knew in her present state she was too upset, too emotional to succeed.

She closed her eyes, focused on her center of power and took a long, deep breath. On the exhalation, she concentrated on calming her mind, stilling her chaotic thoughts. After a moment, the sounds of birdsong twittered into her consciousness. She shifted and tried to refocus. A moment longer and the ruffling of leaves accompanied the scurry of small animal feet into her awareness. She rolled her head, heard her neck pop, and took another deep breath. For an instant, her mind went quiet. She sighed, then turned her focus on her magical center.

A breeze blew over her face, bringing with it the scent of wood smoke and leather. Arlana's heart danced, thumping faster. An image of black hair, seductive blue eyes and a firm mouth turned up in a mischievous grin. The touch of strong, sure fingers on her neck, her shoulders, caressing her breasts. The whisper of heated words into her mind, against her lips.

Her eyes popped open and she groaned. This wasn't working. How in the name of the Goddess was she supposed to focus when her mind kept wandering back to Oric? She shifted, straightened her back, squared her shoulders and closed her eyes again.

After a moment, her eyes snapped open and her shoulders slumped. "Damn it!"

"Is there a problem, my lady?"

Arlana's stomach dropped and her body tense. "I told the Guardian I wasn't to be disturbed." Her voice came out steady at least, but not as stern as she'd hoped.

"I didn't consult with the Guardian before seeking you out."

She heard him stepping closer, surprised and embarrassed that she hadn't heard him before he spoke. She could almost feel the heat of him. She shot up from the tree stump but didn't turn around. "What do you want, Oric? Is there a problem?"

"The only problem is you wandering off into the woods without an escort. This forest holds many dangers, not the least of which is the forest people. And it is still my duty to see to your safety. For the time being."

She didn't flinch at the shot, but she wanted to. "I need to be alone now. I have to focus myself for the spell tomorrow."

There was silence, long enough that she half turned to see if he'd left. He hadn't.

"I will leave you to concentrate," he said very quietly, "but there is something I must say first."

"Oric—"

He cut her off with a curt hand gesture. "It must be said now. You've had your chance, stated your position. Now I will explain mine." He took a deep breath. "When I was about twenty-four, I met a woman. I fell in love with her. Or so I thought at the time."

Arlana turned away and closed her eyes. She didn't want to hear this. Goddess, she didn't want to hear about this.

"I wanted to ask her to marry me. You would have been around fourteen at the time. The same year you ran away."

Arlana bit her lip to keep silent. When she didn't respond in any way, he went on.

"This woman, Gretta, was from a simple background. The necessary duties of my position required I associate with people of power and wealth. That way of life made her uncomfortable. She lived with it because she cared for me, but I always knew she wanted a quieter life. For a time, I hoped maybe I would be able to give her that life. But reality intruded, and I knew for certain I would never be able to live any other way than I was living.

"After one particularly difficult evening for her, I faced the fact that I could not marry her. I would never have been able to give her what she wanted, what she deserved. Bringing her into my life would have destroyed her, slowly but inevitably. After a long, sleepless night, I made my decision. And I had one more thing to resent you for. The next day, I ended our affair—for her sake."

Arlana sucked in air, clenched her hands together until her nails bit into her palms. Every word about this other woman, this woman he'd hoped to marry, was like an arrow in her. She clamped down hard on her emotions, but her throat closed up and her lips trembled. "Then you understand," she murmured, her voice thick and choked.

"I understand the reasoning."

She nodded and tried to force her voice to sound light and positive. "Perhaps, when I've released you, you can find her again. Without the difficulties of your duty, maybe…" She had to stop when her throat squeezed too tight for words to get through. Her heart hurt so much she was afraid it would constrict until she stopped breathing all together.

"She is married now," Oric said, his tone neutral. "She lives in the country with her farmer husband and three children. I bumped into her in the market six months before setting out to meet you. She was very happy with her life. When I walked away, I realized I hadn't felt even a hint of the old emotions. I was not jealous of her husband or the life he gave her. I was happy for her. That was all.

"That's when I knew, Arlana. I knew my life was linked to yours irrevocably. You were my obsession, my future, my life. Though I tried to deny it, at that moment, I knew deep in my soul you were my destiny. No other woman would ever be able to supplant you in my life."

Arlana pressed her fingers to her lips to keep from sobbing out loud. "You must have hated me," she whispered.

*No. I wanted to. I tried to. But I couldn't. I knew before we ever met that I would always be by your side. Now I understand why. And it is not because of my duty as First Protector.*

Arlana turned slowly to face him, her heart hammering. "Oric, I'm trying to do what's right for you. You have to understand."

He skirted around the tree stump, closed the space between them and gripped her shoulders, pulling her flush to his body. "All I understand, Arlana, all I have ever understood, is that I love you. I love you more than my life, more than I ever loved Gretta, more than anything. I will always love you, no matter what you try to do to me." *If you release me from my duty, I will find a way to stay in Czanri. If you try to have me banished, I will haunt the edges of the city. Wherever you are, I'll be there. You won't be able to ignore me, or forget me, or get me out of your life.* "I do not want a normal life, Arlana, if you are not in it. I do not want anything but you. And I would walk through fire, face all the gods in the heavens, sacrifice anything you asked to be with you."

He kissed her before she could protest, his mouth hard, demanding. Desperate. *You will never be rid of me, fayria. I love you too much to let you go.*

Tears flowed freely over her cheeks, mixing with his kiss, salting the exquisite flavor of his mouth. He wrapped his arms around her, as unyielding as rock, as gentle as a breeze. And she was lost.

He eased back just enough to look into her eyes. He wiped his thumb over her cheek, across her tears. "Do you love me, Arlana? Did you mean it when you said it this morning?"

She nodded, unable to speak aloud. *Yes, Oric. I meant it. I love you so much it hurts. But...*

He shook his head before she could say more. "That is all that matters, fayria." Cupping her cheek, he brushed her lips briefly with his. He stared down into her face for a long, quiet moment. Then he said, "I will be there when you finish tomorrow. We will decide where we go from there." He dropped his arms and stepped away. "I will leave you now to prepare. If you need me, call."

His face remained serious, intent as he studied hers. Then he turned and left, but he whispered one last comment into her mind.

*Be safe.*

Arlana's knees gave way and she dropped to the soft earth. She stayed that way for a long time.

# CHAPTER TWENTY-NINE

S he passed possibly the longest night she'd ever endured. As the sun rose, Arlana blinked at the pink horizon. The sky was cloudless through the tree branches, promising a warm, bright day.

And she was going to stop it.

She'd slept only a little, spending most of the evening and the cool night in meditation, preparing for the spell, pulling in the necessary power. She would stop time in one small space, with the help of the orb. By stopping a single instant in a confined space, she lessened the risk if something went wrong. The orb's power, combined with the guidance of the orb sorcerers, would allow her to focus on a specific instant in a specific place. Without them, she would have only been able to cast this spell in a broad, general way.

Of all the fears she'd struggled with through the night, her deepest was that she would miss the precise moment and the traveler would be gone. She had no idea what would happen then or how the orb might react. She was nervous enough about what would happen if she did succeed. To worry about what might happen if she failed was too overwhelming to consider. So she'd pushed those thoughts aside, leaving room only for confidence and concentration. She was born for this. She wouldn't have been born if she weren't capable of succeeding.

She would succeed.

She rose from the tree stump that had served as a meditation stool through the night. Stretching, she felt bones crack along her back and sighed at the release. Extending her senses, she noted the presence of the forest people, far enough away to be harmless, but still closer than they'd been all night. They were gathering to the cottage, their movements measured and cautious. A flash of chaotic mental noise gave away their fear, their awe. Even they knew something significant was to happen today. Little did they know she was planning on meeting their god in person.

Arlana glanced around the quiet forest, letting the sounds of morning bird song, the scent of mossy earth and oak, the feel of cool, damp air seep into her. She took a deep breath, let it out slowly. And the calm she'd worked all the night to gain flowed through her blood. Her heartbeat was slow and steady, her breathing deep and even, her mind focused and sharp. She took a few moments to savor the feeling of balance. Then she returned to the cottage and the rest of her group.

Wisps of gray smoke floated up from a small cooking fire as she neared the campsite. Whypp sat on a log next to the fire, poking the kindling with a stick. He looked up when she stepped up to the fire.

"Good morning, my lady."

"Good morning, Whypp. Did you sleep?"

"Some. You?"

"Some." She smiled and sat next to him.

"Are you ready then?"

"Yes."

"Are you afraid?"

"Not now." She glanced at him, but he kept his gaze on the fire. "Are you?"

His lips lifted. "No. It's hard to scare the likes of me, my lady. I know death's first name."

They sat in silence until the others joined them. Oric was first, the Guardian last. Arlana studied Catarin across the fire, frowning at her ashen appearance. The orb was pulsing in her hands, but it wasn't unusually misshapen. In fact, Arlana would swear it was more balanced than she'd ever seen it, with or without her help. She was still lending some strength to the balance, had opened herself to it at a level that wouldn't distract her concentration. But it shouldn't have been enough to balance it that much. And if it were more balanced, why did Catarin look so haggard?

"Did you sleep, Guardian?" Arlana asked, trying to keep the worry from her voice.

Catarin's smile was shaky and wry. "It was a troubled sleep, Prophesied One. I would not call it restful."

"Are you up to this, Guardian?" Oric asked quietly.

He was sitting beside his mother, and for the first time, Arlana noticed the many similarities in their features. Oric bore a striking resemblance to his mother when she took the time to notice it.

Catarin patted his leg. "I have to be up for this, don't I? Do not worry, my son. I'll be fine."

Oric placed a hand over his mother's and held her gaze for a quiet moment. It was the first time Arlana had ever seen them act like mother and son. A sudden sadness tightened her chest, but she forced it away, pulling her calm and focus around her as armor.

"Oric? How much time do we have left?"

His gaze turned inward, then he said, "Less than half an hour now. We should prepare."

Arlana nodded. "You should know the forest people are moving closer. They're close enough to attack now, though they seem to be holding off. You three should be prepared." She looked from Oric to Whypp to GeJarn, where he stood to one side of the fire. "Oric, can you protect them both from the mental attacks?"

"Yes. We'll be on guard, my lady."

"Okay." She turned to Catarin. "Shall we?"

Catarin nodded and stood with Oric's help.

Arlana and the Guardian went to take their places just at the door to the cottage. Arlana let the Guardian move ahead, staying back so she could talk with Oric. *She doesn't look well, Oric. This will be a strain on her.*

His nod was barely discernable. *She will do what she must. She has for more than two hundred years. And you? Are you truly ready?*

*Yes.* She faced him. *This will look odd to you and the others. You'll probably feel some of the resonance of the spell. It will appear as if the Guardian and I disappear, and then in the next instant, if all goes well, we'll be back. To you, only a second should pass. If the forest people do attack, you won't have to defend on your own for long.*

*I am not worried about the forest people.* He reached out and touched her cheek. *Only a second will pass? It will feel much longer, fayria.*

Arlana smiled and reached up to grasp his hand. Her grip tightened when she felt the gate forming.

She spun toward the oak ring in time to see the black, light-eating rectangle take shape. The bond that linked her to the orb pulled taut. And then he stepped through the gate.

"Pgar," she hissed, already forming a defensive shield around herself and her group. Whypp and GeJarn were at her side and Oric stood just in front and to the left of her by the time the sorcerer moved away from the gate. *Catarin, are you okay? How is the orb?* She didn't dare take her eyes off Pgar, but Catarin's gasp had been too sharp and loud to ignore.

*By the gods.*

The shock in the Guardian's voice nearly pulled Arlana's attention from the blood sorcerer.

"You are supposed to be dead," Catarin spat.

Arlana knew then her fears about Pgar were true. She tilted her head and studied his half-smile, half-leer. "Should I call you Gavin?" she murmured. His black eyes flickered, his upper lip twitched, the skin around his eyes pinched, but those were the only outward signs of strain.

"It hardly matters now, does it, Arlana? You will be calling me master before the day is out."

Oric took one step forward but was stopped by a cautioning hand from Whypp. Pgar barely glanced at him, though Arlana saw the rage spark in the depths of his eyes.

"You've found a way to be in the presence of the orb?" she said, diverting his attention back to her. She didn't want the sorcerer to focus his rage on Oric again.

"Strange, isn't it? The very link that binds you and me, the link you have been using to stabilize the orb, gives me added protection from its pull. You are giving me the ability to resist."

"I haven't been using the…" She stopped, realizing abruptly why the orb stabilized more when she opened to it. The link brought Pgar's power, his tie to the spell, into the mix and brought the orb that much closer to balance. Through her, the orb regained two of its missing elements instead of just one.

But with that, the orb should have been completely stabilized. The truth of that shocked her speechless. Only three of the original members of the spell were missing. Catarin had replaced the Guardian. Pgar, through her, had been brought back into the spell, and she replaced the sorcerer that had died after prophesying her part in all this. So why was the orb not fully stable? What was left to be done? Why did they still need to meet the traveler?

She didn't get the chance to voice any of these concerns aloud. From behind Pgar, through the still open gate, a dozen GeMorin warriors stepped out into the oak ring. They lined up behind Pgar and the gate collapsed.

"A small guard this time, Pgar," Arlana said, wariness replacing her moment of shock.

"They will be all I need." His look skimmed over her small group, contemptuous and dismissive. When he looked at GeJarn, however, the look turned to ice. "You have betrayed your blood oath, GeJarn. Your life is forfeit now."

Arlana started to speak out in the healer's defense, but GeJarn spoke first.

"If I had broken a valid blood oath, like the one I gave to the Lady Sorceress Arlana, then my life would be forfeit to my clan leader." GeJarn faced the GeMorin clan leader, dropped to one knee and bowed his head. "I would give you my reasoning, before you take my head, GeNol."

GeNol stepped forward, passing Pgar only when the sorcerer waved his consent. "Speak, traitor." GeNol's deep voice rolled through the oak ring like thunder. The blue tattoos of his position rippled with the flexing of his biceps.

GeJarn didn't raise his head as he spoke. "A blood oath, given by the clan leader in good faith, with the permission of the clan, binds us for life. We forfeit our heads if we so break this oath."

GeJarn's voice took on a rhythmic cadence as he spoke, a tone that reminded Arlana of a storyteller's voice.

"Only three things may sever this bond of blood. Death of the clan leader. Permission of the one to whom the oath was given." GeJarn looked up then and met GeNol's gaze. "And the use of deceit to forge the original bond."

GeNol's heavy brow ridges lowered over narrowed eyes, the only change in his expression. "Explain."

"The plague that brought us to near extinction, the plague that this sorcerer claims to have cured, the reason our ancestors first gave him our blood oath… It was a creation of the blood mage, cast upon us by his magic and ended when we were weakened, designed to gain our oath. He dealt us a dishonor. The blood oath is not valid."

GeNol turned very slowly to face Pgar. The GeMorin standing behind Pgar looked to one another, then took a single step forward, forming a semi-circle around the mage.

"Will you deny this charge?" GeNol asked.

Since first meeting the GeMorin, Arlana had never heard them address Pgar without calling him master. The epithet was obvious in its absence. Pgar must have noticed it as well. His black-eyed gaze bore into the GeMorin leader.

"You question me? On the word of a traitor?" He spoke so quietly it was difficult to hear.

"GeJarn, will you hand up your head to me if your claim is proved a lie?" GeNol didn't turn to look at the healer when he asked.

GeJarn stood, stepped within easy reach of GeNol's saber and pronounced a stream of guttural-sounding words that Arlana could only assume were in his own language. GeNol nodded, satisfied with whatever GeJarn had said.

"You understand the implication of what the healer has just said?"

Pgar nodded, quick and sharp. "I've heard the pact of soul-forfeit before. And so I ask simply for his proof. If he has none, then he has sacrificed his future lives for naught."

"GeJarn?" GeNol faced him, his hand on the hilt of his saber, and waited patiently.

Arlana found GeMorin expressions so difficult to read, it was hard to tell whether GeNol cared if the healer produced proof or not. He didn't seem concerned with the outcome.

"The proof comes from the Lady Sorceress's own vow. When I explained the circumstances behind the blood oath, she looked into Pgar's mind and found the memories of his deceit."

"Impossible!" Pgar shouted.

Arlana flinched at Pgar's outburst, but the GeMorin remained unmoving. GeJarn's focus shifted to the sorcerer. "You have never been able to read my thoughts, Blood Mage. For a very long time, we did not understand why. The Lady was able to explain to me that I had a natural gift, a gift you mistakenly assumed came from my abilities as a healer. I would probably have remained unaware of it, but for Lady Arlana's assistance."

Pgar snarled. "And what is this gift, traitor?"

"The gift of seeing. I can see things beyond my own experience, beyond my own existence. It is a rare trait among my kind. We've been so many generations without a seer that the signs and knowledge of the gift were all but forgotten. But the truth of this gift's existence in our clan is still in our oral history."

"What the hell is he talking about, GeNol?" Pgar demanded.

"It is said that seers are born into the clan when their presence is necessary for the clan's survival. It is thought that those born with this gift are old souls, nearing the final stages of their rebirths among the clan." GeNol looked GeJarn over. "There is a way for you to verify your gift."

GeJarn nodded. His gaze turned inward and his hands fell loose to his side. When his eyes opened again, he said something in his native language. GeNol's eyes flared wide and he unsheathed his saber. The other GeMorin followed GeNol, metal scraping against metal as a dozen sabers were pulled free. GeNol swung his weapon and settled the tip at Pgar's throat.

Arlana's gaze jerked from GeJarn to Pgar. The blood sorcerer had gone pale, but he didn't flinch away from the weapon's sharp point.

"He has given us the proof of his gift, Blood Mage. He has spoken ritual words, potent, magical words that would destroy the speaker if he were not truly gifted. This is not a thing that can be misinterpreted. GeJarn is a seer. As a seer, he would not have to take Lady Arlana's word concerning the fact of your deceit. He would see the truth of it for himself. How do you answer this charge? Do you deny his claim?"

Pgar glanced down at the saber and the weapon moved away despite GeNol's straining arm muscles. "Do not threaten me, GeNol. It would not go well for you and your clan to have me as an enemy."

Arlana watched the muscles along GeNol's back ripple as he fought for control of his saber. When he failed, he relaxed and let the weapon's deadly tip fall to the ground.

"I would not have you as enemy of my clan, but I will no longer have you as ally. Or master. The blood oath is broken." He said something in his native language, then moved away from the sorcerer. All of the GeMorin moved from their positions behind Pgar to flank their leader. Even GeJarn.

Pgar snarled viciously, but the GeMorin simply stared, expressionless as far as Arlana could tell.

"Seems you've lost your servants," Whypp said, leaning one shoulder casually against a tree. "Guess that means our little band now outnumbers you. Wouldn't put a bet on your chances now, Lord Sorcerer."

Pgar's glare turned to the assassin, but Arlana stopped his attack with a word. "Don't." When he faced her, she said, "He's under my protection. Don't think to harm him."

He looked back at Whypp. "Another time then, assassin. When you're not so protected."

Whypp smiled. "As you say, Lord Sorcerer."

Pgar snarled, took a step closer to the assassin and was stopped by Arlana's shield.

"Enough!" she said. "I don't have time for these games. Why are you here?"

"Isn't it obvious?" His glare moved past her to Catarin and the orb. "I've come to claim what is rightfully mine."

"How?"

"How?" He raised brows at her simple question. "I think the better question is, how will you stop me?"

She stared, never dropping her gaze. "I'll stop you. I have before. I will now. And you are decidedly outnumbered, as Whypp pointed out. You no longer have your GeMorin to help."

"We both know I don't need the GeMorin, Arlana. The orb is mine by right. I will take it back. The Guardian is too weak to protect it. And if she is killed, you will be too busy trying to control it to be able to stop me from doing whatever I please." His gaze skimmed over Oric. "To anyone I please."

"I've been threatened with this before, Pgar. I won't be any more lenient this time around."

"Lenient? You presumptuous insect! I have power you have yet to comprehend. I will not be so easy to stop this time."

A saber rested against Pgar's throat. "You will find this saber more difficult to deflect than GeNol's, Blood Mage," GeJarn growled from behind him. "I can block more than your telepathy. Not for long, maybe, but long enough to make sure you're cut wide open. It might kill me to do it, but believe me when I say I would take pleasure in the sacrifice."

"You gotta like these GeMorin," Whypp said.

Pgar glanced down at the saber, then back to Arlana. She could see the rebellion in his eyes. He'd fight her until it was too late for her to see her task done. He'd die in the effort and just as her death would affect the orb, so his death would have a disastrous affect on its stability. As she looked deep into his black eyes, she knew he understood this and would use it if he had to.

"Why?" she whispered. "Why would you risk all for this? The very existence of our world?"

"It is the ultimate power, Arlana. And it is within my grasp. Do you think I care who or what is destroyed in this war? I don't. Deaths are required to attain greatness. And I will be great, Arlana. I will possess the orb no matter how long it takes, and I will rule this small world."

Arlana sighed and shook her head. How could she reason with that logic, with a man so greedy for power he'd turned to blood magic, so hungry for control that he wanted to be a god? He would risk everything for power. She didn't understand it. She hoped she never would. "Leave, Pgar. You have no business here." She started to turn away.

"No! I will not allow you to destroy the orb!"

Arlana turned back, her mouth falling open. "I haven't come here to destroy the orb."

"No? You hope to." He moved forward, letting the saber at his throat push against his skin.

At a look from Arlana, GeJarn moved the weapon away.

"You think I can't read any of your thoughts through the link anymore," Pgar said, "but you're wrong. I can still sense some things."

His gaze flicked to Oric, then back to her. "You're hoping to dispose of the orb. Here. Now. I've felt the power you're pulling in. The very air twitches in anticipation of the spell you're getting ready to cast. I don't know what the spell is, Arlana, but I know you mean to dispose of the orb. And I won't allow it. The orb is mine!"

"You're wrong. Again. I haven't come here to destroy the orb. I don't think it's even possible."

"Ah, but we both know you're capable of things that aren't supposed to be possible."

"Why would you see it saved, Pgar? It'll do you no good. I'll never let you have it."

He smiled and Arlana felt her blood run cold.

"That is yet to be determined, lady."

*Fayria, the time draws near.*

Oric's voice whispering through her mind pulled her gaze to him. She blinked, then nodded. *Thank you.* "I'm afraid I no longer have time to argue this point with you, Pgar." She turned toward the cottage and Catarin. "Don't try to stop me."

"Why, Arlana?"

The challenge in his voice spun her around. But instead of the attack she'd expected, she got more questions.

"Why is time so important to the destruction of the orb? Why must it be done here? Why now?"

She was about to wave away his questions. She had to begin the spell and didn't have time for explanations, but then an idea dawned. "Do you really want to know?"

"Of course," he hissed.

"Very well. Then you shall see."

"Arlana!"

"Prophesied one!"

Oric and Catarin's protests came simultaneously. She raised a hand to quiet them. Her gaze locked with Pgar's. "Come closer, Pgar. You're about to watch me do something impossible. Again."

He snarled at the cockiness in her tone but didn't hesitate to move closer. When he stood before her, his gaze darted to Catarin and the orb. Sweat beaded on his brow and upper lip.

"Is it difficult to be this close to the orb, Pgar?" Her voice oozed sweetness.

"Not as difficult as it would have been without you. *Love.*"

Her humor was snuffed out beneath his taunt. "You'll have to get closer still, Pgar. Can you handle it?"

"Without trouble."

Arlana turned back toward Catarin. She felt the Guardian flinch when Pgar settled into position just the other side of Arlana. "The orb?" she asked under her breath.

"Is…pulling at him. But it is under control." Catarin's voice was ice.

*Fayria?*

Arlana turned at the sound of Oric's voice in her mind. The fear she felt from him wasn't even hinted at in his expression.

*Is it wise to bring him?*

*More than wise. His physical presence stabilizes the orb better than I could have done otherwise. The spell will be easier this way. Don't worry, Oric. All will be well.*

He nodded, his expression never changing. *I will signal when the precise moment occurs. I will see you in a moment, my love.*

*A second. No more.* She turned back to the door of the cottage. Catarin and the orb stood to one side of her, Pgar to the other. She pulled in the last of the power she required, settled it, calmed her mind and focused on her center. "I'll be drawing from both of you," she told the two beside her in a quiet, calm voice, "to stabilize the orb. And then to use it. Don't try to interfere with the spell or deflect me when I use your energy." She looked sideways at Pgar. "It will kill you if you do."

She turned her entire attention to the spell then. Focused, calm, her mind moved inward and she began to murmur the words that would stop time.

# CHAPTER THIRTY

Arlana had told Oric this would look strange to him and the others. She didn't realize how strange it would look to her. The area around the cottage faded away until all that was left was gray. Not the gray of storm clouds or fog, but a gray that was void of everything. The cottage, the focus of her spell, was the only solid thing remaining.

Heart thumping, Arlana took a deep breath and stepped through the cottage door. The Guardian and Pgar followed close behind. The inside of the cottage had changed. And yet it hadn't. One instant it appeared exactly as she'd seen it, dusty and unused. The next instant it was warmer, cleaner and filled with signs of daily life. The two images superimposed on one another, making her head ache with disorientation when she tried to sort them out. Instead, she ignored the odd nature of their surroundings and focused entirely on the man sitting at a small chair near the hearth.

He rose when they entered, said something in Browan and turned to face them.

Arlana had a split second of warning. She caught the orb just as it slipped from Catarin's hands. She wasn't fast enough to stop the Guardian's fall as she fainted. The stranger was. Catarin leaned forward against an invisible hand, her entire body limp, her eyes closed, her face so pale it was nearly transparent. The man moved close and took Catarin in his arms, disconnecting her from the invisible barrier that had cushioned her. He stroked a soothing hand over her hair and stared into her face for a long moment.

Again, he said something in Browan, looking up at Arlana as if for the answer to a question. She shook her head. "I don't speak Browan." At his frown, she said, "Pgar, tell him I don't speak his language because of the Browan custom."

When he didn't respond, Arlana turned to look at him. He was almost as pale as Catarin, his eyes so wide they bulged from his head. "Pgar?" He didn't even react to his name. He simply stared at the man holding Catarin. Slowly he started to shake his head. He started talking, low and fast, but he also spoke in Browan. Frustrated, Arlana closed her eyes, said a silent apology to Oric, and hoped the spell for language comprehension would work in this in-between-time place.

She opened her eyes again, relieved to be able to understand Pgar's litany. "You're dead. You died. You're dead. Even the orb couldn't find you. You're dead!"

He looked at Arlana, his entire body trembling. "You've killed us! You killed me!" He lunged toward her, slammed against her shield and fell backward onto the packed earth floor. He stayed there, the stunned shock on his face almost as surprising as his words.

"What the hell is he talking about?" she asked the air.

The stranger answered. "He's talking about me. I'm supposed to be dead."

She swung around to study him. The traveler. He was a tall, lanky man with long, sharp features that were both attractive and exotic. He had white hair and blue eyes. Without having to extend much, Arlana could tell he was a powerful sorcerer. Very powerful.

She frowned. "Traveler?" She gasped as the reactions of the other two finally made sense. "You're Owen! You're the one who was meant to be the Guardian."

The man smiled, charming and kind. "Yes. And you are a very bright woman…"

"Arlana. Lady Sorceress Arlana von Fordin of Fordin Barony of Karasnia."

"Karasnia? They've let an enemy into the country?"

"Our countries aren't at war now."

"Ah." He nodded, as if this explained something.

Catarin shifted and groaned in his arms. He lifted her easily and set her in the chair before the hearth.

"I suspect this was something of a shock to her." He caressed her cheek. "Gods, she's even more beautiful than I remembered." He looked back at Arlana and smiled. "And I've developed a very good memory in the last two hundred years."

"I have a lot of questions for you, Lord Sorcerer."

"Please, call me Owen. And I have a fair few questions for you as well, Lady Arlana. The first being, why did you not already speak my language? I assume you are working with these two." He glared at Pgar where he still sat stuttering on the floor, but his look softened when he glanced back at her. "And I see you have the orb. It is unbalanced?"

"Yes. I…we've been able to stabilize it some, but it's still not… right. Which is one of my questions for you. But first, I should tell you why I've been working with the…with Catarin. Pgar—Gavin as you'd know him—is not my ally. He's an enemy. But he's tied to the orb and so is part of this. I didn't speak your language because it's considered illegal now to allow someone from outside Browan to learn the Browan language. Out of deference to the people here, I never performed the language spell. Most either speak Karasnian or speak to me through a translator."

"Not allowed to teach the language? That happened after I…left. It wasn't a part of the time I entered either. Strange custom to develop."

"I think it started because of the orb."

Arlana took a deep breath and told Owen what she knew of the orb and of Browan now. How the emperor had been overthrown fifty years after Owen's supposed death and how a senate ruled Browan now. How Catarin had taken his place as Guardian. The fact that Gavin had also survived the chaos of the orb's formation and had been living in Bthak ever since. That the Sorcerer Derek had been killed by the formation of the orb but had survived long enough to direct them to the prophecy of her birth and to look to her for help with the orb. She explained that she'd only just come to Browan in the last few months and was still learning about the orb. And that she'd used it to stop time, to stop the moment when their two times met.

"This explains a lot, Lady Arlana. I've felt, for a long time, that this moment was coming. But I didn't know what to expect of the moment. The last thing I expected was to see three people walk through my cottage door and stay there."

"Stay there?" She moved to the small table and sat, resting the orb delicately on the wooden surface.

"I'll explain more after you've finished, but it has to do with the way I encounter the physical aspects of your plane of existence while I move backward through time."

Since she was anxious to hear his explanation, she finished her story as quickly as she could. She tried to remember everything, to tell him anything that might be significant. He took all of the news in stride, seeming to know some of the background. Other bits of information seemed to clarify something for him. But nothing surprised him, or provoked much of an emotional response, until she mentioned Oric and Hilda.

"Who was their father?"

His knuckles had turned white where he gripped the tall back of the chair he'd placed Catarin in.

"They had two different fathers. She was directed to both by a vision."

He nodded and sucked in a breath. "So she didn't form a life bond with either man? She didn't…"

Arlana smiled, amazed at the cause of his distress after two hundred years away from Catarin. "No. She hasn't had any mate, life-bonded or otherwise, since you…as far as I know."

"She told you about me?" His white-knuckled grip relaxed.

"Yes. Some. Not everything. I guessed the rest."

He looked down at the top of Catarin's head. "I told myself if she survived it was only right that she find another lover eventually. And I had no right to be jealous if she did." His smile turned wry. "I suppose I wasn't listening to myself very well." He stroked a finger over her temple. "Guardian?" he murmured. "That must have been so difficult for you. You were so young, and not nearly powerful enough for the burden."

Pgar made a guttural sound, pulling their attention away from Catarin. Arlana turned to watch him staggering up from the floor. She was shocked to see his hair now white. When he looked up, his eyes were also a startling blue. She frowned, not sure why she was surprised to see he'd used a spell this whole time to change his hair and eye color. The change made his appearance no less frightening.

Her frown deepened. This was the first reaction she'd seen from Pgar for what seemed a long time. She couldn't actually feel time passing, though. Her story must have taken awhile to tell, yet Catarin was still unconscious and Pgar was only now beginning to move. The blood sorcerer she'd known all her life, the man with black eyes and black hair, wouldn't be shocked speechless for this long just by the sight of an old enemy. But he'd never even tried to interrupt her. She couldn't begin to imagine why he'd let the spell coloring his hair and eyes drop either. Except that perhaps this was how he preferred to face Owen.

She watched him warily as he steadied himself, then glared across the cottage at Owen.

"How did you survive?" he snarled. "Where did you survive?"

"I could ask you the same, Gavin." Owen shifted so he stood in front of Catarin, blocking her from Pgar's view. "I was flung forward in time when the orb spell finished in that chaos you created. My entire being was altered so that I moved backward through time, at odds with everything around me. My only consolation in all this was that I believed you dead. I'm sorry I was mistaken in this."

"You're not the only one. I believed you dead too when I couldn't locate your mind anywhere in this part of the world."

"Locate my mind?"

Pgar ignored the question. His now blue eyes darted to Catarin. "She thought you were dead too, you know. She lived as if you had died."

"If you think you can taunt me with jealousy the way you used to, you're wrong. Two hundred years is a long time to learn from your mistakes. And to grow out of your youthful passions."

Despite his words, Owen reached a hand back to rest possessively on Catarin's slumped shoulder. Pgar followed the move and he smirked.

"You're as full of meaningless rhetoric now as you were then,

Owen. And no more the wiser for your travels, I'll bet."

When Owen took a step closer to Pgar, Arlana rose from the table and moved between the two men. "No fighting. It would disrupt my spell and kill us all. I won't allow it."

Pgar mumbled something distinctly unflattering under his breath, but stalked away to the opposite side of the cottage. Owen moved back to Catarin's side. Arlana picked up the orb again—just in case.

"Good. Now, Owen, before Pgar…Gavin does something stupid, you should know that there was another side effect of the orb's formation. It ripped open the minds of everyone within its range at formation. Because of that, all Browans now possess some degree of telepathy. Some are stronger than others. Gavin is quite strong. I'm very strong—though my gift doesn't come from the orb. Oric, Catarin's son, is probably the strongest telepath ever born. He's the one who's heard your approach for years."

"Heard my approach? Fascinating. I'd love to talk with this man." He looked around the cottage. "I suppose that will be impossible." His sigh was resigned.

"I'm not so sure. First, you need to explain some things to me, about moving backward through time, about what you've learned in the last two hundred years." She looked down at the orb, still pulsing and not quite stable in her hands. "Because I still don't know exactly why I'm here. They insisted—the orb sorcerers—but…"

At Owen's wide-eyed stare and Pgar's curse, she explained that the sorcerers were still somewhat conscious and cognizant. Though they had trouble with control, they were capable of communication. But only with a strong telepath. "Catarin never heard them. But then, neither did Oric until after they started talking to me. I've been tied to the orb since my birth, so it knew me when I arrived. I must have triggered the reaction that started their efforts to communicate." She met Owen's gaze and smiled a bit bashfully. "I suppose I left a few things out of my tale."

"Yes." His brows dipped, his mouth curved in a half frown that was almost a smile. His eyes widened again, suddenly. "Gavin, can you read my thoughts?"

Pgar smirked. "Ever since arriving. And they're as boring as ever."

"As ever? You mean to say you've always been capable of this?"

The blood mage's eyes darted to Arlana, then back to Owen. "The…accident with the orb made my skills stronger. But yes. I've always had this ability."

Owen started to pace in front of the hearth. "That would explain it then," he muttered, ignoring Arlana's and Pgar's stares.

"Explain what?" she asked after he'd crossed in front of the hearth at least twenty times without explaining.

He looked up as if surprised to see them, then he relaxed. "I'm sorry. I'm not used to having people to talk with anymore. I tend to go into my own thoughts." He made a vague gesture toward Pgar. "But you see, I didn't know this when we were creating the spell. It was an unknown element not accounted for." He began pacing again. "I don't think it would have altered the outcome too much, except that the spell was disrupted. The tie to Gavin, his telepathy an unknown element in the spell, must have been what caused the opening of telepathy among the Browans." He stopped. "Why just Browan? This didn't spread into Karasnia or Bthak?"

Arlana shook her head.

"I stopped it as much as I could."

The quiet sound of Catarin's voice swung Owen around. He dropped to his knees beside her, cupping her cheek in one hand.

"I couldn't completely contain it," she said, gripping his hand and speaking in an urgent, hurried voice. "I did try, Owen, I swear it. I managed to keep it within the borders, to keep it that contained. But it was as much as I could do."

"You did very well, my love. Very well." He studied her face, ran his hands over her cheeks, into her hair. "I can hardly believe I'm seeing you again. I was afraid…afraid you'd been killed."

"I thought you were dead too." Her eyes widened. "By the gods," she breathed. "Owen." She threw herself into his waiting arms and clung to him, her hands running over his shoulders and into his hair.

Arlana smiled and dropped her gaze to the floor to give them some semblance of privacy.

Pgar raised his brows. "You find this charming, do you, Arlana?" he muttered in Karasnian.

*Yes.* She met his mocking gaze. *I find it very charming.*

He grunted in disgust and turned away.

After awhile, Catarin pulled back from Owen and looked around the cottage. "What's happened?"

"We were just discussing that. Lady Arlana was telling me of some of the side effects of the disruption in the orb spell."

Catarin nodded, but her gaze darted to Pgar. "And what of him?"

Pgar spun around and snarled. "What of me? What of me? Do you think your lover is now going to dispose of me for you? I'm not so easy to get rid of, Catarin. You should know that already."

She looked away, her mouth forming a hard line.

Owen cupped her cheek. "We still haven't decided what's to be done about anything, love. Lady Arlana still doesn't know what brought you all here to begin with."

"The orb sorcerers insisted."

"Yes, but why?" He turned from his crouched position next to Catarin to look at Arlana and the orb. "Do they speak to you now? Can they explain what this is all about?"

Arlana focused on the orb, but the sorcerers were strangely quiet. She looked back at Owen and shook her head. "Perhaps if you tell us more about your experience."

He shrugged. "There is really very little to tell considering the time lapse. I've spent most of that time secluded here in the woods. When I first arrived in the future, I was so disoriented that I wandered for days, a babbling idiot. After a while, when I could think coherently again, I started to notice the strangeness around me. People didn't seem to see me, and I had trouble seeing them. I would walk up to someone, there would be a moment when our gazes met and there was acknowledgement of another presence, and then the moment would pass and they would walk through me, or disappear before me. As I came to notice this oddity, I started to fall back into madness. People appeared to be walking backward sometimes, or simply disappearing, the days felt strange, the flowers grew back to seed from bloom. I was staring at a clock for hours before it came to me what had happened."

"A clock?"

"A mechanical marker of time. Quite ingenious. But it took me a very long time to realize that, in relation to me, the clock was moving backward. That's when I realized the disruption in the orb spell must have…altered the way I moved through time. I presumed I was in the future because of the differences in Czanri. It is, you say, some two hundred years since the orb disaster. So I must have been flung more than four hundred years into the future. I've been able to mark time by counting days and years. Even in reverse, I still experience a day and a night. So I know I've been moving through time this way for more than two hundred years."

"How did you come to be living in the forest?" Arlana moved back to the table bench and sat.

"Once I discovered my predicament, all of the oddities around me made more sense. I stayed among people for perhaps a year, learning what I could of their society. But the difficulty of walking among those moving in a different timeframe grew too disturbing. I had to move where I wouldn't encounter so many people. So I moved here. I remembered this cottage had existed in the forest, but when I found the spot, the cottage had been reduced to rubble. So I rebuilt it in that future time."

"It's moving backward in time with you." Arlana's mouth gaped at the strangeness of that. But it helped explain the anomalous energy surrounding the cottage.

He nodded. "I found, after a while, that although I couldn't control my movement through time, I could influence a small space around me through a variation on the orb spell. So I set up an area of space—this cottage—to move with me. Otherwise, I would lay a stone one moment and the next it would be where it started. Very disheartening."

Arlana exhaled. "That must have been very difficult for you. Weren't you lonely?"

"Of course. But better lonely than mad."

Catarin laid a hand on Owen's arm and squeezed. "Perhaps this is why we're here, my lady," she whispered, keeping her gaze locked on Owen's. "To bring him back into our timeline."

"That's ludicrous!"

Pgar's shouted exclamation made Arlana jump.

"Why would a prophecy more than a thousand years old bring about the birth of someone like Arlana merely to bring this one man back? Power like hers could not come about for something so… unimportant."

"Unimportant to you maybe," Catarin hissed. "That doesn't mean it's not important."

Arlana raised a hand when Pgar opened his mouth to retort.

"Enough." She turned to Catarin. "Guardian, while bringing Owen back into our timeline may be a side effect of all this, I doubt it's the entire reason for my being here." She stood and raised the orb to eye level, studying it. "But for the life of me, I can't understand why else they want us here."

Owen rose from his crouched position. "You said it isn't stable yet, despite the replacement of the three missing elements. Or at least, the use of suitable substitutes. Maybe the key is in that. Maybe the orb requires me back as Guardian in order to stabilize."

Arlana looked past Owen to Catarin.

"I am weak, my lady," Catarin said. "I can't really control it anymore. If not for your help, it would have killed me very soon and with my death, the destruction of the world as the orb broke free of all control."

"But with my help, the orb is still controlled."

"You were still not part of the original spell. Owen was. He would be the best to replace me as Guardian. Perhaps only someone with your power could stop two separate timelines long enough to reclaim Owen. Maybe that would provide the orb with the balance it needs, and prevent the possibility of it ever going out of control again."

"You're assuming," Pgar said, "that I'll allow it to continue to feed off me through Arlana."

"I don't think you have much choice, Gavin," Catarin said.

"You underestimate me, Catarin. You always did. Everyone always did." His voice dropped. "I have more power, more skill than you can imagine." He looked at Owen. "I haven't simply been counting time over the last two centuries. I've learned more, grown more powerful, studied and trained. You couldn't stop me so easily now. Either of you."

"But I can." Arlana's simple statement snapped his head around, focusing his glare on her.

"You're still young and there's a lot you don't know."

He paced closer, stopping when he was near enough to brush against the orb. She noticed for the first time that he didn't find the proximity difficult. She sucked in a breath. Pgar's lips curved up.

"I would have taught you so much," he said. "I would have given you everything."

"I never wanted your everything, Pgar."

He shook his head. "Young. And stupid." He glanced down at the orb. "They've gone quiet? They don't pull at me now." He reached out and gripped the back of her neck. "The laws of our world don't work the same in this in-between time. Have you noticed? You'd find it more difficult to stop me here and still maintain this moment of frozen time."

A large, long-fingered hand dropped onto Pgar's shoulder. "I wouldn't find it so difficult, Gavin." Owen spun the blood sorcerer around, forcing him away from Arlana. "I haven't spent the last two hundred years counting time either."

The two men glowered at each other. The hair on Arlana's arms rose with the building of power. "Stop! I told you already, if you fight here, it might kill us all."

"It would be worth the sacrifice," Pgar growled.

Catarin launched out of her chair toward Owen.

He raised a hand and gestured her away. "This has been a long time in coming, Catarin. Gavin and I must settle our differences."

"Would you kill us all, destroy the orb, to do it?"

Owen didn't glance in her direction. He kept his gaze on Pgar. "I wouldn't mind destroying that damned orb after all the damage it's done."

"I would rather the orb not be destroyed," Pgar said. "But I also won't allow you to control it, Owen. Not you."

The first shock of power came from Pgar. It hit Owen's defensive shield and ricocheted around the room in a dangerous arc. Arlana stopped the bolt with an encompassing shield that forced the energy into the ground.

"Damn you both," she roared, fear slicing through her chest. "Stop this nonsense now!" But she could see her words weren't getting through to either man. Another attack, another defense and the very air shuddered. Arlana raised a hand to stop them, then realized that by casting another spell, she'd only make things worse. Panic bubbled into her system. She and Catarin exchanged a frantic, helpless look as another attack shimmered through the room.

For the first time since entering this in-between time, the orb came alive in Arlana's hands, pulsing more wildly than before, its shape distorting. Around them, the cottage walls began to blur, fading in and out of existence, showing only the gray nothingness beyond. The few furnishings in the room started to distort, like melting candle wax one moment, then hard, misshapen steel the next. The ground beneath them rolled, but the two sorcerers never broke eye contact, never slowed their fight.

Catarin stumbled close to Arlana. "Prophesied one! You have to stop them. They'll destroy each other this time."

"If I try to use a magical attack to stop them, I'll only make matters worse."

Catarin's gaze dropped to the orb. "Something is wrong with it."

"The spell I've cast is starting to fray at the edges."

"No. There is something else. Can you speak to the sorcerers now?"

Arlana closed her eyes and tried to focus on the orb and not on the nausea rolling in her stomach as she tried to keep control of the time spell. She came up against a wall of such silence it was near deafening.

And then she heard the chanting. It started low, in the very depths of the orb, a rumbling sound of power. Underneath the chanting she heard voices, trying to tell her something. She listened, strained. And then she heard it.

"They're going to try to pull him back in," Arlana breathed, her gaze darting to the two dueling sorcerers.

"What? Who? Which one?" Catarin's voice rose with each word. "Why?"

"To stop the fight, to keep them from destroying it." She turned to look at Catarin, her pulse pounding. "It's the reason they brought us here. This whole time, they've wanted him, needed him back."

Catarin's mouth rounded in an "O". She shook her head. But before she could voice her denials, the house around them shook so violently it drove Arlana against the table and Catarin to the ground. Arlana screamed as pain seared through her, dropping her to her knees. Catarin crawled to her and tried to lift her by her arms. Arlana screamed again.

"Lady! Lady, what is it?"

Catarin was shouting in her face, but Arlana could barely hear her over the roaring in her ears. "The spell. It's tearing apart. Oh Goddess, I can't hold it much longer."

She doubled over as searing hot pain raced through her once more, stealing her breath. She clung to the orb, folding around it until it rested against her stomach. She turned her focus completely over to the orb, to controlling the spell. The orb sorcerers continued to chant at the back of her consciousness, pain fired her muscles and she could barely feel Catarin's grip on her shoulders. She sent up a silent, desperate prayer to the Goddess that she'd be able to hang on, to control the spell long enough to end it. As tears streaked down her face, she began to mouth the words to restart time.

# CHAPTER THIRTY-ONE

Oric watched, his gut knotted into a hard ball, as Arlana, the Guardian and Pgar seemed to disappear. He could still see the cabin, but it was blurred at the edges, as if it was an illusion and not a stone and mortar building. He tried to swallow but his mouth had gone dry. Only a second. That was all. Only a second.

It seemed like the longest second of his life. And then he felt the change. His sense of time blurred. For the first time ever, he couldn't pinpoint the moment. It felt almost like two different moments were overlapping one another. Then the walls of the cottage started to tremble and the blurred edges got fuzzier.

"Something's wrong." He barely realized he'd spoken out loud. He stepped forward, and suddenly he felt time again, as it should be. And two seconds had passed. He stared at the cottage. Fear knifed into his gut and stole his breath. No. Gods, no. He couldn't drag his gaze away. There was no movement from within the cottage, no sign that they were alive.

He was on the balls of his feet, ready to run into the little building, when the walls exploded outward. He hit the ground hard, the air forced from his lungs in a painful grunt. Stone debris and shards of wood arrowed through the air over his head. And then it was over.

He lay silent, listening for the sounds of… He wasn't sure. Death. Slowly, he raised his head. Terrified to look, more afraid not to, his gaze swept over the debris littering the forest floor toward the place where the cottage had been. His heart squeezed so tight he wondered how he could still be alive. If Arlana were dead, he doubted he'd be able to live too much longer.

A plume of gray dust filled the air where the cottage had been. He held his breath, felt time moving normally again. Even in the area of the cottage. *Arlana?* He almost pulled back the question, almost couldn't bring himself to send a thought out. When nothing but silence came back, he felt his world begin to crumble.

He was staring into the gray dust, his vision blurred by tears, when a shadowy figure appeared. He watched, unable to move, unable to breathe. His fingers dug into the soft mossy ground.

She stumbled out of the dust, staggered a few steps and dropped to her knees. When she looked up, she looked right into his eyes. And Oric felt like he'd been touched by a piece of heaven. He pushed to his feet, tripped on his way over to her and collapsed on the ground at her side. "You're alive." He ran his hands through her hair, over her face, across her shoulders. "Are you hurt? I felt the spell go wrong." He cupped her cheeks in both hands and lifted her face until their gazes met. "Are you all right, fayria?"

Arlana nodded and gave him a weary smile. It was all he needed. He kissed her. Gentle. Tender. Passionate. Then he pulled her into his arms and held her close, promising himself he'd never let her go again.

"What happened?" he murmured, stroking a soothing hand along her spine.

"The traveler was the sorcerer Owen, the one originally intended to be the Guardian. He and Pgar…Gavin, fought. That's what disrupted my spell."

"And the others? The orb?" He looked over the top of her head as two more shadows emerged from the choking gray dust. When Arlana shifted in his arms, he dropped his gaze.

Her hand lay open in her lap, and in the center of her palm sat a small gold ball, no bigger than the size of a rosebud. He stared at it for a moment before he realized. "The orb?"

She nodded.

"But…how?"

She raised her head. Her eyes were red-rimmed but dry. "They wanted Gavin back. They wanted the real Guardian back. They've got them both now."

Oric frowned. He looked up at the sound of footsteps nearby. The man was a stranger, but he was holding Catarin's hand. Oric's frown deepened as he studied the man—tall, lanky, but muscled, roughly kept white hair, long narrow features, sharp, intelligent blue eyes.

"You must be Owen," Oric said to him in Browan. The man bowed his head in greeting.

"And you must be Oric." Owen's glance moved between Catarin and Oric. "You look a lot like your mother."

Oric continued to frown as he got to his feet, helping Arlana to stand with a steadying hand. She still held the orb on her open palm, staring at it.

"Perhaps one of you should explain what's happened." He directed the comment to Owen and his mother, in Browan, but it was Arlana that answered.

"The orb sorcerers pulled Gavin…" She looked up. "Pgar back into the orb. While he was distracted by the fight with Owen, the orb sorcerers started the spell to bring him back into his original position inside the orb. Unfortunately, both the fight and the orb's spell raged against my…" She stopped, cocking her head to one side. "What?"

His shock must have been plain on his face. "You're speaking Browan, Arlana," he murmured, half afraid someone who was not a friend would overhear.

"Oh, yes. Sorry. I had to use the language spell."

She continued speaking in Browan, much to Oric's growing distress.

"Owen doesn't speak Karasnian. He didn't even know about the ban on teaching Browan to outsiders. I didn't have time to explain and neither Pgar nor Catarin were in any condition to translate for me just after we arrived." She switched back to Karasnian. "I don't think it will matter much now. But if it will make you more comfortable, I can pretend not to understand Browan. And I won't use it after today."

"Perhaps this will help," Owen said, switching to Karasnian.

Unaccented Karasnian, just as Arlana's Browan was unaccented.

At Oric's glare, he said, "I've just performed the same spell that gave Arlana the ability to use Browan. I can speak in Karasnian now if that will help."

Oric grunted, nodded his head and turned his attention back to Arlana. His lips lifted in a wry half-smile. *Ferdinand would be disappointed to lose his post as your official translator.* At her relieved grin, he said aloud, "Finish your story, fayria." His mother stiffened, sucking in a sharp breath, but Oric ignored it.

After a darting glance, so did Arlana. "There's not much more to it. As far as I know. Gavin is now part of the orb. And I think they've reclaimed Owen as the Guardian."

"They have," Owen said. "Despite my lack of participation in the process. Since I was already tied to the spell, I assume it didn't take my conscious efforts to return me to my original position, just as they could pull Gavin back without his consent."

Owen's gaze turned thoughtful, speculative.

"What of my mother then?"

"Catarin is still tied to the orb," Arlana said. "She replaces the dead sorcerer. But as she's the only element not of the original spell, the orb is almost completely stabilized. At least as stable as it will ever be." Her gaze dropped to the orb again.

"And now that I am no longer trying to control the orb, my waning strength should return," Catarin said.

"It should do more than return, my love. You should be a stronger magician now than you ever were before, because of your tie to the orb."

Owen reached out and pushed a lock of hair behind Catarin's ear. Oric scowled. His mother blushed. She actually blushed.

Before he could absorb this strange new view of his mother, a deep rumbling started at the very edge of his telepathic senses. His gaze darted to the orb. It pulsed in Arlana's palm, but unlike before, its shape didn't distort or twist. GeJarn and Whypp cautiously joined them, both their gazes locked onto the orb. The remaining GeMorin, who'd come up to circle them, dropped to their knees and bowed their heads. Even GeNol. Oric looked around. Just beyond the GeMorin circle, the forest people stood, staring and silent, the chaos that marked their thoughts unusually calm.

"What is it?" Oric asked.

The answer came from a very unexpected source.

"We are whole…"

The voice, or voices, rose up out of the depths of the orb, more collected and cohesive than Oric had heard them before. There was one sound, one real voice, but it was subtly made up of many voices.

And this time, they spoke aloud, not just through telepathy. Everyone in the vicinity heard them.

"We are whole," the orb repeated. "As whole as we will ever be. Our thanks, prophesied one."

"How?" she whispered, her voice breaking before she could say more than the single word.

"Gavin. He is with us now."

"Is he…?"

"He is as he was meant to be. He is one with us. His talent, though not a conscious part of the spell, was a part of it nonetheless. We were meant to have it, in order to communicate. Now we can. The Guardian does not have telepathy. He will find our new voice easier to understand as well."

There was something like humor in the orb's voice, but it was hard to tell amid the strange echo following it.

"Now what?" Arlana looked up when she asked, her gaze wide. "Was this the reason I was born? The entire reason for my existence, a thousand-year-old prophecy? To bring you balance, to return Gavin and Owen to you?"

The orb was silent for a moment, its gold color pulsing, ribbons of midnight blue and deep purple racing over its surface. Finally, it answered. "As we now are, we see much. We see the future time that is, the future time that can be, the past as it was and could be. We know more of paradoxes. And we see the possibilities. But the decision is yours."

"What decision? I don't understand."

"'She will hold the fate of the world in the palm of her hand.'"

The orb's quote from the prophecy drew everyone's gaze to Arlana's palm and the small glowing ball in its center.

"You have a choice. It is yours to make."

"What choice?" Arlana begged. "What am I supposed to choose between?" And then she was silent, her gaze focused inward, as if listening, or watching something. She frowned, shook her head. Then her eyes widened. "I see."

She looked back at the others, her expression clearing. "I must choose whether I will send Owen, Catarin and the orb into the past, to make sure certain elements are put in place so this timeline proceeds as we have perceived it. Or," she dropped her gaze, "I can destroy the orb."

Owen sucked in a breath. Oric cursed, low and quiet. Catarin's eyes widened. The others exchanged nervous, edgy looks.

"Can you do that?" Oric asked. "Can you destroy the orb?"

"I'm the only one who can." Her eyes were pinched and her mouth drawn into a tight line. "I hold the fate of the world in the palm of my hand. If I destroy the orb, the timeline as we know it will no longer exist. Things will change, though not even the orb can predict exactly how or to what extent. They may change for the better. The power of the orb is so great that it's dangerous for it to exist. There will always be those like Pgar who would seek to control it for their own gain.

"But if I destroy it, the prophecy of my birth will never be given to the world. And I'll probably no longer exist as I am now. Though the orb says that's not a certainty. I may be exactly as I am, but my gifts would never have been prophesied and my journey here wouldn't have happened." She frowned and her voice dropped to a quiet murmur, as if she were talking to herself. "The orb may still be formed in the past. If I destroy it now, there will be no reason for the Browans to search me out and it could well lead to the destruction of the world anyway. But is allowing the orb to exist now any less dangerous? The world survives for at least another two hundred years. But what after that? The orb could still be taken and used to alter this timeline to the detriment of everyone."

Oric placed a hand on her arm to draw her attention. "I would this timeline continued as it is, my lady. If we cannot predict the changes, wouldn't it be best to leave things as they are?" *Besides, I do not want to lose you to a time paradox, fayria.*

*But what of the world, Oric? This isn't about what either of us wants. It's about what's best.*

*Your own logic is telling you what is best. We know you've succeeded in preventing the orb from going out of control and destroying the world in this timeline. It is, I think, better to go with the present we know and understand, than to alter existence in a way that we can't predict.*

She sighed. *I feel the same. But I wasn't sure if I felt that way because it was right.* She looked into his eyes. *Or because I didn't want to lose you.*

Oric cupped her cheek, running his thumb across the smooth skin over her cheekbone. *You will do what is right, fayria. You always do.*

*You'll lose your mother, Oric. If I choose to preserve this time, I'll have to send both Owen and your mother back in time with the orb. She's the prophet who foretells my coming.*

He studied his mother. She stood with her hand still firmly clasped in Owen's. She looked more…content. More at ease than he'd ever seen her. She looked younger too. *She will be happiest with him, won't she?*

Arlana nodded. *They were lovers before the orb accident separated them. Catarin said they'd have been life-mated. I think they already are.*

*She was always more the Guardian to me than my mother. I would see her happy. And I will enjoy knowing that she is happy, somewhere.*

Arlana smiled, rubbed her cheek against his hand, then stepped away. She faced Owen and Catarin. "Would you be prepared to do as I decide? To take up the task I'll give you to preserve this timeline?"

Oric watched his mother exchange a glance with Owen.

Owen smiled and faced Arlana. "I've been disconnected from my own time for too long to return now, my lady. If I could have Catarin by my side, I would travel to any place, any time you sent me."

Catarin's smile glowed beneath the shadowed forest canopy. "I will go where you send as well, prophesied one. As you see fit."

"I'm glad to hear it." Arlana handed the orb to Owen, placing it gently in his hand. "This cottage must be rebuilt, to move forward in time. It will give you a familiar place to live. The orb will guide you in the rest, to make sure you complete the necessary tasks to keep this timeline intact." She placed her hand over Owen's, covering the orb. "But before you leave, I'd like to heal one of Browan's wounds." She closed her eyes.

The silence that followed made Oric's skin tingle. GeJarn knelt with the other GeMorin now. Whypp hovered near the edge of their line, his gaze darting from the forest people, who were still strangely quiet, to the sorcerers at the center of the GeMorin circle. After a prolonged moment, Oric felt something slide across his internal senses, skipping over his telepathy. Then the forest people dropped to their knees.

Each of them held the same expression of wonder and awe as they stared wide-eyed at Arlana. Oric opened his mind, just a bit, and was surprised enough to open it more. "You've given them control," he murmured. "They can control their telepathy now."

She smiled. "It was the least I could give them. They'll require time to adjust. They've never been able to think without minds interfering. This will disorient them for a while. But I think in the long run, they'll be grateful for it."

Awed, Oric watched as the forest people stumbled to their feet, muttering aloud in hushed tones as they backed away from the rubble of the cottage and the power of Arlana. They vanished into the forest, not even a faint after-murmur of mental humming left behind.

Whypp raised an eyebrow, looked from Arlana to the forest and shrugged. He moved to a spot beneath a large oak and sat, pulled out a dagger from some concealed spot in his clothing and began cleaning his nails with the tip. Oric wasn't the least surprised by the assassin's easy acceptance of the situation. He envied it, but he wasn't surprised.

The GeMorin rose to their feet. The protective circle they'd formed dissolved as the goblins clumped together, talking in the hushed, guttural sounds of their language. Oric turned his attention back to Arlana, Owen and Catarin.

Arlana and Catarin were standing off to one side, talking quietly. His mother glanced at him, frowned and looked away. Scowling, Oric stepped toward them. He was stopped by a gentle but firm grip on his arm.

"Give them a moment, Oric. I think there's something Catarin wished to discuss with Lady Arlana before we left."

Oric glowered at the two women. If his mother tried to interfere with his relationship with Arlana again, he'd…

"My father's name was Oric."

His attention swung back to Owen—the Guardian. "What?"

"My father's name was Oric. Catarin only met him a few times before he died, but they got along quite well."

"Are you saying she named me for your father?" Oric wasn't sure how to feel about that. He was standing here, talking to the man his mother had always loved, a man who was no relation to him, and being told that his name was a legacy of this man's.

Owen shrugged. "I don't know. I'd like to think so. I'd like to think you would be much like the son Catarin and I would have had if we'd been given the chance." He smiled. "Obviously, you don't feel the same way just yet. It's too bad we won't have more time to talk. I understand you've been hearing my approach for a long time now."

Oric grunted an affirmative. Despite himself, he could grow to respect this sorcerer. The man seemed to be honorable. And he obviously loved Catarin. Reluctantly, Oric had to admit he might even have grown to like the man, given time.

He extended a hand to Owen and grasped his upper arm tightly. The grip was very old, used among Browan warriors centuries earlier, taught to Oric by his first weapon master. Owen raised a brow but returned the gesture, his grip firm.

"I will rely on you to take care of her, Lord Sorcerer," Oric said before releasing Owen's arm.

"You have my word of honor that I'll always look after her."

Oric's head jerked in a satisfied nod. They stepped apart when Arlana and Catarin rejoined them.

Arlana and Oric stepped back as Owen began to chant the spell that would take him and Catarin back a thousand years into the past. Catarin caught and held Oric's gaze. She smiled and raised a hand in a silent goodbye.

"Be safe," Arlana murmured.

And then they were gone.

Arlana and Oric stood for a long moment, staring at the place where the Guardian and Catarin had been. She looked around, half expecting the world to alter in some way as they stood there watching. When it didn't, she let out a pent-up breath.

Oric turned to face her, smiling. "So you've set things right, then, my lady."

The husky sound of his voice sent tingles through her belly. She grinned. "It looks like it. We're all still here at any rate."

Oric's smile was slow and knowing. "Yes." The smile faded. "What did Catarin say to you before she left?"

Arlana's smile brightened. He looked nervous. After all they'd just been through, he was nervous about what his mother had said. "She asked me if I'd changed my mind about you."

"And you said?"

"I said yes." His shoulders slumped with relief. The gesture made her heart dance. "Then she told me to make sure you were happy."

"And you said?" He pulled her into his arms.

"I said yes." She tilted her face up to his, meeting his kiss. She broke away when she realized there were still a dozen GeMorin and an assassin hovering nearby. Heat crawled over her cheeks at Oric's husky chuckle.

"So what's in store for us now?" he murmured.

His hands slid up and down her back, gently stroking away her last remaining fears. "Now? I still have a lot of work to do here. Browan has a lot of magical wounds that only I can heal. I used the orb's knowledge to heal the forest people, but I'll have to discover how to heal the rest on my own. And then there's the senate to deal with. I'm not sure how they're going to feel about the fact that I sent the orb back in time. Then there's..." He silenced her by placing a finger across her lips.

"I meant, what's in store for *us* now?"

"Oh. I don't know."

He rubbed his finger over her bottom lip. "I have an idea then."

"Yes?" Her heart pounded as her breathing deepened.

"Yes." He met her gaze. And in Browan, he murmured, "Marry me."

Arlana didn't think her heart could pound any harder without breaking out of her chest. "Are you sure?" His smile was touched by a vulnerability she'd very rarely seen in him.

"I have never been so sure, fayria." *Marry me. Spend this life with me.*

"Yes." She rose on her toes to kiss him. *Yes.*

*I love you, Arlana.*

He hugged her close and all her uncertainties faded beneath the glow of his love. When she met his lips again, Arlana knew she'd found the place she was always meant to be. Her destiny. Held tight in Oric's arms.

# EPILOGUE

Merig, sorcerer to the Fordin Court, older than most even imagined, mentor and teacher to generations of magicians—most recently the most powerful sorceress ever born—felt an ease he hadn't felt in years. He walked along the quiet game trail, letting the dappled sun warm him and the leafy canopy soothe him. He hadn't walked in Fordin Forest for the pleasure of it in more years than he cared to remember.

This wasn't entirely a pleasure walk. But he could easily mistake it for one.

She stood in the middle of the game trail, patiently waiting. Her golden hair hung to her ankles and flowed around her like a cloak. She wore a loose gossamer robe of ebony cinched at the waist with a braid of flowers. She looked serene and yet dangerously lovely, like a mountain lioness standing atop a rocky cliff. Magnificent and untouchable.

Merig smiled. "Why do you appear to others as a crone and yet to me always as a beautiful young maid?" He stopped near enough to breathe in the earthy flowery scent that always seemed to surround her.

She smiled back, her golden, liquid eyes crinkling at the corners. "Because I like you, Merig. I always have."

"My lady is too kind." He bowed his head in acknowledgement.

Her laughter carried high and sweet on the summer breeze. "There are many who would disagree with you."

"Only those not happy with their fate."

"Mmm… Perhaps. You've come to ask about her."

He nodded, though she hadn't really asked a question. "I know she's succeeded in this task. I felt it. But what for her now?"

"Now, she will marry."

Merig's brows rose at this pronouncement, the only outward sign of his surprise.

"She will live a long, long time with the Lord Commander Oric and bear him three children. She will outlive him, obviously, but by then she will be contented with the time they were allowed together."

"Will you take her then?"

"No. She will have one or two more things to do before she comes to me again."

"Tasks as difficult as this one?"

The golden eyes unfocused and sparks of silver and red flashed in their depths. "Some. Not all." Her voice dropped, growing more resonant. "She will have help along the way. The GeMorin are loyal to her now. They will stay that way for centuries. But she has much to learn before she is ready."

Merig waited for the sparks to disappear and the golden eyes to refocus before he spoke again. Then he smiled. "She will make you a fine apprentice, my lady."

"Yes." She grinned. "Though I've always thought it a shame you were not the one to be my apprentice. We would have made a fine pair."

He'd thought himself too old to blush, but the compliment heated his cheeks nonetheless. "Now you flatter me. But I'm not nearly powerful enough for that purpose, and I well know it."

"I still think it unfortunate. But you're right. Arlana will be a fine apprentice." She grinned at Merig, taking his arm to continue down the game trail. "Fate couldn't ask for a better right hand."

# About the Author

Isabo Kelly is the award-winning author of numerous science fiction, fantasy, and paranormal romances. She also writes best-selling paranormal romance under the name Kat Simons. Her life has taken her from Las Vegas to Hawaii, where she got her BA in Zoology, back to Vegas where she looked after sharks, then on to Germany and Ireland where she got her Ph.D. in Animal Behavior. Now Isabo focuses on writing. She lives in New York with her Irish husband and two beautiful boys, working as a full time writer and stay-at-home mom.

Don't miss out on new releases from Isabo! Sign up for her Newsletter here: http://eepurl.com/caxHa9

For more on Isabo and her books:

Website: http://www.isabokelly.com
Facebook: http://www.facebook.com/IsaboKelly
Twitter: https://www.twitter.com/IsaboKelly